17876

LOUP C

D0457513

3-9-06

MY MOTHER'S DAUGHTER

a novel

JUDITH HENRY WALL

simon & schuster
new york london toronto sydney singapore

SIMON & SCHUSTER
Rockefeller Center
1230 Avenue of the Americas
New York, NY 10020

Simon & Schuster and colophon are registered trademarks
of Simon & Schuster, Inc.

Designed by Jeanette Olender
Manufactured in the United States of America

ISBN 0-684-83766-8

acknowledgments

I am deeply grateful to Bill Stein, director of the
Nesbitt Memorial Library, for making Columbus, Texas,
and its history come alive for me. Thanks also go
to Columbus residents Frances Seifert, Ilse Miller,
Lois Burk, and Mary Grant Weimar for sharing
their memories with me.

I am indebted to my longtime friend Paula Baker.
Grayson's pilgrimage in chapter 46 is dedicated to her.

Others who provided assistance are Dawn Heston
of Texas Women's University, Suellen Smith, JoAnna Wall,
Peggy McFarland, Colonel Wilbur Wiltze, and
Lesa Bethel Mulligan, M.D.

I am fortunate to have a wise and caring editor in
Chuck Adams.

And as always, I am grateful that Philippa Brophy of
Sterling Lord Literistic is my agent and friend.

*this book is dedicated
to my brother-in-law, and my hero,
Russ Burson.*

cissy

My brother Buddy never stopped wondering about our birth parents. He was certain that finding out who they were would give us essential knowledge about ourselves and somehow change our lives for the better. We would be happier, more confident. We would have a heritage and lineage. We would be more comfortable with ourselves.

Who were those other parents, and why had they given us away? Would we ever meet them? Did they ever think about us?

For many years, I wondered along with my brother, who was older than me by a year and a half. The romance and mystery of birth parents gave Buddy and me endless hours of shared longing and speculation, mostly spent on a dusty old mattress we'd dragged in front of the round attic window.

When our cousin Iris was with us, we would focus instead on the comings and goings of the neighbors who lived in the gingerbread-laden homes that occupied our tree-lined street. But when it was just Buddy and I stretched out in front of the round window, we focused on mythical, what-if worlds—on the places where birth parents might dwell.

Sometimes we imagined them together, but mostly we dealt with our birth parents separately, reasoning that a couple who had given away their children would not still be together. Buddy conjured up scenarios with our father an undercover CIA agent in Russia—or falsely accused of a crime and locked away in prison.

Usually, however, we thought of him as dead. It was tidier that way. He might have been killed in Korea. Or swept out to sea during a hurricane like the one that had torn away the county courthouse when our grandparents were young. I preferred a scenario in which he was killed in a fiery car crash as he raced to be with our mother the night I was born.

Mostly, though, we passed our time daydreaming about the woman who had given us birth and trying to find excuses for her. Death worked well here, too. Maybe she had wanted to keep us but died giving me birth. I imagined a woman who looked remarkably like Audrey Hepburn, kissing us good-bye and promising to watch over us from heaven. I would cry unashamed tears, seeing all this unfold in my mind's eye. She was young and beautiful, her dark hair spread on a white pillow. A white-collared priest, thrown in for drama, was praying in Latin.

Or maybe she was still alive but suffered from amnesia. Someday she might remember that she was the mother of two children and hire a private detective to find us. She might even be a grand duchess, with Buddy heir to a defunct Russian throne.

At times, I could close my eyes and actually feel our birth mother's presence. She smelled of flowers. Her caress was gentle and her voice sweet. The longing that filled my young breast was quite real.

Of course, up there in the little attic alcove, I felt disloyal succumbing to birth mother daydreams. Our adopted mother worked very hard at motherhood. She was always saying how lucky she was to have us for her very own children. Without us, no one would have ever called her "Mother." She and Daddy never would have been parents.

Our daddy probably would have understood our need for birth parent daydreams, but Mama would have been hurt. She had earned the right to be first and foremost in our affection. And in my heart, I knew our birth mother wasn't a grand duchess or a grand anything else. She was probably the daughter of sharecroppers—just some poor, ignorant girl who feared humiliation and hadn't the means or courage to raise her own children. Whether she was alive or not had little bearing on our lives.

As the years went by, I came to realize that understanding ourselves had little to do with learning about our birth parents. When I was twelve, I drew a line across my life and stopped wondering. The true mystery in our lives had to do with the undercurrents that swirled about the people who had adopted us and given us a home and a name.

The happiness we yearned for would not come from finding an angelic birth mother but in pleasing the complex woman who was raising us. We seemed to have disappointed her in some deep, profound way. Why did our mama sigh? Had her heart broken when she came to realize that she would never have children of her own? Or maybe the fear that our aunt Justine would someday swoop into town and reclaim Iris stole away her youth and laughter.

Buddy and I had always known that Iris was the beloved one. Iris was the daughter of our mother's sister and therefore related by blood—not a daughter, but the closet thing our mother would ever have to a blood child. We had grown up accepting Iris's special status as rightful. After all, Buddy and I loved her, too. From earliest memory, Iris had been the center of our lives, of our family. She loved us all without qualification. She spread joy in her wake. She made our mother happy in a way that Buddy and I never could. And more than anything, we wanted our mother to be happy.

one

Justine was coming home!

Martha Claire paused in her weeding and sat back on her haunches to relish the thought. At this very minute her sister was on a ship crossing the Atlantic Ocean.

And surely before the year was out, Grayson also would come back to her. Her life could begin anew.

She stretched a bit and rubbed at the small of her back before returning to her task. Whether Justine noticed it or not, when she came down the front walk for the first time in two and a half years, she was going to be greeted by weedless flower beds and a perfectly manicured yard.

And inside, the house was well on its way to being spotless. By the time Justine walked through the front door, every curtain in the entire house would be freshly laundered, starched, and ironed. Daddy had refinished the front door and was even putting down new linoleum in the kitchen and upstairs bathroom. Mother had recovered the seats of the dining room chairs. Justine's bedroom was freshly painted.

Yesterday, Martha Claire had gone across the river to pick wild blackberries so Granny Grace could put up Justine's favorite preserves. Granny Grace already had rows of watermelon pickles, spiced peaches, and pickled okra on the pantry shelf, waiting for her granddaughter's homecoming. Martha Claire would help her grandmother and mother prepare all of Justine's favorite food. Nothing boiled, Justine had written. She was sick of boiled food. For her first meal home, she wanted pork roast, mashed potatoes and gravy, fried okra, sliced tomatoes fresh from the garden, cole slaw, and corn bread—with chocolate cake *and* apple pie for dessert. And please have a watermelon chilled. She hadn't tasted watermelon for two whole summers.

Martha Claire decided to cut back the petunias, which had gotten leggy. The lantana and periwinkles were in full bloom, though. Across the yard, the magnolia tree was laden with huge, waxy blossoms, and the stand of crepe myrtle was a mass of pink. The freshly painted gazebo and the picket fence around Mother's rose garden shimmered whitely in the sunshine. It was a beautiful yard—one of the finest in Columbus, as was the house, which had been built by Martha Claire's great-great-grandfather.

Had Justine missed any of this? Martha Claire wondered as she surveyed their childhood home—the place she herself loved best on this earth.

What letters her sister had found time to write described the wonder of being in London, of meeting people from everywhere, of doing her small part for the war effort. If she wrote about the war itself, it was only to complain about the hours spent in bomb shelters. Only at the end would she dash off a few words about missing her family back home.

Grayson's letters, on the other hand, had been mostly about missing her, words that Martha Claire would read over and over again. Of course, if he wrote anything about where he was or what he was doing, the censors would mark it out.

Now that the war was over, however, her husband's letters were more about human tragedy than longing. His unit was involved in the repatriation of prisoners liberated from the concentration camp at Dachau. He was overwhelmed with the horror they had found there, overwhelmed with the task at hand but dedicated to it—passionately so. He did not know when he was coming home.

Martha Claire tried not to be resentful. She had seen pictures of those poor souls in the newsreels—living skeletons in filthy rags with empty eyes—ghastly pictures that made her look away. But her husband had been gone for three endless years, and his father wasn't well.

It was time for Grayson to take over the family store. It was time for him to make a home with his wife and put the war behind him.

Martha Claire wondered what Justine planned to do now that the war was over. Their parents hoped their younger daughter would settle down in Columbus—or at least someplace not too far away. That's what Martha Claire wanted, too, her sister close by, if not in Columbus, then no farther away than Houston, where Justine had worked in a photography studio before enlisting in the Women's Army Corps. Martha Claire had missed her sister as much as she had missed her husband, in some ways more. She was always thinking of things she wanted to tell Justine. Sometimes she even had imaginary conversations with her sister.

Her body longed for her husband, but she had a hard time imagining conversations with him. Grayson was only a year older than she was, but she felt as though she had been frozen in time while he had grown older. And sadder. More serious.

Martha had been Grayson's wife for three years and one month, but she still lived with her parents, still had no home of her own, still didn't feel like a wife. Everything in her hope chest was brand-new. Their wedding gifts were still in their boxes. The only time she had shared a bed with her husband had been on their honeymoon and the few weekends they had together before he shipped out.

But surely by next summer she would have her own house and garden, she told herself as she returned to her weeding. And a baby on the way. Oh, yes, definitely a baby on the way.

Justine had always claimed that she would never get married, never be any man's wife, never belong to anyone but herself. Martha Claire would smile knowingly at her sister's remarks. She knew that deep in every girl's heart she longed to have a man love her enough to stay with her always and have children with her.

Sometimes Martha Claire worried that Grayson no longer loved her in that special way. Maybe he had been gone too long and seen too much.

At least, a girl didn't have to worry about her sister not loving her. No matter what, she and Justine would always be sisters, would always have each other.

Martha Claire began making mental lists of all the things she wanted to do with Justine. Loll on the beach on Galveston Island. Float the river. Make a pan of fudge and eat it all themselves. Visit their high school friends. Ride the bus to Houston for a day of shopping. And she wanted to crawl into her sister's bed late at night when the house was dark and their parents and Granny Grace were asleep. That's when she and Justine always had the best talks. Whispering made it more fun, more private. Sometimes, they had even shared a pirated bottle of their daddy's homemade beer and smoked a clandestine cigarette while they imagined the time when they would be rich and famous and return to Columbus to visit the home folks in furs and diamonds, riding in a chauffeur-driven Rolls-Royce.

"Caught you daydreaming, didn't I?" her grandmother's voice said from the porch. Martha Claire shaded her eyes and look up at her grandmother, who was smiling down at her and holding two glasses of lemonade.

Martha Claire scrambled to her feet and wiped the sweat from her forehead with the back of her hand. "How does it look?" she asked, stepping back to survey her handiwork.

"Pretty as a picture. Now, come up here in the shade and have a glass of lemonade with your granny. Can you believe that this time next week we'll have our Justine back home with us!"

Martha Claire sat with her grandmother in the newly varnished wicker chairs. "The place hasn't looked this good since your wedding day," Granny Grace said. "Gracious, how we scurried around when you decided that you just had to marry Grayson before he reported for duty!"

"Do you think Justine will stay in Columbus?" Martha Claire asked.

"Now, don't you go getting your heart set on that sister of yours comin' home to roost," Grace warned her granddaughter. "After two and a half years in London, with all those palaces and people from all over the world, I expect our little town is going to seem pretty small and countrified. But this is where her heart is, honey. Justine will always need to come back home from time to time—to remember who she is."

two

The porter shook Justine's arm. "Wake up, miss. Next stop's Columbus."

Justine struggled to an upright position, with every cell in her body protesting the act. Her muscles were stiff and sore, her stomach churning and raw, her head throbbing, her mouth foul, her eyes dry and scratchy. Grandpa Mayfield would say she wasn't worth shooting.

Her grandpa had died while she was away, she reminded herself. He would not be waiting at the station with the others. Someone else was living in the little house south of town where her daddy had been raised. Granny Grace was the only grandparent she had left.

She looked out the window in search of something familiar. There were cattle grazing in fields defined with barbed wire, stands of trees with tangled underbrush, farmhouses in need of paint attended by barns and clusters of dilapidated outbuildings. It was so different from the English countryside—not pristine and picturesque. Waiting at a crossing was a dented pickup truck with an ancient farmer at the wheel. Sitting in the back was a colored boy, wearing overalls and no shirt, his wide-eyed gaze focused on the passing train. And for an instant, her photographer's eye framed a picture.

"'Bout fifteen minutes now," Jessie the porter was saying. "I'll come back and help you off."

She nodded and sagged against the seat.

"Hang on jus' a little longer," Jessie said, his voice soothing. "You'll be jus' fine when you get home to your people."

But Justine knew she wasn't going to be just fine at all. She had envisioned a different sort of homecoming, with her smiling and smart in her uniform as she stepped down from the train, retuning home from war for a visit with her family before getting on with her life—not sick and scared, with her future in jeopardy.

On the ship, she had tried to convince herself that she was suffering from seasickness. And the crossing had been a rough one. Two of her three roommates also spent most of the voyage in their bunks. Only pudgy little Ruth from Detroit had been spared and had done her best to care for the rest.

Of course, the seas had also been rough two and a half years ago, when Justine made the crossing from New York to Dover as a member of the Women's Army Corps with orders for London, where she would serve as a file clerk in a military police command. She hadn't been sick then, just scared to death of storms and German submarines.

She'd been through a great deal since then, though, Justine reasoned. She wasn't as healthy, for one thing. She had smoked and drunk too much. She never ate breakfast, even though every letter from her mother reminded her how important it was to start each day with a nourishing meal. And she was pale as the underside of a fish from the lack of sunlight.

The cramped quarters she was sharing with three other WACs were far below deck—in the deepest bowels of the ship where the air was heavy and claustrophobia was at its worst. Justine found herself wondering if any holdout submarines with swastikas on their sides were still swimming around out there, if icebergs came this far south, if she could even muster the strength to make it topside to a lifeboat should the ship founder.

By the third day, however, she wouldn't have minded going down with the ship. Nothing she ate or drank stayed down. She would retch so hard it felt as though she were turning inside out. When the nausea receded, she would crawl inside a cocoon of semiconsciousness. The third or fourth day out, her darling Billy was inside the cocoon, waiting for her.

She knew that he was only a hallucination brought on by serious dehydration, by days without nourishment, by fear of what awaited her at the end of the voyage. But she didn't allow reason to chase him away. She needed the comfort of his presence. Billy Baker from Brisbane. An RAF tail gunner. She had called him her "Billy Boy." Just a wartime romance. She wasn't about to fall in love with anyone, much less a boy with the life expectancy of a gnat.

Except as the tide of war began to change, she had begun to think that Billy just might make it through, that he just might be alive to celebrate the armistice with her and to wonder what they would mean to each other in a world where there was no war.

In the cave of her bunk bed, she would close her eyes and drift with Billy, back to their favorite Westminster pub, the Toad in the Hole, right off Regents Square, where they drank, sang, and laughed away the hours. At the corner table, grizzly old Hugh played the harmonica: "As Time Goes By," "Chattanooga Choo Choo," "Baby Face," "Danny Boy." The air was thick with cigarette smoke and smelled of damp wool, stout ale, strong cheese. Every night was a party. Justine went whether Billy was in town or not, to have a half pint or two. When he wasn't there, she missed him. When he was, it was glorious. Billy knew the words to all of Hugh's songs, which he sang in a haunting tenor voice, and his laugh was infectious, his grin adorable, his dart game legendary. Maybe a bomb would fall on them tonight, or he would fly away tomorrow and never come back, but for now they were absolutely *alive*. Every time they said good-bye, she wondered if she'd ever see him again.

She never allowed herself to think about all that talk about them publishing a weekly newspaper in Australia's Northern Territory. She lived for the present, for the magnificent present filled with laughter and poignancy and death all around. The past had grown dim for her. Only at occasional stabbing, nostalgic moments did she think of her family back home in Columbus, Texas. Every moment in the here and now was a gift.

When the air raid sirens began to wail, they would race toward the entrance of the Baker's Street tube. That last night, he grabbed her arm and there in the middle of the wet, black pavement, drew her into his arms. She could feel his heart pounding, the shock waves from exploding bombs traveling up her legs, a cold misty rain settling into her hair. The air was filled with the smell of burning wood and diesel fumes, with the pandemonium of fire sirens, men yelling, women calling frantically to children. Billy held her so tightly, she could barely breathe. And they kissed. God, how they kissed. She wanted to fuse with him, even if it meant dying with him. She had wanted the war to end and for it to go on forever.

Now, down in the belly of a troopship that was transporting her to the rest of her life, Billy was with her again—at least a vision of him. And she was grateful. Sometimes she was aware of the other women yelling at her to shut up while she talked to him and sang pub songs with him and told him over and over that she loved him, only him, forever and ever, that she was sorry she'd never said the words before. She should have that night in the street when he'd kissed her. She should have said them then, because she had felt them. All the way to her toes, she had felt them.

The last morning of the voyage, Ruth helped her shower and put on her uniform and led her up the narrow steps to the deck.

Under the benign eyes of the Statue of Liberty, Justine filled her lungs with fresh air for the first time in seven days. But soon she was heaving again, leaning over the rail, Ruth grabbing her hat before it fell into the water. Justine was past being embarrassed. It was all she could do to keep from lying down on the deck and wishing herself dead.

As they docked, a military band played "The Stars and Stripes Forever." Throngs of people were cheering, many waving American flags. Her family wasn't among them; they were waiting in Columbus. But the people on the docks were just like them—Americans who were ecstatic that the war was over and their own were coming home.

Justine wanted to be happy. She wanted to sing and cheer and feel hot tears of joy and relief flowing down her cheeks. But mostly she was afraid. She had lived for the present, and now her future was in jeopardy. As she retched, she prayed that it would dislodge the tiny spark of life that had taken up residence inside of her and send it floating away to its doom.

In Grand Central Station, at a first-aid station set up to care for the continuing waves of returning military personnel, she confessed her condition to a medical corpsman. He took her pulse and administered a bottle of IV fluids, but he wouldn't let her stay on the cot. Others were waiting. If she needed further medical care, she would have to go to a hospital.

At least she wasn't as dizzy as before, she thought, as she went in search of a Western Union office. After she'd sent a telegram to her parents, she stumbled through the masses of uniformed humanity in search of a place to sit. Finally a lanky major with artillery brass on his collar gave her his seat and brought her a cup of hot tea from the Red Cross canteen. He spoke with a comforting drawl—probably a fellow Texan, but she didn't have the energy to ask.

She risked two sips of the tea, then set the paper cup under the bench and willed her stomach not to reject what she had drunk. The back of the bench was only shoulder high, and she needed desperately to rest her head. So she sat on her duffel bag facing the bench and laid her head down on the seat, using her arms as a pillow, one hand clutching the camera bag where her precious Rolleiflex resided. If she weren't so sick, she would be photographing the historic return of American servicemen after World War II. Closing her eyes, she tried to invoke another image of Billy, but the IV had made her lucid. Her Billy Boy wouldn't come. He had slipped back into her memory.

If Billy hadn't been shot down, she probably would have married him and lived with the dirt and isolation of the outback, birthing lambs and babies and newspapers. Would she have been happy or hated him in the end?

The acoustics in the huge vaulted space were amazing. Justine could pick up pieces of conversation from distances a football field away— happy voices, going-home voices. By holding very, very still, she was able to keep the nausea at bay but knew better than to risk a third sip of tea.

To distract herself, she thought of her hometown with its wonderful trees—stately native pecan trees with their annual bounty, towering magnolias with their waxy blossoms and heady perfume, and best of all the huge spreading live oak that evoked respect and awe. She conjured up images of the meandering river that wrapped itself around the north half of the town and of the domed courthouse surrounded by a handsome iron fence.

But the iron fence was gone. Her mother had written that the town donated it to the war effort. Most of Columbus's iron fences had been donated, including the ones around the family home on Milam Street.

She thought of her room at the top of the stairs, imagined herself in her bed with smooth white sheets, her mother's cool hand on her forehead. She wanted to go home. God, how she wanted it!

But she could not stay. She had to move on. Columbus was her past, not her future.

She would find a way to deal with her problem. Better to have been killed by a bomb in London and go out with glory than to endure stagnation in a backwater Texas town, no matter how pretty that town happened to be, no matter how much she loved the people who lived there. Columbus had afforded her and her sister an enchanted childhood, but adulthood there would be a different story, especially for a woman. She wasn't going to waste her life cooking pot roasts and singing hymns.

Somehow the hours passed until her train was announced. The officer with the drawl helped her on board and asked the porter to look after her—the porter before Jessie, who hadn't come on board until Atlanta. The train had been full of returning servicemen, with some passengers forced to sit on luggage stacked in the vestibules. The elderly porter had taken one look at Justine and managed to secure a seat for her, then he found an army nurse on board to take Justine's pulse and assure him she wasn't going to die on his watch.

Out of Atlanta, Justine had two seats to herself and a pillow Jessie had smuggled from a sleeping car. She was too weak to sit up, too weak to make her way to the ladies' lounge when the next wave of nausea hit. She would put her mouth over one of the paper bags Jessie had supplied and heave whatever sips of water she had taken in hopes of keeping herself hydrated. Now her journey was almost over. She was only minutes from home after being away for a lifetime.

She stumbled into the ladies' lounge to rinse out her mouth and splash water on her face. The reflection in the mirror was ghastly. Her hair was matted, her skin ashen, her lips chapped to the point of bleeding. Her uniform hung on her body like a sack. She found a comb in her purse and tried to pull it through her tangled hair but gave up. She glanced out the window and realized the train was crossing the Colorado. *Her* river. Right under this very bridge, she had fished with her grandfather.

Grandpa Mayfield was dead and buried. Boys she had grown up with would never come home. The iron fences were gone. She could never go back to the Columbus of her childhood, yet as the train grew closer there was a part of her that longed to retreat to the simplicity and sanctuary of that other time.

She made her way back to her seat and watched out the window as the train rolled into downtown. She could see the roof of the opera house. The courthouse dome. The hotel. The old brick water tower. The train station was just ahead. Columbus was all around her.

She was *home*.

She could see her family standing on the platform—Mother, Daddy, Martha Claire, and Granny Grace—all dressed in their Sunday best, their faces anxious and excited as they looked for her in the passing windows.

She drew back, not wanting them to see her just yet. Her heart swelled painfully. She did love them. She would always love them, always come back to them.

She put on her hat and hung her purse from her shoulder. Jessie collected her things and guided her down the aisle. He went down the steps first and helped her down. She and a colored soldier were the only passengers getting off at the Columbus station. His family was there, too, looking vaguely familiar. Both families were waving and rushing toward them.

"Thank you, Jessie," Justine called as the porter scurried back on the already moving train.

"Good luck to you, miss," he called back.

Martha Claire arrived first. Her sister. The other half of herself for so many years. Her even lovelier face was registering shock. "My God, Justine, what happened to you?"

Justine could tell how wasted she was by the feel of her sister's arms around her body and by her daddy's arms engulfing her. Next came

Granny Grace, who was thanking God that her Justine had come home safe and sound.

Then her mother took Justine's face between her hands. "Oh, Justine, what have you done to yourself?" Polly Mayfield asked.

Polly's arms came around her daughter. Justine leaned into her mother's embrace. She had traveled all those miles for this moment.

"We'll work it out, my darling," her mother whispered. "Somehow, we'll work it out."

three

Polly Mayfield sat on the side of her daughter's bed and took Justine's hand. "Feeling better?"

Justine nodded.

She did look better, Polly thought, now that she'd had a bath and slept most of the day. But dark circles rimmed her eyes, and her cheeks were white as her nightgown. Doc Hadley had checked her over and said not to worry. She needed rest and lots of fluids, even if they made her throw up.

"Then I guess we'd better discuss what we're going to do," Polly said, looking down at Justine's ringless fingers. "I don't suppose you're married?"

Justine rolled her head back and forth on the pillow. No, she wasn't married.

"And no man is going to arrive in the next few weeks to make an honest woman of you?"

Once again, Justine rolled her head.

"And your young man is dead."

Justine propped herself up on an elbow. "What young man?" she demanded.

"The one who flew with the Royal Air Force."

"How do you know about him?" Justine asked.

"You mentioned him in a letter about six or eight months back. You apologized for not writing for so long and said you'd been sad because a friend in the RAF had been killed—or at least that's what we gathered. Part of the letter had been marked out by a censor."

"I'd forgotten about that. You wrote back, asking about him."

"You never mentioned him again, though. Did you love him, Justine?"

Justine fell back on her pillow. "I don't know. Maybe. It hurt when he was killed. A lot."

"And then you found someone else?"

"Not someone to love," Justine said in a small voice. Then turning her face to the wall, she said, "I'm sorry, Mother. Please don't hate me."

Polly allowed herself a sigh and stroked Justine's shoulders and back, soothing her, telling her that she was disappointed but could never hate her own daughter, that she would always love her no matter what and that somehow they would work things out.

How could this have happened? Polly wondered. Justine, of all girls. The last thing Polly would have expected of her.

Actually, though, for different reasons and morality aside, Polly had always assumed that neither one of her daughters would ever disgrace herself and the family in this manner. Martha Claire was the sort of romantic girl who saved herself for marriage, who regarded the wedding night as a sacrament. Justine was simply too self-possessed. No boy had ever turned her head. She never flirted, never dated, never seemed the least bit interested in boys, except as pals. Polly had assumed that someday that would change and her younger daughter would find a man who didn't care if the woman in his life ever went into a kitchen and never wore a skirt if she could help it, but Justine would have to be on her own first. Maybe she had gotten enough of that in England, though. Maybe she had intended to settle down with the man who got her pregnant, but things just hadn't worked out. Polly would like to know what happened. Had her daughter's grief over the death of the young airman left her needy and vulnerable? Had some man made promises he did not keep? Or had the Justine who had always taken every dare simply thrown caution to the wind? As Polly looked down at her reticent daughter, however, she doubted if she would ever know.

It certainly wasn't the homecoming Polly had envisioned for her daughter, but then other mothers' children had come home in caskets, she reminded herself. After the doctor had left, they finally sat down to dinner without the honoree. Martha Claire's in-laws had been invited, but Polly called the Stewarts and suggested they drop by tomorrow, explaining that Justine was exhausted from her trip and a bit under the weather.

All that food! They had been cooking for a week.

Months ago, Walter had painted Justine's room, varnished the floors, and put in a new light fixture in preparation for her homecoming. Then Polly had helped him put everything back exactly as Justine had left it. Polly looked around at the cluttered room with its mementos of adolescence. It looked like a boy's room, with a rock collection and a baseball mitt in the bookcase, a BB gun and fishing pole leaning in the corner. Instead of dried corsages and dance programs, two bulletin boards were filled with photographs that Justine had taken—of family members, the opera house, the Walnut Street bridge, sunsets, surprisingly beautiful close-ups of insects. Polly's favorite was a photograph of Martha Claire. Justine had captured her sister just at dusk, sitting on the porch railing, her gaze focused past the front gate on some private horizon, her sweet young face pensive. Polly saw not only her older daughter's beauty in that photograph, she saw Justine's pain. It had captured Martha Claire as she was moving away from girlhood and into other dominions, no longer Justine's cohort but Grayson's sweetheart. Polly remembered well how difficult it had been for Justine when Martha Claire started wearing dresses to school, when she stopped roaming the countryside with her sister and was either with Grayson or thinking about him.

Polly was certain that Martha Claire had been thinking about Grayson at the moment that picture was taken. Justine had seen it, too. Whether it was the lighting or Justine's perspective, the picture was a sad one.

Polly wondered if she should have explained to Justine that young love had a way of settling down, that Martha Claire would once again need her sister's friendship just as much as before.

She leaned forward and rubbed her cheek against Justine's shoulder, and Justine rolled into her embrace. Polly pressed her lips against the smooth young skin on her daughter's forehead and fought back tears. All she wanted out of life was to raise her children well and protect them from harm. Should she feel responsible for what had happened to her willful and yet more vulnerable child? But then, Justine was one of those people who expected more out of life and was, therefore, destined to disappointment.

Enough of pondering, though, Polly decided, adjusting the pillow behind Justine's head. The unthinkable had happened to her daughter, and she had to figure out some way to deal with it. "Does this man know he is going to be a father?" she asked.

Justine's chapped lips formed the word no.

"Don't you think you should give him a chance to do the right thing?"

Justine closed her eyes. "No," she whispered.

"Are you absolutely certain of that or are you just being a martyr?"

"I am absolutely certain."

"He's married, then?"

Justine sighed but didn't answer.

Polly took a breath, cleared her throat, and said the words she had been composing in her mind.

"I have been thinking over your situation and have decided that you *are* married, Justine—to a British soldier you met during the victory celebration when everyone was dancing in the streets and kissing everyone in sight. It was a whirlwind courtship, and you had a simple little wedding in a country church with only the minister's wife in attendance. Then, just weeks later, the poor boy was killed trying to defuse one of those undetonated German bombs that were still scattered about London. Your husband was an only child, and his parents were killed in the Blitz, so you have no remaining ties to England. You'll have to decide on a last name—for you and the baby."

Justine struggled to sit up, an astounded look on her face. "My God, Mother, no one is going to believe a cock-and-bull story like that. I would have written to you if I'd gotten married, or sent a telegram, made a transatlantic phone call. You would have told the neighbors and put an announcement in the newspaper."

"It all happened so fast, and then he was dead," Polly went on, honing her story, which made her feel genuinely sad. The young man had not existed, but he could have—a son-in-law she would never know. She patted Justine's hand sympathetically. "You had to deal with your private grief before you told anyone, and by then you realized that you were in a family way. Doc Hadley said he'll put whatever name you want on the birth certificate. People might whisper, but no one will know anything for sure. You have to think of what's best for the child, Justine. It's better to have a father's name, even if it's a made-up one."

"What about what is best for me?" Justine demanded.

"And what might that be?"

"Not to have a baby at all." Justine's chin was lifted in defiance. She was daring a challenge, maybe even wanting one.

"It's a little late for that," Polly said, smoothing back her daughter's hair—fair hair that couldn't decide if it was supposed to be red or blond, just like Martha Claire's, just as her own had once been. Justine's hair needed shampooing in the worst way. Tomorrow, if she was up to it, Polly decided. Then they would sit in the backyard, and she would brush her daughter's hair until it was dry and shone with the sunlight.

"I could get rid of it," Justine said, her voice lowered to a cautious whisper. "Doc Hadley said he wouldn't do it, but there's that colored woman over in Freedmantown."

"Yes. Aunt Sally Washington, with her potions and voodoo. She must be close to ninety now, but I've heard she still does abortions on her kitchen table—mostly for colored girls, of course, but I expect she does an occasional white girl now and then when she shows up at the back door in the middle of the night. I imagine that's where poor Sadie Marie Cordell went. You would probably live through it, but do you really want to take that risk? And do you really want to wonder for the rest of your life about the baby you never had?"

"I want a different kind of life," Justine insisted. "I'm not like Martha Claire. You know that. I want to be a photographer and make my own way in the world."

"You should have thought of that back in London," Polly said, not unkindly. She'd had dreams once herself. She was going to study music at a conservatory in St. Louis and become a concert organist and not just play hymns on Walnut Avenue Methodist's decaying Hammond. But she didn't have the money and life got in the way, and the life she'd ended up with was a good one. She would not go back and change it if she could. Now all she dreamed about was living to a ripe old age with Walter at her side and grandchildren in her lap—and playing the Easter anthem so magnificently that she felt the rapture even if no one else did.

Before the war, Justine had refused to follow her sister to college and had taken a job in Houston as an assistant in a photography studio. People couldn't believe that Polly and Walter Mayfield had allowed their daughter to do such a thing—a young girl like that, just out of high school, living alone in a big city. Walter had had a fit, of course, but Polly knew there was no point in telling Justine she couldn't go. She would have gone anyway.

As it turned out, Justine hated the job. All she did was take pictures of babies and develop film. She probably would have come on home and found some nice boy to marry if it weren't for the war. As early as 1941, even before the Japanese bombed Pearl Harbor, Mrs. Roosevelt and General Marshall were pushing for the creation of a Women's Army Auxiliary Corps. As soon as Justine heard about it, she knew she would sign up the moment it became a reality and begged her sister to join with her. After Pearl Harbor, though, after war became a reality, Martha Claire decided she would marry Grayson the minute he graduated from Texas A&M, before he began his military service. A&M was a military school; Grayson would graduate as a second lieutenant in the artillery.

After Martha Claire's wedding, Justine traveled to Fort Des Moines, Iowa, where she received her military training. She spent the first part of her military service working in the processing center there, all the time champing at the bit for an overseas assignment. A subdued Martha Claire dutifully wrote tediously long letters to her husband and sister. When Grayson's father had a heart attack, she began working at Stewart's Dry Goods. Polly was sorry about Mr. Stewart's ill health, but working at the store was certainly better for Martha Claire than sulking around the house all day.

Justine came home the following summer to say good-bye. She celebrated the Fourth of July with them but was like a horse straining at the starting gate. Martha Claire was sad and quiet for the three days they had Justine with them. At the station, when they put a smartly uniformed Justine on the train for her journey to Boston and embarkation to England and the war, Martha Claire had broken down and thrown herself in Justine's arms. "Promise me you'll come back to Columbus," she begged. Justine hugged her sister and promised. But she hadn't promised that she would come home to stay.

In London, Justine had taken pictures of the war-torn city and the people who lived there. Polly didn't know anything about photography, but anyone could look at those pictures and feel something. Some of Justine's photographs had been published in a London newspaper. And one of them had ended up in *Collier's* magazine—almost a full page with Justine's name in little letters underneath. It was a picture of two little girls having a tea party with their dolls in the middle of a bomb crater, with bombed-out buildings all around.

Collier's had paid Justine an astounding one hundred dollars for that picture. An issue of the magazine, opened to the picture, was displayed on the Queen Anne side table in the parlor. The local newspaper had run a story about Justine taking pictures in London. "She'll never come back to Columbus now," Martha Claire had predicted mournfully.

Poor Martha Claire, Polly thought. Her older daughter wanted her life to take up where it had left off, with both her husband and her sister back at her side. If only she'd been able to get pregnant before Grayson left, she would have managed the separation better. That had certainly been her plan. Until the war came along, Martha Claire had been convinced that if she wanted something badly enough and worked hard enough, she could make it happen. After all, she had been elected homecoming queen, graduated valedictorian of her high school class, been named outstanding student at Mary Hardin Baylor College, and gotten the boy she wanted to fall in love with her. But she had waited out the war childless, and now her unmarried sister was carrying a misbegotten child. How in the world was Martha Claire going to react to that?

Polly hoped that her son-in-law arrived home soon and that his would be a more joyous homecoming than Justine's. But at least Justine and Grayson had both survived, when fifty-one young men from Colorado County had not. Grayson had lived though horrendous fighting in Africa and Europe. Justine had survived the bombs in London. And now there would be a baby. Polly felt a swelling in her breast at the thought of a grandchild in her arms. She had already decided there would be no late-night crossing over the tracks into Freedmantown. She would raise the child herself if she had to.

"You don't have to decide anything right now," Polly told her daughter, "but you need to keep in mind that you have responsibilities—to the life growing inside of you and to your family, to your sister especially. Martha Claire plans to stay in Columbus. Manufacturing a husband would give her a way to hold her head up."

"It's not *her* problem," Justine said defiantly.

"You know better than that, Justine Mayfield. Dirty linen is a family matter, especially in a little town like Columbus."

Justine's shoulders sagged, and the defiance drained from her face. "Do Martha Claire and Daddy know what's going on?"

"I think they've guessed. I'm going to talk to them now."

"Oh, Mother, do you have to?" Justine said, her eyes filling with tears.

"Yes, dear, I do. They have a right to know. Your grandmother, too."

Polly kissed her daughter's forehead. "I love you, my darling girl. You have no idea how much we missed you, how much we worried about you. We thought of you constantly, wondering if you were all right and what you were doing. Every evening, when your daddy gave the blessing, he always ended it with 'Please, Lord, bring Justine and Grayson home to us safe and sound.' Your poor sister was so lonesome with both of you gone. At least while you were still in Houston, you and Martha Claire could see each other on weekends. But when you went off to England, you might as well have been on another planet. You girls were always each other's best friend. Martha Claire has never found herself another best friend, Justine. She's been counting the days until you came home."

Justine put her arms around her mother's neck. "I love you, too, Mother, but I can't be what you want me to be."

Polly turned out the lamp. From the doorway, she said, "Don't underestimate the value of a home and a family who will always love you, no matter what. It's probably your most precious possession."

"I have to be someone," Justine said into the darkness.

"Everyone is someone," Polly said and closed the door.

four

The glow of the streetlight silhouetted the branches of the magnolia tree outside the bedroom window. Justine remembered the day Grandpa Hess had planted that tree. She and Martha Claire had watched—two little girls in pigtails, sitting cross-legged in the grass, with Granny Grace watching from the porch. Their mother's father had died not long after that, and Justine, Martha Claire, and their parents had moved from their smaller house on Walnut Street to live with Granny Grace in the big house on Milam Street where their mother had grown up.

And now that tree shaded her bedroom window, a legacy from her long-dead grandfather. She would leave a legacy, too, with her photographs. They would live after her. If there were ever a retrospective of her work, it would include only a few of the pictures she had taken thus far. Only a handful were the kind that made people mentally crawl inside of them, the kind that evoked a genuine emotional response. The little girls playing in the bomb crater was one such picture. She had known as she was taking it that it would be. If she hadn't joined the WACs and gone to London, that moment never would have been captured on film.

Grandpa Hess had been the first dead person Justine had ever seen, in a wooden casket downstairs in the parlor, with the smell of embalming fluid still in the air. Granny Grace had pulled aside the white net and leaned forward to kiss him. Justine had pulled on her grandmother's skirt, not wanting her to touch a dead body. She'd seen death many times since, but it never failed to stun her that someone could be alive one instant and dead the next.

She reached down and touched her belly and thought of the life that had planted itself in there, a parasite that could suck away her hopes and dreams. And she thought of Sadie Marie Cordell, whose family lived across the alley. Sadie Marie was a quiet, plain girl with a flat nose and thick glasses. One morning, there had been a special assembly so the principal could announce that Sadie Marie had died of a ruptured appendix and they should all pray for her family and her immortal soul. Word got around, though, that Sadie Marie had been pregnant—by her cousin who lived down on Matagorda Bay. Mrs. Cordell had taken her daughter someplace—probably to Freedmantown. That night Sadie Marie bled to death in her bed. The next day, a neighbor saw her father burning the mattress out behind the shed. Justine and Martha Claire had sneaked over there to see the charred pieces of cotton batting that still bore traces of Sadie Marie's blood. The wages of sin were death. No doubt about it. Right there in front of them was the proof. Justine had clutched her sister's hand and marveled that Sadie Marie could ever have been so stupid.

"I hate you," Justine whispered to the presence under her outstretched fingers. She wanted to get rid of it but not enough to risk her own death. A girl gambled everything by letting a man into her life. If she didn't marry him, she became an outcast, a fallen woman. If she married him, she became someone else—a wife, like Martha Claire had become. The return address on Martha Claire's letters had said "Mrs. Grayson Stewart." That name had nothing to do with Justine's sister.

Justine turned on the lamp and looked over at the bookcase. Her old Kodak box camera was there beside a rusty pair of roller skates. She had delivered groceries and raked leaves to earn money for film and processing but never had enough. She agonized over each snap of the shutter. Would the resulting picture be worthy?

In Houston, she had worked for a disgusting old man who patted her fanny and tried to put his hand inside her blouse, but she put up with him because he taught her about f-stops, film speed, composition, lighting, depth of field. He taught her about developing and how to make the most of her negatives. On her own, she learned to take pictures with abandon; once an instant passed, it could never be revisited.

She put her knowledge to use in London and had gotten better with each roll of film. For the rest of her life that was what she wanted—to get better and better while she photographed life, like Dorothea Lange and Margaret Bourke-White.

She rolled onto her side, pulled her knees up to her pregnant belly. "Go away," she groaned. "I don't want you."

Tears rolled out of her eyes, and the nausea was creeping back. If she could have turned back the clock, she never would have gotten on that morning train to Dover, never would have fallen into the abyss.

Justine woke to the sound of her sister whispering from the doorway, "Justine, are you awake?"

Without opening her eyes, Justine nodded. She felt the bed sag as Martha Claire sat beside her and asked, "Are you feeling better?"

It was daylight. Justine had slept through the night when she'd thought she couldn't sleep at all. She opened her eyes and regarded her sister's distraught face. *Feeling better?* She took inventory. "I guess," she said.

Martha Claire had put a tray with tea and toast on the bedside table. "Mama said this was all you'd be wanting this morning," she said, looking imploringly at her sister. "Is it true?"

"So it seems," Justine said, propping herself up with a second pillow.

"Did some man force himself on you?" Martha Claire asked, her eyes wide. Green eyes—a more startling green than Justine's.

"No, nothing like that."

"Then if you loved him, why didn't you get married?"

Justine accepted the cup of tea from her sister and took a couple of sips. "I never said I loved him."

"I'm your sister, Justine. I know that you wouldn't have done something like that with a man if you didn't love him."

"Things were different over there. The war changed everything. We had too much to drink, and it just happened. I wish it hadn't, but it did, and I'm sorry. Very, very sorry. And that's all I'm ever going to say about it."

"But we've got to decide what we're going to tell people."

"I don't want you telling anyone anything," Justine said, putting the cup on the tray and lying back on the pillows. "Maybe I'll just go off someplace to have it and put it up for adoption. I wish I hadn't come home. Then no one would have to know anything."

"Why did you, then?"

"By the time I figured out what was going on, I was too sick to think of anything else."

"Well, now that you're here, you can't give away a baby," Martha Claire said. "We would all spend the rest of our lives wondering about it and feeling sorry."

"And if I don't give it away, I'll spend the rest of my life wishing I had. Actually, I came home with something else in mind. I didn't want anyone to know. Not ever. I was going to sneak across the tracks and let that old colored woman do whatever it is she does. But Mother knew the instant I got off that train. Can you believe that? Doc Hadley at least had to poke around, but Mother takes one look at me and knows."

"You can't do *that,* either, Justine," Martha Claire said, a hand on her breast, her eyes wide. "Remember Sadie Marie."

"Of course, I remember Sadie Marie! But at least things got settled for her, didn't they?"

Justine felt tears welling and turned her back to her sister. She hated crying. Hated feeling sorry for herself. Hated herself. Maybe she deserved to die like stupid ole Sadie Marie.

Christ, what a mess she had made of things! She didn't know what she was going to do and felt more helpless than she had ever felt in her entire life. But she didn't want to think about it right now, and she certainly didn't want to discuss it with her sister, who had never done anything wrong in her entire life. She wanted to tell Martha Claire to go away and leave her alone, but she was choking on her sobs and couldn't say anything at all.

Martha Claire began rubbing her sister's back and shoulders, telling her that it wasn't the end of the world, that they just had to be sensible about things.

Then Martha Claire started talking about how much she had missed Justine, how in some ways she had missed her more than Grayson. She had never really lived with Grayson. But Justine had been a part of every day until she went off to work in Houston, and even then they still visited back and forth all the time. She could always tell Justine everything; she only told Grayson what she wanted him to hear.

Justine felt herself relaxing under her sister's touch. They used to give each other back rubs all the time. And shared all their secrets. But no longer. Life would never be like that again.

"I hoped that when you got back home, you would realize that Columbus is where you belong," Martha Claire was saying. "If you stay here, I'll help you with the baby. Maybe that's why you got yourself pregnant in the first place, because in your heart of hearts you knew that you belong here with your family. Now, with a baby on the way, you'll need us more than ever. But we will have to tell people that you got married and your husband died, just like Mother says. He got blown up by a leftover bomb."

"Go away, Martha Claire," Justine groaned.

Without consulting her parents or sister, Martha Claire managed to get a brief obituary included in the next issue of the weekly *Colorado County Citizen* before it went to press on Wednesday afternoon: "Sergeant Major Philip Benston Dover. Born July 12, 1921, in Liverpool, England. Killed in the service of his country June 4, 1945, in London, England. Survived by his wife, Justine Mayfield Dover, of Columbus."

Of his own volition, the editor bumped a story about the ball-moss blight off page one for a story about the war's last hero. He told how a hometown girl serving as a WAC in London had danced in the streets with a young British soldier during the V-E celebration and married him three days later—only to be widowed soon after when he was killed defusing an undetonated bomb that had fallen in a south London neighborhood.

Martha Claire thanked God when she saw the story. A story in the newspaper made it true. Her parents and Granny Grace were over-joyed.

Justine burst into tears when she saw it.

"I'm sorry you're upset, Justine, but I had to do something. I just had to. Maybe you don't give a plugged nickel about this family's reputation. Maybe you think it won't affect us all when you get big out to here with no claim to a husband."

Justine blew her nose and handed the newspaper back to her sister. "It's okay. You did what you had to do. But why *Dover?*"

"I thought his name should sound English," Martha Claire explained.

Justine nodded and turned her face to the wall. "Do you want me to rub your back?" Martha Claire asked.

Justine gave her a muffled "No" and buried her head deeper in the pillow.

Neighbors and family friends began showing up at the front door in their Sunday best—the men with hats in hand, the women carrying casseroles, pies, bouquets of freshly picked flowers—to pay their respects to the grieving family. The phone rang continuously with folks saying how sorry they were and asking what they could do to help out. Reverend Huxley stopped by to ask about a memorial service. A reporter from the *Houston Post,* with a photographer in tow, arrived. He wanted an interview with Mrs. Philip Dover and a photograph of the young widow holding her dead husband's picture but had to settle for a photograph of the Mayfield family's handsome Victorian home with a funeral wreath on the front door. It was printed the following day next to a picture of Justine from a Columbus High School yearbook, along with an overwritten article that relied on interviews with neighbors and friends of the Mayfields: "A tomboy in high school, Mrs. Dover was the only woman from Colorado County to enlist in the Women's Army Corps. A friend recalled that Mrs. Dover had always wanted a career and claimed she would never get married and keep house."

Through it all, Justine stayed upstairs in her bed. She never should have come back home. She knew that now. She should have taken her chances with a coat hanger. She felt as though she were sinking into a quicksand bog from which there was no escape.

Justine and Martha Claire had always been known as "the Mayfield sisters." Everyone called them that back when they were two freckle-faced, fair-haired girls riding their bicycles up and down shady streets and county roads, roller-skating around the square, canoeing the river, playing hide-and-seek in the evenings with the neighborhood children.

And they daydreamed about leaving someday—going to New York, Hollywood, Paris. The Mayfield sisters would never settle for ordinary, never become boring proper ladies who did nothing more exciting than go to teas and club meetings. *Never.*

Even then, Justine should have known better, though. Martha Claire enjoyed pleasing people. She had learned how to bake a pie by the time she was ten and didn't mind wearing Sunday clothes. She always did her homework and had never once been sent to the principal's office. She was pretty and perfect and everyone loved her.

Justine hated school and church with equal passion and was frequently truant from both institutions, even though her own mother was the church organist. Her teachers passed her to the next grade to avoid having to deal with the defiant girl for another year. Her frustrated father would threaten to take the razor strap to her if she didn't straighten up but never could bring himself to take the strap down from its hook by the bathroom mirror. Her mother was calmer. Polly assured everyone that she admired Justine's free spirit and that the girl would have to grow up soon enough.

Justine watched while perfectly intelligent girls turned into pink-frocked dunderheads in the presence of boys, and decided she was never going to play that game. If a boy ever tried to kiss her, she'd sock him in the nose. "Then no boy is ever going to marry you," Martha Claire warned.

Justine blew up. "Haven't you been listening to me? I don't want to be some man's wife. I want to be *me.*"

In high school, Martha Claire started curling her hair and flirting. She made straight A's and was voted both the most intelligent and the most beautiful girl in her class. Justine still played hooky and rode her bicycle all over Colorado County. She smoked cigarettes with the boys behind the school, never made an A or even a B, except in physical education, and was never voted the most anything. People would shake their heads over Justine and marvel at the difference in the two sisters. Justine surely was taking a long time to settle down. But she would eventually. A girl couldn't stay a tomboy forever.

When Martha Claire and Grayson started keeping company, old ladies whispered behind their fans about what beautiful children they would someday have. Justine knew that the era of the Mayfield sisters was over. Whatever she did with her life, she would do it alone.

five

I must have been about nine when my aunt Justine asked me if I thought her name would have been inscribed on the plaques honoring Colorado County's war dead if she had died in London during the war. We were taking an evening stroll around the square and had stopped in front of the courthouse to pay our respects. That was in the years when Justine still came back to us. Justine's visits were more important than Christmas. As soon as one was over, we began planning for the next.

"Well, if you had choked to death on a fish bone, they probably wouldn't have included your name," I speculated. "But if you'd died in the bombing, I'd think they would have had to. You were a soldier, after all, just like the men."

Justine shook her head. "No, even if I'd died rescuing Winston Churchill from Nazi assassins, I don't think my name would be there—unless you and Iris circulated a petition and wrote letters to the newspaper. Then the city fathers might have reconsidered and added my name right down there," she said, touching a place right under "Sgt. Benjamin William Younger." The Youngers were country folk who lived out by Saints Peter and Paul Catholic Church and came into town on Saturday with eight or ten children in the back of the pickup.

"Did you know Benjamin?" I asked.

"Yes. He hardly ever opened his mouth except for spelling bees. I'll never forget the day he deposed Zellie Rae Baumert as fourth-grade spelling queen. Miss Edmondson gave me three slaps on my hand with a ruler for jumping up and down and whistling."

With a grin on her face, Justine rubbed her hand. Then she grew somber and touched Benjamin's name on the original plaque. A second plaque held the names that had been left off the first one. All total, fifty-one names were inscribed.

"War is so confusing," Justine said. "Really sweet boys like Benny Younger never *came* home, and those of us who *did* will never get over it. Yet, we wouldn't have missed it for the world."

"I'm glad you didn't miss it," I told her. "If you had, you never would have met Sergeant Major Philip Benston Dover, and then there never would have been an Iris."

Justine smiled and nodded.

"It's sad that Iris will never know her father," I said. "Of course, Buddy and I don't know our real father, either, but we have Daddy."

"And so does Iris," Justine reminded me.

Justine took my hand, and we walked on. I never thought of my aunt as a widow lady, even though that was what she was. The only other widows I knew had white hair and put flowers on graves. But Justine only had known her husband for a very short time—like in one of those sad movies with Irene Dunne or Susan Hayward. My cousin Iris didn't even have a picture of her father. Someday, she was going to England and track down his relatives to see if they had a picture of him.

Other ladies wore dresses downtown, but Justine—in spite of her widow-lady status—always wore slacks, like Katharine Hepburn. In fact, she reminded me of Katharine Hepburn, with her long legs, big stride, and plain-speaking ways.

I remember wishing that I could have been a little like Justine, but the truth of the matter was, I didn't have the nerve to be different. Of course, Buddy and I were the only adopted kids in town, so we could never be just like the other kids.

"If you had died in the war, there wouldn't be an Iris to help with the petition to have your name added to the memorial," I reminded her, looking back over my shoulder at my cousin, who had stopped to visit with one of the old men who came to sit on the park benches on warm summer evenings.

Justine hugged me and laughed her wonderful, big brassy laugh. "You're right, my little sweetie pie. Good thing I dodged all those bombs. If I hadn't made it back from the war, you would have had to get my name on that monument all by yourself."

"Buddy would have helped me," I pointed out. "People would pay more attention if a boy asked them to sign a petition."

Then suddenly Justine wasn't laughing. "Listen here, Cissy Stewart, don't ever think that because you're a girl you can't do things."

Of course, because of her, I already knew that. Justine shunned convention and had never let being a woman hold her back. She had even photographed the war in Korea, and her pictures had been in newspapers and magazines all over the world. She had won a national award for her picture of a little Korean boy in torn clothing, sitting in the snow by his mother's dead body. He was holding his mother's hand, and you could see the thick snot running out his nose, the dirt on his face, the puzzlement in his eyes. It was the sort of picture that you couldn't forget about after you had turned the page. A lot of Justine's photographs were like that.

Granny Grace said that Justine had graduated from high school by the skin of her teeth. Yet, she had grown up to be a famous photographer. She was a woman who hadn't paid much attention to ministers and teachers and still got to do exactly as she wished. She was the exact opposite of my mother, who had made straight A's and paid a great deal of attention to what other people expected of her.

I was not a young Justine in the making. I knew that even then. I hadn't the courage to alienate my mother and flout convention—probably more because of my mother than of any respect for convention. I had a need to please her that came from deep inside of me. I was, above all, Martha Claire Stewart's adopted daughter. And perhaps, even though I loved Justine very much, I also shared my mother's disdain for a woman who would leave her daughter for someone else to raise. Justine was able to travel the world and become a famous photographer because my mother was raising her daughter.

Of course, it was quite impossible to imagine Justine as a Columbus matron, keeping house with an apron tied around her waist, making casseroles and cakes for covered-dish socials at the church, or putting on a hat and white gloves to attend club meetings with all the other ladies. And Iris did have both a legend for a mother and a doting aunt to care for her. Her life did not seem deficient in any way. She was a happy, sparkling girl who enjoyed people and didn't have a shy bone in her body. At that moment, she was hunkered down in front of old Mr. Barnhart, listening to some story about the good old days she'd probably heard many times before. When she laughed at something he said, the look on the old man's face was one of absolute delight. Then Iris jumped up, kissed his wrinkled cheek, and came skipping in our direction with pigtails bouncing. I looked up at my aunt Justine's face as she watched her daughter. Other than their strawberry blond hair and green eyes, the only way in which my aunt and my mother were alike was the way they looked at Iris, never with censure—even if her hair was mussed and her face dirty—always with adoration.

Since earliest memory, a picture of my aunt and my mother hung among the gallery of framed family pictures that marched up the staircase wall. The picture had hung there since before I was born. It had been taken when the Mayfield sisters were teenagers—fifteen and sixteen, probably. Tall, athletic Justine was wearing a plaid skirt, white blouse, and saddle oxfords. My mother, clutching a straw handbag, was dainty in a ruffled frock and high-heeled white pumps.

After the falling-out between Mama and Justine, Mama burned that picture in the backyard. I found its absence jarring and thought about the picture that wasn't there far more than I would have if it still occupied the space above the fourth step. Even after it was replaced with a studio portrait of Iris, Buddy, and me, I thought about it. The wall didn't seem right without it.

In my mind's eye, I can see that picture still. The Mayfield sisters portrayed there were so pretty, so fresh-faced and young, their arms linked forever in sisterly affection, with no foreshadowing of the schism to come. When that picture was taken, they thought they would have each other for a lifetime.

"I think you'd make a terrific army wife," Justine told her sister as she hammered the lid back on the paint can.

"Why do you say that?" Martha Claire demanded.

"Just think of all the 'finishing' you got over at Mary Hardin Baylor College for young women. You probably know as much about etiquette as Emily Post."

"Don't make fun," Martha Claire said as she worked the paintbrush back and forth on the layers of newspaper that protected the floor from drips.

Justine carefully lowered her pregnant body onto the wooden crate that held the photo enlarger she'd ordered from Sears and Roebuck. They could just roll her to the hospital when it came time for this baby to be born. She'd always felt like a cow next to her dainty sister. Now she felt like an elephant—and still with a month to go.

"I'm not making fun of you, Martha Claire," she said with great earnestness, hoping that just once her sister would follow her advice. "I really mean it. Officers' wives have to know all about etiquette and protocol and how to dress appropriately and entertain beautifully so their husbands can get promoted. You and Grayson would be a great team. With you managing the home front, he'd probably be a general someday, and a general's wife is like royalty. All the other officers' wives have to stand up whenever she walks into the room and serve on whatever committee she says. And I remember back in Grayson's cadet days at A&M, you used to say the most glorious sight you could possibly imagine was Grayson in his uniform."

"We were young and courting back then," Martha Claire insisted with a scowl that creased her smooth forehead. "Now we're married and have to plan for the future."

"Oh come on!" Justine scoffed. "You can't tell me that when he finally steps off the train into your waiting arms you'd just as soon he'd be wearing slacks and a tweed jacket. I don't think so. The fantasy is for him to be in uniform, isn't it?"

Martha Claire shrugged. "Sure—coming full circle. He left here in uniform; he'll come home in one." Then she got a wistful look on her face. "I think about that moment a lot. I wish he would surprise me and get home for Christmas. I've been married three and a half years and never spent a Christmas with my husband."

Even wearing old clothes, with her hair tied up in a bandanna, Martha Claire was lovely—like Greer Garson in *Mrs. Miniver*. Justine had never known anyone who was so comfortable in her own body, her own face, her own smile. Justine would find herself staring at Martha Claire, waiting for the next smile. Everyone did that. Martha Claire's pretty face and effervescent moods were constant sources of fascination. In high school, she could turn any boy to putty with one of her smiles. Girls, too. Everyone wanted to be Martha Claire's friend. She was the center of every gathering. No wonder Grayson had fallen in love with her. Lots of other boys had, too. But Martha Claire had zeroed in on Grayson the first week of her sophomore year in high school, when he marched up onto the stage and sang "When the Moon Comes Over the Mountain" at a back-to-school amateur hour, and she never wavered in her aim. She bought Kate Smith's recording of the song and played it over and over again. She told Justine that she had decided that someday she was going to marry Grayson Stewart and have his babies.

Always before, Justine and Martha Claire had been a team. Then suddenly, in the course of one week, Justine realized she would face the rest of her life without her sister at her side. Grayson did have a surprisingly nice voice, and he had looked nice up on the stage in a suit and tie, but he was still the same old Grayson Stewart he had always been. Just another dumb boy. He wasn't even a very good football player. And Justine could beat him in a footrace any day of the week. She could hold her breath underwater longer than Grayson and make more baskets in a row. In fact, Grayson had always been her pal more than Martha Claire's.

She tried to hate Grayson, but eventually she realized she had been railing against the inevitable. In spite of perfect report cards, her sister was just like all the other girls in Columbus who knew the words to every sappy love song sung by Bing Crosby and sat around embroidering flowers on pillow cases for their hope chests. Martha Claire was bound and determined to waste her intelligence and charm and prettiness. If not Grayson, she would marry some other hometown boy and live a boring, conventional life.

Justine reached over and stroked her sister's hand. "I know how hard these past years have been for you, but now the most important thing is for you and Grayson to be together again. I want you both to be happy, and I worry that if you make Grayson stay here and spend the rest of his life doing something he doesn't want to do, neither one of you will be."

Martha Claire shook her head. "If Grayson stayed in the army we'd spend our lives as homeless vagabonds. We'd always be living among strangers, and our children would be born God-knows-where. I want to live here, and before the war Grayson did, too. Columbus is our home."

"He's not the same man that he was before the war," Justine warned. "You know that, but you're being stubborn. For God's sake, Martha Claire, the man's been off saving the world. He's been through hell. He deserves a chance at happiness."

"Other men have come back home and settled in. What makes Grayson so different?"

"Other men didn't have a military education," Justine pointed out. "You know how he took to all the regimental stuff up at College Station. He was the corps commander, for God's sake—the number one cadet! And now he's a captain with medals on his chest. He has a chance for a distinguished military career, and you want him to be a shopkeeper!"

Martha Claire sighed her exasperation. "What's so bad about being a shopkeeper? Our daddy has tended his pharmacy for twenty-five years. Grayson's family has always had that dry goods store. He'll get back here and remember what it was like to grow up in Columbus. He'll want the same for our children."

"Living in Columbus isn't some sort of guarantee, you know. If he were my husband, I would set him free, even if it meant losing him."

Martha Claire's head jerked up. Anger flared in her eyes, but her reply was calm. "This is where Grayson and I belong. It is the best place in the world for a family. You know that as well as I do. Just think of all those canoe rides on the river. Think of the Saturday matinees, the county fair, the Friday night football games. Think of living among people you've always known. Why would I want to live anyplace else?"

"So that when you're on your deathbed, you don't have to be sorry that you lived such a limited life," Justine snapped back.

"Is that what you think of Mama and Daddy? That they are limited?"

"They aren't, but their life is. Oh, Martha Claire, you can't imagine what it was like over there—history and war and life all mixed up together. Even with the Blitz, England was splendid. And now the war is over. I can go to Paris, Rome, Casablanca, Copenhagen. I can go anywhere I want! There's a whole big incredible world out there, and I want to see it all. Once you did, too. You were going to be a famous actress with your name in lights and your picture on the covers of magazines."

"Good grief, Justine! That was just a childish daydream!"

Silence fell over the room, with its smell of paint and turpentine. Sounds of children's laughter drifted up from the sidewalk below the window. With one hand on her pregnant belly and the other rubbing at her aching back, Justine asked softly, "What do you daydream about now?"

Martha Claire's face went soft as she said, "I dream about Grayson coming home. And having babies. Living in a wonderful old house with a big front porch and a garden all around. Maybe someday Grayson will be elected mayor, and I'll be state president of the United Daughters of the Confederacy."

Her piece said, Martha Claire stood abruptly. She walked around the room, inspecting the walls she'd just painted, signifying the end of the conversation.

Poor Grayson, Justine thought. He would have to hang up his uniform and put on a vest and tie, as his father had done when he came home from World War I, the way men had always done, she supposed. Grayson would spend his years stocking shelves and selling shirts when he could have had a different sort of life.

And she herself was facing the same sort of prison, here in this very room. Not that it wasn't a nice room, over their father's pharmacy, with two windows in the front that looked out on the square and a storeroom with no windows where she would set up her darkroom.

Justine remembered when Maybelle Owens had opened a beauty shop up here, to support herself and her two children after her husband ran off. When she died of pneumonia, the children went to live with relatives over in Tyler.

Justine sighed and stared down at her belly. She didn't hate the baby anymore. It hadn't asked to be conceived. But she did hate what was happening to her life.

She would open a photography studio to support herself and her child. They would live in what once had been servants' quarters over a carriage-house-turned-garage behind the family home. Everyone had pitched in to make it livable. Martha Claire and Daddy painted. Granny Grace made curtains and a bedspread. Mother had scrounged around in the attic for furniture and household goods. Justine had decided to wait until after the baby was born to move in. Right now, she took comfort in having her mother just down the hall, and she was afraid of the permanence that the apartment and these rooms over the pharmacy represented.

She still had her dreams, but she felt as though she were sliding out of control down an icy slope. She couldn't stay here, but she didn't know how to leave. How could she be a mother and have a life of her own?

She stared at her backward name that was already painted on one of the front windows: JUSTINE MAYFIELD-DOVER, PHOTOGRAPHER. She'd borrowed the hyphen from Margaret Bourke-White. How strange to have a different name, as though she really had been married. Her mother talked about the mythical Philip Dover as though he had really existed. He'd been raised by his grandparents, Polly had told their next-door neighbor Mrs. Carpenter. Philip's grandfather had owned a bakery in Liverpool. Philip had worked there after school.

Dover. Beautiful Dover. Strange that Martha Claire had chosen that name. Justine closed her eyes and saw the castle ruins. She had stood on the edge of the white cliffs with the wind whipping her hair around her face and the taste of the sea in the air and actually seen France across the strait.

Poor Grayson, she thought. She felt for him from the bottom of her heart. His sentence was for life. Hers would not be, she vowed.

six

Martha Claire stood with her parents and grandmother at the nursery window, peering through the glass at Justine's newborn baby—an absolutely beautiful baby girl, asleep in a bassinet. The nurse drew back the blanket so they could see tiny fingers and toes. Martha Claire was transfixed. *A baby*—surely the most wondrous thing in the world, what she herself wanted more than anything.

Had the baby's little mouth already nursed at Justine's breast? Martha Claire felt a tingling in her own nipples at the thought, and rubbed at them, imagining a baby at her breast. She longed to hold this child, to kiss her sweet face and inhale her baby scent. Soon, she would have her own baby, but in the meantime she would have her sister's child to fill her heart. Iris was her name. Beautiful little Iris.

She and her mother had stayed with Justine throughout the night while the pains ripped though her body and made her cry out time and again. Hour after hour it went on, her screams echoing up and down the hospital corridor. In between the pains, Martha Claire wiped the sweat from her sister's brow and rubbed her back. Justine hadn't cried out at all when Doc Hadley set the arm she had broken in a fall from the porch roof, but she had screamed like someone possessed all through that long nightmarish night.

Martha Claire wished that Grayson were here with her now to see perfect little Iris in the first hours of her life. He had called from New York yesterday, before Justine went into labor. He was accompanying his command to Fort Bragg, North Carolina, and would muster out there. In just a matter of days he would be home.

She wouldn't have slept last night even if Justine hadn't gone into labor. Now that the time of her husband's return was actually at hand, she felt uneasy. Afraid, even. Grayson had become a stranger to her, someone she used to know. He had been involved in the repatriation of displaced persons, including the poor souls liberated from Nazi death camps—from Dachau, Buchenwald, Auschwitz, Bergen-Belsen. The newsreels at the movies reflected his letters—ghastly pictures of skeletal people with empty eyes staring at the camera, pictures so horrible that Martha Claire had to look away. And stacks of unburied dead— more than ten thousand bodies at Bergen-Belsen alone. Grayson wrote about broken, diseased people who had no possessions, no family, no spirit; people who had lost everything. His heart was heavy for the suffering of others when she wanted it to be light and filled with hope and love and thoughts of her and the wonderful future that awaited them. Of course, he wrote at the beginning and end of each letter how much he loved her, how much he wanted and needed her, but his words seemed rote—a man writing the words a wife might expect to see. What if Justine was right? What if he ended up hating her for insisting they spend the rest of their lives in Columbus, where no one could ever completely understand what he had seen and felt, not even his own wife?

Being with Grayson once had seemed the most natural thing in the world. She had been a virgin when they married, but just barely. They had had their secret place in a riverside grove, where they took off their clothes and did everything short of going all the way. She enjoyed their mutual beauty as much as the touching and kissing. One night she insisted that he sneak up to her room so they could undress in front of the cheval mirror that stood in the corner of her bedroom and admire the reflection of their embracing bodies. "When we're old, we must remember how we looked tonight," she had whispered.

Justine had wanted Martha Claire to join the Women's Army Corps with her. They could serve together, she insisted, and do their part for the war effort.

For a heartbeat, Martha Claire had been tempted. She could keep her childhood promise to her sister. They would go off together before she settled down with Grayson. But what if he never came back? What if he died over there? If that happened, she wanted him to die as her husband. She wanted his child to love and raise.

She abandoned her plans for a big wedding at some point in the unknown future and decided to marry Grayson in her mother's rose garden the same week that she graduated from Mary Hardin Baylor and the day after he had graduated from Texas A&M and received his commission as a second lieutenant in the United States Army. With luck, she would be pregnant by the time Grayson shipped out. Then no matter what happened, she would have their child to raise and love.

Grayson had been reluctant about the hurry-up wedding. Everything was so uncertain, he told her. Maybe they should wait until the war was over. He wanted their wedding to be a time of unfettered joy, with their future assured. If he was killed over there, he didn't want her to face life as a widow.

"But I need to be your wife," Martha Claire explained. "I couldn't bear to send you off to war otherwise."

They all worked around the clock to get the house and garden ready for the wedding. Martha Claire had fretted about the weather, but her wedding day arrived fair and blue. The air was filled with the scent of wisteria, magnolia, and rose blossoms. Her wedding dress had been worn by her grandmother and her mother before her. Grayson was married in his cadet uniform, complete with high boots and jodhpur breeches. Martha Claire's roommate from Mary Hardin Baylor played the violin from the freshly painted gazebo. In front of family and friends, with her sister at her side, Martha Claire had proudly said the words that bound her to Grayson for a lifetime. Justine had tried valiantly to be happy for her. "I wish we could have stayed kids forever," she said as she hugged her sister good-bye.

"You'll get married, too, someday," Martha Claire said. "We can live next door and raise our families together."

The newlyweds spent their wedding night in a tourist court outside Sugar Land on the way to a honeymoon on Galveston Island. "Make me pregnant," she whispered as Grayson entered her body for the first time. "Give me a baby, please."

For one week, they walked for miles along Galveston's great empty beaches, gorged themselves on fresh seafood, reveled in the awesome beauty of ocean sunsets, made love morning and night—lovemaking made even more intense by their impending separation. Afterward, they would hold each other and talk about the future with tears and assurances. He would come back to her. They would be happy. Their love was forever. But Grayson became distant at times, and she knew he was thinking not about their mutual future but his own more immediate one. He tried to hide his excitement, but she could hear it in his voice, see it in his eyes. He wanted to go, as did Justine. They both would rather go to war than stay in Columbus with her. This knowledge ate at her and altered the nature of her love for them.

After she and Grayson returned to Columbus, they spent one night together in her parents' house—a strange, inhibiting experience after all the privacy and passion in their beachside bungalow. The next day, Grayson rode the train to Fort Sill, Oklahoma, where he would attend the twelve-week battery-officer training course.

Three times, Martha Claire made the seven-hour train ride into southwestern Oklahoma, getting off in downtown Lawton and walking to a nearby hotel. Grayson would catch a ride into town and meet her there. He would have to be back at the base the next morning, leaving Martha Claire to her long ride home.

She and Grayson had not conceived a child on their honeymoon or during her three visits to Lawton. Their last night together, in the Lawton hotel, she had prayed with such fervor that she grew lightheaded, first in the privacy of the bathroom, then kneeling beside the bed. She asked Grayson to join her, which he did willingly. Together they prayed. He wanted a baby, too. He was thrilled about what lay ahead and scared to the depths of his being. A baby would make facing death easier.

As he thrust his way into her body, she was beyond lust. She was floating in a high celestial space with brilliant light all around. If God loved her at all, He would give her a baby. She could almost feel it happening inside of her. She was filled with rapture and hope.

Two weeks later, Grayson was in Boston, awaiting embarkation to Africa, and Martha Claire was staring down at a telltale show of blood on the crotch of her underpants. She wept bitter tears, her dream of a baby reduced to a bloody stain. And a deep-seated fear became embedded in her soul. What if there would be no baby ever? At some level, that thought remained with her always. The specter of childlessness would catch her unawares and turn her heart to ice. Who would she be if not a mother?

She thought of the town's childless women. They were objects of pity. People lowered their voices to discuss a woman's childless state: *Poor Betty Jane. She never could have children, you know.*

Because she was a naturally positive person, though, Martha Claire was able to keep fear at bay. After all, she and Grayson had been married only a short time, had been together only twelve nights, all told. They had just been unlucky. He would come home, and she'd have a baby within the year.

For three and a half years she had waited for his return, prayed for his return, longed for his body, read and reread his letters. Waiting became a way of life. And fear became her constant companion, fear that the dreaded military sedan would pull up in front of the house, with a solemn-faced officer coming to the door.

Grayson had been wounded when a mortar shell hit his jeep and killed his driver. He had been in southern France then, after fighting with the 45th Division up the Italian boot. There had been some worry that he would lose an eye, but he hadn't written about that until the danger had passed.

When Grayson's father had a heart attack, she began helping out down at the store. She was grateful for the structure it gave her life and often wondered what she would have done with herself if poor Mr. Stewart had remained healthy. Working at the store was only temporary, of course. When Grayson returned she would become a full-time homemaker and mother.

She had saved all of Grayson's letters—a trunk full of V-mail letters —photographs of letters, actually, with the heavy black blocks where the censors had made their deletions. Hundreds of letters. He wouldn't have saved hers, of course—he would have no way to do that.

Now his letters weren't censored. The war had ended. For months now, she had almost resented his letters when they arrived. In spite of transportation problems and the nationwide stevedores' strike, other men had already returned, especially now that there was peace on both fronts. How could she complain, though, when what he was doing was so noble and good? But what if he had volunteered for extended duty to put off his return? Was he punishing her for refusing to leave Columbus and denying him a military career?

He had been gracious in defeat, however, writing that Martha Claire was exactly right—there had been an implied promise on his part that they would make their home in Columbus. He had a responsibility to her and his parents. Stewart's Dry Goods had been a Columbus institution for two generations. After all, he could continue his military service on a part-time basis in the Texas National Guard. It wasn't as though he was hanging up his uniform forever. They would have a good life in their beloved Columbus.

When he'd called last night, she hadn't recognized his voice. Who was this man saying her name? He sounded so far away, his voice coming to her over a sea of background voices and static. "It's me," he said. He was calling from the pier in New York City. The ship had just docked. He explained about Fort Bragg. He would call as soon as he knew more.

"I love you, Martha Claire," he said. "You are my life."

His voice broke. He meant what he said. But there had also been resignation in his voice. He wanted her *and* something else, and he was having to settle for just her. She had won, and she had lost.

But they would heal themselves with a family. She wanted three, four, maybe five children. She would bring Grayson here to the hospital to see this precious newborn child. Before they made love even, they would make this pilgrimage together, to the place where their own babies would be born. When he saw the miracle of Iris, he would better understand where their love would lead them.

She had rented a two-bedroom house next door to her in-laws and finally unpacked her and Grayson's wedding gifts. She painted every room, refinished furniture, made curtains, all the while so full of anticipation it made her dizzy at times. After she made up the bed for the first time, she stretched out on it and closed her eyes. It wouldn't be long now. Life would begin anew. "I love you, Grayson," she had whispered, imagining him here in her arms, undressing her, covering her body with kisses.

Martha Claire was alone now at the nursery window. The others had gone to fuss over Justine, but Martha Claire didn't want to leave. Not yet. Iris was her baby, too. Grayson would take over management of the store, and Martha Claire would care for Iris while Justine worked at her new photography studio. *Soon,* she hoped. She had already bought a secondhand crib and rocking chair.

During Justine's labor, Martha Claire had asked about notifying the father. Surely a man would want to know that he had a child.

Justine had exploded. "The man does not exist! Do you hear me? He does not exist. This child does not have a father. I am having this baby all by myself, and I don't ever want to have it brought up again."

"Hush," Martha Claire said. "Someone will hear you yelling like that."

Then Justine's yelling turned into screaming as her body arched in another contraction. "Does she really have to make that much noise?" Martha Claire asked her mother.

"Yes, dear, she does," Polly said, clutching Justine's hand.

Justine's screaming finally turned to gasping. "God, how long was that one?" she wanted to know.

"I forgot to time it," Martha Claire said. "At least tell us that you loved him, Justine, that this baby's father wasn't just some anonymous soldier you met one night in a bar."

"Go to hell," Justine said.

"Justine!" Polly snapped, but already Justine's body had arched in another contraction. "It won't be long now, honey," Polly had promised.

It was, though. The contractions became longer and longer, with only seconds in between, and the nurse periodically asking them to leave the room so she could check Justine again. Then Doc Hadley came to do the checking. "She's doing fine," he assured them. "First babies just take a while."

At first, Martha Claire had been certain that if her sister would just calm down, things would move along more quickly. But as the hours went by and Justine became delirious with exhaustion, she changed her mind. Her mother asked if she wouldn't like to sit with her father and grandmother in the waiting room.

She stayed on, of course. It was her duty. She was Justine's sister.

Nothing Martha Claire had seen in the movies or read in books, however, prepared her for watching her sister's seemingly endless suffering. At times, she even wondered if Justine would die, but her mother, Doc Hadley, and the nurses did not seem concerned. And even while she witnessed hour after hour of her sister's agony, listening to her screams, praying that the ordeal would soon be over, Martha Claire imagined how it would be when her own time came. Grayson would be at her side, marveling at her bravery. If he could endure a war, she could endure childbirth. She would welcome each back-arching pain. She would suffer anything to have their child.

Finally, the nurses came and wheeled Justine into the delivery room. Thirty minutes later, Doc Hadley brought the baby out into the hall for them all to see. "A fine girl," he had announced. "Almost eight pounds."

The baby was more than fine. She was exquisite. Martha Claire pressed her fingertips against the glass. Iris should be *her* baby. Justine didn't want to be a mother. Maybe she would go off and have her career and leave Iris for her sister and brother-in-law to raise.

seven

The minute Martha Claire saw Grayson stepping down from the train, she realized that her sister had been right. She was indeed getting back a different man.

He had seen horrors she couldn't imagine, been places she would never go. Even though she'd seen every newsreel, read newspaper accounts, and sat with her parents every evening by the radio to listen to the evening news with Edward R. Murrow, Gabriel Heatter, H. V. Kaltenborn, or Lowell Thomas reporting from London, she would never understand how the war years had been for her husband. She had wanted to believe, though, that once he was home the years would roll back, and they would be newlyweds again. They would begin anew, this time without an impending war and separation hanging over their heads.

However, now that Grayson was actually in her arms once again, she realized that the part of him that was young and carefree had died over there along with his comrades-in-arms. There was a part of him she would never be able to know, when once she had known him completely.

But oh, how sweet it was to have his arms around her once again, to hear his voice, to lift her face for that first kiss.

"All that kept me alive was thinking about this moment and being with you again," he said, burying his face in her hair. No woman could want more than that from her man.

"My darling, my darling," she whispered. "We'll never be apart again. Never."

Reluctantly she relinquished him to his parents, who were sobbing uncontrollably. His father had suffered two heart attacks and gone from robust to fragile while his son was at war. All he wanted, he would say again and again, was to live long enough to see his boy safely home. If he was granted that wish, he could die a happy man. Martha Claire had tried to warn Grayson in her letters, but there was shock on his face as he embraced his father's frail body.

Then Martha Claire's parents stepped up to embrace their son-in-law. And Granny Grace. Only Justine was missing. But they would go by the hospital later to see her and the baby.

No one could stop crying. Even the stationmaster was wiping his eyes. Except for two boys still in the hospital over at Fort Sam Houston, Grayson was the last Columbus serviceman to come home from the war.

They had dinner at his parents' house. With his parents, in-laws, and wife hanging on his every word, Grayson told them that Africa had been majestic and humbling. He would like to have met Rommel. Desert warfare was army against army without the ravished countryside and destroyed cities that he'd seen in Europe. He would like to return to Italy and France someday, after the wounds of war had had a chance to heal. Even with war all around, the timeless beauty of the towns and countryside had touched him deeply, as had people who welcomed them as liberators. When his dad asked him if many of the men from his original unit had been killed, he answered, "Most of them."

After dinner, he pulled gifts from his duffel bag. For his father, there was a German helmet he had found in the rubble of a burned-out barracks. For Polly and Granny Grace, he had bottles of French perfume they probably would never open but would treasure always. For his mother and Martha Claire, he had exquisite music boxes from Austria. For his father-in-law, Walter, he had Swiss chocolates in a tin shaped like a grandfather clock. And he presented Aunt Orna, the family's longtime housekeeper, a handmade lace handkerchief from Belgium. Then he put his arms around Orna and told her she still made the best peach cobbler in the state of Texas and he was so sorry about her grandson, who'd been killed at the Battle of Midway.

Orna wiped her tears on her apron and said she wished she could have died in his place.

"I wish I could have known him better," Grayson told her. "The colored soldiers fought bravely. You can be proud, very proud."

As they said good-night, he promised his father, "I'll be down at the store in the morning."

At the hospital, they viewed Justine's baby through the nursery window. "She's lovely," was all Grayson said.

Martha Claire wasn't sure what she had expected, but his reaction was disappointing. "I wish she were *our* baby," she told him.

They walked silently down to Justine's room, where Grayson politely kissed his sister-in-law's cheek, congratulated her on a beautiful baby, listened to her rant a bit about being held captive in a hospital for ten whole days when poor women had babies at home and went back to cooking and scrubbing the very same day. Then she stopped abruptly. "Your husband is exhausted, Martha Claire. You need to take him home."

During the short ride, Martha Claire's palms began to sweat, and her stomach tied itself in knots. She hadn't been this nervous on their wedding night.

With great seriousness, Grayson carried her across the threshold, then he walked through the house. "I thought you said it was run-down."

"It was a month ago."

"You did all this?"

"Daddy helped with the floors. I wanted our first home to be pretty." Martha Claire looked around, trying to see the little house through his eyes. Had she made it too fussy? Maybe she should have chosen a stripe to slipcover the sofa instead of a floral print and drapes instead of ruffled curtains. Tomorrow she would put away the doilies she'd crocheted for the coffee and end tables.

Martha Claire lit candles and opened a bottle of champagne. "To my husband," she said, lifting her glass.

He picked up his glass, then put it down again and buried his face in his hands. Martha Claire held him while he cried, unsure of the source of his tears. Finally, the sobs subsided, and she felt all the energy drain from his body.

She helped him out of his uniform and drew a bath for him. He was asleep by the time she crawled into bed beside him.

"Where are we going?" Grayson asked.

"It's a surprise," Martha Claire said, trying to sound merry when she was so nervous she felt almost ill. It felt strange to be driving with her husband as a passenger, but that wasn't why she was nervous—at least not the primary reason. She was taking a risk, something that went against her nature.

Grayson had been home almost two weeks—two very polite weeks. Mealtime was a strain. Sitting in the living room after dinner, they were like two old people, listening to the news, Martha Claire with her sewing basket, Grayson with the newspaper or a book. He was quiet and withdrawn. And so thin. He looked and sounded older. Deep lines radiated from the corners of his eyes; his voice was less animated, his skin weathered. She wanted him to talk about the war and make her understand why he had changed so, but he said he couldn't. "Will you ever?" she asked.

"I don't know," he'd answered.

They had made love at dawn that first morning. He cried again and said he was grateful to have lived to come home to her. So many had died. It didn't seem right that he had lived to return home to his wife when others had not. Good men. Better men than he. Braver men. Martha Claire stroked his back and kissed his tears. The first time was just something to get over with, she told herself. Next time would be different.

And it had been. That same evening, they came together again, quietly, carefully, without tears. And every night since, it had been so. Martha Claire was left longing for the abandonment of their honeymoon, when their bodies had fused like streams of molten lava.

It was a beautiful evening, with a warm breeze and full moon. The river was at its romantic best, all silvery in the moonlight. Theirs was the only car on the gravel road.

When she turned down the rutted lane, Grayson sighed. At the end of the lane, in a riverside stand of willow, was an abandoned duck blind—their special place, where they had come to spread a blanket, drink forbidden whiskey, take off their clothes, experience flesh against flesh. Martha Claire wanted to revisit those times of high passion and endless kisses. She had a blanket in the trunk, a flask in her purse.

She stopped the car. "Please," she said.

He put his arms around her. "Ah, sweet Martha Claire. We didn't leave the magic down by the river."

"Then where is it?" She was crying—not pretty crying. Great hiccupping sobs escaped from deep inside of her. *Where had the passion gone?*

"We have to start all over again," he said, caressing her hair, her back, her wet cheeks. "There's no way to go back to that other time. We can't be those two lusty youngsters necking among the cattails."

"What will happen to us?" she asked.

"We will make our home together, raise a family, help our parents as they grow older. We'll run the store as best we can. If we make enough money, I hope we can travel some. I'd like to take you to Europe. And Africa. Other places. Peacetime travel."

"Do you still want to stay in the army?" she asked, her voice small. "If it's what you really want . . ."

He buried his face against her neck. "It's all right, Martha Claire. I won't make you leave Columbus. I want more than anything to make you happy. That's all I want out of life—to make you happy."

And his mouth found hers. The kiss was salty. Deep. Full of need. *Oh, yes,* she thought. *Please.* And they did revisit that other time and were able to satiate themselves with youthful ardor. At last she could kiss his body with abandon and make him cry out in passion.

Curled in the circle of his arm as he drove them home, hope flowed in her veins. Tonight was *the* night. She felt it as never before. Their first child had been conceived. She even laced her fingers across her belly, already protecting, already loving.

Polly and Grace kept assuring Justine that the baby was just a bit colicky. She would get over it. It just takes time. And as Justine endured endless nights and miserable days, she felt genuinely sorry for the poor little creature. She didn't doubt for a minute that Iris truly was suffering from tummy aches or birth trauma or whatever it was that gave babies colic. Justine was too exhausted to cope, though, too exhausted to care. If asked to choose between a million dollars and an uninterrupted night's sleep, she would take sleep. She wanted to sleep for one hundred years, or at least long enough that the baby would be grown and gone.

For months, Justine had warned Doc Hadley that she absolutely would not breast-feed the baby. She simply could not be tied down like that. He nodded his graying head and said that would be just fine. But when the baby arrived, he insisted that Justine needed to nurse for a week or so, "just to get the baby off to a good start."

The second day home, holding a crying infant to her shoulder, she called Doc Hadley to inform him that the baby didn't like her milk. How did one make formula?

Of course the baby liked her milk, the doctor said. It wasn't the reason for her colic. He suggested Justine pump her breasts and let her mother take over the night feedings. But just the idea of actually *milking* her unbelievably tender, swollen breasts sent shudders through Justine's body.

Justine yelled at him, accusing him of torturing her, of punishing her for not wanting to be a mother, of being mean and hateful. When she ran out of words, he told her good-bye, and the receiver went dead.

Her mother and grandmother showed her about rocking, jiggling, and pacing, activities that Justine performed by the hour. But Iris cried on. The only thing that quieted her was sticking a nipple in her mouth. Justine felt like a cow. Her world had been reduced to two hideous, red, raw, cracking nipples and a miserably unhappy baby. When the baby took hold, there was an instant of sharp pain that shot all the way to Justine's toes. Then the baby would nurse greedily for a short time, fall asleep with her mother's nipple in her mouth—and start crying the minute Justine put her down. So Justine sat by the hour, cold and miserable in the uncomfortable spindleback rocker, with one of her nipples either being sucked on or simply occupying the mouth of her marginally asleep infant. Justine wept when the radio station signed off for the night. Didn't radio people know there were women out there who needed the talking and music to keep them from going crazy? She was a prisoner. A recluse. She didn't even get dressed. All she wore was milk-stained flannel gowns, wool socks, and a pad between her legs to catch the globs of blood that her poor, traumatized body kept passing.

Her mother, sister, and grandmother came often and did what they could. If it weren't for the nursing, they could take the baby home with them. The one week of required breast-feeding turned into two, then three. Justine insisted that she had to wean the baby, but Doc Hadley wouldn't hear of it, not until she and the baby were getting along better. Polly and Grace concurred. Justine would have done it anyway, but she didn't know how to make formula and sterilize bottles. Didn't even know where one bought the necessary paraphernalia. Couldn't face the thought of making herself presentable enough to go to a public place and buy what she needed.

Out of desperation, Justine began emulating her mother and grandmother in their endless stream of baby talk, which did seem momentarily to distract the baby from her wailing. Justine talked to Iris in a syrupy, coochy-coochy-coo voice, explaining to her daughter that she was ruining her mother's life, that she would rather be anyplace in the world than stuck here in a garage apartment behind the house where she had grown up with a baby who cried all the time. She was supposed to be in New York by now, or some other major city outside of the state of Texas—Chicago, San Francisco, even Kansas City—beginning her career as a newspaper photographer.

During the baby's seventh week of life, however, in the middle of Justine's desperate baby talk, Iris smiled at her.

Justine was suspicious. Probably it was just gas. "Were you smiling at me?" she demanded.

Iris did it again. The smile was lopsided, silly, and absolutely precious.

"Does this mean that you are actually a human being?" Justine asked in wonder.

Iris smiled one more time, then promptly closed her eyes and fell asleep.

Justine stared down at her daughter's angelic face, at the tiny hand clutching her finger, and felt something stirring inside her breasts that had nothing to do with milk coming down. Carefully, she picked up the sleeping infant and put a cheek against her silky head.

"Oh, my God," Justine whispered as understanding dawned.

This wasn't supposed to happen, but it had. She was in love.

Falling in love with her baby did not end the colic or cure Justine's exhaustion. But now that she and the baby "had come to terms," Doc Hadley finally sanctioned supplemental feedings, and Martha Claire raced off to buy bottles, a sterilizer, and the ingredients for formula. Justine danced around the room with her baby. "I've been granted trustee status," she explained to Iris. "They're letting me go to work."

Justine put an announcement in the newspaper offering an opening month special on baby pictures and began practicing on her daughter. Polly and Grace made sure she had customers that first month—nine in all. Some of the mothers had their older children photographed as well. The following month Justine photographed her first wedding. Martha Claire organized her life around caring for her husband and her sister's baby.

Martha Claire still wasn't pregnant. She'd had two periods since Grayson's return even though they made love most nights, sometimes with passion, other times dutifully. She found herself thinking more about the drama going on inside her body—of legions of sperm searching for an elusive ovum—than orgasm. In fact, at times she simply turned off the part of her mind that dealt with her own responses and concentrated instead on squeezing every available sperm from her husband's body.

eight

They had just crawled into bed when the phone rang.

Grayson hurried down the hall to answer it, with Martha Claire following behind, the skin on her brow tingling with apprehension. No one called after ten o'clock unless there was a problem.

Standing behind her husband, she could hear his mother's hysterical voice. Frank couldn't breath, Lily was shrieking. He was turning blue.

Martha Claire called Doc Hadley while Grayson pulled on trousers and raced out the door in his bare feet. By the time Martha Claire had thrown on her robe and joined him next door at her in-laws' house, Lily was cradling her husband's body in her arms, kissing his face, telling him how much she loved him, what a good husband he had been. Grayson was kneeling beside his mother, his face in his hands.

They were in the dining room, with an unfinished game of cribbage and two half-empty cups of tea on the table. The mellow music of Guy Lombardo and the Royal Canadians was coming from the living room radio. Both Lily and Frank were wearing bathrobes.

Martha Claire put one hand over her mouth and the other against the wall for support. *Frank was dead.*

Sometimes she had a hard time convincing herself that she liked her mother-in-law, but she had been genuinely fond of Frank. And she admired the love and affection the senior Stewarts obviously felt for one another. Sometimes she had wondered why in the world Frank adored his spoiled, self-centered wife, but he had. And Lily obviously had enjoyed her role as a helpless little wife who totally depended on her big strong husband, a role she continued to play even after Frank needed help getting up and down the stairs.

How would Lily manage without Frank, Martha Claire wondered. And how would his passing affect her own life, her own marriage?

Martha Claire turned off the radio and immediately wished she hadn't. The silence was worse. Now all she could hear was Lily's pitiful whimpering and Grayson's sobs.

She went to stand behind her husband, to put her hands on his trembling shoulders and kiss the top of his head. "My poor darling," she said, "I'm so sorry. He was such a good, kind man."

Doc Hadley arrived and called the undertaker. Lily wailed as she watched her husband's body being carried out the front door. She clung to her son and asked, "What will I do without him?"

Neighbors had come out of their houses and were standing on their porches in their bathrobes.

Lily refused Doc Hadley's offer of an injection for her nerves and asked for a glass of whiskey instead. Martha Claire tried to get her to go home with them for the rest of the night, but Lily started up the stairs, the glass of whiskey in hand. She wouldn't sleep, she told them, but she wanted to lie in the bed she had shared with her husband for more than thirty years. She would feel closer to him there.

"We can't leave you here alone, Mother," Grayson had protested.

Lily didn't answer. They listened to her footsteps walking down the hall, the bedroom door closing behind her.

"Oh, God," Grayson said as he sank down onto the bottom step and buried his face in his hands. Martha Claire sat on the next step up and held him against her breast. She wanted to say that it was a good thing they were living next door, to point out how awful it would have been if they had been living at some distant military posting. But she didn't; it would seem like gloating. And surely he realized it was so without her pointing it out.

He refused to leave his mother in the house alone, so they went upstairs to Grayson's old room and laid down together on his narrow bed. Martha Claire felt weariness seeping through her body but fought against sleep. How could she sleep when her father-in-law had just died downstairs and her husband was overcome with fresh, raw grief?

Eventually, however, she felt herself drifting away and curled against her husband's body.

When she woke, first light was streaming through the window, and Grayson was gone. She lay there for a time, remembering why she was there, dreading the day that lay ahead. And she remembered creeping up there one day to Grayson's forbidden bedroom while he and his parents were away. She had stretched out on this bed and experienced such a thrill.

Downstairs, she found Lily and Grayson dressed and sitting at the kitchen table drinking coffee. Grayson had already called Aunt Orna and told her they would be needing her the entire day. Lily was making a list of people who needed to be called. Her preacher from the Lutheran church. Relatives. The two elderly saleladies who worked at the store. The newspaper. Friends.

Martha Claire hurried home to dress, then came back and prepared breakfast. Over breakfast, they talked about arrangements. Frank had been an infantryman in World War I, and Lily wanted Grayson to arrange for a rifle squad and a military salute. She wanted a flag covering his casket that would be folded and presented to her. And she didn't want Genevieve Fuller to play the organ. Genevieve hit more sour notes than sweet ones these days; it was time for the church to find a new organist. Would Martha Claire please ask her mother to take care of the music? And she wanted Grayson to sing "In the Garden," if he was up to it. Then Lily went upstairs and brought down a poetry book.

"I don't much like poetry, but your father told me that you should pick something out of this book to read at his funeral," she told her son. "He didn't want scripture or a sermon, but the preacher won't take too kindly to that. There's a list of pallbearers written on the flyleaf. He also said you were to have all his books. I never could figure out why a man would have so many books. All they did was collect dust. But then, he didn't sleep well at times and said they kept him company in the night."

That afternoon, with the Stewart home full of friends and relatives offering condolences, Aunt Orna asked to speak privately with Martha Claire. The two women went out into the backyard and sat in the shade of a gracious elm on wooden lawn chairs in sad need of painting.

Orna had carried a folded newspaper with her and was using it to fan herself. A tall, angular woman with large hands and feet, Orna Green had worked for the Stewart family ever since Martha Claire could remember. Her own mother had help only once a week, but Orna had worked for Lily Stewart every afternoon, after working mornings for the banker's wife.

"Is there something wrong?" Martha Claire asked.

"I can't work for Miz Lily no more," Orna said, her dark face impassive.

"But why?" Martha Claire demanded, shocked. "My God, Orna, she needs you now more than ever."

"I'm sorry, Miz Martha Claire, but I've worked for Miz Lily more than thirty years now, and I need my rest."

"Can you afford not to work?"

"I'll keep working over at the Andersons' in the mornings and take in ironing in the afternoon," she announced, the newspaper waving back and forth, her face covered with a sheen of perspiration. "I've got the rheumatism in my knees and can't do all that scrubbing and cleaning and cooking for ten hours a day like I used to."

"I can understand your wanting to cut back, but why not keep working for Miss Lily and stop working for the Andersons? After all these years, I really think you owe it to her, at least until she gets herself together."

Orna's jaw jutted out just a bit. "When I lost my husband, Miss Lily expected me to come to work the afternoon of his funeral. Mr. Stewart, though, he told me to take the week off and paid me for it anyway. And Mr. Stewart, he had me pick out a brand-new suit from the store to bury my George in. And he came to the funeral—the only white person there. I can't tell you how much I appreciated that man. I never would have left while Mr. Stewart was alive. A good man like that deserved a clean house and a good meal in the evening when he came home from work. Every Friday afternoon, Miss Lily would hand me a five-dollar bill. I'd have to go by the store to get the rest of my wages from Mr. Stewart. He called it 'our little secret.' Miss Lily expected me to clean and cook for twenty cents an hour, like my mama made working for her mama. Well, Mr. Stewart is gone, and I'm not working for no twenty cents an hour. And I'm not cleaning the burned oatmeal out of that pan no more. Every morning, she burned the oatmeal and never once put the pan to soak. It sat there all morning long getting hard as a rock. Every afternoon, the first thing I did was scrape burned oatmeal from the bottom of that pan."

"I'm sure that my husband will see that you get your proper wages," Martha Claire pleaded.

"I'm sorry, but I jus' ain't working in that house anymore. I'll help out until after they put Mr. Stewart in the ground, then that's the end of it."

"But what's going to happen to her now?" Martha Claire asked, looking toward the house that Orna was no longer going to clean.

"She's a younger woman than I am. She can go up and down those stairs a whole lot easier than I can, and maybe she'd remember to turn the fire off under the pan sooner if she's the one who has to clean it. But I suppose you'll have to find someone else to work for her. You won't find a woman stupid enough to stay on for thirty years, though."

"Could you help me find someone else?"

"No, ma'am, I can't do that. Maybe it's not a very Christian thing to say, but I wouldn't wish Miz Lily on the devil hisself."

The back door opened, and both women looked toward the house. Lily came out on the back porch and leaned over the railing. "Orna, what in the world are you doing out here? People are wanting refills on their lemonade."

Orna sighed and hauled herself to her feet. "I jus' wanted you and Mr. Grayson to know. I'll help with the funeral lunch, but that's the end. I'd appreciate it if you'd wait to tell Miz Lily until after I'm gone," she said.

Martha Claire nodded. "I'll see that you get your wages."

"Yes, ma'am," Orna said as she started toward the house, then she paused and looked back at Martha Claire. "My granddaughter is going to the Negro college over in Waco—to Paul Quinn College. Our Delane is making a teacher of herself and won't have to do housework all her life like her granny."

"I know that makes you very proud, Aunt Orna."

"Yes, ma'am. It does make me right proud."

The screen door opened again. "Orna, *people are waiting!*"

Somehow Grayson managed to sing about Jesus walking in the garden for his mother. Sitting beside her weeping mother-in-law, Martha Claire closed her eyes. She hadn't heard Grayson sing since before the war.

She remembered "When the Moon Comes Over the Mountain" at the school assembly—ten years ago. She had loved him that long now. And would love him forever. But she feared she would always love the memory of the boy more than the man he became.

She wished they had a piano so she could accompany him at home in the evenings. It would give them something to do after dinner other than read the newspaper and listen to the radio.

The Lutheran minister had convinced Lily that he must conduct a complete funeral service or people might think Frank had not been a Christian. She had written out the things she wanted him to mention in a eulogy and suggested scripture readings.

The service ended with the poem Grayson had chosen to read for his father.

"My father didn't have a college degree, but he was the best-read person that I have ever known. This was one of the poems he had dog-eared in a well-worn volume. It's 'Abou Ben Adhem' by Leigh Hunt:

> Abou Ben Adhem [may his tribe increase!]
> Awoke one night from a deep dream of peace,
> And saw within the moonlight of his room,
> Making it rich and like a lily in bloom,
> An angel writing in a book of gold:—
> Exceeding peace had made Ben Adhem bold,
>
> And to the presence in the room he said,
> 'What writest thou?' The vision raised its head.
> And, with a look made of all sweet accord,
> Answered, 'The names of those who loved the Lord.'

'And is mine one?' said Abou. 'Nay, not so,'
Replied the angel. Abou spoke more low,
But cheerily still; and said, 'I pray thee then,
Write me as one that loves his fellow-men.'

The angel wrote and vanished. The next night
It came again, with a great wakening light,
And showed the names whom love of God had
    blessed,—
And, lo! Ben Adhem's name led all the rest!

Grayson had planned to say a few words about his father, but apparently decided to let the poem speak for itself. He came to sit beside his mother, and Polly gently pumped away on the organ, playing a soft dirge while the minister offered his final prayer.

After his father's funeral, Grayson retreated inside himself. In the weeks that followed, he left early for the store and stayed late. Lily often came to dinner, and he would reminisce with her about his father, but when it was just him and Martha Claire, however, their conversations were perfunctory. No, he didn't want a glass of wine. Yes, he'd heard about the General Electric strike and Admiral Byrd's flight over the South Pole.

Grayson repaired and painted his father's small outboard and fished away Sunday afternoons. He needed time to come to terms, he told his wife. He was all right, but he needed to grieve on his own.

Martha Claire spent as much time as she could with her mother-in-law, who was coming to terms in spite of herself. She didn't like wearing black, and overt grieving interfered with her social life. She wasn't one to miss club meetings and church events and wasn't about to give up bridge and canasta. Not that she didn't get weepy from time to time, and she was lonely to the point of tears when she woke in the night and Frank wasn't there. But after a time, sadness became a bore, and she decided to remember her husband fondly and talk about him often but also to work on her bridge game.

It wasn't long until she was "keeping company" with Robert Vandecamp, a widower who worked at the abstract office. He took her to church and to the movies and most evenings came to sit on her porch or play cribbage at the dining room table.

The cleaning lady Martha Claire found to work for Lily was just a high school girl who came after school every day to clean and cook and did the laundry and ironing on Saturday. "You need to be nice to her, Lily," Martha Claire warned. "Times have changed, and Mary will quit if you don't treat her with respect."

"If there's one thing I can't stand, it's uppity niggers," Lily grumbled.

Mary got along surprisingly well with Lily, however. Lily would follow the girl around the house, telling her to do this and that, while Mary went about her business without saying a word. Sometimes Martha Claire wondered if the girl were hard-of-hearing, but whatever the secret of Mary's patience, she endured, a fact that made Martha Claire supremely grateful. She saw to it that Grayson paid Mary a bit over the going rate and that all of Lily's unneeded clothing and household goods were given to the girl.

With her mother-in-law taken care of, Martha Claire could once again devote herself to Justine and the baby, who grew more adorable by the day.

Martha Claire was determined to get Grayson out of his funk. Sometimes he didn't want to make love, and that was particularly upsetting. How could she get pregnant if her husband didn't reach for her in bed? When she reached for him, he would kiss her and tell her that he loved her, then roll over and fall asleep.

Sometimes Grayson would stare off at nothing, forgetting she was even in the room. Martha Claire tried to make light of it. "A penny for your thoughts," she would say, and he would smile at her. "I'm just tired," he'd answer.

Two months after his father's death, she splurged on a rib roast and cooked a fine dinner. She put on a nice dress and set the table with the good china and candles in silver holders. When Grayson arrived, she greeted him at the door with a kiss.

"I don't care what we talk about, but we have to talk about something," she said. "I can't stand the silence anymore."

He held her close for a long time. "I'm so sorry," he said.

"No need to be sorry. You had to get through your grief, but now I need my husband back."

They ate dinner first, making careful conversation about striking coal miners, the weather, the new treatment for tuberculosis. Grayson told her the roast was perfect. She was a fine cook. A wonderful housekeeper.

Over coffee, he stared at the flickering candlelight and began to talk in earnest. It was strange, he explained, to suddenly become his father, to become the Mr. Stewart who owned Stewart's Dry Goods, to see the rest of his life laid out in front of him, a replication of his father's and his father's before him. But it wasn't such a bad life, he supposed. The store had been a second home to Grayson when he was growing up. If he wasn't off playing with his friends after school, he was at the store, straightening merchandise or sweeping the floor and watching his father wait on people and ask about their lumbago or an ailing relative or tell a joke, share a bit of gossip. Everyone liked Frank Stewart, but Grayson wasn't as comfortable with people as his father was. Evenings, he and his father listened to the news while his mother got in Aunt Orna's way out in the kitchen. After dinner, his father helped him with homework and taught him to play chess. His dad gave him books to read: *Treasure Island, Huckleberry Finn, Great Expectations, Uncle Tom's Cabin, Ivanhoe, Anna Karenina.* His dad hadn't gone to college but he understood those books better than any of Grayson's teachers. And such a patient man. Grayson would never be that patient. He got irritated when people couldn't make up their mind after trying on ten pairs of shoes. He had thought he would be better prepared for his father's death. He had known it was coming. And after all, it wasn't like it was his first brush with death. God, he'd seen so much dying and death during the war—hundreds, maybe thousands of dead people. He had seen instant death and prolonged dying. And such suffering. Cruelty of the worst sort imaginable. Little children who starved to death or were gassed to death in their mothers' arms. His dad hadn't died like that. Or suffered much. No one had ever been cruel to him. But still, Grayson was having a hard time getting used to the idea that he would never see his father again or hear his voice. Just today, down at the store, he had tried to make sense of an invoice from the notions supplier. He wasn't sure what buttonhole twist was. And bias tape, seam tape, bobbins, sharps. He hadn't known there were so many different kinds of knitting needles and crochet hooks, so many different kinds of ladies' stockings.

Grayson paused. "I know I'm rambling. I guess that was just a long way of saying I miss my dad and am having a hard time filling his shoes."

When he was finished, she took him upstairs without even doing the dishes.

nine

Every passing month was anguish for Martha Claire as she waited to see if her period would start. She was not one of those women who started every twenty-eight days like clockwork, a circumstance that prolonged the monthly wait to find out if she was pregnant. As the time drew near, she became obsessed, going into the bathroom every twenty or thirty minutes to check. Each time there was no blood, she dared hope. Thirty-three days was the absolute outside. She had never gone longer than that. If she had not started by the thirty-third day of her cycle, she could be certain. Grayson's fourth month home, she went thirty-one days. But after that, she never got past thirty.

Was this a pattern for the next twenty or thirty years of her life, until menopause set in and she no longer needed to pray and make bargains with God? It would be a relief of sorts, she supposed, but oh, to go through her entire life barren, never to feel life growing inside of her, never to give birth and hold a baby of her own in her arms.

The sight of a pregnant woman hurt her physically, making her feel inadequate and incomplete. It was so unfair. Why couldn't she conceive a child? Justine had had an accidental baby. Other women got pregnant without even trying. Martha Claire wanted a baby more than anything and had schemed and planned for one. She felt her faith wavering. Was God cruel or did He even exist at all? But still she prayed. A prayer ran almost constantly through her mind, begging God for a baby. He could shorten her life. Shorten Grayson's. Do any manner of other injustices if He would just give her a baby. One time she even caught herself bartering with Iris's life and fell to her knees in horror.

See what you have done to me, she told a God she no longer loved or even feared.

Martha Claire relished every minute she spent with Iris. She never tired of caressing her niece's downy head, nuzzling her neck, fondling tiny fingers and toes. Iris smiled and laughed on cue. She was captivated by shadows and mirrors. Her changing expressions were a constant source of fascination for Martha Claire Everything about Iris filled her with delight.

Justine kept a playpen at the office and sometimes went for days without dropping Iris by her sister's house. Martha Claire couldn't bear the separation and would spend hours at the photography studio, holding Iris, feeding her, rocking her while Justine took pictures and worked in the darkroom.

Sometimes when she held Iris, Martha Claire actually felt as though she had milk in her breasts. She would touch her nipples, expecting to feel wetness there.

One afternoon, as she stood beside Iris's crib, she found herself taking off her blouse and letting it drop to the floor. Then she removed her brassiere. She stood there, staring down at the sleeping infant, massaging her bare breasts, rolling her tingling nipples between her fingers.

The sensation in her nipples became unbearable, and she worked them harder, to the point of pain. Then she reached for Iris. *Beautiful Iris. Precious Iris.*

Iris stirred in her arms, and Martha Claire nuzzled her face against the baby's neck, inhaling the intoxicating scent of her. The scent of a *baby.*

Martha Claire groaned and staggered backward into the rocking chair. Iris was awake now, looking at her, reaching a small hand toward her face. Martha Claire cupped her right breast and offered the nipple.

Iris's perfect little mouth toyed with it, but she didn't take hold.

"Please," Martha Claire begged. "Just try. *Please.*"

Then the skin on the back of her neck began to prickle, and she realized Grayson was standing in the doorway. Her blouse was on the floor, out of her reach. She had nothing with which to cover herself, to hide what she was doing, so she hunched over the baby and wept.

Grayson felt his heart fill his chest. In a step, he was at the rocking chair, kneeling beside his wife and the baby in her arms.

"Don't do this to yourself, Martha Claire. Iris is Justine's baby. You can't be her mother."

"You don't understand," Martha Claire said, raising her face to him, tears flowing down her cheeks. "I love her completely, and Justine just loves her when she has time."

Grayson put his arms around her and the baby. "I don't want you to be hurt," he said.

"I'm already hurting," she sobbed.

Grayson kissed the top of Iris's head, then buried his face against his wife's breasts and searched out a nipple with his mouth. Yes, he wished milk for a baby flowed there, wished this baby were theirs to love and raise. His poor Martha Claire. She was so afraid. Her fear and her love for her sister's baby consumed her.

She was telling him no. Pushing his face away, but he didn't want to stop. He felt her nipple grow firm against his tongue, heard her intake of breath.

He pulled away long enough for her to put the baby in the crib, then carried his wife down the hall to their bed.

It was the first time since she'd taken him out by the river that he was sure she'd had an orgasm. Afterward, she trembled in his arms. "I love you so much," she whispered.

"And I you, my darling girl," he said.

"Will you still love me if we never have children of our own?"

Grayson kissed her lips, her eyes, her hair. God, how he ached for her. "I will love you forever," he said solemnly. Even though he still brooded about the life they might have had away from here, he meant those words with all his heart. If his sacrifice brought them a good life, then it was a worthy one.

As he held his troubled wife and kissed her sweet face, caressed her golden hair, he realized that a good life depended in great measure on her happiness. There would be other satisfactions for him, of course. A river full of fish was just a few blocks away. Deer and game birds were abundant in southern Texas. There would be football games at College Station. Texas politics would always provide an interesting sideshow.

The Gulf and its beaches were only a Sunday drive away. And he always had a book open and waiting for him like a trusted friend. But those things could not fill his heart. Spending his days tending store would be tolerable, however, if he could come home to a contented wife. It seemed, however, that only a baby was going to fill Martha Claire's heart. For her, he had given up the prospect of ever-changing vistas and agreed to spend the rest of his life rooted in a small Texas town, but his sacrifice was not going to make her happy. As he rolled onto his back and covered his eyes with his arm, he felt a wave of intense jealousy for a baby that had yet to be conceived, that might never be conceived. She loved that baby more than she loved him, and it alone could make her life complete.

As Justine became busier, the playpen at the studio frequently went unused. Her sister kept the baby at her house while Justine made portraits of children, high school beauty queens and football players, couples celebrating golden wedding anniversaries.

With her first two hundred dollars, Justine bought a 1936 De Soto and cast her net wider. She photographed prize bulls, weddings, schoolchildren, church choirs. In the red glow of her darkroom, as she watched the faces of smiling children, wrinkled elders, and demure brides materialize in the developing tray, she vowed this was just an interim stage in her life. She could not go on doing this forever.

When she had time, she focused her camera on other subjects—on the sweating bodies of quarry workers and cotton pickers, rodeo cowboys atop bucking broncos, old men whiling away the hours at the domino parlor, the children of Freedmantown swimming naked in the river, the weary women of Freedmantown shuffling back across the tracks after a day of cleaning houses for white ladies, a railroad engineer framed in the window of his locomotive, sad-faced clowns from the seedy one-ring circus that set up just across the river. More and more she had a sense of the power of her craft. The scenes and faces she captured were more intense than real life, an instant in time frozen forever for future contemplation. She displayed some of these photographs, along with those of brides and babies, on the walls of her studio. Everyone who came through her door stopped to admire them, to say how remarkable they were, but it was the photographs of brides and babies that paid her bills.

Two days before Iris's first birthday, Justine was photographing her first out-of-town wedding in Texas City, a refinery town on the Gulf Coast. The bride was the cousin of the chief of Columbus's volunteer fire department. Justine had photographed his daughter's wedding the month before. From the cousin's wedding would come others. From weddings came babies. She felt as though the script of her life were being written for her.

The Gulf Coast was flat as a pancake, but the church sanctuary was built over a first-floor fellowship hall and the broad front steps offered a fine view of the busy harbor, the nearby Richardson Refinery, and the huge Monsanto chemical plant. Maybe she would prowl around a bit after she was finished here, Justine thought. She'd heard that high-quality industrial photographs were always needed for company annual reports.

She stood in the back of the church during the service, waiting to take a triumphant picture of the newlyweds coming down the aisle. She adjusted her camera and wondered if it would be unseemly for her to stand on a pew. The bride was saying "I do" when Justine heard an explosion.

And instantly the entire building began to shake, the stained-glass windows to implode.

Justine was thrown to the floor and rolled under a pew to protect herself from the shards of flying glass. People were screaming, calling out in pain.

A bomb, Justine thought. *Dear God, another war!*

She grabbed her camera and was the first person out the door, with only one thought on her mind. *Iris.* She had to get home to her child.

But the sight that greeted her was not of war. Not a blitzkrieg. No invading airplanes flew overhead. But plumes of orange smoke were rising over the harbor, with burning pieces of debris arching across the heavens like Fourth of July skyrockets.

People were running toward the harbor. Excited voices were yelling about the explosion. A ship had blown up.

Justine ran to her car for a different camera, different film, and prepared to join the river of people racing toward the pier for a view of the burning ship. But suddenly she remembered the small airfield she had passed on the way into town. An aerial photo would be more dramatic. She could probably sell it to one of the Houston newspapers, unless some other fast-thinking photographer scooped her.

She drove fast, hoping to get to the airfield before the roads were clogged with emergency vehicles. The last hundred yards, she drove across a field to avoid the growing pandemonium on the highway.

A pilot who looked too old to drive a car, much less fly an airplane, took her up in a vintage open-cockpit biplane. He flew so close to the burning ship that Justine choked on the orange smoke as explosions continued to erupt from the vessel. She wondered what in the world it had been carrying and how many people had been killed. Thank goodness she had plenty of film.

They had just finished a flyby of the shore that allowed her to photograph the crowds of people watching the spectacle when she realized the chemical plant was on fire. She yelled at the pilot and was pointing in that direction when the Monsanto refinery exploded.

An instant later, the concussion reached the airplane. Justine screamed and held on for dear life as the plane rocked about wildly. As soon as the pilot got it under control, with a feeling of absolute horror, Justine raised the viewfinder to her eye and photographed the huge fireball rising over the refinery. The people on the pier had been incinerated. They hadn't had a chance. Hundreds of them.

The fireball looked like the pictures she'd seen of atomic explosions. Fire was everywhere. Every warehouse. Every oil storage tank.

She screamed profanities to the heavens. Or maybe they were just in her head. All those people. Dead in an instant. As her mind tried to deal with the horror, her hands were automatically inserting another roll of film into her camera. She kept on snapping the shutter, hardly thinking about what she was doing. Frame after frame, roll after roll, of profound tragedy worse than anything she had witnessed in London.

Finally, her film exhausted, the pilot flew Justine to the Houston airport. By then she knew her pictures were too important for a state newspaper. She made arrangements to have the film on the first flight to New York and called *The New York Times*'s newsroom to say that film documenting the Texas City disaster was on its way, to have someone meet the plane.

It was only then that she thought to call home. Her mother answered the phone and began weeping hysterically. "My God, Justine, when we didn't hear from you, we thought you were dead."

If she had run down to the pier to take her pictures, she would be, Justine realized. And she began to cry. "Oh, Mother, it was so horrible."

She bought more film in Houston and flew back in the biplane to Texas City, where she took pictures throughout the night of the rescue efforts, the devastation, the dead laid out in rows. The following day, her photographs of the Texas City explosion that killed more than five hundred people and injured more than three thousand were on the front page of *The New York Times*. The ship had been a French freighter—the *Grandcamp*. The company that owned the freighter insisted that it had been carrying fertilizer, not explosives. Already a controversy was brewing. Could fertilizer explode?

A Mr. Silverstein at the *Times* wanted Justine to stay on the scene as more and more dead were pulled from the rubble. And he wanted pictures of the mass funeral at the high school football stadium. "You're doing a great job," he told her. "Really great."

She willed herself to stay dry-eyed throughout the service. She was there to document. After the film was on its way, she would cry.

Everyone in town had lost someone. The only reason she herself was still alive was because she had decided to try for a scoop. But she was too busy to ponder. There was so much to do, with a picture at every turning.

Her pictures had gone out over the wire, which meant they were in newspapers all over the world. She hadn't felt this alive since London. She tried to catch an hour or two of sleep curled up in the backseat of her car but couldn't wind down. Her eyes would not stay closed.

Her postwar life had finally begun.

She thought of her baby at her sister's house. Today was Iris's first birthday. She should drive home and check on her baby, give her a birthday hug. Or at least call, but the phone lines were down. She would call again when she took the next batch of film to the Houston airport, she promised herself.

At that moment, what she wished more than anything was that she was in a London pub drinking a half-pint with Billy. Wartime London seemed closer and more real than Columbus, Texas.

Six days after she'd left to photograph a wedding, Justine drove home to Columbus, to a sleepy Sunday afternoon and empty streets. She felt disoriented after the intensity of Texas City.

She stopped first at her sister's little house, but no one was there, so she drove on home. Her father was dozing on the front porch in his favorite wicker rocker. Justine walked quietly up the steps, shocked at his appearance. Her father wasn't well, she realized. His skin was as gray as his hair. And he was thin. Wasting. When had this happened? she wondered. Why had she not seen it?

Her father was older than her mother by more than ten years, but Justine had always thought he'd seemed younger. Polly Mayfield had been plump and matronly for as long as Justine could remember. Walter Mayfield had always been tall and slim—an athlete in his youth, when he'd played semipro baseball and basketball in the Texas industrial leagues. But now her father looked ancient, a man near the end of his life.

He opened his eyes and realized he was not alone. "So, you came back to us," he said with a chuckle and tilted his cheek in her direction for a kiss. "I wondered if you'd flown on up to New York City with your film."

"I might have, if it weren't for Iris."

He nodded. "She took her first step at her birthday celebration. We all clapped for her."

Justine pondered this piece of information. She had missed her daughter's first birthday and her first step. Should she feel guilty?

Justine sat on the stool in front of her father and took his hand. "Are you happy, Daddy?" she asked.

"Sure, honey. What makes you ask?"

"Did you ever want anything more?"

"More than what?"

"Than living here? Than filling prescriptions and running a drug-store?"

"Sure. I wanted to play major-league baseball. But the call never came, and I was afraid if I kept your mother waiting one more season she'd up and marry someone else. Do you still want to leave us, Justine?"

Justine nodded.

"What about Iris?"

"Maybe she'd be better off with just one mother."

"Martha Claire loves Iris, all right," Walter agreed. "You'd think she was the child's mother, but she isn't."

"She should be," Justine said, holding her father's hand against her cheek. She would not stay and watch her father die, she vowed. Then her grandmother. Her mother. There would always be some compelling family reason to stay on. She could see that now.

"I love Iris, too," she said.

"I know, honey. We all love her. I wouldn't have missed this past year with that little gal for the world. She has stolen her old grandpa's heart for sure."

ten

I am not going to cry, Justine promised herself. Crying would just make her feel worse. This night would pass. Someone would come dig her out of this snowdrift and she'd be just fine.

She reminded herself of the guys at the front in foxholes. At least she was dry. And she had a better chance of living through the night than they did, except the incoming fire seemed to be creeping closer. It wasn't just the North Koreans now. The Chinese communists had come swarming across the Yalu River, half a million strong, creating a whole new war, one the United Nations forces were losing. The Eighth Army had been run out of Seoul. Marines had to be evacuated by sea. The U.N. forces were in shambles.

She pulled her gloved hands inside the sleeves of her parka and tried to remember if she had ever felt this cold before. Certainly not in south Texas. It had been damned cold in Iowa during basic training, but most of her military training had been indoors, learning how to take dictation, type, operate a switchboard. And in London during the war, she'd felt shivering cold and damp all winter long, but not so cold that she wondered if she would lose her toes—or freeze to death.

The jeep's canvas top and sides kept out the snow but offered scant protection from the cold. But then, her bones had turned to ice days ago. Whenever she walked she felt as though she were walking on ice daggers. Her toes, fingers, nose, and ears all felt as though she could break them off like icicles. And she hadn't taken off her parka in days. Or her boots. Hadn't bathed or changed her clothes in more than a week.

She jumped when a shell hit too damned close—less than a mile away, she guessed. Should she abandon the jeep and start walking?

Yes, she would do that if another shell came that close. She'd rather freeze than be blown to bits.

The concussion had caused some of the drifted snow to fall away from the windshield, but all she could see was swirling snow. The jeep leaned so far to the right that she had no choice but to lean against the metal supports for the canvas cover. It was not only uncomfortable, it was like leaning against bars of ice.

Her driver, Han Woo, had gone for help when they slid into the ditch, but that was hours ago. She checked the glowing hands on her watch—almost three hours ago. If he didn't come back soon, the vehicle was going to be completely buried in the snow, and no one would ever find her.

What if Han Woo had gotten lost? Or frozen to death? Stepped on a land mine? Been hit with a mortar shell? Decided to go back to his village and family?

She'd been on her way to photograph the Second Division commander, General Porter, at his command post. Would anybody notice that she had not shown up?

The driver had taken the flashlight, so she had no way to look at the photograph of Iris she carried in her pocket, but she took it out anyway, clutching the leather folder against her heart.

Last summer, photographing the arrival of wave after wave of troops at Pusan, she'd thought she would die of the heat. How could a place have such extremes? And why in the hell had she come back here?

When the war broke out, she had begged to be sent to Korea and photograph Texas boys at war. Clyde Whittington, her boss at the *Houston Chronicle,* said he'd think about it. Almost hourly, Justine would ask him if he'd decided yet. When he finally said no, she negotiated—just for a week or two, then she would come home. When he said no to that, she threatened to quit. She would get the *Post* or some other newspaper to send her.

"So what happens if you get yourself blown to smithereens?" Clyde asked, a soggy, unlit cigar stub hanging from the corner of his mouth.

"Then there'd be a public outcry. We'd lose our readers. I'd lose my job."

"Nothing is going to happen to me. You know very good and well they won't let me within miles of the action. But think of the publicity a home-grown woman war correspondent would bring. People will buy the paper out of curiosity. I'll send copy, too. A woman can get a different angle on things. The boys will admit they're homesick and miss their moms."

"Look, Justine, you got me great pictures of Congressman Johnson out on the stump, hunkering down with farmers and hugging babies and grannies. And your photo of Babe Didrikson winning the Ladies' Open was a classic. But that stuff is soft news."

"What about Texas City?" Justine demanded. "That was hardly 'soft news.' Those pictures were good enough for you to hire me. Now, give me a chance at the real stuff, Clyde."

"We're talking about *war,* Justine, and you are a woman—and this *is* Texas. Our readers aren't going to take too kindly to us putting a young woman in harm's way. And what happens when you need to pee or take a crap? And don't tell me that Margaret Bourke-White did it. That was in Europe, where there were front lines. In Korea, the war is all around. Those little buggers don't play by the rules. And Bourke-White was older than you, already well known. It was worth the risk. You're just a kid."

"I'm almost twenty-eight, Clyde."

"Well, you look like a kid. And what about your little girl? What happens to her?"

"Nothing happens to her. My sister will take care of her like she always does."

In the end, he relented. She had stayed a month that first time, leaving in September after Allied troops landed behind enemy lines at Inchon. In spite of the disastrous retreat to Pusan, it looked as though the tide was turning. Everyone was predicting that the war would be over by the end of the year. Justine had no expectations of returning, especially after MacArthur announced that U.N. forces had captured Seoul, the South Korean capital.

But the last week in October, China entered the war on the side of

North Korea. Before she had a chance to discuss a return trip with Clyde, Mr. Silverstein at *The New York Times* called. He'd seen some of her pictures from Pusan. He'd like to send her back.

She'd jumped at the chance, of course, not imagining that the sweltering, sticky country where she'd spent the summer could turn into the brutally cold place where she now found herself. Would she have stayed away if she could have foreseen the misery she would face? Until now, she would have thought of the pictures she had taken and decided they had been worth the misery. But sitting in a snowdrift, with enemy fire coming ever closer, she realized she had risked her life by coming back.

It was January 5, 1951. She was twenty-five miles south of Seoul, where the Allies had dug in after the retreat. Justine hugged her body and curled herself into as tight a ball as she could manage. It hurt to breathe. Were her lungs frozen? Maybe she was already dying. She put the leather folder to her lips and kissed it. "I love you, baby," she whispered.

She thought about trying to pray her way out of this mess, but if there was a God he'd probably given up on her years ago. If there was a heaven, she'd have a lot of explaining to do before St. Peter opened the gate. Suddenly, she had an image of Billy Baker from Brisbane, sitting on his duffel outside the Pearly Gates, waiting for her to show up. Maybe he could help her plead her case. She was not a bad person, but she had done bad things. The worst thing that she had ever done had led to the best, to Iris, her wondrous child, the center of her life.

Darling Billy. Funny how he still popped in and out of her mind. This war wasn't like that war, though. There was no pub. No singing. No nights in the Tube with all that discomfort and humanity.

She imagined Iris and Billy here with her, the three of them all cuddled up together, keeping each other warm. Billy and Iris would like each other, she decided. But how were they going to get to know each other in a snowbound jeep? She mentally relocated them to Columbus and imagined them sitting on the porch swing, with Billy teaching Iris how to laugh like a kookaburra bird. Justine felt a smile tugging at her lips and began to sing about the kookaburra sitting in the old gum tree.

Then she pushed away thoughts of Billy and concentrated just on

Iris. If she was going to die, she wanted her last thoughts to be of Iris's precious face. The very best times in her life had been going home to her daughter. When she parked in front of the house on Milam Street, the front door would fly open and her daughter would come racing down the steps and throw herself in Justine's arms.

All of her people lived in that house now. After her daddy died, Martha Claire and Grayson had moved in with Mother and Granny Grace. It was a four-generation house, great-grandmother, mother, daughter, and granddaughter all under one roof. Of course, when Justine was there, Iris stayed out in the garage apartment with her, but the big house was Iris's real home now. When Justine thought of her daughter, she pictured her there.

Justine jumped as the incoming fire came terrifyingly close. The jeep tottered a bit, threatening to roll over completely. Where in the hell was Han Woo? How warm was all that padded clothing he wore? Maybe she should pray that he was all right, that he would find his way back to her. She wondered if it was appropriate to address the Christian God when praying for a Buddhist.

She closed her eyes and called up an image of both deities—of a white-robed bearded God on His throne and a massive cross-legged Buddha, the two of them sitting side by side. "Please look after Han Woo," she implored. "I don't care which of you manages it, but he's a gentle little person with all his bowing and smiles, and I'd hate for him to die trying to save me."

If she died tonight, would Iris even remember her? Iris wasn't yet five. Probably her mother's memory would fade until she would have to look at pictures to remember her. Or maybe she wouldn't bother. After all, she had Martha Claire.

Martha Claire would always take care of Iris, always love her. Columbus, Texas, was a dead end for grown-ups but a terrific place for kids. Maybe Iris would be better off without a sometime mother who dropped in and out of her life.

But Justine didn't have the strength to stay away. If she lived through this night, she would keep going back to see her daughter. She didn't deserve Iris, but she loved her with an intensity that filled her up and made her whole.

Another explosion shook the jeep. Her ears rang like church bells. The time had come to find someplace safer or freeze to death searching. She pushed on the door, but with the weight of the snow piled against it, it would not budge. She pushed with her feet, her arms, her shoulders, even her head. She tried again and again, then fell back into her corner. She was sitting in a snow-covered tomb.

The cold was really getting to her, like a drug, taking over her blood and brain.

She opened the leather folder and kissed the picture she saw so clearly in her mind's eye. Iris with her sparkling green eyes and strawberry-blond curls. Iris, who skipped rather than walked, who was silly and dear and surrounded by love.

Then she saw another image—Iris in Martha Claire's arms. There was a rightness about that image. "Take good care of our baby," Justine said as she closed her eyes, prepared to sink into a peaceful slumber. Not such a bad way to die, she decided, except it seemed as though someone was calling out to her.

She opened her eyes and listened. Yes, a voice over the wind, calling "Mrs. Dover." Someone was pushing away the snow, trying to open the door.

"Mrs. Dover?"

The voice was familiar. "Yes, I'm in here," she called out.

The door opened and a gloved hand reached inside. "It's Captain Russell," the voice was saying.

She remembered the name—and the man. General Porter's aide-decamp, Captain Cameron Russell.

"We found your driver wandering around lost. We've been looking for you."

He pulled her out of the jeep, and she fell against the wonderfully sturdy bulk of him. His face was covered with a snow mask, but she remembered how handsome he was. A regular Gregory Peck, wavy hair and all. And she smelled like an outhouse.

eleven

My *aunt Justine* used to tell how people back east always thought she came from Alabama or Georgia. "You sound Southern," they would insist. Justine would explain that east Texas was right next door to Louisiana, and our drawl—and our ways—were more Southern than Western. We didn't have any cowboys or sagebrush.

Not that we had antebellum plantations with white-columned verandas where we lounged about sipping mint juleps. Spanish moss was not dripping from the trees. But most of Columbus's original settlers had come from Louisiana and Arkansas, and they had grown cotton and owned slaves.

After the Civil War, white folks lived on one side of the railroad tracks and black folks—or "colored people," as polite white children were taught to say—on the other side in Freedmantown. That division still exists today. Our schools are no longer segregated, but our cemeteries certainly are. Black citizens continue to bury their own in the Willing Workers Cemetery. White folks are buried across the road in the Odd Fellows Cemetery or St. Anthony's, depending on whether they were Catholic or Protestant. Paupers are buried in the Old City Cemetery, alongside the tottering graves of some of the town's original settlers.

Our town was established in the 1830s on the banks of the Colorado River by families from the Stephen F. Austin Colony. Our Colorado River should not be confused with the mighty river that carved the Grand Canyon. Our river generally loops its way lazily across the coastal plain to the Matagorda Peninsula on the Gulf Coast.

The decision to build a town on that particular bend in the river probably had something to do with the majestic live oak trees that offered huge canopies of shade, a welcome relief from the relentless summer sun. Some folks claim that Colorado County's first district court session was held under the live oak that still stands just east of the present-day courthouse. Magnolia trees were brought to town after the turn of the century and now surround the courthouse and grace many of the older streets. And we make the best pies imaginable from the pecans that fall every autumn from the native trees that are found in abundance both in town and in the surrounding countryside. Our town is defined by its stately trees.

The Columbus of my childhood hasn't changed greatly from the days when my parents were young. Even today, in spite of Wal-Mart and the fast-food restaurants that now blemish the outskirts of our little town, vestiges of old Columbus still survive, attracting a steady trickle of tourists who exit from the interstate highway to visit the museums and stroll around the historic square. In May, they come in larger numbers for the Magnolia Home Tour.

An antiques store occupies the building where my grandfather once operated his pharmacy and, for several years, my aunt Justine had a photography studio on the second floor. A dress shop is in the building that once housed Stewart's Dry Goods. Other businesses are gone, too—Berger's and Fehrenkamp's groceries, the Orphic Theater, Smitty's Sandwich Shop, the pool hall, the domino parlor, the cotton gin, the Live Oak Hotel, the depot—but many of the old buildings that housed them are still standing, occupied by tearooms, gift shops, even an art gallery. The old brick water tower is now a museum. The courthouse, Stafford's Opera House, and the Stafford Mansion right next door look pretty much the same.

Sometimes, just at twilight, I turn my back on the ugly new bank building north of Courthouse Square, so that only the courthouse and the old buildings on the west and south sides of the square are in my line of vision, and I can almost see us three kids on our bicycles, riding barefoot, a nickel in our pockets for a cherry phosphate at the Sandwich Shop. We would wave to people sitting on benches or strolling along, perhaps enjoying an ice cream cone or on their way to the Orphic.

After our phosphates, before darkness fell completely, we would turn our bikes down Milam Street, toward the big old Victorian house where our mothers, Grandma Polly, and Granny Grace had all grown up. In spite of its cracking paint and sagging front porch, living in such a house had given our family a certain prestige. Our family was "old Columbus," our parents descended from original settlers. Since my brother, Buddy, and I were both adopted, we didn't actually have old Columbus blood flowing in our veins, but I felt proud of our family's history nonetheless, and proud that we lived in such a wonderful house with its gingerbread trim, high peaked roof, round gable window, and—best of all—the broad front porch where we spent at least a part of every summer evening, visiting with the neighbors, listening to the radio, even playing cards by the light of a lamp set in the parlor window. The house would someday belong to Iris, but at that point in our lives, it belonged to Buddy and me just as much as it did to her.

❧ ❧

"There is no place on earth I would rather live than this house," Martha Claire announced as she and Grayson stood back to admire the newly refurbished parlor. For weeks now they had been refinishing the floors, papering the walls, reupholstering the side chairs. They had just finished rehanging the pictures, replacing books on their shelves, replacing her mother's upright piano, her grandmother's Victorian settee and Queen Anne occasional tables, the corner cabinet that her great-great-grandparents had brought when they came west from Louisiana to join the Austin colony, and the Chippendale card table with its four handsome slate-backed chairs that Martha Claire had bought at an estate sale and Grayson had helped her refinish.

"Well, that's one room down and ten to go," Grayson said with less enthusiasm than his wife. He wished that his mother-in-law had sold the house when her husband died rather than invite him and Martha Claire to move in with her and Granny Grace. What at first seemed a way to save money was in reality a fiscal albatross. He hadn't realized the extent of the decay and termite damage to hundred-year-old lumber and hadn't understood the serious problems that came with antiquated wiring and corroded pipes. It would take years of work and more money than he could possibly provide to restore the once-grand house to its former glory, which clearly was what his wife had in mind.

Martha Claire had her hands clasped in front of her, a look of pure pleasure on her face as she took in the formal front room that was used only when the preacher came to visit or the women of the household entertained their respective bridge or music clubs or held a committee meeting for one of the daughter clubs—the Daughters of the American Revolution, the United Daughters of the Confederacy, or the Daughters of the Republic of Texas. The spacious corner room off the kitchen—what Martha Claire continued to call the "morning room"—was where the family gathered after dinner to play cards or to watch *Your Show of Shows* or *Arthur Godfrey's Talent Scouts* on the new television set.

Now that the parlor was complete, the broad entry hall would be next, he supposed. Then the other rooms. The exterior. He had years of work ahead of him.

Martha Claire wanted the house to look the way it had when her great-great-grandfather built it as a wedding present for his daughter—a house with six bedrooms to accommodate all the grandchildren he hoped she would provide him. Her great-great-grandfather had owned a cotton plantation east of town and more than one hundred slaves. His plantation house had burned down before the turn of the century, but his daughter's house had endured now for almost a century.

Grayson had inherited a dry goods store that was barely able to pay their bills and those of his widowed mother in her fortunately smaller, sounder home. He and Martha Claire would have a difficult time if it weren't for the government check he received every three months for his service in the Texas National Guard and the generous check that Justine sent every month to cover Iris's keep. But that was all needed just to live; there was nothing left over for restoring an old house.

After he had gotten over the shock of another war just five years after the end of the last one, Grayson had found himself guiltily hoping his guard unit would be called up—even though he still had nightmares about the last war, even though he would rather die himself than kill again. But he would enjoy a stateside assignment. Martha Claire could put her house project on hold and run the store, and with his active duty salary, they could put some money in the bank and not always be living month to month. Of course, it was restlessness more than financial concern that fostered such thoughts. Truce talks had begun, however, and he couldn't bring himself to hope that the fighting would continue just so he could have a reprieve from the numbing routine that had become his life.

Justine was in Korea for a third tour, this time covering the truce talks in Panmunjom. She had written that she lived in a tent city, with tent movie theaters, tent showers, tent hospitals, tent conference rooms, tent mess halls, even a tent chapel. Justine's pictures of the first released American POWs crossing the bridge over the Imjin River had appeared on front pages all over the country.

Martha Claire had decided that there was a man in Justine's life—based on what, Grayson was unsure. As a result, his wife worried constantly that her sister would fall in love, settle down, and take Iris from them. He feared that, too. Iris was the most delightful child imaginable. She was the light of all their lives—his mother's, too. Iris made them climb down off their adult perspectives and return to wonder and silliness. They were able to see the world through her eyes and realize once again that trains, crawdads, and Christmas trees were indeed magical things. If Justine took her away, their universe would collapse.

Already Grayson was anticipating Iris's delight over the finished parlor. With sparkling eyes, she would say how lucky they were to have such a beautiful room in their house, making the effort and expense almost worthwhile. He glanced at his watch. Granny Grace and Polly had taken her with them to make Sunday afternoon calls on shut-ins, which would take most of the afternoon. "All it needs now is an Oriental rug for the floor," Martha Claire was saying. "Then the room will be complete."

"Don't hold your breath on that one," he said as they walked down the hall toward the kitchen, their footsteps echoing on the wooden floor.

They sat at the big round kitchen table drinking lemonade and munching on sugar cookies. It was oddly quiet in the big old house. The television and radio were silent. There were no footsteps overhead. Grayson wanted to talk about taking a trip next summer, even if just for a few days at the beach, or perhaps driving over to visit his cousins in Tyler or Martha Claire's cousin in Shreveport—anything to get out of town for a while—but Martha Claire was full of plans for modernizing the kitchen. He only half listened, occasionally reminding her that they couldn't afford this or that, that they would have to rewire before she could install an electric stove.

But dreaming about the house was good for her, he supposed. It distracted her from the other problem. It occurred to him that she longed to restore her family home as much as he wanted to spend significant time someplace else, to escape for a while. It seemed doubtful if either one of them would get their wish.

Grayson always knew without being told when his wife's monthly period came. She would become quiet and withdrawn and didn't want to be touched, didn't want to talk about it, wouldn't let him share her sadness. Then, a few days later, she would become hopeful once again. Month after month, it was always the same.

She was asking him if they could put down new linoleum themselves or needed to hire someone to do it when there was a knock at the front door. Grayson pushed back his chair and walked back down the hall, wondering who could be calling on this quiet Sunday afternoon. He hoped it wasn't Reverend Huxley soliciting for the building fund or inquiring about Grayson's spotty attendance, now that Martha Claire had talked him into affiliating with the Methodist Church.

When he opened the door, it was Doc Hadley standing on the front porch, holding a baby in his arms—a very small baby wrapped in a faded green shawl. "Hello, Grayson," the doctor said. "I've got someone here I want you and Martha Claire to meet."

Grayson heard Martha Claire call, "Who is it?" But he couldn't seem to answer.

"It's Doc Hadley, Martha Claire," the physician called back. "You got a minute?"

Grayson stepped to one side and allowed the physician into the entry hall. Doc Hadley looked rumpled and tired; his necktie protruded from his pocket. Grayson could hear Martha Claire's footsteps coming from the kitchen.

When she arrived at her husband's side, Doc Hadley pulled the corner of the shawl from the infant's face. "It's a girl," he said. "She was born this morning."

Martha Claire took a hesitant step closer. "Whose baby is it?" she asked.

"Yours, if you want her," the doctor said.

Grayson stared down at the tiny newborn face. *Their baby if they wanted her?* As the words sank in, he had to grab the newel post to steady himself.

"But where did she come from?" Martha Claire asked.

"Can't tell you that," Doc Hadley said in his usual brusque way. "All I can tell you is that she's a love child—there wasn't a rape or anything like that—and her parents are not from hereabouts. That's all you're ever going to know about this little girl's history. If you take her, it's with a clean slate."

Martha Claire cleared her throat before she responded. "Grayson and I will have to talk it over," she said.

"I don't have time for talking over. This baby needs someone now. If you're not interested, I'm driving her over to the Baptist Children's Home in San Antonio."

"But something as important as taking in a child needs to be discussed," she insisted.

"I don't see it that way, Martha Claire," Doc Hadley said, his voice stern. "You either want a baby or you don't."

Then the doctor fell silent, and the only sound in the hallway was the ticking of the mantel clock from the parlor. The two men watched Martha Claire, trying to take a reading from her frowning face, and waited.

His wife was lovely still, Grayson thought, even in a faded housedress with her hair tied back with a kerchief. Her skin was as satiny smooth as a girl's, the line of her jaw as young, firm, and lovely as before. But she had changed in other ways. Two vertical lines now permanently resided between her eyebrows. Her chin had lost a degree of its tilt, and her eyes a measure of their sparkle. She seldom teased, seldom laughed out loud, was seldom spontaneous. She who once had the bearing of a dancer now let her shoulders sag more often than not, and instead of walking along with a merry bounce, her step had become deliberate. Once she had refused to let anyone in her presence be glum or out of sorts and would tease and cajole them into a good humor, but now she was quiet and distant. Only when she was singing or playing with Iris could Grayson see glimpses of the lively, vivacious girl with whom he had fallen so deeply and completely in love.

But in spite of Martha Claire's diminished spirit and his own diminished expectations, in spite of the longing for distant places that sometimes filled his chest and pulled him down, he still loved his wife, was still touched by her beauty, still wanted to spend his life with her at his side. And if that life was to be forever lived in this small, rural town with its rules and scrutiny, he knew it would be more fulfilling if they took in this small nameless child with her secret history.

Grayson also knew full well the debate that was raging in his wife's head. On one hand, there was her perpetual worry that Justine would take Iris away. No matter what happened with Iris, however, Martha Claire wanted a baby of her own more than anything, a baby that no one could ever take away.

But a *foundling?*

People in Columbus sometimes took in the orphaned children of relatives, but Grayson could not think of a single family who was raising a foundling. Martha Claire had always cared deeply about what other people thought. It was as much a religion with her as the one she practiced at the Walnut Avenue Methodist Church. In fact, he suspected that the time she devoted to church activities was motivated more by her need to have people think of her as a good Christian woman than by any desire to do the Lord's work. And what would those people whose opinion she so valued think of a baby whose mother had given her away, a baby who was most likely born out of wedlock—an illegitimate child? Would such a child be accepted into their narrow little world? Or would it be tainted? An outcast? Would her presence in their family somehow make it seem less respectable?

Tears were making their way down Martha Claire's cheeks. She looked at Grayson, a helpless, questioning expression on her face.

His heart was pounding so hard, he put a hand to his chest in a useless attempt to quiet it. All he could offer was the smallest of nods. It was Martha Claire's decision. He couldn't ask her to become the mother of a child she could not fully accept as her own.

Martha Claire took a step closer to the doctor and to the newborn infant he held in his arms. She reached out and touched the baby's cheek, and the expression on her face softened. A small whimper escaped from her parted lips. Suddenly, she was gathering the baby into her arms and putting it to her shoulder.

Grayson's knees gave way, and he sank to the bottom step. *At last, a baby for Martha Claire.*

She came to stand by him and put a hand on his shoulder. He wrapped his arms around his wife's legs, buried his face against her stomach. He felt so blessed, so at peace. This wasn't the way he would have chosen for Martha Claire's prayers to be answered, but it would do. Yes, it would do.

When the doctor cleared his throat, Grayson managed to scramble to his feet and shake the man's hand. They would get a phone call about the legal stuff from the secretary in the county judge's office, Doc Hadley said before leaving them with their new child, his five-minute errand concluded, their lives forever changed.

Then they were alone in their quiet house with a sleeping baby, with *their* baby, suddenly parents after years of longing. "Oh, Grayson, isn't she beautiful?" Martha Claire said, her voice filled with such reverence.

Grayson was aware that in the years to follow he would look back on this day as one of the most joyous of his life, and the source of that joy was the look on his wife's face. He already loved his nameless daughter because she was theirs. Later, he knew he would come to love her for herself, in the same manner that he had come to love Iris for the inquisitive, completely honest, and delightful little human being that she had become. But on this first day of his daughter's life, he loved her because she had done something he had not been able to do. She had made Martha Claire happy.

They were laughing and crying at the same time now. With their baby between them, they shared salty kisses and touched the baby's tiny fingers, stroked her head and cheeks, stared with adoration at her newborn face.

"What do we do now?" he asked.

His question sent Martha Claire into action. She sent Grayson to borrow enough Pet milk from the neighbors to last until the grocery store opened in the morning. Then she dispatched him to the attic for Iris's crib, the trunk of carefully folded baby clothes, and a box that held baby bottles and a sterilizer.

Granny Grace, Polly, and Iris had already heard the news by the time they came rushing up the front walk. Right behind them were Reverend Huxley and Lily Stewart. Grayson was proud of his mother, who seemed genuinely pleased about the baby and showed no disdain when he told her they would never know where the child came from.

For the rest of the day, Martha Claire held court in the parlor as a constant stream of visitors came with casseroles, flowers, hand-me-down baby clothes. Polly said it was providential that the parlor was completed in time for this wonderful event.

Iris never left the baby's side. Whoever was holding her, Iris was alongside. "Is she going to be my sister?" she asked.

"No, honey, she is your cousin," Granny Grace said.

"I'd rather have her be my sister," Iris insisted.

"She will be just like your sister," Granny Grace explained. "Martha Claire will need you to be a big sister to the baby, and she'll need you to help take care of her."

"Can we call my mama and tell her about the baby?" Iris asked.

"No, honey, your mother is still on the other side of the world. We'll have to wait until she calls us to tell her the news."

When the last of the visitors had said good-night, Granny Grace asked her family to join hands in the middle of the parlor and give thanks to the Lord for the miracle that he had wrought. When she finished, Iris said, "I think we should thank Doc Hadley, too. It was awfully nice of him to give us a baby."

Grayson set up the crib in the corner of their bedroom, and Iris insisted on making a pallet on the floor right beside it so she could sleep next to the baby. Already she was calling her new cousin "Sissy."

In bed, Grayson curled his body against Martha Claire's. He was exhausted but knew he was too elated to fall asleep. He wanted to celebrate their good fortune by making love, but with Iris in the room, he supposed that was out of the question. He contented himself with kissing his wife and holding her in his arms. "Do you think we did the right thing?" Martha Claire whispered.

"Oh, yes. You're glad, aren't you?"

"Yes, but a little scared. I wish I knew something about her."

"All you need to know is that she is ours and no one will ever take her away."

"As soon as Iris is asleep, you can carry her to bed," she whispered and pushed her body against his. While they waited for Iris to fall asleep, they surreptitiously kissed and caressed.

Their lovemaking that night was so infinitely sweet and full of promise, it made Grayson weep. He loved and was loved in return. He was a husband and father. Life was good.

He was just drifting off to sleep when the baby whimpered. "Let me," Grayson told Martha Claire. "I'll come get you if I need help."

He carried the baby downstairs and warmed her bottle, then sat in the rocking chair. "Thank you, sweet child," he told her with tears in his eyes.

He had cried more today than he had in years. They were happy tears, though, not like when his father died. He wished his father could have lived to see his granddaughter. Grayson kissed his baby's forehead, rubbed his cheek against her soft little head, inhaled her baby scent. He felt sad for whatever heartbreak had brought her to them, but like Iris, he was so very thankful that Doc Hadley had brought her to their door.

"I will be the very best father I can possibly be," he promised his daughter.

The following Sunday, the baby was christened Cecilia Claire Stewart, but from the first day Iris's name for her cousin stuck, only they would spell it with a C, Martha Claire decided. Their baby would be "Cissy."

Every time the phone rang, Iris raced to answer it, hoping it was her mother. Finally, when Cissy was a week old, Iris was able to share the news. "You've got to come right home and see our baby," she said. "I named her Cissy."

twelve

No one understood what Martha Claire had gone through in the minutes after Doc Hadley offered her a baby, and she could never explain it, not even to her mother or husband.

She immediately realized that taking the baby would in many ways be a good thing. Iris would have the equivalent of a little sister, and theirs would be a better and stronger family. Surely Justine would never even consider taking Iris away from the security of such a family. And a baby would ease the anguish of Justine's visits, when she took Iris to stay with her in the garage apartment for days or weeks on end.

Last fall, after Justine announced that she was taking Iris to Dallas for an entire week, Martha Claire found herself wishing that something would happen to make Justine cancel the trip. Maybe she'd be offered an assignment too prestigious to pass up. Maybe she'd come down with pneumonia or influenza.

Martha Claire knew that, as Iris grew older, Justine planned to take her away for even longer visits, even to spend time with her in New York. Maybe the day would come when Justine decided to keep her for an entire summer or a whole year. Maybe, someday, Iris would never come home.

Sometimes, Martha Claire had thoughts even more troubling than wishing her sister came down with the flu. Sometimes darker, more ominous images crept their way along the folds and creases of her mind.

Justine had returned to Korea for the third time, again putting herself in harm's way, although maybe less so this time, since the truce talks were under way. But the fighting continued, and once again Martha Claire had found herself guiltily imagining a telegram or phone call informing the family that Justine had been killed—a telegram or phone call that would make Iris irrevocably hers.

That morning, as she had looked down at the newborn child in Doc Hadley's arms, Martha Claire thought, *If I take this baby, maybe I can become a better person; maybe I can stop wishing my sister would die.* With that thought, she had reached out and taken the baby in her arms and vowed that she would pray every night that her sister lived a long and healthy life. Taking this child would be both a blessing and an act of contrition.

Even as she had looked down at the newborn baby who could be hers to raise, while Grayson and Doc Hadley waited with bated breath for her answer, she thought about the baby she really wanted, a baby that she herself had carried and birthed. What if she took this baby and immediately became pregnant? If that were to happen, she absolutely would not shortchange her own baby to care for this one. Her mother and grandmother would have to look after this poor child. Martha Claire would devote herself to her own child—and to Iris. She would never slight Iris. She loved Iris as though she were her own. In her heart, she knew that Iris had become more her child than her sister's.

In the months that followed, Martha Claire realized that her husband assumed the baby had put an end to her monthly lapses into depression. And maybe Cissy did help some, but mostly Martha Claire did a better job of concealing them. Because of this child, she was supposed to be a whole woman now. She knew, however, that nothing on this earth would ever cure the emptiness inside her except a baby conceived in her own body.

Six months after Cissy joined their family, Doc Hadley returned with a two-year-old boy in his arms. "This little boy is Cissy's older brother," he announced. By this time, Cissy was a sweet, easy baby who delighted in patty-cake and peek-a-boo.

Holding Cissy on her hip, Martha Claire watched Grayson approach the little boy as carefully as he would a wounded bird, his hand outstretched, his expression gentle and full of hope. The boy was a pretty child, with dark eyes and hair like Cissy's.

Without taking his eyes from the boy's face, Grayson asked Doc Hadley, "What's his name?"

"They call him 'Buddy.' He's healthy. Not talking much yet, though."

"Hello there, Buddy," Grayson said, taking the boy's small hand and shaking it formally. Then he took the child from the doctor's arms. "My, what a nice big boy you are," he said. "Do you like cookies? I'll bet this nice lady here might have a cookie for you."

In the kitchen, Martha Claire put Cissy in the playpen she kept by the pantry and gave the doctor coffee and a piece of pie and the boy a cookie, which he nibbled while sitting on Grayson's lap.

"The boy needs a home, too," Doc Hadley pointed out.

"Who's been taking care of him?" Martha Claire demanded.

The doctor shook his head. "No questions. This one comes with a clean slate, too. I just thought it would be nice for a brother and sister to be raised together."

Martha Claire was leaning against the sink, her arms folded across her chest, her forehead creased with a frown. "Why in the world didn't you tell us that Cissy had a brother when you brought her?"

"'Cause if there'd been two kids, you wouldn't have taken either one of 'em," the doctor said.

Martha Claire sighed. He was right, of course. And she wasn't sure she was going to take a second one now. With Cissy, it had been all but a foregone conclusion. But she really didn't need this other child.

And just the other day she'd read an article in the *Ladies' Home Journal* about a woman who became pregnant for the first time at forty after being married almost twenty years. Martha Claire was only thirty-one. What if she took this little boy and got pregnant? She already had her hands full with Cissy and Iris, and Granny Grace had had a stroke and needed help doing the simplest tasks. Her mother and Grayson's mother were both helping out down at the store now, leaving her to look after her grandmother and the children and manage all the cooking and cleaning. The only household help she could afford was a colored woman to do the ironing. And there were so many things she wanted to do to the house. She was beginning to think their money problems were never going away. They hadn't done a thing to the house since they'd finished the parlor. Grayson worked hard at the store, but he wasn't a born businessman like his father had been. She didn't see how they could afford to take in another child.

But there was such longing in Grayson's eyes. A boy to play catch with and take fishing—every man wanted that, she supposed. As it was now, poor Grayson lived in a house with five females.

Justine was involved with some man—an army officer she had met in Korea who was now teaching at West Point. What if Justine decided to marry this man and settle down to a normal life? If she did that, she would want her daughter with her. Then Martha Claire would have only Cissy.

"Think of Cissy and Buddy as insurance in case Justine ever decides to raise Iris herself," Doc Hadley said, as though he had read Martha Claire's mind.

Her mother was standing in the kitchen door, watching the drama unfold, saying nothing. Grayson, too, would say nothing. If Martha Claire told Doc Hadley to take the boy away, that would be the end of it. But where would he take him? To an orphanage? Back to a mother who either didn't want him or wasn't capable of caring for him?

She walked over to Grayson and took the child from his lap. Such a sturdy little boy. At least someone had been feeding him. The boy was looking at her, his big, dark eyes questioning, as though he, too, were waiting for her answer. Then he offered her a bite of the cookie in his hand. Martha Claire took a small nibble and told him, "Thank you."

What kind of woman would she be if she said no? Did she really have a choice?

"Oh, I suppose," she said. "But no more, you hear? Don't you come bringing me another brother or sister six months from now."

"You can count on that," Doc Hadley said. "Mighty fine pie, Martha Claire."

Justine's footsteps echoed on newly varnished wooden floors as she walked through the empty house. It was a fine old house, probably the same vintage as her family home in Columbus. But this house was devoid of gingerbread trim and in perfect condition—a stately house on West Point's Thayer Road.

She wondered how many families had lived there over the years. The house was at least one hundred years old, maybe older. Tours of duty at West Point probably averaged three years. That meant that more than thirty families had once called this place home. She thought of all those officers' wives overseeing teas and entertaining the general and his wife at sit-down dinners in the formal dining room. When the wives hosted their bridge club, there would have been card tables set up in the living room and on the sunporch. Their lives hadn't been greatly different from those of the ladies of Columbus, Texas. Both sets of ladies played by the rules, maybe not exactly the same rules, but close. The West Point wives even had their rules assembled in a book. Cameron had given her a copy. *The Army Wife* discussed at great length the intricacies of courtesy calls, calling cards, receiving lines, seating protocol, formal and informal invitations, thank-you notes, dress codes, and the like.

"Why have you brought me here?" she asked her handsome, uniformed companion, even though she already knew the answer. It always came down to a scene like this. No matter how carefully she explained that she would never be any man's wife, that she had no intention of settling down, that her love came with no promise of clean socks in the bureau drawer or apple pie in the oven.

"What do you think of it?" Major Cameron Russell asked, the forehead of his achingly handsome, wonderfully sincere face creased in a worried frown.

The poor darling, Justine thought sadly. Things weren't going the way he had imagined. She was supposed to fall in love with West Point, the ritual of military life, and this house. She was supposed to have seen how gracious all those wives were at the general's reception and to have decided that joining their ranks wouldn't be the end of the world after all. And the women really had been lovely. The reception in the upstairs ballroom at the officers' club had been orchestrated perfectly, with everyone playing their roles flawlessly. No one had too much to drink. No voice was raised. No wife's neckline was too low. The general and his lady in the receiving line had welcomed Justine graciously and asked her and Cameron to dine with them during her next visit.

Justine kept thinking how well Martha Claire could have managed in this world. What a pity she had not let Grayson follow his heart's desire. What a pity Cameron was forcing Justine to chose between him and a life of her own.

Justine rubbed Cameron's frown lines and brushed her lips against his. A part of her wanted to be angry with him. Why hadn't he believed her when she told him how it was for her, how it would always be? But in the two years since they had met in Korea, she had come to love him very much—and come to depend on him loving her in return. It was wonderful to close her eyes and imagine the next time they would be together. She loved the anticipation. He did, too. He would come dashing through the door of her apartment, sweep her into his arms, kiss her as though his life depended on it as he backed her down the hall to the bedroom. After the first round of lovemaking, they would dress and go out to dinner, then come back and start all over again. As far as she was concerned, they had the perfect relationship. Why couldn't he see that marriage would end all that, would kill the anticipation? But then, the military expected its officers to marry. He had been too long a bachelor. His next promotion could very well depend on his marital status.

She'd always been a sucker for a man in uniform. Something quite fine happened to a man when he polished his shoes, shined his brass, and put on a uniform. She thought of Billy Baker from Brisbane in his RAF uniform. Of course, Billy and Cameron had been cut from different cloth. Cameron was an officer and planning to make the military his career. Billy had been an enlisted man who planned to run a newspaper in the outback. Billy always managed to look slightly cocky in his uniform; Cameron looked every inch the professional soldier. But each in his own way had been splendid. She had loved walking into a smoke-filled pub on Billy's arm; she loved walking into a smart restaurant on Cameron's.

She walked over to one of the living room windows, which offered a fine river view. West Point was such a perfect place, to the point of being otherwordly for someone who had grown fond of the disorder and bustle of Manhattan. No trash ever littered the post's streets. No lawn or shrub ever went untrimmed. No vehicle ever speeded. Children and dogs were well behaved. Military posts were about order and predictability, and there was comfort in that for the women who lived there, she supposed. But it was a false comfort. When their husbands were killed in combat or died of a heart attack, they and their children were evicted from their stately quarters and banished from this well-tended world. Justine had long ago decided she would make her own way in the world, a way that depended on no one but herself.

She had deliberately kept Iris and Cameron apart. She didn't want to play family with him, didn't want him to get the wrong idea. But he had anyway.

"You're barking up the wrong tree," she finally told Cameron, but with such regret. He would move on now, find someone else to marry—Justine realized that. Of course, it was time, but God, how she was going to miss him.

"Would it really be so awful living here with me?" he asked. "And Iris? We could be a family."

Justine closed her eyes and imagined the picture he was painting. She did not fit. She could love Cameron away from this regulated, spit-and-polish place, but not here, not in a world where she would have to become someone else.

"Honestly now," she asked, "can you see me in here, sitting at the head of a table, wearing a proper tea dress and careful hair, asking the ladies if they wanted one lump or two?"

"You wouldn't be pouring," he corrected. "The wife of the ranking officer does that."

Justine smiled. "See there! I would disgrace you. I not only don't know the rules, I wouldn't play by them if I did. You'd never get to be a general. Oh, Cameron, I told you all along that we weren't going down that road."

"I know," he admitted. "But I hoped you would change your mind. I can't imagine loving anyone but you, Justine. I want to see you every day instead of once in a while."

"If we were together every day, love would die—at least the kind of love we have. It doesn't work that way, my darling."

But could there have been another kind of love for her, she wondered, the kind of love her parents had shared—comfortable and constant? Both her parents had given up on their dreams to settle down. Her father stopped playing baseball and finished his pharmacy training. Her mother took the money she had saved for a year at a music conservatory and made a down payment on a building across the street from the courthouse, so he could open a drugstore. On the balance, had they been satisfied with their choices, or had they just convinced themselves that they were? Probably the answer was someplace in between. They loved their children and cared sincerely for one another, but at times they surely must have sighed and wondered how it might have been.

She crossed the entry hall into the living room and ran a finger along the edge of the mantel, where children's stockings would hang at Christmastime. "If you will recall, the first time you saw me I was wearing fatigues, a helmet, and combat boots. That was the woman you were attracted to, and that woman doesn't belong in this house. Do you really want to turn me into someone else?"

"You're turning me down before I've even proposed."

"You do need to get married, Cameron. I could see that at the reception this afternoon. You were the only unmarried field-grade officer there, and career officers are expected to have a proper, sherry-sipping wife at their side. In your heart of hearts, you know that I will never be a proper wife, but the gentleman in you feels obligated to make the offer. Well, you don't have to. All those good ladies I met this afternoon will help you find a wonderful wife. And I'm not being sarcastic, either. She *will* be wonderful. You will be just right for each other."

"But I live for the times we are together," he protested, not yet willing to admit defeat. "What will I do without you in my life?"

A part of her wanted to throw her arms around him and tell him he didn't have to, that she would put aside her dreams and live the sort of life he wanted, which would be wonderful in its own way. But even if she were willing to give it a try, she knew it never would work.

She took his dear, earnest face in her hands. "You will live on, my darling, and you will be a fine husband to a fine, worthy woman. You will love your children and be a wonderful father. And every once in a while, when you hear Lionel Hampton singing 'September in the Rain' or take a sip of really good champagne, you will think of me and smile. Now, what do you say we go upstairs to the master bedroom and screw one last time for old time's sake."

"There's no bed."

"Since when did you let that stop you?"

thirteen

From earliest memory, Buddy and I knew that we were adopted. Of course, in a little town like Columbus, there would have been no way to conceal the fact, but Mama and Daddy must have started telling us in the cradle, fearful we would learn from someone else. We loved to hear the story about how Doc Hadley brought us to them, and how happy our arrival in their lives had made our parents.

On our birthdays, Mama always said that our birth mother would be thinking of us on our special day. Even now, on my birthday, I still wonder if there is a woman out there someplace thinking of the day she gave birth to a baby girl and gave her away, but it is only a passing thought, not something I dwell on. Mostly I think about Mama and all those celebrations around our dining room table.

On our birthdays, she always cooked our favorite meal and baked whatever kind of cake we requested. Iris always asked for white cake with white mountain icing; Buddy changed from year to year; and after pondering my choices, I usually selected German sweet chocolate, which wasn't a pretty cake but tasted the best. The table would be set with Granny Grace's crocheted tablecloth, the good china, and the sterling flatware. Back then, kids didn't have major birthday parties with clowns and balloons, but we could invite a friend or two to dinner, and the honoree would sit in Daddy's chair at the head of the table. I don't remember any of the presents I received on my birthday, but I remember how special it was sitting in my daddy's chair and how silly it seemed to have him sitting in mine. And I remember Mama standing beside me, leading the singing, smiling as I blew out the candles, telling me how proud she was to have such a fine big girl as her daughter.

Mama was an intense mother, often grabbing us children mid-sentence to smother us with kisses and hugs. And she was always grooming us—combing, straightening, retying, sending us back upstairs to rewash faces and scrub fingernails. And she reminded, praised, fussed, chastised. Somehow she always knew when it was report-card day and met us at the door with her hand outstretched. She also knew when we told fibs, even tiny ones. If I claimed that I'd already eaten three bites of liver, she knew that it had been only two—two very tiny ones. She never forgot to hand out vitamin pills in the morning, and she always checked our throats for redness at the first sign of a cough. She was never without cough drops, Band-Aids, and Kleenex in her purse. My daddy sometimes accused her of mothering him along with us kids. And she did, reminding him to drink his juice and feeling his forehead if he looked feverish. That was who she was—a mother.

And my cousin Iris was a fiercely devoted niece to her mothering aunt. Iris taught Buddy and me from an early age that our job in life was to please our mother. That's what good children did. We were to rub her neck when she was tired and brush her hair in the evening when the family gathered to watch television. We were to do our chores without being told and compliment her cooking. We were to make our beds every morning and never, ever leave clothes on the floor or a chair. We were to mind our teachers and do our best at school to make our mama proud.

Pleasing Mama was something I took very seriously. I thought that if I could be a good enough girl and show my mother how much I loved her, it wouldn't matter to her so much that she really wasn't Iris's mother and that Buddy and I were adopted.

We didn't need to worry about pleasing Justine, who periodically swooped into our life with hugs and gifts and wonderful tales and enchanting photographs of faraway places. My aunt was someone to have fun with. Her visits to Columbus were magical times for us kids. Everyone in town knew Justine, and when we walked downtown, people stopped her on the sidewalk to say how much they enjoyed her photographs and could she believe how big us kids were getting to be.

If Justine had not been famous, she surely would have faced censure for not raising her own daughter. But celebrity seemed to give her special dispensation. Famous people were allowed to play by a different set of rules; after all, how could Justine take all those pictures if she never went anyplace? Folks were proud to know Justine Mayfield-Dover, proud that she still called Columbus home, proud she remembered their names, proud when a picture of their town made its way into one of her magazine spreads. Our bridge had been in *Life,* our courthouse in *Southern Living,* our county fair in *Saturday Evening Post.*

Every day was an adventure when Justine was with us. We would roam through the town cemeteries while she told us about the people buried there—relatives, murderers, saints, crazy people, little children. She recounted their sad and happy stories, making us laugh and cry for people we had never known but who had been a part of our town. To this day, whenever I go to the Odd Fellows Cemetery to tidy up around family tombstones, I can hear Justine's voice telling us all those stories, like the one about Ike Towell, whose grave was adjacent to those of my Stewart predecessors. Ike had been the city marshal and enforced segregation by drawing a line down the middle of the floor in the train depot and beating the bejesus out of anyone who disobeyed—black or white. He composed his own dubious epitaph, which Justine claimed was an attempt to win over St. Peter:

> Here rests Ike Towell
> An infidel who had
> No hope of heaven
> Nor fear of hell
> Was free of superstition
> To do right and love
> Justice was his religion.

Justine said she had learned the history of Columbus by poking around those old cemeteries and asking her parents and grandparents questions about the people buried there, and it was her responsibility to pass all that on to us. She told us about the flood in 1913 that washed away the original black cemetery and showed us where the victims of the 1873 yellow fever epidemic were buried in unmarked graves.

The Catholic cemetery was new to Columbus, built on land donated by Mrs. Cecilia Hanak so that Catholics could be buried on holy land. "Does that mean the other people are buried on unholy land?" Iris wanted to know. "All land is holy," Justine told us. "The Catholics just haven't figured that out."

Sometimes we hacked down the weeds in the tiny unkempt Jewish cemetery, with its handful of tombstones marking the graves of those long-ago merchants whose descendants had decided not to stay on in a small, very Christian town.

Often we would roam the countryside in the family station wagon. Justine showed us the house over in Glidden where a family of black people were killed by an ax murderer, and ever since black mothers have told their children that they'd better behave or the ax man would get them.

With a sense of reverence, we all touched the very oak tree where two colored boys were lynched back in 1935, and looked up into its branches, imagining those last horrible moments for the boys.

Justine drove down rutted lanes so we could poke through deserted farmhouses and encouraged us to weave tales about the people who had lived there, to imagine what their hopes and dreams might have been.

She took us on the train to Houston, where she would buy us new shoes at Krupp and Tuffly's and take us to lunch at the wondrous Forum Cafeteria. She took us to the beach at Galveston and to the Brenham creamery to eat the richest ice cream in the state of Texas.

Justine turned somersaults and cartwheels on the lawn and played kick the can and hide-and-seek with us and all the neighbor kids. She would sit cross-legged on the old mattress in the attic and tell ghost stories by candlelight.

Sometimes, Justine would insist that my mother do a recitation from her high school days. Mama would protest, of course; that was part of the ritual. Then she would give in, take a deep breath, and grow younger before our eyes as she recited from memory passages from

Mark Twain, Henry Wadsworth Longfellow, Elizabeth Barrett Browning. It was difficult to reconcile this impassioned, captivating woman with the one who frowned when she saw a cobweb and fretted when we didn't clean our plates.

When she had the chance, Mama went along with us on our excursions, but not very often. First Granny Grace was sick and shouldn't be left alone. And in the last years Iris came to us, it was Grandma Polly who needed looking after. And there was always the housework, which was like a second religion with my mother. Most of the women in our part of town had a black woman who cleaned and did the laundry, but Mama took her ironing over to Freedmantown and took care of the rest herself. We kids helped with the chores, but still there was a lot for Mama to do, and she wasn't one of those people who could leave things until later. Never once, in all the time we were growing up, do I remember leaving the dishes undone so we could rush off to a ball game or the drive-in movie. If we had plans for the evening, we had an early dinner and didn't walk out the door until the last dish was put away and the kitchen floor was swept. And Mama was always doing something to the house—hanging wallpaper, painting, making curtains. She couldn't afford to pay someone to fix up the house, so she and Daddy did what they could themselves.

I used to dream about how lovely it would be to find a box of money and give it to my mother so she could make her house the prettiest one in all of Columbus—like it used to be when Granny Grace was a little girl.

As much as I adored the time we spent with Justine, I sometimes stayed home with Mama while Justine took Buddy and Iris on the adventure of the day. And it wasn't just that I felt sorry for my mother and all the work she had to do; I cherished the times with just her and me and enjoyed being my mother's little helper. I didn't want her ever to doubt that I loved her, and especially that I loved her more than Justine.

When Granny Grace began what my mother referred to as "slipping away," I helped her to the bathroom and up and down the stairs and constantly tried to bring her watery old eyes into focus, to bring a smile to her inattentive face. I loved my great-grandmother very much, but looking back, I'm sure a great deal of my motivation for looking after Granny Grace was that it brought words of praise from my mother. To hear my mother say she didn't know what she would do without me was more important to me than even straight A's on my report card.

One Saturday morning I couldn't make Granny Grace wake up. I don't think I ever had truly thought through the term "slipping away" to its inevitable conclusion, for her death came as a terrible shock to me. Afterward, I had a difficult time reentering the world of childish pursuits. I checked out books from the library but didn't read them. I couldn't bring myself to jump rope or play jacks when my Granny Grace was dead in the cemetery. Mama even took me to see Doc Hadley, who took my face in his hands and told me that I was a little girl and it wasn't good for a little girl to ride her bicycle out to the cemetery every single day on the way home from school. He said that from then on I could go to the cemetery only once a week, on Sunday afternoon, and if he heard I was going more often he would have to give me an anticemetery shot right in the butt, with a very long and very fat needle.

Then, like always, he let me listen to my heart with his stethoscope and gave me a handful of tongue depressors and a roll of gauze so I could play doctor with my dolls. Even back then, I knew that I wanted to be a doctor when I grew up, just like Doc Hadley.

"Close your eyes," Iris instructed her mother, aunt, and grandmother at the doorway to the attic stairs.

Polly obliged and allowed herself, along with her daughters, to be led up the narrow stairs. At the top of the stairs, there was much whispering among the three children and a scratching sound as a needle was placed on a record. The music of "The Yellow Rose of Texas" burst forth, and Iris announced that the women could open their eyes now.

"Oh my," Polly said as she took in the transformed attic. All the trunks and castoff furniture had been pushed to the corners, and crepe paper streamers were draped from rafter to rafter. In front of the round window, three chairs were covered in blankets and bedecked with more streamers. "I would have dressed up if I'd known this was going to be such a fancy affair," Polly said, patting her hair and untying her apron.

"Okay now, those are your thrones," Iris said, and the three children led the women to their places, with Polly given the center chair. After cardboard crowns covered with tinfoil were placed on their heads, the children lined up in front of them and bowed ceremoniously. With a nod from Iris, six-year-old Buddy and four-year-old Cissy carefully served graham crackers and glasses of green Kool-Aid to their honored visitors. Then they were presented programs carefully printed by Iris and featuring artwork by Buddy and Cissy.

Iris welcomed their majesties to the Royal Theater and introduced the opening act. For the next hour, the children sang current favorites such as "Hernando's Hideaway," "Aba Dabba Honeymoon," and "Doggie in the Window," along with the ever-popular "Dixie" and "A Bicycle Built for Two." They performed the "Bunny Hop" and the "Hokey Pokey," and for the main presentation of the afternoon, they performed their version of "Little Red Riding Hood," with Buddy playing the role of the wolf, Iris as the old granny, and Cissy in the title role.

After each performance, Polly and her daughters clapped and cheered enthusiastically. She could remember watching similar presentations, usually staring Martha Claire as a princess, with Justine and their playmates in supporting roles, but nothing as elaborate as this. Iris was not only an imaginative child, she was an industrious one. Polly knew that just cutting and putting up all those streamers must have taken her days. And obviously, she had spent a great deal of time in rehearsal, teaching her two young cousins their parts. Iris had lots of friends her own age, but she always found plenty of time for Buddy and Cissy. She was their self-appointed nursemaid, guardian, and teacher. Currently, she was helping Buddy with his reading, but Cissy was learning faster than her older brother. Buddy was a bit slow, Polly feared. Martha Claire insisted not, claiming that Cissy was just exceptionally bright, which was true. There was no doubt, though, that Cissy was going to outshine her brother.

The program concluded with a song dedicated to the memory of Granny Grace: "I Dream of Granny with the Soft White Hair." When the final bows had been taken, the three women went back downstairs for a cup of tea before starting dinner.

"When I'm on my deathbed, I want to remember all that," Justine said. "Iris can get those two little guys to do anything."

"Iris is pretty much in charge of us all," Polly said with a laugh.

"She's a better mother than I am," Martha Claire admitted. "She bosses Buddy and Cissy around like they were hers. And they love her so. It's hard for them when she's away," she added, ignoring her mother's frown.

Yes, Polly thought, Buddy and Cissy missed Iris when Justine took her on a trip. They all did. Justine planned for Iris to go to New York for Christmas this year—and to fly all by herself. Martha Claire was having a fit about that, but only behind Justine's back, of course. When Justine wasn't around, Martha Claire sometimes would go on and on about what a negligent mother her sister was and how phone calls and visits didn't take the place of someone who was with the child every day and took care of her when she was sick, and who crawled in bed with her when she had bad dreams. Justine thought it was enough to come down here and play for a couple of days or a week, then say tah-tah and go running back to her highfalutin career. And with polio sweeping the country, what was she thinking of, taking a child some-place like New York City, which probably had more germs than any-place else in the world?

The irony of it was, of course, that because Justine wasn't a full-time mother, Martha Claire had the privilege of filling in for her. She absolutely doted on Iris, and Iris loved her aunt and wasn't shy about showing it. She hovered around Martha Claire, fixing her cups of tea, making her bed in the morning, running errands for her, helping with Buddy and Cissy. But the pure and simple truth was that Martha Claire was jealous of the love Iris also had for her mother. Iris was always overjoyed when Justine called on the telephone, and would count the days until her mother's next visit. Martha Claire refused to understand that she and Justine weren't competing for Iris's love. The child loved them both, but in different ways. Martha Claire was for every day, Justine for fun and trips. Polly was certain that Iris herself didn't think in terms of whom she loved more. She simply loved.

Martha Claire had adored Iris from the outset, but of course, they all had. Iris had brought life to this old house. Iris made them come out on the porch to look at sunsets and make wishes on shooting stars. She planned Sunday afternoon excursions to the round house in Gillian, the Frelsburg country store, and Fayetteville Lake. Iris had so much love to give. Polly wished that Martha Claire could understand that. Iris had enough love for everyone.

Martha Claire both delighted in and disdained Justine's visits. She hated the nights when Iris abandoned her own pretty bedroom—with its ruffled curtains, quilted bedcover, and hooked rug, all of which Martha Claire herself had made—and slept with her mother in the garage apartment. Justine and Iris would watch television with the rest of the family, then say good-night and head across the backyard. Martha Claire would lie in her bed, waiting until the light from the apartment windows no longer reflected on the walls of her bedroom. Sometimes the lights stayed on until after midnight, even on school nights.

Martha Claire preferred the evenings when Justine would tell Iris to go on upstairs to her own bed, that she and Martha Claire needed to have some time alone. And the two sisters would sit at the kitchen table, drinking beer or iced tea, talking about people they knew and how much they missed their daddy and grandparents, remembering the days back when, worrying about their mother's occasional dizzy spells. She had fainted at Granny Grace's funeral and scared them all to death. Doc Hadley had changed her medication, though, and she seemed to be doing better.

"You work so hard on the house and taking care of everyone," Justine said. "It isn't fair that you have to do it all."

Martha Claire shrugged, not knowing what to say. Of course, she had to do it all. Justine had a *career*.

The day had been hot, but the night breeze coming through the kitchen windows was refreshingly cool. Martha Claire lifted her glass and took that first lovely sip of cold beer.

"Are you happy?" Justine asked.

"I'm where I want to be," Martha Claire said. "I wish this were what you wanted, too. Life would be easier if I had you here to help."

"I'll try to come more often," Justine promised. "But I can't live here, Martha Claire. You know that, don't you?"

"I suppose. Sometimes I wish I hadn't kept Iris for you. Then you might have stayed on in Columbus. But I really didn't take Iris for you, did I? I took her because I wanted her. What about you?" Martha Claire asked her sister. "Are you happy?"

"I'm doing what I want to do, but I pay a price. I miss being with the people I love. I get so homesick sometimes, I feel like I've got a disease."

"Do you ever think about Iris's father?"

Justine shook her head.

"Would you tell me if there was a man in your life?"

"There have been several."

"But what about the man you met in Korea—the army officer. You really liked him a lot. I could tell by your voice when you talked to him on the phone."

Justine offered a sad little smile. "Yes, I liked him a lot. I guess you could say that I was in love with him."

"Why didn't you marry him?"

"An army officer needs a proper wife, Martha Claire. You know that. I would have spoiled things for him."

"I was so worried that you were going to get married and take Iris away," Martha Claire admitted. "I wanted you to be happy, but it would have killed me if you had taken Iris away." She tried to force back the tears that were threatening, but they came anyway.

Justine knelt beside Martha Claire's chair and embraced her. "It's all right," Justine soothed. "I will borrow my daughter from time to time, but she belongs here with you and Grayson. This is her home. Mine, too."

"But don't you miss him?" Martha Claire asked, wanting to know more about this man her sister had loved.

"I still think about him, but he's married now, as he needed to be. He needed a gracious wife, one who played by the rules. I've traded what you and Grayson have for independence, and that makes me sad sometimes. But we all make choices."

"What about some other man—a man who doesn't care if his wife 'plays by the rules'?"

"Yes, I knew a man like that once, but his plane was shot down over the English Channel."

"Was he Iris's father?" Martha Claire asked.

"No," Justine said, then drained her glass and pushed back her chair.

fourteen

"No, sweetheart, think now—nine times seven?"

Buddy looked down at his lap and shrugged. "I don't remember," he said, his voice an agonized whisper.

Martha Claire held back a sigh. "Okay, then, what is ten times seven?"

Moving his lips, Buddy counted by tens on his fingers, then looked up at his mother. "Seventy?"

"That's right," Martha Claire said brightly. "Now, if ten times seven makes seventy, wouldn't nine times seven be seven less than seventy?"

Buddy looked at his mother's face as though trying to decide if this was a trick question or if the answer really was yes.

"I want you to think of ten piles of apples," Martha Claire said. "Each pile has seven apples. That's seventy apples in all. If you took away one of those piles, wouldn't you have seven fewer apples?"

Buddy nodded.

"So how many apples would that be?"

She waited while Buddy used his fingers to count back from seventy. "Sixty-three?" he asked anxiously.

"That's right, son! Seven times nine is sixty-three." Martha Claire leaned back in her chair, pleased that she had finally gotten him to say the right answer but exhausted from the effort.

Theme music from *Wagon Train* was coming from the television in the next room. She went to the door and asked Grayson to please turn down the sound, then closed the door. Back at the kitchen table, she said, "Now, we just figured out that nine times seven is sixty-three, so what is seven times nine?"

Again the downcast eyes and the shrug.

Martha Claire held a wave of irritation in check. "Okay, let's think of those nine sacks, each with seven apples. We could take those sixty-three apples and divide them up a different way. We could put nine apples in seven sacks, instead of seven apples in nine sacks. Multiplication is like addition, Buddy. You can turn it upside down. If you add three to two, it's the same as adding two to three. Multiplication is the same. You can turn the problem upside down and get the same answer. Seven times nine and nine times seven get you the same answer. Do you understand?"

"I think so," he said in a small voice.

Martha Claire reached over to caress his soft cheek. Such a beautiful child. At eight years old, Buddy had a wonderful head of thick curly black hair, huge dark eyes, and perpetually rosy cheeks that stood out against fair skin. Buddy was more beautiful than his sister, but he had none of Cissy's quick intelligence.

But Buddy could learn, and he would learn. Martha Claire would see to that. Grayson said she pushed the boy too hard, that he needed more time to run and play, but she couldn't bear the thought that their son might be held back a grade, that he might be branded a dummy, that people might think she hadn't helped him enough with his homework and drilled him endlessly on his spelling lists and multiplication tables, that she hadn't gone over the next day's assignment in his reader. Grayson helped some, too, and Iris when she was finished with her own homework. Even Cissy, who was a precocious second-grader, would help her brother with his reading. Together, they would get him through the third grade and all the grades to follow.

Martha Claire remembered a boy who had been branded a dummy during her own grade-school days. Dirk Sutherland had been held back two grades and was physically the largest child in her fifth-grade class, as tall as the teacher even. During spelling bees, he wouldn't even try to spell the words. His papers were never displayed on the bulletin board. Everyone called him Dumbbell Dirk. Martha Claire wasn't going to let anything like that happen to Buddy. He was going to learn and stay with his class in school. Only the children of sharecroppers were held back. If his sister could learn, he could, too.

"I'm sorry, Mama," Buddy said.

"Why, sweetie?"

"That I can't remember things."

She opened her arms, and he came to sit on her lap. Soon he would be too big for this, she realized, and she held him tighter, kissing his neck and hair. "Life isn't fair, my darling boy. Some children have to work harder in school than others. Some grown-ups have to pick cotton to make money to feed their children, while other grown-ups just have to count money at a bank to earn money to feed theirs."

"I love you, Mama," he said, curling his body to fit more closely against hers.

"And I love you, Buddy. You are a good boy, and you can run faster than any other child in your whole class. Maybe you aren't the best at arithmetic and spelling, but you can run very, very fast. Now, go watch *Wagon Train,* and remember that nine times seven is sixty-three."

"And seven times nine is, too."

"That's right! You think that if I ask you in the morning, you will still remember?"

"I'll try, Mama."

"I know you will."

She watched him hurry across the kitchen to join the others in front of the television. If his teacher just spent more time with him, he would do better, she decided as she put the tablet and pencils away. Buddy wasn't dumb. It just took him a bit longer to learn multiplication tables and other things.

Poor Dirk Sutherland had never learned any multiplication tables, and he was a big clumsy boy, hardly able to run at all. His family had moved away before the war, and Martha Claire had no idea what had happened to him. She couldn't imagine him married or holding down a job.

But why in the world was she thinking of poor Dirk Sutherland, Martha Claire wondered with a shake of her head. Buddy was nothing like Dirk. Dirk had been retarded and unable to learn much of anything. Buddy could learn just fine; it just took him longer. And he wasn't the least bit clumsy. He ran surprisingly fast for the big sturdy boy that he was. And he already could hit a baseball a country mile. She was beginning to understand how important those things were for a boy like Buddy. Even if he wasn't smart, other children accepted him because of his prowess on the playground.

She took a last look around the kitchen to make sure everything was tidy, then turned out the light and went to join her family in the morning room.

"I'm sorry, Mrs. Richardson, but I can't give your money back on a dress pattern that you've already opened and used."

"But I didn't use it," she protested. "I opened it up and decided it was too complicated."

"But the pieces are all wadded up," Grayson pointed out. "No one else would buy the pattern now."

"They can be ironed flat," she insisted. "I'm certainly not going to keep a pattern I can't use. And I'd like to trade this piece of red corduroy for the hunter green."

Grayson took a breath to compose himself and pointed to the sign over the counter: NO RETURN ON PIECE GOODS UNLESS PURCHASED BY THE BOLT. Years ago his father had made that sign and put it in a frame.

Grayson wanted to raise his voice and tell this annoying woman that he no longer needed her business, that she could take her piddling purchases and go elsewhere. But he couldn't do that, of course. She would tell all her friends that he had been rude and unreasonable, and the truth of the matter was he couldn't afford to lose even one customer, piddling or otherwise.

"But I am not returning the corduroy," Mrs. Richardson asserted. "I am *exchanging* it."

Grayson could feel his blood pressure rising, but he drew in his breath and forced himself to use his calm, reasonable voice. "But I would have to sell the red corduroy on the remnant table at half price," he pointed out. "If I turn around and give you three yards of green corduroy, I would be losing money on the transaction."

In the end, of course, he ended up exchanging the fabric and giving

Mrs. Richardson her money back on the pattern. All total, the transaction cost him two dollars and eighty-seven cents. Some businessman he was!

He was no good at dealing with the Mrs. Richardsons of the world. Maybe if his mother or mother-in-law had been there, they might have fared better with Mrs. Richardson. But Polly wasn't well and came in only when she was up to it, and Lily mostly worked mornings, leaving her afternoons free for bridge games and club meetings. Ethyl Woodson, who had been hired by his father more than forty years ago, had finally retired and moved to Tyler to live with her sister. Most of the time now, it was just Grayson in the store, measuring out piece goods, selling shoes and underwear, and every now and then a dress or suit. He had decided to cut his overhead by not replacing Miss Woodson, which meant he was more a prisoner than ever in what he still thought of as his father's store. The times he would be able to sneak off with his fishing pole or go to the library for an hour or so of browsing would be few and far between.

His New Year's resolution for 1960 had been to be more innovative at the store. His mother kept telling him that doing things the same old way wasn't working. "Your father didn't need to change things around," Lily pointed out. "Our only competition was the Sears and Roebuck catalog. Now folks think nothing of driving to Houston to buy their clothes and goods." But here it was August and he hadn't had a sidewalk sale or so much as rearranged the store fixtures or replaced the cracked mirror in the dressing room. Stewart's Dry Goods still looked exactly as it did in the 1930s vintage picture of his father and the store employees that hung behind the cash register.

What he really should do was specialize in children's clothes and shoes, which still moved fairly well, and get rid of adult clothes and the fabric and notions department. But he was reluctant to do that. Coming down here six days a week was disheartening enough the way it was, but at least he could talk sports and politics while customers tried on shoes or browsed through the racks. With a changeover to children's wear, he would be dealing almost exclusively with mothers and children. Mothers with children in tow—even if they had an interest in sports or politics—were too busy saying "Stop chasing your sister" or "Leave things alone" to carry on a conversation.

If he had to run a store, he'd rather it be a sporting goods store, but Columbus was too small to support such an endeavor. He had laughed when his mother suggested that he eliminate fabric and notions, which never made much money anyway, and add a small sporting goods department. She also suggested that he carry only men's and boy's shoes and ready-to-wear since he'd never been any good at selling dresses and ladies underthings.

Now he was considering her ideas. He could partition off the back and carry shotgun shells, decoys, fishing lures and line, bats and balls, shuttlecocks, swim goggles and fins. Not full lines. Just the everyday stuff that people had to replace from time to time.

But would it be worth the effort? He would still be a shopkeeper, and a mediocre one at best. He was never going to make any more than a marginal living, never going to be able to fix up the house for Martha Claire or pay for Buddy's and Cissy's college education. Maybe a few changes would make a difference, though. And it would be a change, not just plowing the same furrow over and over again. Maybe he should at least try.

He would discuss it with Martha Claire when he got back from guard camp, he decided. Tomorrow he would be traveling with his unit to North Fort Hood for two weeks of maneuvers, and in spite of the heat and mosquitoes, he looked forward to the time away from the store.

After two weeks he was generally ready to come home, though, ready to see the children and have a home-cooked meal, ready to make love to his wife. Maybe if he had committed to a military career he would have longed for the life of a small-town shopkeeper. Sometimes he wondered if he was one of those people whose glass was half empty instead of half full.

He did find contentment, though, in books and nature, and the children brought him happiness. He liked taking them fishing, liked teaching them the names of birds and trees. And he liked watching Buddy play ball.

The center of his universe was still Martha Claire, would always be Martha Claire, even though he wasn't sure why that was so. Youthful ardor was pretty much a memory, and at times he still wondered what life would have been like if he'd never come back to Columbus after the war. Whenever he thought of his wife, though, it was with tenderness.

fifteen

"Hey, Martha Claire, are you high on something?" Justine asked as she stretched out on the blanket and covered her eyes with her arms.

"What do you mean?" Martha Claire asked.

"You seem so up. I haven't seen you run around and play with the kids in ages. You were actually *frolicking* out there in the surf. And last night you played hide-and-seek out in the yard and sat in your husband's lap on the porch swing. You've laughed more in the past two days than you have in years. You even look younger. What's going on with you? You and Grayson discovered a new position or something?"

Martha Claire actually laughed. "It's just nice to have you home for two whole weeks. And Mother is doing better now that Doc Hadley has convinced her to take those nitroglycerin pills. Grayson's sports corner down at the store is beginning to turn a profit. Buddy passed fifth grade. And it's a beautiful day to be with my sister and our children on Galveston Island. Just look at that sky. And have you ever seen the ocean such a beautiful shade of blue!"

Justine raised herself on her elbow and regarded her sister. "If I didn't know you so well, I'd swear you were having an affair."

Martha Claire stopped laughing and gasped. "How dare you say such a thing!"

"Sorry," Justine said. "I know you wouldn't do that. It's just that women I've known get all silly like you are when they're in love. I've been that way myself a time or two." She lay back down, allowing the warmth of the sun and the sound of the surf and children's laughter to lull her.

Yes, something was definitely going on with Martha Claire. She hadn't protested that it was too windy for a day at Jamaica Beach or that she needed to finish painting the front porch or was too busy to be gone for a whole day. She'd just said it was a great idea and started making lists of all the stuff they'd need to take along. She'd even dug around in her bureau and found a bathing suit to put on, much to the children's amazement.

"Can you keep a secret?" Martha Claire asked in an oddly girlish voice.

Justine uncovered her eyes and regarded her sister. With knees hugged against her chest, Martha Claire was staring dreamily out to sea. The wind was teasing her hair, which shone absolutely golden in the sunlight. Her profile was as pure as a Raphael Madonna. She hadn't looked this lovely on her wedding day.

Justine reached for her camera and managed to snap the shutter before Martha Claire was aware what she was doing.

"Hey, that's not fair," Martha Claire said with feigned indignation.

"Of course I can keep a secret," Justine said, closing the camera back in its case. "Did I ever tell anyone that it was you who stole that jug of homemade brew off old Mr. Logan's back porch?"

Martha Claire groaned. "God, that was the sickest I've ever been in my life. Mother thought we had food poisoning."

Justine sat up. "So what's the secret?"

Martha Claire leaned forward and lowered her voice, even though they had the beach all to themselves. "Well, it may not be anything, but I'm almost five weeks late with my period. I've never been this late before, not in my entire life."

"You think that you're *pregnant?*"

"Yeah. Wouldn't that be something, after all these years? I have an appointment with Doc Hadley tomorrow. I wasn't going to tell anyone in case it's another false alarm, but this time I feel so certain. And you've already noticed how different I am—that just confirms it, doesn't it?"

Justine regarded her sister's slim figure. Her breasts were as small and compact as ever, and obviously she wasn't suffering from morning sickness. She'd been up at dawn this morning, baking cinnamon rolls for breakfast and deviling eggs for the picnic basket. "Remember how sick I was when I was pregnant with Iris?" she asked.

Martha Claire's face clouded. "Not everyone gets sick. And you didn't want to be pregnant. I do. And besides, I'm having other symptoms."

"Like what?"

"I'm light-headed sometimes and don't have much appetite. Mostly, though, I feel hopeful."

"Well then, I hope you're right, if that's what you really want."

"I know it's difficult for you to understand, Justine, but I've never stopped hoping," Martha Claire said. "Motherhood is no big deal for you, but it's the most important thing in the world for me."

Not trusting herself to respond, Justine rose and starting walking toward the surf, then broke into a clumsy run, with the soft sand holding her back. She was aware of the children waving their arms and coming toward her, thinking she had returned for more fun riding the waves. But she raced into the water and began swimming as soon as it reached her belly. She swam and swam, past the breaking waves, until she could look back and her sister was only a speck on the distant beach.

But Martha Claire's words followed her. *Motherhood is no big deal for you.* The words had stabbed like a knife.

The next day, Martha Claire prepared for her doctor's appointment as carefully as any bride prepared for her wedding night. She shampooed her hair and gave herself a pedicure. She lingered in her bath to shave her legs and underarms. She dusted herself with bath powder that had been sitting unopened on the shelf since Cissy had given it to her the previous Christmas. She looked lovingly at her nude body in the mirror. "Don't let me down this time," she implored.

She wished she hadn't said anything to Justine yesterday. For weeks, Martha Claire had been holding her secret close to her heart, not wanting to say anything in case it wasn't true. After all, she'd had false alarms before—but nothing as hopeful as this. When four full weeks had passed, she had allowed hope to blossom, allowed herself to imagine a reconfigured life, to think of the surprise and joy her secret would bring to her husband of nineteen years. A baby that came of their love and their marriage! And she imagined the look on the children's faces when she told them. Iris was fourteen now, in her first year of high school. Buddy was almost twelve and Cissy almost ten. They would all be so thrilled.

Martha Claire found herself touching her stomach every few minutes, caressing the microscopic infant that surely must be growing there, loving it already, feeling herself caught up in the miracle. And she had gone into the bathroom constantly to make sure it wasn't yet another mistake, another disappointment after nineteen years of disappointments.

She and Grayson never talked about a baby anymore. He thought she had put all that behind her and found fulfillment with the three children they were raising. And to a degree, she had. She knew she had been blessed: she loved Iris, Buddy, and Cissy—adored them, in fact. But Iris had come from Justine's body, and Buddy and Cissy from some unknown woman's—two women who hadn't wanted their babies, when she herself had prayed for one every day of her married life.

Dressed and ready to go, Martha Claire paused at the bedroom door, put both her hands over her belly, and closed her eyes. *Please, God, I've worked hard to be a good mother to these children. If you care about me at all, let this be true.*

Martha Claire regarded Doc Hadley's cluttered office, with medical journals stacked on the table, desk, and floor. Pictures of babies he had delivered over the years all but covered one wall in a random, thumb-tacked montage. Hundreds of babies. A faded picture of a smiling, six-month-old Iris was tacked up in the far corner. Every time Martha Claire saw that wall, she wished that a picture of *her* baby would be up there someday. Maybe now, her wish would finally come true.

On the bookshelf behind his desk, a framed picture of Doc Hadley's long-dead wife presided over pictures of their three daughters and their grandchildren. Rumor was that a young doctor from Dallas would be joining him in the next few months and would eventually take over his practice. Martha Claire hoped Doc Hadley would be the one to deliver her baby. He had delivered her and taken care of her all her life. She couldn't imagine having anyone but him.

Doc Hadley had seemed impressed when she told him she was thirty-four days late with her period, and agreed that even for her, with her history of fluctuating cycles, that was a significant symptom. He had conducted her pelvic examination with his usual briskness, then told her to get dressed; he would talk with her in his office.

Martha Claire could hear voices coming from an adjacent examining room and a child crying. Not a baby. An older child. She hoped the doctor wouldn't take too long in there. As Granny Grace would have said, she was as nervous as a long-tailed tomcat in a room full of rocking chairs. Her heart was pounding, her palms sweating. *Hurry up, old man,* she implored. *Come in here and put my heart at ease. Tell me what I need to hear.*

What if he had forgotten about her sitting in here? Should she go tell the nurse to remind him that she was still here, waiting?

But then she heard the examining room door opening and closing, his footsteps on the wooden floor. She took a deep breath as the door to his office opened.

"Sorry to keep you waiting, Martha Claire," he said, lowering himself into his desk chair. "Little Mickey Tisdale has the worst case of poison ivy I've seen in years."

Martha Claire held her breath while the doctor took off his glasses and cleaned them with his pocket handkerchief. When he put them back on, he looked across the desk at her. "You're entering menopause, Martha Claire."

"*Menopause?* But I'm only thirty-nine years old."

"Yes, that's a bit young, but not abnormal. You're healthy as a horse, and I'll put you on hormones to prevent hot flashes," he said, reaching for his prescription pad. "You should have no problems at all."

"Are you saying that I'm not pregnant?"

"Yes, I'm afraid so. I'm sorry to have to disappoint you again, but at least you won't have to keep worrying about it anymore. Looks like you're never going to have a baby, Martha Claire. But, then, you've got Iris and Buddy and Cissy. Surely getting pregnant is not as important to you as it once was."

"Couldn't you be mistaken? Maybe I should see a specialist in Houston."

He shrugged. "You can see all the doctors you want, but it isn't going to make you pregnant. Now, you go on home to your family and count your blessings. You've got a fine husband and three lively young'uns to raise."

He handed her a prescription and said something about what a good little ballplayer Buddy was turning out to be. "But actually not so little," he said with a chuckle. "The way that boy is shooting up, we're all going to be looking up to him pretty soon."

Martha Claire knew she was supposed to get up now and leave him to his other patients, but she felt as though her body had turned to lead. *Menopause.* No baby, ever, in her entire life.

She didn't realize she was crying until Doc Hadley was thrusting a handful of tissue at her. He had come around the desk and pulled a chair close to hers so he could put his arms around her and pat her back. He was saying something about reading in a medical journal that even nuns in convents who had never been with a man and knew they never would be pregnant still got depressed when their reproductive years came to an end. The wisest thing he had ever done in his forty-two years of practicing medicine was giving her Buddy and Cissy. She was a wonderful mother, and it did his old heart good to see those two youngsters growing up happy in such a fine home. Martha Claire pressed her face against his starchy white jacket and sobbed her anguish. *Never have a baby.* When they buried her out there in Odd Fellows Cemetery, they would be burying a barren women. All that useless praying and hoping and dreaming.

She sobbed on and on, painful sobs that came from deep inside of her, from a broken heart and a womb that would be forever empty. Finally Doc Hadley called out to his nurse, who brought him a hypodermic needle to inject in Martha Claire's hip. Even as the nurse was leading her to a cot in the back room, Martha Claire could feel blessed oblivion flowing through her veins. Maybe when she woke up she would find it had all been a terrible dream.

It was night when she awakened, and she was home in her own bed with Grayson at her side. He must have sensed her wakefulness, for immediately he had taken her in his arms and caressed her and told her it didn't matter, that she was more precious to him than anything in the whole world, that he loved their life just the way it was, but he was so sorry, so very sorry that she had been disappointed like that.

"Do Mother and Justine know what happened?"

"Yes, but not the children. When Doc Hadley called, I closed the store and went to bring you home. Tell me, my darling, what can I do or say to make you feel better?"

Martha Claire considered his request. And she thought of Doc Hadley's words—that at least it was over and she wouldn't have to face the monthly torment ever again. "Just keep on loving me," she said. Then she kissed him. It was to be a kiss of dismissal, a kiss that said she was okay and he could go back to sleep now and leave her to her thoughts, to the anguish that only she could feel, but the kiss turned into something else altogether. She found that she needed very much the reassurance of passion to reaffirm her womanhood. And this night, his love filled her more completely than it had in a very long time. Not for years had it been like that. She wondered, could it be a new beginning, free of other expectations, with loving just for loving's sake?

She clung to him for a long time afterward, relishing the scent and feel of him, this husband for a lifetime.

sixteen

"Are you sure everything is all right?" Martha Claire asked.

"My goodness, Martha Claire, you've only been gone since this morning. The children are home from school. Cissy is across the street playing with the Williams girls. Iris put a roast in the oven and is out in the yard playing catch with Buddy. You and Grayson forget about us and have a gay old time for a change."

"Did Iris remember to change the bandage on Cissy's knee?"

"Yes, she did. And Cissy knows she isn't to roller-skate again until it heals up. Now, stop worrying and enjoy yourself, or at least pretend like you're enjoying yourself for Grayson's sake. He's been looking forward to this reunion for ever so long, and the man deserves a weekend away with his wife."

"I wrote the phone number of the hotel there on a pad by the phone."

"Yes, it's right here where you left it. I'm fine. The children are fine. The house is fine. Lily's perfectly capable of looking after the store on her own. For heaven's sake, Martha Claire, get off this phone and go make yourself pretty for your husband."

Martha Claire hung up the phone and sat on the bed for a time, staring across the room at her reflection in the dresser mirror. Yes, she worried too much, and they had only driven up to College Station, for God's sake. But her mother wasn't well at all. Doc Hadley said her heart was all worn out, and it was a miracle she had lasted this long. Polly could no longer go up and down the stairs, so they had moved the television and morning room furniture into the dining room, with the dining room table pushed to one side, and moved Polly's bedroom furniture downstairs to the morning room.

If it weren't for Iris, Martha Claire wouldn't even have considered leaving town. At sixteen, Iris was as responsible as any adult and would take good care of her grandmother and cousins.

Martha Claire smiled at the thought of Iris. She was such a blessing. In sixteen years, Martha Claire had never had a moment's trouble out of her niece, who had always been more like a daughter to her. Yes, she would relax and have a gay old time. She took a deep breath to start the process.

Hanging on the closet door was Grayson's dress uniform, freshly dry-cleaned, the moth hole in the sleeve rewoven, silver oak leaves on the shoulders. He was now a lieutenant colonel in the National Guard, and a battalion commander. There had been a ceremony at the armory, and a general drove over from Austin to pin the oak leaves on him.

Tonight they were attending the twentieth reunion of his class at Texas A&M. Tomorrow, class members and their wives would attend the annual homecoming festivities and a football game against Texas Tech, with the men being honored during halftime.

As one of the organizers of the weekend reunion, Grayson had been writing back and forth to former classmates for more than a year and driving up to the College Station campus to make arrangements. Martha Claire had bought a new dress for the occasion, and her mother insisted that she have her hair styled and do something about the gray that was starting to dull the strawberry blond. Once she had been voted the prettiest girl at Columbus High School, but that was a long time ago. She'd changed more than Grayson, who still had his military bearing and a full head of thick brown hair.

She studied her shorter, fluffier hairdo in the mirror. It did look better, she supposed, even though the color seemed a bit brassy.

Iris had helped her shop for a dress at Foley's in Houston and insisted she buy a black velvet sheath that showed she still had a decent figure. As soon as Grayson got out of the shower, she would put on her makeup, doing more than her usual dab of lipstick and touch of rouge.

Her mother had said that Grayson deserved this weekend, meaning that Martha Claire didn't provide many occasions just for the two of them to be together. It had been years since she'd spent the night alone with him in a hotel room, and the thought of coming back here a bit tipsy and making love without having to whisper was a wonderfully appealing one.

Grayson was singing the Aggie War Hymn in the shower, which brought another smile to Martha Claire's face. She held the smile for the mirror's benefit. She did want to look pretty tonight and was glad now that she'd let Iris talk her into the black velvet dress—and the glittery rhinestone earrings and satin pumps. Of course, she needed everyday clothes far more than she needed something fancy, but sometimes practical considerations had to take a backseat. Her mother was right. Grayson was entitled—they both were.

When she finished getting ready, Martha Claire did a little pirouette for Grayson's benefit. There was admiration in his eyes as he came to attention and offered her a snappy salute.

Grayson wore fatigues or khakis to his National Guard meetings, and Martha Claire hadn't seen him in dress blues for years. He looked so handsome, it took her breath away. She'd forgotten what a really fine looking man her husband was.

"I hope you arranged for a photographer at this shindig," she said. "I want a picture of us looking this good to keep forever."

Martha Claire remembered many of the men and their wives from the military balls she'd attended at College Station during Grayson's undergraduate years. At dinner, they sat with Bobby and Ruth Mitchell, who now lived in Fairbanks, Alaska. Bobby and Grayson had roomed together their senior year and served together in the same artillery battalion in France. The two men had corresponded occasionally over the years, but this was the first time Grayson and Bobby had seen each other since the war. Martha Claire and Ruth chatted about their children, but mostly they sat quietly while the men reminisced about fallen classmates and the war years. It was the most Martha Claire had ever heard Grayson talk about the war, but she realized this was a carefully edited version, with little reference to the horror she knew both men had experienced.

After dinner, there was a memorial service for fallen classmates. It was conducted in the form of a roll call, with someone answering for each of the men who had died during World War II and the Korean War. It was a haunting, solemn experience, and Martha Claire had to keep dabbing her eyes. So many names, so many young men who never came home. How lucky she was that Grayson had. She prayed that Buddy would never have to go to war.

After the roll call, she and Ruth headed for the ladies' room. When they returned, Bobby was commenting about how good Grayson looked, with not even a scar from his wound. "I thought for sure he was going to lose an eye after his jeep took that hit," Bobby told his wife. "I guess he would have if we hadn't been able to get him on a medevac flight to England."

A flight to England?

Martha Claire replayed the words in her head to make sure that was what Bobby had said. Grayson had never been to England. Martha Claire glanced at her husband, waiting for him to correct Bobby's statement.

But Bobby was still talking, explaining to his wife how Grayson had been wounded during the battle for the town of Le Luc—five or six days after the beachhead in southern France. The Germans had massed a strong defense of the town. Their battalion had been moved in as reinforcements. They were low on fuel, so they walked fifty minutes and rode ten. The roads were so pocked with shell craters it was hard to know which was worse, riding or walking. Grayson was just getting back into the jeep for his ten-minute ride when the jeep took a hit. The driver was killed. Grayson had taken some shrapnel in his right eye and was given emergency treatment at a field hospital, then evacuated to a hospital north of London, where he could be treated by an eye surgeon.

Martha Claire tugged on Grayson's sleeve, but he didn't meet her gaze, didn't say that Bobby was mistaken, that it was some other officer who had gone to England for eye surgery.

She put down her cocktail and mentally retreated from the conversation, going over what she had just learned. Grayson had been in England during the war.

Suddenly the band was playing, and Grayson was pulling her out on the dance floor. The music was from their era—"Sunrise Serenade,"

"Falling in Love with Love," "Begin the Beguine," "Perfidia"—music they had danced to when they were young and filled with high hopes and sweet longing. Their bodies fit together just as perfectly as they had back then. Martha Claire closed her eyes and let the music take her. So many times they had danced like this, with Grayson in his cadet uniform, always with the expectation of afterward, when they would play the agonizing games of young sweethearts who were almost certain they would not go all the way but relished the temptation and gloried in each others' bodies, in the feel of moist, firm flesh and unending kisses.

When Grayson provided her with another bourbon-laced drink, she accepted and anticipated the warm buzz it would bring. She mentally pushed puzzlement aside. She would think about Grayson and England another time. Tonight she wanted to feel young and in love. She wanted to be alone in a motel room with her handsome husband in her arms. She wanted to be hot and wanton, to depart from the quiet, routine sex of the marriage bed.

In the station wagon, on the way back to the motel, she turned on the radio and found a love song to keep the mood alive. Paul Anka sang "Tonight, My Love, Tonight," and Grayson put his arm around her and sang along. She snuggled up against him, nuzzling his neck and stroking his thigh.

In their room, they drank whiskey from a flask and danced naked in front of the dresser mirror. They promised each other that they would have other nights like this, away from home and inhibitions.

The next morning, they nursed their hangovers with aspirin, coffee, and a walk around the campus. Martha took a picture of Grayson in front of the Academic Building and listened to him reminisce as they walked along. He wished that he had appreciated that time of his life more while he was living it. "But those years weren't the best," he added. "The best is yet to come."

"Do you really believe that?" Martha Claire asked.

"Yes, I do. With the children getting older, we can do more things together, and you can help me more at the store. I need you, Martha Claire, to help with advertising and merchandising. You're better at all that than I am. I want the store to be more profitable so we can hire a full-time salesperson and do more things together, so we can travel. We can finish fixing up the house, too, but most of all I dream of going places with you, seeing places for the first time with you and showing you some of the places I've been." He put his arm around her waist and drew her close. "This weekend is just a taste of the future, my darling. I know it is."

She smiled and leaned her head against his shoulder.

That night, during the outdoor barbecue, she mentioned to Bobby Mitchell that she hadn't realized Grayson's injury had been so serious.

"I imagine that he didn't want to worry you," Bobby said. "He was lucky that transportation to England was available. Doctors in field hospitals aren't equipped for eye surgery."

"Was he gone long?"

"I don't remember. Maybe a week or two. We'd already crossed into Germany when he rejoined the unit. Knowing Grayson, he probably insisted on coming back at the first possible moment. I remember, though, that he brought back a couple of bottles of Irish whiskey. At the time, I thought it was the best stuff I'd ever tasted in my life! Headquarters company was bivouacked in what was left of a barn, and there was a big old moon shining through a hole in the roof, and here comes Grayson in spanking-clean fatigues, with a patch over his eye and two bottles of whiskey, wanting to know where to find his company. I wasn't about to tell him until he shared some of that whiskey with me. We'd lived that long and were starting to actually think we would make it to the end and come out alive, and we drank to that—to living. Except you never quite get over the fact that you lived when so many good men didn't. You think, *Why me?* Was it just a crapshoot or was there some reason? Or maybe it was all a mistake. Maybe some other guy took a bullet with your name on it. God, all those feelings came back last night during that roll call." Bobby looked away and took a handkerchief from his pocket. Martha Claire patted his arm and left him with his emotions.

She waited until the next morning, when she and Grayson were on their way home, to ask him why he'd never told her about going to England during the war.

"I'm sure I wrote to you about it."

"The letter probably got lost along the way," Martha Claire acknowledged.

The next day, while the children were at school, her mother was resting, and Grayson was at work, she went up to the attic and looked in the battered footlocker where his wartime letters were now stored. Most letters had sections blacked out by censors. Some letters had little more than the greeting and final paragraph of endearments left legible. She found the letter telling her about having to wear a patch over his eye after having a piece of shrapnel removed, but nothing was said about treatment in England. But lines had been blacked out, lines that might have mentioned England.

Then she found herself going back to the beginning, reading in order the hundreds of letters she had received from him. Much of the content was mundane. He wrote about K-rations and the delight of a rare hot meal. He frequently mentioned the difficulty of shaving in cold water, the difficulty of buying soap and razor blades, and how he longed for a hot shower, for dry socks and boots. He never wrote about specific places, or if he did it had been marked out by a censor. But he did write about castles atop distant mountains in Italy and the lush greenness of the French countryside. Numerous times he mentioned the joy of buying or being given a loaf of fresh bread. At least half his letters mentioned some sort of discomfort—unbearable heat, freezing cold, relentless rain, heavy snow. And sore feet, sunburn, a frostbitten toe. The only indications that he actually was a man at war, however, were vague references to "engagements" or "action." As the war progressed into 1944 and 1945, he would mention the arrival of new men, which she now realized indicated that men in his company were being killed or wounded. At the end of each letter was the part she would not read to her parents or his, the part about missing her and the longing he felt, the part she had read over and over.

The tone of the letters did change, however, after the time of his injury. He wrote about returning to her but never mentioned Columbus and the life they had planned. Then he started discussing the advantages of a military career in the peacetime army. He said there was more security in the army than there would be running a store in a little Texas town. They could live abroad. Their children would grow up citizens of the world.

Martha Claire remembered how she had lived for these letters. Often there would be no letters for agonizing days on end, then several letters would arrive the same day. Reason told her that some probably had been lost on the way, going down with torpedoed ships or shot down with airplanes. But it did seem odd that not a single letter mentioned his trip, medical treatment, the time he spent in England, or his return to his unit. Surely every mention of those things would not have caught a censor's attention. Surely not every one of the letters that might have mentioned those things would have been lost.

In the years since, Grayson seldom had talked about his actual combat experiences, but he had shared his impressions of Africa, Italy, France, and Germany, sometimes showing her pictures from books of places he had been during the war. But he never had shown her pictures from England. Not only had he not written about England, he had never said one word about going there. Never. She was certain of that. England was where Justine had been stationed. She would have taken note if Grayson had said anything about England.

Of course, he could have flown directly to a military base and seen only the inside of a military hospital. Yes, that was probably it, she decided.

But apparently he had been there for more than a week, maybe even two weeks or longer, in the same part of England as Justine. Wouldn't he have called his sister-in-law? Or sent her a message? Wouldn't she have gone to see him? Surely a wounded brother-in-law would have warranted a short train ride.

And if Justine had heard from him or had gone to see him, wouldn't she have mentioned it in a letter? Would all mention of such a phone call or visit have been deleted by censors or written in letters that never arrived? Even if Grayson had asked her not to worry the folks back home, wouldn't one of them have mentioned it after the war?

The following morning, without analyzing the reason why, she crossed the backyard and climbed the stairs to Justine's apartment.

How different it looked from those days more than sixteen years ago, when she, her parents, and Granny Grace had painted and furnished it for Justine and the baby she was expecting. In the years since, Justine had carpeted the floor, installed wooden blinds on the windows, and had bookshelves built across one wall. She had added a vintage armoire, and a cedar chest stood at the foot of the bed. The walls were covered with photographs she had taken, mostly of family members, but also ones that captured the town of Columbus—the bridges, the courthouse, the massive live oaks, the opera house, Stewart's Dry Goods, the brick water tower. Over the bed was a wonderful picture of Buddy, Cissy, and Iris sitting on the porch swing, and one of Martha Claire and the children taken on the beach at Galveston, on the day before she learned she wasn't pregnant and would never have a child of her own.

Having no idea what she was looking for, Martha Claire looked in and behind every drawer, opened every cupboard. She looked under the mattress and bed. She shook every book for what might be hidden between its pages. She looked in the pockets of garments and behind the footed bathtub.

Finally, she sat at the kitchen table and began to go through a shoe box that held pictures Justine had taken in London during the war—photographs of people digging through bombed-out buildings, medics carrying the injured on stretchers, people emerging dazed from bomb shelters, doctors and nurses in a hospital working over the charred body of a child.

And there were carefully labeled pictures documenting the bombing damage to buildings and landmarks: Admiralty Arch, Eaton Square, Victoria Station, Harrod's Department Store, Carr's Hotel, St. James Church, the House of Parliament, Havis Wharf.

One picture in particular captured Martha Claire's attention—of a soldier and little boy kneeling beside a dead dog, with debris all around and bombed-out row houses in the background. Justine had written on the back: "Charlwood Street, 150 houses destroyed by parachute mines."

The focus was on the grief-stricken face of the boy. The man's face was turned toward the boy. If Martha Claire's perusal had been a more casual one, she might have passed right over it, taking it for a candid picture of two unknown people—an American soldier comforting a grieving child in war-torn London.

But this American soldier had a bandaged right eye, and she recognized the familiar line of his cheek and jaw. It was a picture of her husband, and her sister had taken it.

seventeen

Martha Claire slipped the photograph in her apron pocket and left her sister's apartment. With what she considered truly amazing calmness, she helped her mother bathe and put on a fresh housedress. Then she installed Polly in front of the television with a basket of mending to keep her occupied while she changed her mother's bed, started a load of laundry, picked some vegetables from the garden, and made a pot of soup.

At lunch, when her mother asked if she had a headache, Martha Claire wanted to say no, that it was another sort of ache. But she simply shook her head.

"You need to eat your soup, dear," Polly said. "You're looking a bit peaked."

Martha Claire lifted a spoonful to her mouth but knew she wouldn't be able to swallow and returned it to the bowl. She took a sip of water instead.

While her mother rested, Martha Claire cleaned the oven and scrubbed the kitchen floor.

When the children got home from school, she admitted that she didn't feel well and was going upstairs to rest. She told Iris what to cook for dinner. It was Buddy's turn to do the dishes. Cissy was to take her grandmother a cup of tea and dust the downstairs before she went out to play. Grayson was having dinner with his mother, she reminded Iris. Be sure to have him help Buddy with his homework when he got home.

In her room, Martha Claire pulled down the shades, took off her dress, and crawled beneath the covers.

When Grayson came upstairs to check on her, she pretended that she was asleep. But he sat on the side of the bed and felt her forehead. "Do you want me to bring you a tray?" he asked.

"I'm not hungry," she said, not looking at him. Later, they would talk, when there would be no interruptions.

She actually dozed some during the evening, waking to the sound of laughter and footsteps running up and down the stairs. Normal sounds.

She desperately wanted Grayson to have the right words, to put forth some believable explanation for the photograph.

But what if he could not?

She waited until he had turned out the light and settled his head on his pillow before she told him that she had found a picture of him that Justine had taken in London. He had been comforting a boy whose dog had been killed.

So often throughout their marriage they had held difficult conversations in their bed, under the cover of darkness. Somehow darkness offset tension and brought a sense of reasonableness to such a discussion. Should they fix the roof or replace the aging Buick? Should they tell Buddy he couldn't play football unless he did better in school? How could they get Cissy's nose out of a book and get her to spend more time with her playmates? At what age and under what circumstances would Iris be allowed to go on car dates? Where would they find the money for a nursing home if Polly got too sick for Martha Claire to care for at home? But never once, in twenty years of marriage, had the nighttime discussion been about trust.

Grayson didn't say anything at all for long, silent minutes, then finally his disembodied voice said into the darkness, "I met her for a drink at a pub."

"That picture wasn't taken in a pub."

"No, it was taken afterward. The next day actually, after an air raid."

"Why did neither of you mention something as remarkable as seeing a relative from back home in London during the war—not in a letter or after the war? Not a word. Not a single word. What reason could you possibly have for not mentioning it? There was no letter at all from England. Why didn't you want me to know that you'd gone there?"

"It all happened so suddenly," he said. "Just hours after I was injured, I was on my way to London. Almost as soon as I arrived, I was having surgery. Probably I decided to wait until I knew the outcome of the surgery before I wrote. Or maybe I needed to keep it all to myself. I'd had some close calls before, but not like that. My driver's chest was blown open. I tried to help him, but blood was gushing out of my eye. I thought I was dying, too. It wasn't something I could put in a letter home to my wife."

"So you told Justine?"

"Yes. She was there; you weren't."

Their arms were so close she could feel the warmth from his flesh. She shifted her weight, eliminating the risk of an accidental touch. "Did something happen between you and my sister?" she asked.

"Not in the way that you mean. The air raid sirens were going off, but it seemed like the bombing was miles away. Justine helped me figure out how many shillings to leave for our tab, and we were putting on our coats—then suddenly the building was caving in. We managed to crawl down to the cellar and ended up trapped down there. Buildings were burning all around us, people screaming, and no matter how many pieces of rubble I moved, I couldn't find a way out. She made me promise that I would kill her rather than let her burn to death. I promised. It wasn't something either one of us wanted to talk about afterward."

"And nothing else happened? Do you swear on the lives of the children that you didn't decide to have a last fling before the flames got you?"

"No, we didn't do that, but would it have been so terrible to want that sort of human comfort in the face of death? Justine represented home to me. Hearing that soft south Texas voice made me think of you. Before the bombing started, I remember thinking how I wanted to sit in that pub all night and listen to her sound just like my wife."

Martha Claire allowed him to take her in his arms, to stroke her back and assure her of his love. But the seeds of suspicion had been planted. She believed him, and she didn't. What he told her was probably the truth. But was there something more he was not telling her?

Deep inside of her, doubt was eating away, but she was probably never going to know if that doubt was justified, so she decided to ignore it. Actually, she was quite proud of herself for coming to this conclusion. She would just put the whole damned business out of her mind.

For a time it worked. Life went on. She nursed her mother and took care of her children. She made love to her husband and wrote chatty letters to her sister that said nothing about the picture she had found. The picture itself she tore into small pieces.

Then one summer evening, while she was sitting at the table paying bills and half-watching an episode of "I Love Lucy," the cloud of doubt began to lift, leaving sickening realization in its stead.

The windows were open, but there was no breeze. Grayson had brought the circulating fan from the kitchen to stir the air. Polly was lying on the sofa propped up with pillows. In spite of the warmth, she had drawn an afghan over her legs. Buddy and Cissy were stretched out on the floor in front of the television. Grayson was in his easy chair, with Iris sitting on the floor in front of him, using his legs as a backrest. Martha Claire paused a minute in her check writing to admire the pure line of her niece's profile. Iris's hair was pulled back into a ponytail, her knees drawn up to her chest. She had a sweet loveliness about her that brought a catch to Martha Claire's throat.

She needed to have a silhouette made of Iris. Buddy and Cissy, too. But Martha Claire especially wanted to capture Iris as she was tonight, at the end of girlhood, poised on the threshold of young womanhood.

Iris was slimmer than Justine had been at that age. And she was a calmer person than her mother. Justine had always been in motion. As a child, she would run rather than walk and was always climbing up trees and onto roofs. She had accepted every dare, even crossing the railroad trestle when a train could be coming down the track at any minute. But with a glance, one could tell that Justine and Iris were mother and daughter. Iris had Justine's long legs and her dimpled chin, her widely spaced eyes and full mouth.

Now, however, Martha Claire was noticing something about Iris that she'd never realized before, or at least never given much thought to, something that now made her put her hand to her heart and catch her breath.

Iris had Grayson's nose.

Iris's nose was shaped exactly like his and matched its tilt, matched the way it curved into his forehead, the flare of the nostrils, the slight indentation at its tip.

Martha Claire studied Cissy's and Buddy's noses, her mother's nose. She reached up and touched her own nose. Everyone's was different. Only Grayson and Iris had noses that were exactly the same.

She realized her mother was watching her. Martha Claire met her gaze, and Polly shook her head slowly back and forth, her message clear. *Whatever it is that you are thinking, let it go. Don't ask questions that are best left unanswered.*

Martha Claire pushed back her chair and walked out to the front porch, where she leaned against the railing and stared out into the night.

Not a leaf stirred. Insects were performing their nighttime chorus accompanied by the soft "who" of a owl from a nearby tree.

Should she have seen it before?

Their coloring was different, Martha Claire reminded herself. Iris had reddish blond hair and green eyes—like her mother and Martha Claire herself. Grayson had brown hair and hazel eyes.

But other ways in which her husband and her sister's child were alike began to crowd into Martha Claire's mind. Their perfect teeth. Their laugh. Their passion for pecan pie. The way they always bounded over the first step when climbing the stairs. Their beautiful singing voices. They were both sentimental and got teary-eyed at the drop of a hat. Both of them wrote with a definite backward slant. They both slept on their back.

Always before Martha Claire had accepted such similarities as nature over nurture, except that Buddy and Cissy couldn't carry a tune. They didn't laugh like Grayson. Their handwriting didn't resemble his. Both slept curled on one side. They weren't particularly fond of pecan pie.

People who were not related could be quite similar, Martha Claire reminded herself, and people who were related didn't necessarily look alike or act alike. Neither she nor Justine greatly resembled either one of their parents. When Martha Claire was growing up, everyone said she looked like Jeanette MacDonald, and she certainly was not related to her.

God, it was all so confusing. But what she was thinking could not be so. The injury that had taken Grayson to England had happened in late summer in 1944. Iris was born in March of 1946, which meant she hadn't been conceived until after the war had ended in Europe, not until the summer of 1945.

Had Grayson gone back after the armistice?

Later, after she had helped her mother into bed, Martha Claire sat on the edge of the bed and said, "Talk to me, Mother."

Polly adjusted the covers and placed her hands across her chest before she took a breath and said, "You have created a beautiful family and allowed me to be a part of it. I've felt so blessed to spend my last years with you and Grayson and the children in the house where I grew up and have lived for most of my life. In all those years, there has never been anything but love in this house. Don't change that now, Martha Claire."

"I am such a fool that I didn't see it before."

Polly put a hand on her daughter's arm. "You haven't *seen* anything. You don't *know* anything. Let sleeping dogs lie."

"Come on, Mother. I saw the look on your face. You've wondered, too, haven't you? Wondered if Grayson were Iris's father?"

Martha Claire was immediately sorry that she had said the damning words out loud, that she had given them flight. They seemed to fill the room and suck away the air.

"If such a thought had ever crossed my mind," Polly said, her voice firm, "I would have put it right out of my head."

"But the thought has occurred to you. When, Mother? Have I just been blind all these years? Has the whole town been laughing at me behind my back?"

"No, my darling. No one has done any such thing."

Martha Claire stared down at her mother, who had once been

plump and pretty and was now little more than sagging, wrinkled skin over bones, her skin as gray as her hair—a woman nearing the end of her days. After a lifetime of caring for those she loved, she wanted a tidy ending for her life.

"So you want me to sweep it under the rug and go on like before?" Martha Claire asked.

"Yes, that is exactly what I want you to do, what I beg you to do."

"I'm not sure I can," Martha Claire said.

Polly squeezed her daughter's hand. "Yes, you can, Martha Claire Mayfield Stewart. For your family, you can do that."

Once the floodgate had been opened, however, Martha Claire could not look at Iris and Grayson without seeing some new way in which they were alike. Their earlobes. Their bearing. They both drank tea without sugar. They both loved church music but squirmed during the sermons.

And there was something else that occurred to her, something that had nothing to do with likenesses.

Before the war, Justine and Grayson had been great friends, always kidding one another and horsing around. In the years since the war, there had been no kidding, just politeness. Her husband and sister actually had very little to do with one another, she realized. She couldn't remember a single time that just the two of them had gone anyplace together, not even for a walk around the block or to sit on the porch and drink a beer. They saw each other only in the presence of other family members, which seemed more ominous than if they had gotten their fishing poles and headed for the river every time Justine came for a visit.

Finally one night, after the lights were out, Martha Claire summoned the courage to ask her husband if he went back to England after the war.

"Why do you ask?"

She couldn't bring herself to tell him why, in case she was wrong. Her mother was right. Sleeping dogs should be left alone. Just wondering, she had answered. Wondering if he would like to go back there someday.

But the following night, when the silence in their darkened bedroom grew too heavy to bear, she stared up at the ceiling shadows and asked once again, this time making her question more inclusive. "Did you go back to England after the war and have an affair with my sister?"

"No," he said.

"Just *no?*" she challenged. "Not, 'My God, Martha Claire, how on earth can you say such a thing?'"

When he didn't respond, she asked, "Did Justine come to you?"

"No."

"You swore on the lives of the children that nothing happened between you and Justine during the war. Now I want you to swear on their lives that you and my sister did not see each other after the war, that you have never had an affair with her."

She felt his eyes on her face, but she kept her gaze firmly fixed on the ceiling.

"You have to stop this, Martha Claire," he said.

"Then you won't swear."

"No, I won't swear."

"Then I don't want to sleep in the same bed with you."

Silently, he rose from the bed and crossed the hall to Granny Grace's old room.

The next day, Martha Claire avoided looking at him, avoided being alone in the same room with him. That night, he went straight to the spare room.

And the night after that.

Martha Claire moved his clothes into the spare room, and his stack of books and magazines from the bedside table.

More and more, Polly stayed to her bed, the sickness in her heart taking on an added dimension.

The children realized, of course, that all was not well with Martha Claire and Grayson, and tried to be better children. Buddy kept promising he would work harder in school. Cissy dusted the furniture daily and kept her bedroom as immaculate as a nun's cell. Iris baked more pies and cakes than they could eat and, with Cissy's help, took over much of the care of her grandmother.

For weeks, Martha Claire kept her silence, until she could stand it no longer. After the house was dark and quiet, she crept across the hall to the room where her husband now slept and knelt beside the bed. The window was open, but the air in the room was heavy and still. Grayson didn't move, but she could tell he was awake and began telling him all the ways in which he and Iris were alike. And how, when he came back from the war, he and Justine acted like two strangers, when before they had acted like idiots around each other, chasing each other up trees, challenging each other to games of horse out at the basketball goal, making bets about who could catch the biggest fish.

"Maybe the reason you never wrote me about going to England during the war was because you knew that you would be going back there, that there was a very good chance you were going to be unfaithful to your wife with her own sister."

"I'm not sure why I didn't write you about it," Grayson said. "I intended to, but the words didn't come. Maybe I felt guilty because I had told Justine things I had never been able to tell you. I told her that I didn't want to come back to Columbus after the war, that I didn't want the same things out of life that you did, that I had tried to tell you we shouldn't get married but suddenly you were inviting people and painting the gazebo."

"And you went back after the war to finish the conversation?"

He said nothing for the longest time. A freight train's lonely whistle pierced the humid darkness as Martha Claire waited, whatever love was left in her heart for this man ebbing slowly away. *He hadn't wanted to marry her when she thought he loved her more than anything.*

"Well?" she demanded, her voice harsh and cold. "You went back after the war to discuss *the Martha Claire problem.*"

"Something like that," he said.

Martha Claire fell back on her haunches. Grayson rolled to a sitting position with his bare feet on the floor, his forehead resting in his hands. "I wasn't sure what to do," he said, his voice a monotone. "I didn't want to come back here, but I didn't want to hurt you. It was tearing me apart. Justine and I had a lot to drink. It just happened. I never planned for it, and I've regretted it ever since. God, how I've regretted it."

Martha Claire put a hand on the bedpost and pulled herself to her feet.

"I don't know if Iris is my child," he went on, looking up at her, the wetness on his face shining in the moonlight. "Justine told me that she'd slept around after her boyfriend was killed. When you wrote that she was pregnant, it was easy to convince myself it had nothing to do with me. I never asked her who the baby's father was. Justine never said. Like you said, we pretty much avoided each other after the war. After a while, I stopped thinking about it. Now, it seems so long ago. Another time. Other people."

Martha Claire slapped him hard across his face, the sound reverberating in the silent house. "I hate you with all my heart and soul and strength. I want you to leave this house and never come back."

"I would rather die," he told her, falling to his knees in front of her. "Please, if you will let me stay here in this house with our children, I will do so on whatever terms you set. Please, Martha Claire, for their sake. They shouldn't be made to suffer for something that I did. I swear to God that this will be our secret forever. Iris need never know, or Cissy and Buddy."

eighteen

Martha Claire wondered how she could face the rest of her life with the knowledge she now possessed. *Her husband and her sister.* She had no doubt that Iris was *their* child.

The child she and Grayson had loved as their own was in fact *his* daughter—his and Justine's.

She could no longer bear to look at Iris, knowing what she now knew. She was *their* child. The child of their betrayal.

It was too much to endure. She thought about it every minute. The knowledge poisoned her insides and made food taste foul. It stole away her sleep.

She could face life as a widow, but not as a divorced woman. The very word *divorce* sent shivers of revulsion up and down her spine. In towns like Columbus, divorced women were set apart. They were dropped from the ladies' clubs; people avoided them on the sidewalk and in the grocery store. She herself had shunned women who had once been friends, feeling pity tinged with contempt, wondering what flaw in them had caused their husbands to stray.

But Martha Claire knew that, in her own marriage, the fault was not hers. She was blameless. She had waited patiently throughout the war and never entertained so much as a thought about another man. Never in her entire married life had she thought of any man but Grayson. Now the sight of him sent icy daggers through her heart.

The tension in the household became a palpable thing. The children whispered and tiptoed about. When Martha Claire screamed at her mother that no, she was not too much trouble and absolutely was not going to move to a nursing home, Polly cowered against her pillow.

Martha Claire apologized, of course, and told her mother how much they all loved her, how the children would be devastated if she left them.

Martha Claire was tormented with indecision. She did not want to subject herself and her children to a divorce, yet she could not live the rest of her life under the same roof with Grayson.

She wished he would die. Then she could be a respectable widow and get on with her life. Maybe she would even find a gentleman friend, as Lily had, to squire her about. Not to have sex with, of course. She never wanted a man to touch her again. Never. Her insides shriveled at the thought.

And then, in the middle of all this anguish, on an overcast November day, with the children at school and Grayson at the store, she took her mother a lunch tray and found her gasping for breath. Even as she dialed Doc Hadley's number, she knew it was too late.

She raced back down the hall and knelt beside Polly's bed. "Don't go, Mother. I need you. I love you so."

Her mother's last words were little more than a gasping whisper, but Martha Claire understood them. "Grayson loves you," Polly said.

"Don't leave me, Mother," Martha Claire cried, kissing Polly's hands, her face. "Please don't leave me."

Martha Claire began to wail, her voice filling the rooms where her mother had always lived, where she herself had lived most of her life. But suddenly she was alone. Her mother was dead. Her loving presence would never again fill these rooms.

For the present, Martha Claire put thoughts of her crumbling marriage on hold and went about the business of planning a funeral.

Iris waited anxiously for her mother's arrival, hopeful that Justine could mediate whatever the problem was between Grayson and Martha Claire and bring some semblance of normalcy back to the household.

But Justine was traveling throughout the South, photographing the demonstrations against school segregation, and her agency was having a hard time tracking her down. Martha Claire announced that they would not wait on her for the funeral, declaring that a responsible person with a sick mother didn't just go off without letting her family know where she was.

Justine called the day before the funeral to say she had gotten the news and was on her way. The children waited up for her and greeted her with hugs and tears.

"Mama and Daddy don't talk to each other anymore," Cissy told her aunt. "Daddy sleeps in Granny Grace's old bedroom."

Justine looked at Iris. "Do you know why?"

Iris shook her head. "Grayson didn't do anything," she said, wrapping her arms around her mother. "I know he didn't. I don't understand any of it. Sometimes Martha Claire looks at me like she doesn't even know who I am."

Buddy had grown inches since Justine's last visit and was now taller than she was, but he clung to her like a little boy. Justine reached out and brought Cissy into their group embrace.

While the children were fixing her a cup of cocoa and a snack, Justine tiptoed up the stairs and slowly opened the door to the room that had once been her parents', where her sister now slept alone.

"I don't want to talk to you," Martha Claire said from the bed. "Not now."

Justine turned on the dresser lamp. Martha Claire was leaning against the headboard, a pillow behind her back, her arms folded across her chest. Justine sat on the side of the bed. "I need for you to tell me about Mother. Was it peaceful?"

Martha Claire stared at the foot of the bed. "I don't think she suffered much."

"The last time I talked to her, she kept telling me how much she loved me. I'm so sorry I didn't drop everything and come then."

"Oh, but you have your *career*," Martha Claire said, looking at Justine now, spitting out the words, "and that's always been more important to you than family."

Justine regarded her sister's face and was shocked by the hatred she saw there. "Tell me what's going on. What's happened? The children are frightened to death."

"We will talk about it after the funeral."

"I couldn't wait to get here so we could cry for Mother together. I'm sorry you had to make all the arrangements by yourself."

"I've always done everything by myself," Martha Claire pointed out, impassive once again, her face and voice devoid of expression. "I've been at the deathbeds of our grandparents and our parents while you've been off living for yourself. Now, please leave my room. *We will talk after the funeral.*"

Icy fingers of dread tickled at the back of Justine's neck as she backed away from her sister's bed, as she closed the door behind her.

She hesitated outside the door of the room where Grayson now slept. She and Grayson hadn't had a private conversation in seventeen years, hadn't so much as shaken hands or exchanged glances. She needed to talk to him now, needed for him to explain what had happened.

She was aware of Martha Claire's listening ears, though, and went back down to the children.

After she drank a cup of cocoa and nibbled on a sandwich, they went into the room where Polly, beloved mother and grandmother, had died. All four of them sat on the bed and cried together, feeling her presence, saying how much they loved her and how they would miss her for the rest of their lives.

Then Justine had Buddy and Cissy get armloads of pillows and blankets, and the four of them went out to the garage apartment.

"How long has this been going on?" she asked Iris in a low voice after they had made pallets on the floor for Buddy and Cissy and kissed them good-night.

"For weeks. Martha Claire and Grayson and Grandma stopped smiling or talking. Grayson moved into the spare room. I swear, Mother, he hasn't been seeing another woman. I'd bet my life on that. I don't know what made them start hating each other. But they do. Or, at least, Martha Claire hates Grayson. She can't stand to look at him or speak to him. I don't know what's going to happen to us. Do you know what happened to them?"

Justine reached for her daughter and held her close. "I'm not sure, honey."

"I'm so frightened," Iris confessed. "We were a good family, and now Grandma is dead and Martha Claire and Grayson hate each other."

Justine pulled the covers over her daughter and kissed her damp cheeks. Then in the darkness, she sat in her rocking chair and stared out the window at the house where she had grown up, at the house that was her daughter's home. She hadn't been truthful with Iris. Of course, she knew what was going on. Somehow, Martha Claire had figured out her deepest, darkest secret.

Justine was not religious and didn't really believe in asking a distant God to intervene in the lives of humankind. Nonetheless, she had prayed the same prayer every night for many years, and that prayer had beseeched God or Whoever to protect her family from the one thing that could destroy it.

After the funeral, Martha Claire asked Justine to come upstairs to her room. She sat on the window seat. Justine sat on the vanity stool. The door was closed. The children had gone home for the evening with Grayson's mother. Justine didn't know where Grayson was. He had been like a shadow all day, hovering behind the children, saying nothing.

"You are no longer welcome in my home," Martha Claire announced. "I will always love your daughter, but I hope I never have to see you again." Martha Claire held up her hand when Justine started to speak. "And don't tell me that I can't possibly know how it was during the war. Grayson has already done that. He told me about the bombs and being trapped, about the two of you almost dying. Well, I wish you *had* died. Everyone has had close calls in their life. A close call didn't give you the right to have an affair with my husband. My own sister, for God's sake! How could you? You might as well have plunged a knife in my back. You are a Judas. I loved you, and you betrayed me."

"You are right to blame me," Justine said. "Grayson was in a fog. I could have stopped it, but I didn't. And I told him if he had an ounce of sense, he'd tell his father to sell the store and give you an ultimatum."

Justine began to pace, fighting down the need to lash back at

Martha Claire, but the words came out anyway. "You were always so goddamned self-righteous. You never did anything wrong in your life, never screwed Grayson until you said 'I do.' I wanted to be just like my sister. I played by the rules and never made love to a man I loved very much. And then his plane was shot down. He was dead. Just like that," she said, snapping her fingers, "he was no more. There wasn't even a dead body or a tombstone. I didn't have the memory of lying naked in his arms. I wish like hell he were Iris's father, but he's not. You know what Grayson and I talked about? We talked about you, about how much we loved you. We talked about how in the hell we were going to get you to grow up. How could we convince you to take a risk, to at least give military life a try. Maybe I shouldn't have let him come back to England, but we didn't plan for anything to happen. I swear to God, we didn't. We got drunk and maudlin, and it just did. It wasn't a love affair. It was just two lonely, confused people who needed to touch another human being. I closed my eyes and turned him into an Aussie named Billy. And he turned me into you. I know it was wrong, but it wasn't wrong enough for you to throw away a damned good man and ruin your wonderful family. Afterward, I told Grayson that I was really sorry because we had destroyed a really nice friendship. And I begged him not to go back to this backwater Texas town. I told him he didn't have to settle for life as a storekeeper and Lions Club meetings every Wednesday. But I knew that was exactly what he was going to do. He was going home to spend the rest of his life paying penance for what we had done."

But Justine could tell by the hard, ugly look on her sister's face that she wasn't listening, that nothing Justine could say would make a difference.

She knew that she had lost her sister. And even more than her mother, Martha Claire had always represented home. No more.

They stared at each other for a long moment, silence all around them. Then suddenly Martha Claire began to shriek. "How dare you come back here year after year! It makes my flesh crawl to think of it. What kind of a monster are you?"

"But I gave you my daughter," Justine protested. "Do you think I wanted to? When you didn't have a baby of your own, I knew that was *my* penance. I had to let you raise Iris. But now that's all changed. I'm taking her with me, Martha Claire. I wish I could take Buddy and Cissy, too. This house isn't a fit place for those children."

Martha Claire went white. "You will not take her," she said through clenched teeth. "Iris is *mine!*"

Then she marched out of the room and down the stairs. She picked up the telephone and called Iris home from Lily's house.

Justine watched from the upstairs railing as Martha Claire paced back and forth across the entry hall. When Justine heard footsteps on the front porch, she hurried down the stairs.

The door flew open, and there she was—Iris, the child they would both die for.

Martha Claire presented an ultimatum. "You are the child closest to my heart. I have loved you and cared for you since you were born. I dream of the day I can hold your baby in my arms. But now my sister wants to take you away from me. I want you to know that if you go with her, you will never be welcome in this house again."

Justine felt as though her heart were being twisted from its moorings as she watched her daughter look from her mother to her aunt and saw realization dawn in her lovely young face. She was going to have to choose. She could no longer have them both.

For an instant, Justine wavered. Maybe she should back off. Maybe she should make the noble gesture.

She knew, however, that now, every time Martha Claire looked at Iris, she would think of who she was. Her love for Iris would be forever tainted.

Iris had no answer, of course. Not then. She ran upstairs to her room and slammed the door. Justine went alone to her backyard apartment and waited.

In the night, Grayson went to Iris's room. She was still dressed, lying on top of the spread, a pillow clutched to her chest.

He sat on the side of her bed and held her hand. "You must leave," he told her.

"But what about you and Martha Claire?" Iris said, sobbing. "What about Cissy and Buddy? Why did everything change?"

"It's my fault and no one else's. You must never blame Martha Claire or your mother. You have a right to be happy, and I don't think anyone who stays on in this house will ever be happy again."

He had brought a suitcase and helped her gather the things from her room that were most precious. Then the two of them crept down the stairs and across the yard. He carried the suitcase up the stairs to the landing.

He heard the door open. He knew that Justine was watching through the screen door as he hugged Iris's slim body against his chest and wondered if it was the last embrace for a lifetime with this wonderful, precious girl.

Dearest Iris, who had been a source of such joy for them all. He could not imagine life without her.

When Martha Claire emerged from her room the next morning and realized that Iris and Justine were gone, she crawled into bed with Cissy and wept.

Buddy came to sit on the floor beside the bed and hold his mother's hand and tell her not to cry. "It's not fair," Martha Claire wailed. "I was the one who loved her and raised her. Iris belongs here with me."

Never had Martha Claire felt so alone. Her mother was dead. Her sister and husband had betrayed her. Iris, the child she loved more than anything, was gone. All she had left were these two frightened children who counted on her to mother them.

And she would do that. Somehow, she would be the mother they needed for her to be.

But first she had to deal with other things.

She decided Buddy and Cissy were too upset to go to school. Later, she realized she should have sent them anyway, as they watched with great, fearful eyes as she carried all of Justine's stored memorabilia down from the garage apartment and burned it in the backyard—yearbooks, clothes, albums, toys, photographs, journals, letters, books. She also burned the portrait of the Mayfield sisters that had hung on the stairwell wall for almost twenty-five years.

She thought about burning Iris's things, too, but she couldn't bring herself to do that. Instead, she put everything in boxes and had Buddy carry them to the attic.

Then she prepared lunch and left them to clean up the kitchen.

"I'll be all right," she said, "but I have to be alone in my room for a time."

She stayed for three weeks.

nineteen

In the days after Justine took Iris away, we learned that the Russians had installed missile bases in Cuba.

While the outside world hovered on the brink of nuclear war and other Columbus families were storing emergency supplies in the trunks of their cars and planning evacuation routes in case a missile armed with a nuclear warhead hit the refineries that surrounded Houston, what was left of our family was dealing with its own more immediate crisis. We had no emergency supplies or evacuation plans. How could we leave if our mother wouldn't come out of her room? Three times a day, I would put her meal tray in front of her bedroom door, then knock and tell her it was there. Not a hint of life would come from behind that door except the occasional sound of the shower running or the toilet flushing.

Daddy, Buddy, and I spoke in whispers and kept the volume on the television turned on low while we watched spyplane photographs of missile silos in Cuba and President Kennedy giving an ultimatum to the Russians. All the while, I kept thinking of Mama up in her room. Was she listening to the radio? Did she know that any minute we all could die? Then we would turn off the sound on the television so I could help Buddy with his homework. Daddy would sit in his chair, his newspaper in his lap, ready to turn the volume up again in case Huntley or Brinkley came on with an update. But I noticed that sometimes he would forget to watch the screen and would stare off at nothing. Periodically, he would get up from the chair and wordlessly stroke our hair or touch our shoulders, maybe go out to the kitchen to pour us each a glass of milk.

After I was in bed, Buddy would come to sit on the floor beside the bed with a pillow hugged against his chest, and in hushed whispers, we would speculate about what happened to adopted children if their parents got a divorce. Whom would we belong to then? Where would we live? Was the rift in Mama and Daddy's marriage somehow our fault? Maybe with Iris gone they would prefer not to have any children at all. After all, we'd heard our mother say often enough that we had been adopted so that Iris would not be raised alone. Often Buddy fell asleep on the floor beside my bed, and I would slip the pillow under his head and cover him with a blanket.

In the morning, Daddy would wake us, and the three of us would tiptoe around, taking turns in the bathroom, eating our cereal in front of the television. The Russians eventually backed down, but our mother was still upstairs.

"When is she going to come out?" Buddy kept asking Daddy.

"Soon," Daddy would answer.

Buddy had gotten so big that, at almost fourteen, he looked more like a man than a boy. He was even sprouting whiskers on his chin. Though older than me by a year a half, in many ways he had always seemed more like my younger brother. Our present troubles only accentuated that feeling. Buddy became fearful of making any sort of decision at all, lest some action on his part would somehow plunge our decimated family over the edge of a lurking abyss. I had to help him decide what to wear to school, which chore he needed to do first, even when he should take a bath. I reminded him to get a haircut and rake the leaves in Grandma Stewart's yard. I packed his lunch and made sure he didn't forget his homework.

After school, while Buddy was at football practice, I would ride my bicycle to the cemetery and visit my grandmother's fresh grave. And Granny Grace's, too, where the grass had long since covered the raw earth and tulip bulbs came up in the spring. It bothered me greatly that we hadn't done a proper job mourning Grandma Polly. When my great-grandmother had died, we spent a great deal of time recalling all the things Granny Grace had done for us and all the reasons we loved her. We looked at pictures of her when she was young and beautiful with a handsome young husband at her side, and said over and over again that we would never forget her and would carry her in our hearts forever. But when Grandma Polly died, Mama and Daddy were consumed with the horrible thing that had driven them apart, and Justine's arrival just seemed to get Mama more upset than ever. The worst part was, Grandma had known what the trouble was, and that knowledge made her so sad that she didn't want to live any longer.

In an effort to atone, I would sit beside her grave and tell Grandma Polly that she was the best grandma in the world and that I loved her and missed her and would never in my entire life forget her. Which was the truth. Any love I felt for Grandma Stewart was mostly out of duty. Grandma Polly had been the sweetest grandmother imaginable, and her love for her three grandchildren was uncomplicated and bountiful. I truly believe that she loved Buddy and me as much as she loved Iris. With Grandma Polly, as with my daddy, I never felt adopted. Their love came without my having to earn it.

From the cemetery, I would ride to the store and help Daddy tidy up. Buddy came by after practice, and with Buddy and me pushing our bikes, we walked home with Daddy, stopping on the way to check on Grandma Stewart, who still played bridge almost every day but who seemed to enjoy life less since her gentleman friend, Mr. Vandecamp, had passed away. She also had started to forget things, like to turn off the stove and to comb her hair. Every evening, she complained that Martha Claire hadn't invited her to dinner in weeks or brought her any baked goods and that Iris never came to see her anymore. And every evening, Buddy and I would listen uncomfortably while Daddy explained that Justine had taken Iris to live with her in New York City and Mama was having a hard time coming to terms with her mother's death. "When did Polly die?" Grandma Stewart would ask. "She was a terrible bridge player, you know. She never did understand the takeout double."

For three endless weeks, my mother stayed in her room. Then one night we arrived home to the heavenly aroma of baking bread. To this day, the smell of baking bread makes me think of the time my mother came out of her room.

At dinner that first evening and ever after, not one word was said about Mama's three-week retreat from the family. In fact, words about anything at all were painfully scarce. Grandma Polly and Iris had been the talkers in our family. I tried to fill the void, asking Buddy about football practice and Daddy about his day at the store. I couldn't think of anything to ask Mama, since she'd been sitting up in her room for three weeks presumably doing nothing at all. I announced that four children in my class were absent with the flu and that my next report was going to be on Lewis and Clark. Then the only sounds came from the mantel clock in the parlor and the clinking of silverware against plates. I remember sitting there staring at my plate, desperately trying to think of something else to say, my stomach hurting from the strain. Iris could have gotten us laughing and talking, but I was not Iris. Finally Daddy cleared his throat, thanked Mama for a fine dinner, and pushed back his chair.

The next night was about the same. With Iris and Grandma no longer with us, the remaining members of the family seemed more like four boarders who happened to be taking their meals at the same table. Other than Daddy telling Mama it was a fine dinner, our parents seldom spoke to one another. It was better on the nights that Grandma Stewart came to dinner. She was a regular chatterbox and would start talking about one thing then digress to another and yet another, completely losing her original train of thought. Still, it was infinitely better than silence.

The week after Mama came downstairs, Buddy and I got our first letter from Iris. She wrote that she was going to an all-girl high school where all the students wore navy blazers and pleated skirts. It seemed like a great school with a chemistry lab fit for a Nobel Laureate and a French teacher who was really French and was going to take the entire class to Paris in the spring. But she said that she was terribly lonely for her family and Columbus. Her mother had promised that she could visit next summer if that was all right with Martha Claire.

"Do you think Mama will let her come?" Buddy asked.

"I hope so," I answered, but I wasn't sure. Mama had loved Iris the best, but I knew that in Mama's mind Iris had betrayed her by leaving with Justine.

As those first days of the post-Iris era turned into weeks, and then into months, Buddy and I began to relax a bit. Our parents never kissed, never touched, never smiled at one another, but Daddy returned to what I had come to think of as my mother's bedroom. We reasoned that they couldn't still hate each other anymore if they were sleeping in the same bed. But still, they had little to say to one another, and they never touched—at least, not that we saw—and they never laughed, never went to the movies or dancing with their friends.

As the school year drew to a close, we waited anxiously while Mama decided if Iris could come to visit us. I knew Mama wanted to see Iris more than anything, but Iris had chosen to live with her mother rather than remain in Columbus, and that decision had hurt my poor mother to the quick. I couldn't understand why Daddy didn't speak on Iris's behalf. He should have pointed out that Iris would have left for college in two more years anyway, that they wouldn't have been able to keep her forever, that they were lucky to have had her for the years that they did, that Justine was—after all—Iris's mother. Of course, I didn't know then that the circumstances of Iris's birth disqualified Daddy from making any argument in her behalf.

In the end, Mama decided that no, Iris could not come. Buddy and I could continue corresponding with her, but she wasn't to call on the telephone. And Iris and her mother would never be welcome in this house again.

I don't think I had ever before talked back to my mother, not in my entire life, but that night I told her that she was mean.

Before she had time to say anything in reply, I rushed up to my room and slammed the door. I cried so hard I got sick and threw up on the floor beside my bed. Daddy found me trying to clean it up and held me while I cried some more. When I had calmed down, he told me to go tell Mama that I was sorry.

"But it's the truth," I insisted. "She is mean."

"Go," he said, pointing to the door.

I did as he asked, but had my fingers crossed behind my back. Mama said there were things I didn't understand and asked me to brush her hair. When I got back to my room, Daddy had cleaned up the vomit.

I wish now that I had known the reason why Mama wouldn't let Iris come—not that it would have softened my pain, but I think that even at twelve years of age I would have seen the difficulty of my mother's situation and found some understanding for her decision. Buddy and I did not know, however, and we came perilously close to hating our mother for denying us a visit from someone we loved so much.

I even thought of staying in my room for three weeks in protest, but Mama wouldn't have put up with that. And I didn't have it in me to be sullen or refuse to help her. Now, though, the help I rendered was done out of a sense of duty rather than out of love and respect.

Iris wrote how disappointed she was about Martha Claire's decision and proposed a plan "to keep us close." I was to call her collect on the first Sunday night of the following month—after Mama and Daddy were asleep—and she would explain.

And so, on the appointed night, with a pounding heart and sweaty palms, I crept down the stairs after midnight and carried the phone into the hall closet, where I burrowed behind the coats. With my hand on the receiver, I took a deep breath. What if I couldn't think of anything to say? After all, it had been ten months since Iris had left.

Iris answered on the first ring. "Hi, sweetie," she said, and immediately I began to cry. All that missing overflowed, and all I could do was just sit there like a ninny, sobbing into my mother's gray coat. In a soothing voice, Iris started telling me what once had been my favorite bedtime story—about the day that Doc Hadley gave me to Mama and Daddy and how Iris decided that I was her sissy and she would take care of me and love me forever and ever, how she held me and fed me my very first bottle, and the neighbors stopped by all afternoon long to say what a pretty baby I was, how she insisted on sleeping on the floor beside my crib. "I love you, Iris," I was finally able to say. "I love you, too, my little Cissy," she said. We talked for more than an hour—a magical hour. It was almost like having her there with me.

Her plan, she explained, was for me to call her on the first Sunday night of every month, collect, after Mama and Daddy were asleep. Iris had her own phone, right by her bed. Justine said that we could talk all night if we wanted to.

After that, I kept an ongoing file in my head of all the things I would tell Iris the next time we talked and all the things I wanted to ask her. I needed to know all about her new life, about her friends, her school, her teachers, New York. The first few times, I made Buddy come with me. Buddy was never able to curl up in a corner and just talk, however, never able to bridge the miles and feel almost as though Iris were there with him. After a few awkward attempts at conversation, he would tell her that he missed her and hand the receiver back to me. After a few months, I would just tell him what Iris had said the night before.

Iris wasn't always at home on the first Sunday night of the month. Sometimes she and Justine would be traveling around, and I would have to wait until the following month. But that was okay because I knew there would be a next time. My cousin who had always been like an older sister to me had been reduced to a voice heard only in a dark, stuffy closet, but that voice became a constant in my life and served as an amulet to soften the pain brought by warring parents and an unsure future. So often I found out how I truly felt about things as I expressed them over the telephone to Iris. I said things to her I never would have said to anyone else, like how I wanted to scream at Mama sometimes and call her a mean old witch and how at other times I would look at her face and see the unhappiness there and feel so very sorry for her.

Iris insisted that I was going to come visit her in New York one of these days, and then we would talk about all the places she and Justine would take me. I didn't indulge myself much, however, in that particular daydream. For me, the big dream was seeing Iris back home again.

"Someday we will both be grown up and able to do whatever we want," Iris insisted. "We *will* be together again, Cissy, you'll see. And don't you go making any promises to Martha Claire about staying in Columbus for the rest of your life. You have a right to live wherever you want."

I wasn't so sure about that. Being adopted seemed a special responsibility. I owed my mother more than I would have if I were her natural-born child. She had given me and my brother things to which we weren't naturally entitled. She had given us a name and a home.

With the monthly checks no longer arriving from Justine, money was tighter than ever at our house, and the year after Iris left us, Daddy took a job as area sales representative for a company that made children's shoes. He was gone from early Monday morning until late Friday evening, and Mama took over at the store.

Mama didn't talk about fixing the house up anymore. The best she could do was keep the old place painted and patch the leaks. Rich retired folks from Austin and Houston had started moving to town and buying the old houses and spending lots of money to restore them. Mama insisted that she would never sell her house, though. I wondered if she still wanted Iris to inherit the house when she was gone, or if it would pass to Buddy and me. I wasn't sure if I wanted the lifetime responsibility of my mother's house, though.

Every afternoon after school I worked at the store—Buddy, too, sometimes. But usually he had practice—baseball, basketball, football, track. Academically, Buddy struggled in school, but he was a wonderful athlete.

After we locked up the store each night, Mama and I would walk home together and fix dinner. With Daddy on the road, we didn't have a car during the week to fetch Grandma Stewart, so I would usually ride over to her house on my bike with her dinner in an old Mickey Mouse lunch pail. Daddy thought we should move her into Grandma Polly's downstairs room, but Mama was against it for now, and Grandma Stewart wanted to stay in her own cluttered house with the card table always set up in the front room.

I think if it weren't for Buddy, Mama and I would have simply opened cans of soup or made sandwiches for our dinners, but after hours of running and sweating, Buddy always arrived home with a voracious appetite. Mama and I would finish our own meal and watch him eat second and third helpings.

She let us keep the television on during dinner now. Always before, she had insisted that well-bred people conversed during meals, saying that only common people watched television. My favorite show was *I Dream of Jeannie*. Barbara Eden, with her sweet face and unfailing good humor, made me think of Iris, who in her own way had been a ge-nie of sorts. She didn't grant wishes, but everyone was happier when she was around.

Sometimes after Buddy finished his homework, Mama let him meet his friends downtown at the Sandwich Shop or just hang out in the square. Weekends, if one of his friends had his dad's car, six or seven boys would pile in and head for the drive-in, where they would park beside a car with six or seven girls. Buddy called girls on the phone now, and sometimes he went to sit with a girl on her front porch. But he never went steady like the other kids his age. He said that no girl was ever going to put a ring in his nose, and he vowed that he wasn't going to end up like our daddy.

With Iris gone, Mama had only me to help her around the house and to rub her neck and brush her hair in the evening. Once again, I had be-come Mama's good girl. I liked having her rely on me, but I hated the way she treated Daddy, and I especially hated the tension that ruled the air when he was home.

In the fall, Daddy always tried to make it home on Friday nights in time for Buddy's football games, but often he arrived after the game had started. I would save him a seat and watch for him, feeling a won-derful surge of relief when I finally saw him come around the corner of the stands and could wave my arms to show him where we were. Buddy played defensive end, and already people were saying he might be good enough to get a college scholarship.

Watching my brother play ball made me horribly nervous. I wanted him to do well and was fearful that he would get hurt. But even so, those fall evenings spent sitting between my parents were nice. As we cheered together for our Buddy, it felt almost like before, like when Mama and Daddy still loved each other.

On the weekends that Daddy didn't have National Guard, he took over at the store on Saturday morning. After he closed up, he would work through the list of chores Mama always had waiting for him, spending the rest of the day washing windows, waxing floors, hoeing the garden, replacing rotting boards, cleaning out the rain gutters, trimming trees, painting whatever. He always did her bidding, even if her request was an irrational one—like crawling up on the roof to check the television antenna when the TV was working just fine or re-arranging the fixtures at the store when he'd just done it the month be-fore. She never said thank you, never told him he had done a good job, but was quick to point out something she considered less than satisfac-tory. Buddy thought Daddy should stand up to her, tell her that he had the right to relax on the weekend, but he never said a word. He even went to church every Sunday morning, raising his fine tenor voice in praise.

On Sunday afternoon, if Mama couldn't think of anything else for him to do, Daddy would take Buddy and me on an excursion—usually fishing. I couldn't bear to eat a fish whose death I had caused and was quite certain that if fish could scream, fishing wouldn't be such a popu-lar pastime, but I endured it for my daddy and for the chance to spend time with him. I knew that he missed Iris, who had been his fishing companion from the time she could walk, and that he missed the way things used to be. I felt sadder for him than for Buddy and me. We could grow up and leave our mother's house on Milam Street. I doubted if our Daddy ever would.

I found myself taking my father's side when Mama berated him for things like falling asleep at church, forgetting to buy bread, doing a less-than-satisfactory job of raking the yard, not remembering a cus-tomer's name, not making enough money. "What did he do that makes you hate him so?" I would demand of my mother. "Why can't you for-give him?" After such outbursts, she wouldn't speak to me for the rest of the day, sometimes longer. Then I would say that I was sorry and brush her hair an extra-long time.

Every Sunday evening I baked cookies for Daddy to take on the road. On Monday morning, I would wake up early to fix him break-fast and walk him out to the car. I knew that a man like my daddy, with his college degree from Texas A&M and medals he had earned in the war, could have found a job at the bank or been a manager out at the new gravel company east of town, but he drove away every Monday morning and spent four evenings a week alone in run-down tourist courts because that was what my mother wanted. I could not under-stand how our beautiful family had come to this.

I didn't want to love one parent more than the other, but my feelings for my daddy became more and more tender. Even if he had once done some terrible, hurtful thing to Mama, he had a good heart and had by now surely earned the right to be forgiven. My mother held herself up to be a Christian woman and always marched us kids to church on Sunday morning, but I guess she turned a deaf ear to the sermons on forgiveness. Once I carefully copied Colossians 3:13 and left it on her bedside table: "Forbearing one another and forgiving one another: if any man have a quarrel against any; even as Christ forgave you, so also do ye."

I went back to get it, though, before Mama came upstairs, and tore it into little pieces. I could not forgive her for not forgiving my father, which made me just as guilty as she was.

twenty

He had always wanted to travel, Grayson would remind himself as he drove up and down the state highways and county roads of his sales territory, which stretched across southern and eastern Texas. And he did try to find some satisfaction in what had become his lot in life, as he went from one small town to the next. After he had made his calls on local merchants, dragging his sample cases into their stores and giving his spiel about workmanship, materials, the perfect fit for growing feet, he would visit local museums and drive around, seeing what there was to see.

But after he had visited the Indian reservation in Livingston and the flamboyant old city hall in Lockhart, after he had climbed the lighthouse in Port Lavaca and seen the botanical gardens in the town of Spring, subsequent visits to these communities were less enlightening.

Often he entertained himself by exploring the surrounding countryside, where the barns and country churches were usually more remarkable than the farmhouses. And he enjoyed poking around in country cemeteries, reading the epitaphs, pondering the stories of the people buried there, sometimes striking up conversations with those who came to tend the graves of their loved ones. But even the cemeteries took on a sameness after a time, with the history, sadness, and grief laid out there becoming mundane. He would go to the movies if there was a motion picture theater in the town, but what was a movie unless he could talk it over with Martha Claire on the way home? His second year on the road, Grayson found himself depending mostly on books and television to relieve the monotony of his evening hours.

As much as he hated being away from Buddy and Cissy, and as lonely as he often felt, after a weekend at home with his wife, he was always relieved to be on his way again. But the look on Cissy's dear face as she kissed him good-bye broke his heart. For her and Buddy, there was no escape.

The day that Kennedy was shot, he was in Navasota. He closed up his sample cases and went to his motel to keep the vigil in front of a flickering television screen, hoping against hope that the inspiring young president would live on. When Walter Cronkite made his fateful announcement, Grayson called home. Martha Claire was beside herself, to the point of hysteria, but she didn't want to console or be consoled. She needed to get back to the television. Not even in a foxhole in France had he felt this lonely.

He hated all the jokes about traveling salesmen but did consider taking up with a woman in Tucker, a tiny town just outside Palestine. Pretty, plump Loretta ran a homey little cafe with checkered curtains and potted plants, and her pies rivaled Martha Claire's. He looked forward to Loretta's welcoming smile and liked watching her bustle about, but he couldn't bring himself to deceive Martha Claire a second time.

His hope was that, if he stayed steadfast and true, if he did Martha Claire's bidding without question and proved himself worthy of her trust, she would someday find it in her heart to forgive him. But Grayson hated for his children to watch silently from the sidelines while their mother constantly carped at him. What sort of memories would they have of this awful time? Would it ever get better?

Sometimes he thought about not going home at all, of taking a job on a tanker and sailing to foreign shores. He might have done that if it hadn't been for his children. He had to stand by them and find some way to bring joy into their lives in spite of their joyless mother.

If the blessed day of forgiveness ever came for him, Grayson planned to convince Martha Claire to sell that albatross of a house. They could buy a smaller place and maybe afford to send Buddy and Cissy to college. And before he got too old, he'd like to take whatever courses he needed to get a teacher's license and teach history at Columbus High School. But whether in the big old house on Milam Street or in a smaller one someplace else, he dreamed of his wife once again looking at him with love in her eyes.

Sometimes in the night, when he sensed that Martha Claire was awake, he would put a tentative hand on her shoulder. If she didn't turn away, he would pull up her nightgown and roll on top of her. If he said anything, she would go rigid, but as long as he didn't whisper endearments and didn't try to kiss her, he was allowed to continue. Sometimes he even felt her body respond. Who was she thinking of, he wondered, another man or the man he used to be? His heart broke for her, and he understood full well why she was unable to forgive him. He had committed the one transgression that made forgiveness impossible.

Still, though, he had to hope, and he had never stopped loving her. When he came back to her after the war, he had placed his life and future at her feet, and there it probably would stay until the day he died. He didn't seem to have the will to chart another course.

He longed to pray that a benevolent God would somehow intercede in his behalf but didn't even try. He had left prayer and God back on the battlefields of World War II.

"Remember those times up in the attic when we used to daydream about finding our birth mother?" Buddy asked.

Cissy looked up from her polishing. "Of course, I remember," she said. "We also daydreamed about finding pirate's gold and taking rides on alien spaceships."

They were waxing the station wagon, which Buddy had permission to use tonight—for a date, Cissy suspected, probably with the junior class cheerleader Mabel Warren. Cissy knew that Mabel and Buddy had sat together at the movies a couple of times, and they had danced almost every dance at the last sock hop. Buddy refused to admit he was going on a date, though, even though he had polished his shoes, gotten a haircut, and talked Cissy into helping him make the ten-year-old vehicle look a little more presentable.

"I'd like us to do that," he said, dabbing more paste wax on a faded fender.

"Do what? You're not talking about searching for her?"

"Why not?" he asked.

"We haven't talked about her in years," Cissy said. "Why are you bringing it up now?"

"You always said it wasn't fair to Mom for us to think about our real mother, but I never stopped. We were just kids before. Now we're old enough to really try."

Cissy sat on the open tailgate and leaned forward to use the tail of her T-shirt to wipe her brow. "Buddy, we don't have a single clue to go on. We don't know her name or her age or where she was from. We don't even know where we were born."

"You must have been born someplace close by, since you were only a couple of hours old when Doc Hadley brought you to Mom and Dad."

Mom and Dad. He had started saying that lately instead of "Mama and Daddy." It still sounded strange to her.

He sat down beside her and said, "We could put personal ads in all the newspapers around here: 'Seeking information about a white woman who gave birth to a baby girl October 17, 1950.'"

"Oh, Buddy, what if Mama found out? It would break her heart."

"But we have a right to know."

"Not really. The law protects the identity of women who put their babies up for adoption."

"I asked Doc Hadley about her," Buddy admitted.

Cissy was surprised. He must really be serious about this. "What did he say?" she asked.

Buddy shrugged. "That part of his job was knowing when to keep his mouth shut. He said that doctors take an oath about that. Then I asked him to at least tell me why she gave us away, if she was sick or in prison or something like that. He just shook his head. And he wouldn't tell me if she was still alive. He wouldn't even tell me whether or not he *knew* if she was still alive."

"Let it drop, Buddy. All you're going to do is hurt Mama, and all for nothing. You're not going to find that woman."

"Don't you want to know if she loved us?"

"I suppose I do at some level, but it's not something I think much about. I used to read those reunion stories in the newspaper, where family members are reunited after forty years, and I'd go off on a little daydream. But it's not going to happen, and it would cause pain if it did."

"I also asked Doc Hadley if our birth mother came looking for us, would he tell her where we were."

"And?"

"He said no."

Cissy scooted off the tailgate and went back to polishing. "That should be the end of it, then," she told him.

"I need to know if she loved us," he said stubbornly, still sitting on the tailgate.

Cissy turned, startled to realize he was crying. She put down her wad of rags and pulled him over to the bench that occupied a patch of shade under the hackberry tree. "We have a mother who loves us," she reminded him, rubbing a soothing hand up and down his arm. "And a daddy. We have a home and friends. I think things have turned out pretty well for us."

"You were just a newborn, but I was a year and a half when you were born. I was old enough to walk around and hug her neck and do stuff like that, and *she gave me away.* She didn't know you yet, but she knew me. Why would she do that? I need to find her and ask her why. Maybe she's just sitting there someplace hoping more than anything that we will find her and she can tell us how sorry she is. Maybe it was all a mistake. Maybe she was sick and got better. Please help me find her, Cissy. Please."

"Buddy, you're not making any sense. What if you found her and discovered that she's an awful woman? Maybe the police took us away from her because she wasn't a fit mother. Maybe she was a drunk or a criminal. Did you ever think of that? Or what if you found her and she said she gave us away because she hated kids? No, I will not help you, Buddy. It would be going against Mama to do something like that."

"I don't like James Bond movies," Mabel Warren informed him, "and I promised everyone we'd meet them at the Sandwich Shop."

Mabel was the banker's daughter, a cheerleader, blond, and very pretty—maybe the prettiest girl in the junior class. When her best girl friend hinted that Buddy should ask Mabel out, he'd been shocked. After all, he wasn't the captain of the football team, wasn't the quarterback, wasn't a senior, didn't make good grades. Mabel could have the pick of any boy in the school.

So far, all they'd done was meet at a dance and at a couple of movies. This was their first car date, the first time he'd gone inside her house to say hello to her parents. Their house was old, too, but really nice inside, with thick wall-to-wall carpeting and crystal chandeliers.

He'd already seen *Goldfinger,* but it was playing at the drive-in, and what was the point of having a car on a date if all they did was go down to the square and hang out with the other kids?

Not that he expected much action. She might let him kiss her, but that was probably all. A girl like Mabel Warren probably wouldn't neck with a boy unless she was going steady.

She was wearing a fuzzy pink sweater that showed off her figure, and her blond hair was all fluffed up like cotton candy. Being with a girl like her made him feel ten feet tall. He'd even found himself wondering how many times they'd have to go out before he could ask her to go steady. But first he had to let her know that she couldn't tell him what to do.

"This is the first time I've had the car in weeks," Buddy said as he turned south, "and we are going to the drive-in."

He felt her gaze and knew she was sizing him up. "But what about Sandy and Mark?" she asked. "I thought we were double-dating with them."

"Nope. Just you and me."

"After the Sandwich Shop, everyone is going over to Sandy's house and listen to records." Her voice was sweeter now, and her mouth was screwed into a pout.

Buddy sailed past Walnut Street, past Spring, leaving the downtown and the Sandwich Shop behind.

Mabel folded her arms across her chest, like his mother did when she was peeved at him. "I am not going to the drive-in with you, Buddy Stewart, so you can just turn this car around."

In response, he sailed through the Washington Street intersection.

"What's with you anyway?" Mabel said. "Other boys ask the girl where she wants to go and don't just start driving."

"Well, I'm not like other boys."

"You can say that again! I should have listened to Sophie Lancaster. She said you were like this."

"Like what?" Buddy demanded.

"Stubborn as a mule and cocky as a rooster. You can't stand for a girl to have her way about the teeniest thing, can you?"

"Maybe it's the other way around. I don't like bossy girls."

"Whatever," Mabel said. "You can stop right here. I'll walk back."

Buddy hesitated, then did as she asked. Before she got out of the car, Mabel said, "I'm sorry, Buddy. I think you're real cute, but boys are supposed to be nice to girls. No girl will want to go out with you if you keep acting like this."

When he didn't respond, she got out and slammed the door.

Buddy spun out as he sped down the street. "Bitch!" he muttered. "They're all bitches."

Pretty girls were the worst, he decided, except for his sister. Cissy would be as pretty as Mabel if she weren't so skinny, and she was a hell of a lot sweeter.

Guys were starting to notice Cissy. Only last night, she sat out on the front porch with Joey Huffman for more than an hour, until Buddy went out there and reminded her that she'd promised to help him diagram sentences for English class.

Mabel Warren had been right. Girls started being busy whenever Buddy asked them out. It was one problem he didn't talk over with Cissy, who probably would tell him that he must be a perfect gentleman if he wanted a girl to like him. Well, their father had been a perfect gentleman and look where it got him.

Things weren't as bad now between his parents as they had been right after Justine took Iris away, but Mama was still always after Dad to do this and do that. Buddy loved his father, but he didn't respect him. His father was a wimp.

Sometimes Cissy stood up to Mama, telling her she ought to be nicer to Daddy. Buddy didn't have the nerve to do that, which meant that he was a wimp, too, but only when it came to his mother. The one thing of which he was the most certain was that he was never going to be like his dad.

The following spring, Buddy took a girl from Fayetteville to the Columbus High School junior-senior prom. Sara Ann Masters was a little plump but pretty enough and not the least bit bossy. In fact, she didn't have much to say at all, bossy or otherwise.

After the prom, he drove across the river and down a dirt road. Sara Ann said nothing when he reached down the front of her low-cut evening dress and touched her big soft breasts, but she slapped his hand when he tried to reach under the skirt. "Other girls like for me to do that," he said, which was a stretch. He'd managed to get his hand in exactly one girl's panties after he'd plied her with several cans of pirated beer and right before she threw up all over him and his dad's car. Sara Ann replied, "You don't say," then lifted his straying hand to her mouth and bit it—hard. He had to wear a bandage for weeks to cover up the tooth marks.

His senior year was better. College scouts were driving to Columbus from all over the state just to watch Buddy "the Bulldozer" Stewart play football, and the Houston newspapers were even taking notice of him. And Sara Ann Masters invited him to the Fayetteville homecoming dance and let him put his hands wherever he wanted.

"I wish they weren't making such a fuss," Buddy said as his mother smoothed down his hair and straightened his collar.

"The whole town is proud of you, son," Martha Claire said. "It's your day. Enjoy it."

From their backstage vantage point, Buddy could see the podium at center stage, a row of folding chairs behind it. The audience was filled to overflowing, with people lined up along the wall. Seated in front of the stage, the band was playing "King of the Road."

When the coach told him there would be a public announcement, he had no idea it would be anything like this. His father had even come home mid-week to attend. Dad hadn't come home in the middle of the week since last year when Grandma Stewart fell and broke her hip. Buddy glanced over at his grandmother in her wheelchair. She'd never been to one of his games, even when she could still get around, but when the news came yesterday, she couldn't get to the phone fast enough to call all her friends and tell them about the special assembly honoring her grandson.

His mother looked slim and surprisingly pretty in a flowery yellow dress. When she was happy, Buddy thought she still looked like the young bride smiling out from the picture by her dresser. She was talking to his dad now and straightening his tie, even smiling at him. Cissy said that Buddy's football success had helped heal their family after Iris left and had given them something to share. His parents hadn't missed a single one of his high school games—at home or away. Cissy didn't always attend the out-of-town games, especially when Grandma Stewart needed looking after. She would insist that it was more important for Mom and Dad to be at the games. Grandma Stewart lived with them now, in the downstairs room that had been Grandma Polly's after she got too weak to go up and down stairs.

The principal was getting them lined up to march onto the stage. Cissy was to wheel Grandma Stewart out last and sit with her on the end of the row. Cissy was wearing her pep squad uniform. She looked pretty, too, with her dark, curly hair worn down for a change and not gathered in its usual ponytail. She was smiling at him and offering a thumbs-up from her position behind the wheelchair. Buddy returned the gesture and felt a lump in his throat. This should be Cissy's day, too. This was all happening because of her. He never would have passed anything except PE and shop if she hadn't helped him, hadn't coached him all the way.

The band played the school song as they marched to their places. Everyone in the audience stood and sang. *Dear Columbus Alma Mater, we salute your might.* Buddy felt his neck turning red. He couldn't believe it. Half the town must be out there.

He bowed his head while Reverend Huxley offered a prayer that made it sound as though Buddy had gotten a football scholarship to Texas A&M because he was a God-fearing boy who came from a God-fearing family. He squirmed a bit at that. Buddy only went to church because his mother made him. His dad said when he prayed with the team before a game, he was to pray that he did well and that no one got hurt, but he must never pray that God favor one team over another. That *was* what Buddy prayed for, though. Victory. Creaming the other guys. He was big and strong and surprisingly fast. Creaming was what he did best.

He stared down at his large hands and thick wrists. His birth father must have been a big guy, probably some dumb farm boy with hands just like these, not someone who was expected to go to college.

Buddy kept staring at his hands while his high school coach had his turn at the podium, offering a lengthy chronology of Buddy's high school football career, starting with his freshman season, when he missed more tackles than he made, to his triumphant senior season, when he was named to the all-state team and recruited by every college in the state of Texas—and by several in Louisiana.

Then it was Mr. Lemkey's turn. Lemkey was the A&M assistant coach who had recruited Buddy. His words were less glowing. He called Buddy a big, solid player who had a lot of potential if he worked hard and made his grades. He spent far more time talking about the Texas A&M football program and naming the great players from the past—Joe Routt, Jack Pardee, Heisman Trophy winner John David Crow. Lemkey talked about the A&M players who had gone on to play professional ball and those who had served in the nation's armed forces. Finally, he called Buddy to the podium. "And now, it gives me great pleasure to announce on behalf of the Texas A&M Athletic Department that Buddy Stewart of Columbus High School has accepted our offer of an athletic scholarship and will be playing for the finest football program in the entire nation."

The band struck up the Aggie War Hymn, and the audience rose to its feet, clapping and singing along:

> Good-bye to Texas University.
> So long to the orange and white.
> Good luck to the dear old Texas Aggies.
> They are the boys who show the real old fight.

At the end of the song, everyone cheered. In the front row, the Columbus High School football team stomped and whistled its approval.

The photographers snapped pictures of Buddy and Coach Lemkey shaking hands. Then the CHS coach and Buddy's parents were asked to step forward and be included in a photograph.

When everyone once again was seated, Buddy was left alone at the podium. In a voice quivering with nervousness, clutching the sides of the podium to control his shaking hands, he thanked Mr. Lemkey and said the words that he had rehearsed with Cissy the night before. He had chosen A&M because of its great traditions, because it was his father's alma mater, and because it was close enough to Columbus that his family and friends would be able to attend his games. He promised to work hard and do his best. He thanked his coach, the school, his team, the town.

Then he surprised himself by continuing, adding words to his remarks that had not been rehearsed.

"My mother always said that Columbus, Texas, is the best place in the world for kids to grow up, and I think she's right. I guess all of you know that my sister and I are adopted. We grew up in Columbus because two good people took in a couple of homeless kids and raised them. Cissy and I are the luckiest kids in the world to have ended up in this good town with Grayson and Martha Claire Stewart as our parents. We owe them everything, and I love them very much." Then he hugged his parents, who both had tears in their eyes. Buddy was crying, too. And Cissy.

His words about his parents had been heartfelt. He did love them and was grateful to them, grateful for the life they had given him and Cissy. Maybe his folks weren't perfect, but then neither was he.

Last night, he had allowed himself to imagine his birth mother coming today. He imagined seeing an elegant, slim woman who looked just like Cissy standing in the back of the auditorium and knowing immediately it was her. After the assembly, when he went to find her, she would be gone, but he would know for the rest of his life that she loved him. As he hugged his sister, he scanned the faces in the back of the auditorium, just in case.

"You were wonderful," Cissy said as he held her close.

"God, Cissy, what if I'm not good enough for all this?" And suddenly he wished he could have erased the last weeks and done them over again.

He should have turned down A&M's offer and signed on at one of the small state schools where they didn't expect football players to do much more than show up for class and sign their names on exam papers.

But everyone told him he'd have a better chance of a professional career if he went to a Division I school, and he'd let all those phone calls and letters from coaches, all those promises of glory, go to his head.

Texas A&M. He had grown up wanting to be a Texas Aggie. He would look through his dad's yearbooks at all the guys in military uniform, at the pictures of parades and pep rallies and military balls, and feel the pull of all that tradition. The entire student body stood up at football games, adhering to the Twelfth-Man Tradition, ready to serve if needed. A&M had it all: duty, honor, country, and Texas-style football.

Mr. Lemkey had promised that Buddy would have tutors to help him study and advisers who would make sure he enrolled only in classes taught by professors who understood the importance of football to the school. Mr. Lemkey didn't know, however, that Buddy never would have gotten through high school without his sister's help. How in the hell was he going to manage college? If only Cissy could come with him to College Station, but she wouldn't graduate from high school for another year, and she was hoping for an academic scholarship to the women's college in Denton, where she could study nursing.

"What if I can't hack it at college?" he whispered to his sister, ignoring the press of well-wishers who'd rushed up on the stage to shake his hand. "Everyone will hate me if I screw up."

Cissy put a finger to his lips. "Just do the best you can. No one can hate you for that."

twenty-one

During Buddy's three semesters at Texas A&M, I came to realize that I had not done my brother any favor during those nightly study sessions at the dining room table. I'd always stopped short of working the problems and writing the themes, but he never would have managed on his own without my help.

As soon as I was old enough to take over the evening homework sessions from my mother, I became the most diligent of tutors. When Buddy would push his chair back from the table and insist he'd had enough, I would turn the history lesson into a story or turn the geography lesson into a travelogue of the places we would go someday—anything to help him remember. I'm not sure he ever would have graduated from high school without my help, but maybe that would have been for the best. A big strong boy like him could have gotten a job at the gravel pits or on the docks in Baytown or Texas City. He could have joined the army or the merchant marines.

After he left for College Station, I did what I could over the telephone and through the mail. I overrode my conscience and wrote several papers outright, making them simple enough and including enough mistakes to have been written by Buddy Stewart.

Buddy just couldn't make the leap from the spoken to the written word. Often, he could tell me what he wanted to say, but when I handed him the pencil and told him to write down what he had just told me, he simply could not do it. He was no good at memorizing things, either—spelling words, historical dates, the Gettysburg Address, multiplication tables. He went to college counting on his fingers and moving his lips when he read.

As for football, he did modestly well on the freshman team, but he was beginning to worry that he didn't have a prayer of completing four years of college, no matter how many tutors the athletic department provided. I think he wanted to quit school then, but the whole town was expecting him to become a football legend.

If he couldn't come home on weekends, I'd drive over to College Station on Sunday afternoon, and we would go to the reading room in the library, where I'd help him get organized for the upcoming week as best I could. I had just turned sixteen and couldn't believe my parents actually let me drive up there all by myself, but I think they knew that I was Buddy's only hope.

I loved the drive to College Station, which traversed the sparsely settled countryside, with its quaint old farmhouses and little time-warp hamlets. But I hated the drive back, when I would be the only car on narrow, winding roads for mile after mile of darkness. More than once, I had to swerve to avoid hitting a cow or deer or had to pull off the road when the rain came down so hard I couldn't see. But I would have done anything to help my brother. After all, I was responsible for the mess he was in.

Buddy decided that our birth father must have been dumb and that I got my brains from our mother. Or maybe we had different fathers, and his was dumb as a post. I kept telling him that who they were wasn't important, that Martha Claire and Grayson Stewart were the only parents who mattered, but I think he almost needed to find some reason for the way things were. If he'd had a dumb father, then maybe it wasn't his fault.

His second semester was somewhat better. By then, the athletic department realized they had more of a problem on their hands than they had anticipated. That was in the days before the NCAA ruled that student athletes had to progress toward a degree, and Buddy was put in nonacademic physical education classes and remedial classes that would not count toward a degree but fulfilled his requirements for athletic eligibility. Everyone realized that the best Buddy could hope for was to stay in school until his four years of eligibility ran out, then get drafted by a professional team. Oh, how I hoped and prayed that would happen. I would have given up my own chance at a college education if it somehow would have made things work out for my brother.

He had to go to summer school to make up for a first-semester incomplete in freshman composition, but he was able to do that at junior college in Houston. His sophomore year, he played in most of the games and was cited in newspaper articles as "promising." I was living in Denton by then. Neither of us had a car, and I was now a college student with studies of my own. I told myself that as long as Buddy went to class and showed up for exams, he would be all right. And maybe he would have been, but he frequently cut classes. I suspected his cutting had something to do with all the beer he consumed. His roommate bragged to me that Buddy had the team record for consuming the most six-packs at one sitting.

I spent my childhood watching over my brother and being my mother's little helper. The time had come for me to find other purposes in my life, but it was difficult. It felt as though I should be doing more for them. It felt as though I was succeeding at my brother's expense.

Texas A&M won the Southwest Conference in 1967, earning the right to face Alabama in the Cotton Bowl on New Year's Day. Buddy hadn't been a star, but as the season progressed he proved that he was a solid defensive player.

Even with his specially arranged class schedule, Buddy hated going to class, hated studying, hated taking tests. But he loved playing football. He practiced and played with a passion that exceeded anything he had felt in high school. He told Cissy it was like a religious experience running onto Kyle Field, with everyone on their feet, cheering for the Texas Aggies.

Buddy found himself constantly looking down at his right hand, imagining the Southwest Conference championship ring that would soon reside there. For the rest of his life, he would be able to say that he played on the '67 team. For the rest of his life, he could wear that ring and feel proud.

He went home for Christmas, but the team was required to return to College Station the day after to prepare for the bowl game.

The Cotton Bowl. Just playing in that game was another dream come true. His family and all his friends would be there. Millions of people would be watching on television.

Experience had taught Buddy not to set unrealistic game goals. He simply promised himself that he would hustle and do his best. When he allowed himself to daydream about sacking quarterbacks or picking up fumbles and running for touchdowns, he felt disappointed afterward. It was best to wait until the game was over and find something to feel good about. And find ways to do better. He never got his fill of game films, watching himself making tackles—and sometimes missing them. But he was getting better. Everyone said so. Several sportswriters had indicated that Buddy Stewart had a good chance of making the starting lineup his junior year.

In the locker room, before the Cotton Bowl game, he received a telegram from Justine and Iris. They wished him luck, said they loved him and would be watching and cheering for him and the Aggies. Buddy got tears in his eyes. They loved him. Everybody loved him. In his mind, he dedicated the game to Justine and Iris. And to Cissy. Always to Cissy.

The game was a close one, and Buddy didn't get to play as much as he thought he would. By the fourth quarter, however, there were injuries. Buddy knew he would play the rest of the game.

With the Aggies ahead 20 to 14 in the waning minutes of the game, it looked like victory was within reach. All the defense had to do was hold the Crimson Tide for one last possession.

But on fourth down, in a last-ditch effort, the Alabama quarterback broke loose. Buddy realized that he was the only Aggie with a chance of catching him.

He ran like he had never run before, closing on the Alabama player as he crossed the thirty, then the forty.

Buddy had never wanted anything in his life like he wanted to tackle that guy. His lungs were bursting, but it didn't matter. This was going to be his moment. He would not be denied.

He was aware of crossing the midfield stripe. *Now,* he told himself, before the guy reached field goal territory.

Buddy reached deep within himself for a final burst, and at just the right moment, flew at the guy, knocking his feet out from under him.

Almost instantly, Buddy was engulfed by his fellow players. Hugs that lifted him off his feet. Back slapping. Cheers. All around him yelling and cheering. The cheering from the stands was deafening. All for him. All for Buddy Stewart of Columbus, Texas.

He thought of his parents and Cissy watching in the stands, of the hundreds of friends and neighbors who had driven up from Columbus. He though of the rest of the town, at home, watching on their television screens. He thought of Justine and Iris watching in New York. They would be jumping up and down and hugging each other. He hadn't let them down.

After the game, in the shower, with hot water washing over his aching, bruised body, he cried with the emotion of it all. It was a day he would never forget. A preview of his life to come. A beginning. From now on, he was *someone.*

The next day, his picture was on the front page of the *Colorado County Citizen* and the sports page of *The Houston Post.* When he walked downtown, people stopped him on the sidewalk to shake his hand. His high school coach dropped by the house to say how proud he was of him. His mother had a picture of him in his Texas A&M football uniform framed and put in the store window. His dad and sister were proud, too, but they kept reminding him that finals were coming up, that he needed to spend the remaining week of the Christmas break studying.

Cissy had exams of her own to prepare for and a term paper to write, but she would push her own books and notebooks to one side to help her brother. She made out a study schedule for him and outlined the main points that would be covered on each of his finals. Buddy never ceased to marvel at his sister. How could she know what would be covered on the final examination in a class she had never taken? But she would look over the course syllabus, run her finger down the textbook's table of contents, and start writing. He should learn the major muscle groups and the basic food groups. He needed to review the rules for field hockey, volleyball, badminton, and rugby. He should know the parts of speech and be able to recognize them in a sentence. She wrote out a number of math problems for him to solve and told him to review the organization of the federal government and be able to explain the function of each of its branches.

Buddy promised himself that he would spend at least three hours a day studying, but he couldn't make himself get out of bed in the morning. Afternoons, there was always a touch football game or pickup basketball over at the school grounds with the old gang. In the evening, kids home from college gathered to dance and tank up on beer. Girls who had ignored him in high school would let him dance close and didn't object if his hands strayed a bit.

Whenever he did find time to open a book, his mind would wander. He would find himself replaying the Cotton Bowl game and all the other games of the glorious '67 season. He would stare down at the Southwest Conference championship ring that now resided on his finger and thank God he hadn't gone to a smaller school. Playing football for high-and-mighty Texas A&M was a dream come true. For the rest of his life, he would be identified as someone who played on the 1967 championship team, the team that won the 1968 Cotton Bowl game. Now, when he walked across campus, everyone would know who he was. Rich alumni would buy him steak dinners and slip him hundred-dollar bills. After two more seasons, he would be drafted by a pro team and buy his dad a Lincoln Continental, fix up his mother's house, and send Cissy on a European vacation with Iris.

After a time, the daydreaming would get the best of him, and he would give up on studying, close whatever book was propped in front of him, and head for more entertaining pursuits. Surely none of his professors would flunk a player who had made the game-saving tackle in the Cotton Bowl.

Back on campus, though, Buddy began to worry. He tacked the study schedule on his bulletin board and tried to learn something about each of the topics Cissy had identified. He really did try, but it was a lot of stuff and really boring. He went to tutoring sessions the athletic department arranged, but they only made him realize how little he had learned this semester.

He was on time for each of his finals and struggled to write responses to the questions. Cissy had said that even if he didn't know the exact answer to a question, he must not leave it blank. It was important to write at least a sentence or two to show he knew something about the topic. Sometimes, though, he hadn't a clue. What the hell was the Mason-Dixon Line? An interrogative sentence? He didn't know the difference between a multiplier and a multiplicand, or a dividend and a divisor. He didn't know if he should multiply or divide to find out how many gallons of gas it took for John to drive from Houston to Chicago.

The first week of second semester, when the coach called Buddy into his office, he feared the worst.

"Hell, Stewart, we told you that you had to at least show up for your classes," the coach said in disgust, shaking the grade report for the first semester in Buddy's face.

"But I only missed Monday morning classes," Buddy insisted. "Nobody goes to class on Monday morning."

"You only had classes on Monday, Wednesday, and Friday mornings. That's *one-third* of your classes that you didn't bother to show up for—plus travel days to away games. How can you expect a professor to give you the benefit of the doubt if you can't get your ass out of bed on Monday morning?"

"I thought all my professors supported the football program," Buddy bemoaned.

"Yeah, they're supporters. They could have flunked you, but they didn't. Each one of your professors gave you a D. *You made straight D's!* Your grade-point average is a fuckin' one point, and that means you are beyond probation. It means you are now academically ineligible."

The coach took a breath and stood. "I'm sorry, Stewart, but you've finished here. If you still want to play football, you'll have to raise your GPA and apply at a Division II school. Maybe one of them will take you. I wish you well."

Buddy stood, shook the coach's extended hand, and walked back to the athletic dorm in a daze. This couldn't be happening to him, not after last season, not after the Cotton Bowl.

What was he going to do now? How would he ever be able to face his parents?

He threw himself on his bed, where he stayed for three days, getting up only long enough to go to the bathroom and stumble down the hall to get a candy bar and soda pop from the vending machine. He slept all day, vaguely aware of the comings and goings of his roommate. In the night, he'd stare at the shadows on the ceiling and try to work things out.

Finally, his roommate, Clive Fredericson, a linebacker from Lubbock, pulled a chair over to Buddy's bed. "The coach asked me to talk to you," he said softly. "You've got to leave, Buddy, before they send the campus police to kick you out of here."

Clive helped him pack up and drove him to the bus station.

"You got enough money to get yourself home?" he asked.

Buddy nodded.

He didn't go home, though. He bought a ticket to Denton. To Cissy.

twenty-two

Denton was a long way from College Station, almost to the Oklahoma border, and the bus stopped at towns he'd never heard of—Jewett and Buffalo and Streetman—where he would use the bathroom and buy more candy bars. He looked out the window at the passing landscape and thought about Cissy.

Staring at the ceiling the past three nights, a major truth had evolved. He and Cissy were not really related at all.

Maybe deep down he had known all along they weren't really brother and sister, or even half brother and sister, but hadn't wanted to face the fact that there was no person in his life to whom he was related by blood.

When night fell, Buddy studied his own reflection in the bus window and found reinforcement there for this new theory. Other than the fact that they both had dark hair and brown eyes, he and Cissy weren't alike at all. He was built like a refrigerator, and she was slim as a reed. He was good-looking, he supposed, in a big, rawboned kind of way, but Cissy had a look of quality about her. She was delicate as the china figurine of Marie Antoinette that graced his mother's parlor. Cissy was an angel. A princess. She was as dear to him as life itself.

Cissy was his hope. She had always been his hope; he just hadn't known it.

The phone at her dormitory rang and rang before a sleepy-voiced housemother finally answered. Was this an emergency? she wanted to know. "This is her brother," Buddy said, thinking it would be the last time he said the word *brother* in reference to Cissy.

The woman let out a "Humph," obviously not believing him. He would have to call back in the morning.

"Please, just tell her that Buddy is at the Denton bus station."

Yes, she would do that—*in the morning*.

Using his duffel bag as a pillow, Buddy stretched out on a wooden bench. He was cold and uncomfortable, but surprisingly he could feel himself relaxing and sleep approaching. In just a few more hours, Cissy would be here. With Cissy, he could make a fresh start.

When he woke, she was standing over him. "Buddy, what in the world are you doing here?"

He leapt to his feet and hugged her. "God, am I glad to see you."

"What's going on?" she wanted to know.

He led her to a corner booth in the coffee shop and explained that he was finished at A&M.

She cried a little and told him she was sorry. "What will you do?"

"Get a job here in Denton to be near you. I might even take a class or two over at North Texas State. If I raise my grade-point average, I might be able to play football at Lamar or Concordia. I thought maybe we could rent an apartment and live together." He reached across the table and grabbed her hands. "I can't go back to Columbus with my tail between my legs."

Cissy frowned and shook her head. "Undergraduates aren't allowed to live off campus," she said. "I'd be kicked out of school if I moved out of the dorms."

"Then come away with me," he blurted out. "All that matters is that we're together."

"Buddy, what are you talking about?"

"We don't have the same parents, Cissy. I don't know why it took me so long to figure that out. I'm oversized and stupid. You're little and smart. I'll work hard for you and take care of you. I promise I will. I love you more than anyone."

More tears welled in Cissy's eyes. "Oh, Buddy, whether we're related by blood or not, we were raised as brother and sister. I love you like a brother. I'll always love you like a brother."

"Then just let me be with you. I'll be your brother or whatever you want me to be. I need to be with you."

She covered her mouth with her hands and slowly shook her head back and forth.

Buddy wondered if his life was over, if it would be better to die. Then maybe no one would ever know that he got kicked out of A&M.

Numbly, he allowed her to buy him a ticket to Columbus and to hug him good-bye. Maybe she just needed time to become accustomed to the idea, he told himself. When she thought about it, she would realize they were not related. Neither one of them had ever gone steady, ever had a serious relationship. There was a reason for that. In their heart of hearts, they knew they were supposed to be together.

"I'll call Mama and tell her you're coming," she said. "I'll explain everything. It's just as well, Buddy. Mama needs you down at the store. With me gone, she doesn't have anyone to help her."

As Cissy watched the bus roll out of the station, she wondered if it was a mistake for him to go back home. Maybe she could have gotten special permission to live off campus. After all, no matter whatever notion Buddy had gotten in his head, he was her brother.

She had not been totally surprised by his words, however. She had sensed that something like this might happen someday and had grown quite careful in the way she hugged him. She no longer sat in his lap or padded around the house wearing just a nightie with nothing on underneath.

Sometimes her feelings for her brother were confusing. She'd always been touched by his devotion to her, and there had been disturbing moments when she was deeply aware of his big, strong body. And yes, she, too, had wondered if she and Buddy were truly brother and sister, but whether they were or not did not matter. All that wondering and adolescent attraction was just a phase she had passed through. Now, she was genuinely in love—a pure love without incestuous overtones. Randy Calhoune was a senior pre-med student across town at North Texas State. She'd met him at church. When he smiled, her heart actually fluttered. Yesterday, after the eleven o'clock service, he had asked her out, and she had been floating ever since. This morning when the resident adviser came to knock on her door and tell her about Buddy, she had been hugging her pillow and imagining what it would be like to kiss Randy Calhoune.

For the first time in her life, she was turning her back on her brother. But Buddy was twenty years old, she reminded herself. He needed to start solving his own problems.

But what if he wasn't capable of doing that? What if he was one of those people who would always need looking after?

Cissy went to a pay phone. When her mother answered, she said, "Buddy is on his way home, Mama. He's flunked out of school, and he needs his mother."

Martha Claire drew in her breath, "Oh, Cissy, are you certain?"

"Yes, he was just here. I put him on a bus for Columbus."

"What was he doing in Denton?"

"He was afraid to come home. I told him that you and Daddy would be okay about it. I think we all knew that college might not work out for him. Well, it hasn't, and there's no point in making him feel bad about it. Tell him how much you need him, Mama. He needs to feel important. Tell him you want to make him assistant manager of Stewart's Dry Goods. Have him represent the store at the Chamber of Commerce meetings. Put him in charge of the sports corner." Cissy fished around in her pockets for a tissue. She was crying hard, her chest convulsing with sobs. "Oh, Mama, it just breaks my heart. He's like a lost little boy. He needs his mother more than anything."

She could hear her mother blow her nose. "It will be all right, dear. Thank you for letting me know."

"His bus is scheduled to arrive at four-fifteen."

"I'll be there."

"I love you, Mama."

"I love you, too, Cissy. You are the greatest blessing of my life."

Martha Claire hung up the phone and went back to her kitchen table, where she buried her head in her arms and cried for her little boy. Her poor, poor Buddy.

She thought of that first day when Doc Hadley brought him to the door—a little waif with big brown eyes. He'd sat in Grayson's lap eating a cookie.

She understood well the message of Cissy's call. Buddy needed to be built up, not torn down, which she might very well have done if Cissy hadn't prepared her, hadn't reminded her that Buddy needed mothering.

She dried her tears on her apron, then walked across the backyard to the garage and climbed the stairs. Buddy would live here, she decided as she inspected the empty apartment. He needed both the comfort of his home and the dignity of a place of his own. The garage apartment would be perfect.

Martha Claire had rented it several different times since Justine and Iris left, mostly to men constructing the new interstate highway. Even though the money was nice, she was always glad when they left. She didn't like strangers up here, she thought as she ran her finger across the dusty table.

She remembered that last awful day when she'd carried all of Justine's possessions down to the backyard incinerator and burned them. And she remembered an earlier time, when she scrubbed and painted the apartment with her parents, Grandma Polly, and Granny Grace to make it livable for Justine and her baby. She remembered all those times when she had climbed those stairs to be with Iris. In the years after the Texas City disaster, as Justine moved first to Houston and then to New York, graduating to the realm of big-time photojournalism, the apartment was the place she came back to. Martha Claire remembered staring out the kitchen window, knowing that Justine and Iris were up here enjoying each other in a wonderfully effervescent, come-what-may manner that she herself seemed incapable of experiencing. She had had such mixed feelings—she was so jealous of the love Iris had for her mother that it almost made her ill, but she also was jealous of the time Iris got to spend with Justine. Martha Claire never had enough time alone with her sister, with just the two of them laughing and talking and drinking iced tea or beer until the wee hours of the morning. Yet, she had realized that, if it weren't for Iris, she would be lucky to see her sister once a year, if that often. Justine would come home only for an occasional Christmas or funeral.

At least now she didn't have to be confused about her feelings for her sister, Martha Claire thought as she opened cupboards, checked to see if the refrigerator still worked.

Justine and Iris had been gone for almost seven years now. Martha

Claire didn't want to ever see her sister again, unless maybe it was her dead body in a casket. She hated her own sister that much. Justine had ruined her marriage and stolen Iris.

As much as Martha Claire missed Iris, however, and as much as she hated Justine for taking her away, Martha Claire couldn't imagine what life would have been like if Iris had stayed on—a constant reminder to Martha Claire of a betrayal that had stolen away youth and joy. It was so hard to comprehend that Iris, a child she had loved since birth and cared for as a mother, would never have been born if it weren't for that betrayal.

When Iris wanted to come back for a visit that first summer, Martha Claire had not allowed it. Iris never asked again. Martha Claire knew that Cissy and Iris had middle-of-the-night phone calls. When she realized what was going on, she had wanted to jerk open the closet door and pull Cissy out of there, but she hadn't. The girls had talked once a month for years now. At Denton, Cissy didn't have to crawl into a closet to talk to her cousin. Martha Claire was glad they had each other. She herself had no one to talk to. She had invested all in family. Her best friends had been her husband, her mother, and her sister. Now all she had left was two children who were careful in her presence and acquaintances whose esteem she once had valued. She didn't bother to pay her annual dues to the various ladies' clubs. She now found the meetings boring, and she didn't have time for them anyway, not with Grayson on the road and her having to run the store.

Martha Claire worried that her children thought of her as a mean old woman who was intent on making their father's life miserable and who had deprived them of their beloved cousin. Once Cissy had even called her mean to her face. Of course, she had come to apologize later, but Martha Claire had been shocked. Cissy wasn't one to call names.

How many times she had longed to tell her children what their father had done and see some sort of understanding in their eyes, but there was no justifiable reason to make them share her burden. She and Grayson and Justine had sworn that they would never tell anyone. No one was ever to know that Grayson was Iris's father. Each for their own reasons, they would take the secret to their graves.

Grayson's mother had died in her sleep last spring. Martha Claire hadn't wanted Lily Stewart to come live with them, but what could she say? Her own mother and grandmother had lived with them for years. Maybe if Martha Claire had still loved the woman's son, she might have felt differently, but there she had been, taking care of someone she didn't really like. Of course, they could have insisted that Lily sell her house and use that money for her care. But whatever inheritance Grayson might receive from his mother would be needed for a new car, foundation work on the Milam Street house, and new wiring at the store. So, Martha Claire put up with the endless stream of inane chatter and ignored the smells of old age and infirmity. Toward the end, she did hire a woman to launder the bed linens and sit with Lily during the day while Martha Claire was at the store. When Grayson told her how much he appreciated what she was doing for his mother, she simply shrugged.

After Lily died, they threw out the mattress, moved the bed back upstairs, and put the television, sofa, and easy chairs back in the morning room. Such places were now called "family rooms," but most nights she sat there by herself, her dinner on a tray. The large dining room seemed empty now with just the table, chairs, and sideboard. When Grayson was at home, they ate at the kitchen table, watching a small black-and-white television set she kept on top of the refrigerator.

She didn't hate Grayson like she used to, but she didn't love him, either. She missed her children and didn't like being alone in the big old house at night. As a result, she found herself looking forward to Grayson's being home on the weekends and wasn't such a slave driver anymore. Sometimes they would cook hamburgers on the grill and walk downtown for a movie or an ice cream cone. They talked about buying a camping trailer and vacationing in New England or Yellowstone, but probably that would never happen. They didn't have anyone to look after the store.

Martha Claire had been surprised at the extent of Grayson's grief when his mother died. It had taken hours to track him down, and even on the telephone she could sense the extent of his pain. "Will you be able to drive home?" she asked.

He said he could, but it had taken him half a day, and he admitted that he kept having to pull off the road to get his emotions under control. But Lily Stewart had been such a silly woman, Martha Claire had wanted to protest. By Lily's own admission, she had never voted in an election and hadn't read a book since high school. But she was Grayson's mother, and loving one's mother was innate, Martha Claire supposed, wondering if that innateness extended to adopted children. Would Cissy and Buddy be as upset when she herself died? Would Iris?

Ah, such morbid thoughts. She reprimanded herself with a shake of her head and glanced down at her watch. It was time for her to get dressed and go down to the store. She wanted to get the apartment ready for Buddy, though, and decided any customers who might come by the store this morning would just have to come back later. Folks would probably think she was sick or dead. The store always opened at straight-up nine o'clock, Monday through Saturday.

Assistant manager, she thought with a smile. She would even put an announcement in the paper—with Buddy's picture. Her Cissy was a clever girl, no question about that.

She wondered what Grayson was going to think about Buddy's living in Columbus. He was going to be disappointed about A&M, but they'd always known the boy was no student. Surely Grayson would see that home was the best place for him.

twenty-three

One of Grayson's favorite stops on his travels was the town of New Braunfels, which still retained the German flavor brought by the settlers who founded the town in 1845. The German language was spoken in the schools and churches up until World War II, and whenever old-timers gathered they still reverted to the language of their forebears. The town had some interesting museums, and the German fare in the restaurants was a welcome change from hamburgers and chicken-fried steak.

During his twice-yearly visits to New Braunfels with his samples and catalogs, he always stayed at the Old Germany Motel, which fit his criteria of clean, cheap, and locally owned. Over the years he found himself going back to the same restaurants and motels, sometimes even staying in the same rooms, sitting at the same tables, and ordering the same meals from the menus, getting to know waitresses and proprietors.

The Old Germany was owned by Clara and Clifton Wetzeg, who always greeted him like an old friend. He and Clifton played chess some in the evenings, with Clara bringing them coffee and strudel or a bit of brandy. Sitting on their mantel was a photograph of a handsome young man in a naval uniform—their son Gus, whose ship had gone down in the South Pacific. There had been two other children who had died as infants.

Clara and Clifton were always reaching over to pat one another. They held hands when they took walks in the evening. Clifton referred to her as his "bride." She called him her "darling boy." They shared a passion for polka and every Saturday night crossed the river to the dance hall in Gruene.

The last time Grayson stayed with them, he knew as soon as he saw Clifton that the man was dying. Clifton looked up from his newspaper. "Cancer in my liver," he said without being asked.

"What about treatment?" Grayson wanted to know.

"We'll see," Clifton allowed. "Everyone has to go sometime, you know."

Before Grayson checked out that Friday evening, he sat with Clifton on the bench under a huge mesquite tree that graced the motel lawn. "Clara's a good woman," Clifton said. "You could do a lot worse."

Grayson was too shocked to respond.

"I don't suppose I'll be here when you get back," Clifton went on, "but Clara will. I can't imagine her living the rest of her life without someone to fuss over. She should be looking after a slew of grandkids by now, but it didn't work out that way. We've always liked you, Grayson, and looked forward to your visits."

"This has always been my favorite stop, Clifton. You know that. For me, New Braunfels means a visit with old friends."

"This isn't a bad life here, you know. And Clara would look after you, fatten you up a bit."

"Clifton, I have a wife."

"I know, but I also know that you are not a happy man. It shows in your face, Grayson. I've had my share of heartbreak, but overall I've led a happy life—because of Clara. I didn't used to believe in divorce. I thought that folks had to live with their mistakes and hope for a better hereafter. I don't think like that anymore, though. I'm not even sure there is a hereafter. Seems to me that we should live our lives as though there wasn't."

Grayson stared at the house across the street. One of the old houses. All the old houses in New Braunfels had tin roofs, which made them look like barns, but the roof never had to be replaced. A metaphor for life, he decided. Nothing was all good or all bad. Clifton was right. He wasn't a happy man, but he had come to terms. And there were small pleasures: a phone call from Cissy, the fine meal Martha Claire always had waiting for him on Friday evening, watching his son play football, fishing from the riverbank, sighting a really fine buck in his scope, reading a book by a favorite author. Martha Claire didn't love him anymore, but she would turn into a bitter old woman if he left her. And there was still the dream that she would someday find forgiveness in her heart and come to love him once again.

But what if that never happened?

He wasn't an old man. He had just turned fifty, which surely wasn't too old for change. Or for taking a risk.

Over the next months, he thought about Clara Wetzeg, about her rosy face and round body. He thought about her when he ate lonely meals at small roadside eateries. He thought about her in the night. For the first time since he was a young man, except for momentary forays into erotic fantasy, the woman he longed for was not Martha Claire.

He told himself that, on his next trip to New Braunfels, he would not stay at the Old Germany, but he hadn't made a reservation elsewhere. When he drove into town, the vacancy sign at the Old Germany was lit, and he wavered.

He wondered if Clifton was still alive. Probably not. Probably it was just Clara watching television in the apartment behind the office. Soft, loving Clara. In his mind's eye, he could see the car turning in, see Clara's face when he checked in. But the vision stopped there, and he drove on by and found a generic motel on the highway. He thought about calling Martha Claire and imagined telling her about Clara Wetzeg, explaining that he had not gone back to the Old Germany Motel because he still was in love with his wife. Instead, however, he walked across the highway to a liquor store and bought a pint of Jack Daniel's.

Friday evening, when he arrived home, Grayson was surprised to see a light on in the garage apartment. Had Martha Claire rented it again?

He got his battered old suitcase from the truck and started across the yard. The back door opened. "Buddy's home," Martha Claire said through the screen door.

"Is he okay?" Grayson asked. The semester was only three weeks old, too soon for him to be spending a weekend at home.

"He was expelled because of his grades," Martha Claire said, holding the door open for her husband. "He's been telling people he has a bad knee and decided not to stay in school if he couldn't play football. He even fakes a bit of a limp when he remembers. He's going to work for me at the store."

Grayson went into the bathroom to wash up for dinner, and he stayed for a while, to grieve in private for the death of a dream. Grayson knew that Buddy was a marginal student at best, but after three semesters, he'd almost convinced himself that the school and Buddy had come to terms. Everyone would look the other way and let him play ball. Maybe he could even earn a degree. With some sort of degree, even if he didn't play professional ball, he could have coached high school kids, could have held his head up for the rest of his life.

He splashed water on his face and combed his hair, then stared at his face in the mirror. An unhappy face, Clifton Wetzeg had said. Grayson had wanted his children to be happier than he was—all three of them. Buddy, Cissy, and Iris.

Iris. Thoughts of her never failed to bring pain to his heart. If only he could see her again—even if at a distance.

He carefully hung up the towel and went to have dinner with his wife.

"You look tired," Martha Claire said.

"I'm just hungry, and if I'm not mistaken, that's pot roast I smell. Isn't Buddy eating with us?" he asked, nodding at the kitchen table, which was set for two."

"He'd planned to. But some of his friends came by. They went to the high school basketball game."

"Is he okay?" Grayson asked again.

"I think he will be," Martha Claire said as she lifted the Dutch oven from the stove and set it on a trivet. "Before he came home, he rode the bus all the way to Denton to tell Cissy. She was the one who called and told me he was on his way home."

"I don't think having him work at the store is a good idea," Grayson said and watched Martha Claire's spine suddenly stiffen, her mouth grow tight.

He should have worded his statement differently, Grayson realized. He should have sounded more tentative. *They needed to discuss what was best for Buddy, how they could best help him.* But now Martha

Claire would dig in whether she had reservations about him working at the store or not.

Grayson tried to backtrack. "It's not the store, really. It's the town."

"What's the matter with the town?" Martha Claire demanded.

"There's not much opportunity here for him. Buddy needs to learn a trade. He can't just stay here forever and let his parents support him."

"We won't support him. I'll *pay* him for working in the store," she said. "When I retire, he can take it over."

Grayson shook his head. "He's never shown any interest in that store. We practically had to threaten him to get him to wash the windows or help take inventory. I don't remember him ever voluntarily helping out unless he thought he could talk us out of a pair of new sneakers. When you retire, we'll close the store. It makes less money every year, and you work so hard at it. Buddy won't work hard. He'll put a sign on the door and go fishing."

"I didn't realize you had such a low opinion of your son," Martha Claire said.

"Not low, just realistic. A storekeeper, he is not."

"Like father, like son. Is that what you're telling me?"

"Wouldn't you like for our children to be happier than we have been?"

"It wasn't the store that made us unhappy," she said. "Now, are you going to eat this food or not?"

Suddenly more angry than tired, Grayson hesitated and glanced toward the door. No, he didn't want to sit here in this unhappy home with his unhappy wife, no matter how fine the food might be. Maybe he should just leave. It would take less than two hours to drive back to New Braunfels.

She put her hand on his arm. "Please don't go."

He looked at her for a long moment, then put his hand over hers. And nodded. He would stay.

He took a walk downtown after dinner, strolling out onto the bridge. It was chilly, but the air felt good. He stared down at the water and thought of the things he might have said to Martha Claire. In a way, the store was the root of their unhappiness. The store represented the preordained life he had not wanted. He and Justine had talked about it that night in the London pub, before the sirens went off and all hell broke loose. She'd told him she didn't believe in human sacrifice. Did he really want to spend the rest of his life folding shirts and sweeping the floor just because Martha Claire didn't have the courage to leave home? After the war, he went back to Justine, to finish that conversation.

His unit had been involved in the liberation of Dachau. Thirty-two thousand living skeletons lined the fence and watched them approach. Inside they found more than a thousand corpses, stacked like corded wood, hundreds more stacked inside freight cars. All of the horrors he had lived through over the past three years had in no way prepared him for the hell on earth that greeted him at Dachau. What he saw made him ashamed to be a human being and made him unsure about his future. In a way the nightmare of Dachau pulled him away from Columbus as much as his memories of the achingly beautiful city of Paris. He had experienced too much to live out his life in the doldrums. For better or worse, he had become a citizen of a broader world. He would work for a magazine or newspaper, he decided. Or become a historian and spend the rest of his life trying to ascertain the deeper meaning of the war, of Dachau, and of the millions of dead.

His most immediate need, however, had been to do some small something to reaffirm his own humanity. Or was it just putting off a decision he inevitably must make? He volunteered to stay on and found himself processing concentration camp prisoners, cataloging them like books, trying to figure out where in this world they now belonged. Time after time, he had thought the person sitting in front of him was seventy or eighty years old only to find out he or she was only thirty or forty. Often he couldn't tell if they were male or female, and he had to ask. Heads had been shaved to get rid of lice. Starved women had no breasts. Whatever articles of clothing they had been given to replace the rags they had worn in the concentration camps were too big for their emaciated bodies. Their teeth were rotten or had fallen out. Their eyes had sunk deep into sockets. Many were tattooed. Like cattle. Numbers on their forearms. He was repulsed and sickened by them, and yet he cared for them so profoundly that he wanted to take them in his arms and comfort them. He knew he had to get away for a time or go crazy. Without even knowing if Justine was still in London, he had taken the train to Calais. Yes, she was still there, awaiting her port call, she said when he called. She would meet him tomorrow in Dover.

So many times over the years, he asked himself if he had had other thoughts in his heart when he boarded the ferry for Dover. If he had had longings other than finishing that wartime conversation, he truly had not been aware of them. Not even when he saw Justine was he aware, although the sight of her waiting at the pier filled him with a joy he hadn't felt in a long time. He was both homesick and sick of thinking about home. What was he to do? Could she help him through the maze?

She had already made up her mind about her own future. It was not to be found in Columbus but in a major city like New York, or maybe she would return to London. She loved her family, and Columbus would always be the place she went back to, but she could never live there. She, too, wanted to experience the larger world, to live more fully, to escape from provincialism.

They drank too much that evening. And were filled with the melancholy beauty of the view from the white cliffs. How strange that, of all the names Martha Claire might have selected for her obituary for the husband Justine had never had, she had come up with Dover. The child who was conceived in a quaint inn that had survived the German bombing still bore that name. Iris Dover. *His* child. He had known the truth the moment Martha Claire had written him about Justine's pregnancy, and he had broken out in a cold sweat. *Dear God, what had he done!* He was sick with remorse. Was this all the more reason he should not go back home or was it the last nail in his coffin?

In those years when Justine was still coming back to Columbus for visits, they had hardly spoken to each other—avoided each other, really. And each time he saw her, he was forced to ask himself once again if he had gone to Dover with intent. Somehow it made the act seem less dishonorable if it had just happened and had not been planned.

For most of his childhood, Grayson had known he would someday marry one of the Mayfield sisters, but he didn't know which one.

Martha Claire was the prettier, but Justine was unlike any girl he had ever known. Justine would climb the steepest roof and walk across the ridgepole like a tightrope walker. She relished risk and competition. Until they were teenagers, she had been able to beat him in a footrace. And she could outshoot him with a basketball. Once, just to show off, she walked out on the gym floor at halftime of a junior high boys' basketball game, picked up a basketball, and hit a dozen shots in a row from the free-throw line. If he said something stupid, she told him so. If he was being a jerk, she told him so. Once when he tried to kiss her, she'd told him to go jump off the river bridge. Mostly they tripped each other, jumped out from behind trees to scare each other, and half drowned each other in the river.

Martha Claire, on the other hand, had undergone a metamorphosis in junior high, giving up tomboy ways and pigtails and turning into a breathtaking Southern belle. She was the prettiest girl in town, hands down. Martha Claire also told him when he was being stupid or a jerk, but she did it by saying that she was disappointed in him, that she knew he was a better person than that. In the end, he became the person Martha Claire wanted him to be. He never cursed or spit, drank only in moderation, and cultivated impeccable manners. He even ordered a book on gentlemanly behavior. Texas A&M refined the process. He never felt prouder than when he was in the uniform of the corps with Martha Claire on his arm. Justine would have scoffed at taking a man's arm. She could get around on her own just fine, thank you. She didn't need a man to carry her suitcase or open a door for her. So, ultimately, he fell deeply, spiritually, abidingly in love with the older of the two Mayfield sisters—with dainty Martha Claire. For Justine, he developed a brotherly affection.

During those two days in Dover, however, their childhood was a distant memory. They were now two adults made deadly serious by the years and the experiences they had just lived through.

They had stood on the edge of the cliff, on the very edge of England, and shaded their eyes against the sunlight. Justine put her hand on his arm. "Look there," she said, pointing across the strait into the misty gray distance. "It's France," she said excitedly. "Someday I'm going there."

"Yes, you should—to Paris," Grayson said reverently. "Everyone should see Paris before they die. Sometimes I think I'd like to live there for the rest of my life, except there are so many other places I'd like to experience as well."

While he said the words, he was deeply aware of his sister-in-law's hand on his arm. Very deeply aware. How he would love to be with her the first time she saw Paris.

twenty-four

"Poor Buddy," Iris said. "School was always such a struggle for him, but football made him proud. Is he just devastated?"

"Yes. He wanted to move to Denton and rent an apartment for us to share." Cissy put a hand over her left ear to muffle the dorm sounds—music, voices, water running, toilets flushing.

"Yes, I can see him wanting that," Iris said. "He wouldn't have to go home and would have you to look after him. You've always been his security blanket."

"I told him I'd be kicked out of school if I moved out of the dorm, but maybe I could have gotten special permission to live with my brother," Cissy admitted, tracing with a fingertip the heart carved in the one-armed student desk that sat by the third floor's only telephone. Already there were two girls hovering about, waiting to use the phone.

Cissy never called her cousin without thinking of those years of phone calls initiated from behind the coats in the downstairs hall closet. In the summer it was stifling in there, and her body would be drenched in sweat. But she wouldn't have thought of cutting a call short, not after waiting a whole month to hear her cousin's voice, a whole month of making a mental list of the things she would discuss with Iris. She and Iris seldom exchanged letters; the late-night phone calls were more satisfactory. Cissy was sure her mother thought that she and Iris had grown apart and wondered if she was glad.

Cissy always placed the calls, and Iris would be the one finally to say, "Well, I guess we're about talked out. You go on to bed now, sweetie. Sleep tight and call me next month." They would usually end with words about missing each other, and how they still loved each other in spite of passing years, and that someday soon they would see each other again. Then Cissy would creep back up the stairs. In bed, she replayed every word and felt sad that it would be a whole month until she talked to Iris again.

Now, here in a dormitory in Denton, she still called on the first Sunday of the month, but she didn't wait until the middle of the night. There was no need for secrecy, and no phone calls were allowed after ten o'clock. Of course, some girls risked demerits to make clandestine phone calls to their boyfriends. Or maybe they called out for pizza in the middle of the night and lowered a basket out of the bathroom window to the delivery boy. Several times a week, a group of girls would sit on the floor in the middle of the bathroom, the only room where lights were allowed after hours, and enjoy their contraband pizza over whispered conversations about boyfriends and life. Cissy was never included in these late-night pizza parties. She never made after-hours phone calls. She realized that her dorm mates considered her a bit odd. Her side of her dorm room was impeccably tidy, when her roommate's side was a study in disarray. Before she went to bed, she shined her shoes and ironed her blouse for the next day. She was never late to class, always on time with her assignments, and did her laundry every Saturday morning. Years of pleasing her mother had left their mark, she supposed, or perhaps she was just born predictable and boring.

"Buddy will probably get drafted," Iris was saying. "The war in Vietnam shows no signs of going away. Mom's probably going back in a month or so; her last time, she says. The last time for her last war. If it doesn't end soon, I may end up over there myself, serving my internship in a MASH unit."

"The army might be good for Buddy, but I'd hate for him to go over there," Cissy said. "Mama said he's done more sleeping than anything else since he got home. She really needs him down at the store, but apparently he just wants to wander in and out when it suits him. Do you think I should have him move up here? I could ask the dean of students if something could be arranged."

"No, sweetie, I don't think you should do any such thing. You'd end up cooking his food, washing his clothes, picking up after him. You'd turn into his little mother when you should be having fun and enjoying college life."

"He's decided that we're not really brother and sister," Cissy said softly, checking to be sure no one was within earshot. "He thinks he's in love with me."

Iris said nothing for a long minute. "And you don't want to go down that road?" she finally asked.

"At times, I think I could love him like that, but it wouldn't be right, regardless of whether we had the same birth parents or not."

"Sometimes it's hard to tell one kind of love from the other," Iris said, her words coming slowly, as though she were choosing them with great care. "Buddy adores you, Cissy, because you're a sweet, precious girl who has made life easier for him. And probably the most seductive thing in the world for us females is thinking that some boy or man needs us so desperately that he can't possibly live without us. But the only kind of love you owe Buddy is that of a sister for her brother. He'll find some other girl to take care of him."

"I'm not so sure about that. He's not very nice to other girls. He doesn't trust them. He's afraid of ending up browbeaten like Daddy."

Iris sighed. "Buddy has to work out his problems on his own. If you don't let him, he'll end up ruining both of your lives."

After the cousins finally said good-bye, Lottie Sinclaire beat Rachel Cornell to the phone desk. Rachel's mother, in Gainesville, would have to wait for her Sunday evening phone call until Lottie was done with another seemingly endless conversation with her fiancé.

Rachel Cornell's father had been killed in Vietnam last summer, which set her apart. No one knew how to talk to a girl with a dead father. Cissy sometimes wondered how her dorm mates would react if they knew that she was adopted, if they knew she had never kissed a boy.

Cissy kicked off her shoes and curled up on her bed with her zoology textbook. Margie, her roommate, hadn't come in yet. She was probably still out in the parking lot, necking with her boyfriend in his car until the last possible moment, when the resident adviser flicked the lights, then slowly counted to ten before locking the door. Margie always came in looking as though she'd slept in her clothes. Once she had her sweater on inside out, but Cissy acted as though she hadn't noticed.

Cissy wondered why she hadn't told Iris about Randy Calhoune. She hadn't told Margie, either. Or anyone else, in case he turned out to be not as nice as she thought he was, in case she changed her mind about Buddy and let him move to Denton. Iris's words gave her courage. She had done the right thing for both herself and Buddy. Randy Calhoune had come along at just the right time. Thinking about him gave her resolve. She didn't want to feel all mixed up about Buddy, not when she could be thinking about Randy.

Was Randy thinking about her? Had he already begun to imagine a future with her? She wasn't sure she really wanted to be a doctor's wife, though. Doctors' wives didn't practice nursing. She hadn't had the courage to opt for a career in medicine, like Iris. But then, Iris had gone to NYU. She said her professors and advisers all encouraged her to go to medical school. Girls who went to Texas Women's University still were encouraged to major in elementary education, library science, or nursing.

Nursing was okay, though, she'd decided. Cissy liked the idea of taking care of people, even though she loved her literature and history classes as much as the nursing curriculum. Her mother said nursing was like teaching, something a girl could always fall back on if her husband didn't make very much money or died young. Cissy wanted her diploma to be more than an insurance policy, though. Yet the idea of marrying a young physician and living a comfortable life filled with children, a lovely home, and doing good works in the community was not an altogether unattractive one, especially if the doctor was Randy Calhoune.

Cissy realized that she was part of the first generation of American women whose future wasn't couched in terms of whom she would marry and how many children she would have. The great debate, however, was whether a woman could do justice to both a family and a career. And were there men out there who really wanted a new kind of wife?

But Bob Dylan's words filled the air even deep in the heart of Texas: "The Times They Are A-Changing." On other Texas campuses there were miniskirts, student protests against the war, and LSD. People were performing nude on Broadway. Cissy hadn't read Betty Friedan's *The Feminine Mystique,* but she had read about it. Texas Women's University, with its dress codes and curfews, was a safe haven for girls with a more traditional bent.

When Lottie Sinclaire returned home from a formal dance at North Texas State with an engagement ring on her finger, the news spread through Sayers Hall like a prairie fire, and everyone gathered in the downstairs lounge to hug and squeal and cry. Even the resident adviser joined in, bringing a box of chocolates to pass around.

Lottie was given a seat of honor while everyone serenaded her with "I Love You Truly" and listened in rapture while she told them that she would be married on campus, in the Little Chapel-in-the-Woods, where her mother had been married. She would have an evening wedding with dozens of candles and flowers everywhere. Her wedding portrait would be made in the botanical garden. Her wedding dress would have an Empire waistline and a six-foot train. Her parents wanted her to finish school, but Joey was a senior, and all she wanted was to marry him and have babies.

Every girl in the room, even Becky Clarke, who planned to be an archaeologist and spend her life discovering the buried mysteries of mankind, had envy in her eyes, imagining herself as the princess bride walking down the aisle of the beautiful Little Chapel-in-the-Woods.

After her freshman year in Denton, Cissy would take the remaining three years of her nurse's training at Parkland Hospital in Dallas, where President Kennedy had died. Randy Calhoune would be in Dallas, too. He had grown up in Dallas and planned to go to medical school there.

Dallas. A real city with skyscrapers. The thought of living there both scared and excited Cissy. She would live in the TWU dorm, but as an upperclass student, she would have more freedom. Somehow she would learn her way around. She wanted to visit museums, libraries, and even the fabled Neiman Marcus. Now she wondered if she would do those things alone or with Randy Calhoune at her side.

Gradually, she found herself thinking more about Randy than about her studies. Her eyes refused to focus on the zoology textbook propped on her knees. At the end of her political science class on Friday, she'd realized with a start that she hadn't written a single coherent sentence in her notebook, couldn't recall a single word of the lecture. And she actually liked the class, found the subject matter and the crusty female professor fascinating. But she had spent the entire hour touching the skin on her arms and imagining what it would feel like for Randy Calhoune to touch her there. So far, there had been no touching, only smiles.

She shook her head to bring the words of her textbook into focus. She liked zoology, too. She stared at the pictures of a chick embryo and a human embryo. They looked the same. All races and all species started out pretty much the same. That seemed profoundly important to Cissy.

She had always loved learning—that and being good were the things that defined her: straight A's, with "excellent" checked under deportment. For the last two weeks, however, ever since Randy had stopped her after church and asked if she were related to anyone in Dallas, she had lived in a fog and learned almost nothing.

It had been windy, and Cissy clung to her skirt while Randy explained that an associate of his father's was named Stewart. Aaron Stewart. He'd come from a big family.

He knew her name, Cissy realized. How extraordinary. He must have asked someone.

Cissy had never felt so flattered in her life. Actually, he'd probably had to ask more than one someone. The only people in the congregation who knew who she was were girls from Sayers Hall. And some of them probably didn't know her last name.

Cissy said that she didn't know of any relatives in Dallas, that she was from south Texas. The Stewart name in Colorado County dated back to the Stephen F. Austin Colony. Rufus Jereco Stewart had been one of the founders of Columbus, the county seat.

He hadn't known there was a town in Texas named Columbus, so Cissy explained where it was and how many people lived there. Just a little town, she told him, with a handsome courthouse and wonderful live oak trees.

Randy was tall and slender with wavy brown hair and matching brown eyes. He had a sensitive face, a beautiful mouth, and elegant hands—like a piano player's or a surgeon's, Cissy had thought. He'd asked about her major, if she attended University Methodist regularly; she had asked like questions in return.

That first encounter had been pleasant but hadn't sent her over the edge. Two days later he called to ask if he could drop by the dorm.

Several girls were half watching television in the downstairs lounge, waiting to see who was going to come down the stairs and pair up with the good-looking guy. Cissy could see the surprise in their eyes when she appeared and he stood and said how glad he was to see her again. They walked over to the student union and talked over coffee. She learned that his father and grandfather were both doctors. His mother raised money for the Dallas symphony and a school for deaf children.

"My family has a store," she said. "It still says 'Stewart's Dry Goods' on the front, but now we sell only men's and boys' wear and sporting goods. Our house was a showplace a few generations back, but we can't afford to keep it up, and it's gotten seedy."

On the way home, she wondered why in the world she'd said such a stupid thing. He didn't need to know she lived in a run-down house. On second thought, though, maybe it was best. If he didn't date girls of modest means from small towns he had never heard of, it was best he learned the truth now instead of later.

Randy Calhoune called the following Monday evening to ask if she liked classical music—a guest cellist of some note was appearing the following Saturday evening with the university symphony. Again she found herself being blatantly honest. She had taken piano lessons from Miss Reese, who carried a gun and was such a staunch Confederate that she wouldn't sit on the north side of the church. Cissy had learned to play "Dixie" and a few hymns, but other than being able to recite the names of the great masters, she was sadly ignorant about classical music.

He asked her to accompany him anyway.

She said yes, of course, and that evening shyly told Margie that she had a date with a pre-med student from Dallas. Margie told everyone else. In the days that followed, Cissy was treated with a newfound respect by her dorm mates. She was no longer the little mouse on the third floor who had nothing better to do than study and clean her room.

Cissy spent most of Saturday afternoon fussing with her hair and agonizing over which of her two good dresses was more appropriate for a concert—the navy blue gabardine or the black velveteen. She tried out Margie's mascara and wiped it off. She put on nail polish and took it off. She felt sick to her stomach and hated her hair. She considered calling Randy to say she wasn't feeling well and even rehearsed the words she would say. But he called first. His grandmother was gravely ill; he was heading home to Dallas.

She was almost relieved, even if in truth he had found someone else to take to the concert—a girl who knew Bach from Beethoven and who had grown up in Dallas or Houston and had the perfect dress for every occasion.

She took off her dress, washed off her makeup, and curled up in bed with her books and notebooks. But instead of studying, she closed her eyes and allowed herself to create an imaginary evening with Randy Calhoune during which their shoulders touched while the cellist played so beautifully that tears came to her eyes. Throughout the last selection, Randy held her hand. And while they were still in his car, before he walked her to the dormitory door, he took her in his arms and kissed her ever so gently. Cissy put her hand to her mouth in imitation of that imagined kiss.

He called Tuesday evening to tell her that his grandmother had died. He wouldn't be back in Denton until Thursday. Would she go to the movie with him Thursday night? He was pretty sure *Funny Girl* would still be playing at the Lone Star.

"I'm sorry about your grandmother," she told him.

"Me, too," he said, and his voice broke when he added, "I'm going to miss her a lot."

Cissy felt too excited to study and took a walk around the campus.

A movie would be better, she thought, with not so much pressure about what to wear. But what if he tried to hold her hand? How should she act?

He kept his arm lightly across the back of her seat until the movie was almost over. Only in the last few minutes did he reach for her hand, while Barbra was singing the final song. It felt almost natural.

After the movie, they stopped at Denny's for coffee and stayed for two hours. She told him she was adopted. He told her that he was scared to death about medical school. What if he didn't make his grades? What if he threw up when he cut into a cadaver for the first time?

His dream was to be a plastic surgeon and work with burn patients, but if that didn't pan out, he would settle for being an internist or a family physician.

When he pulled up in front of Sayers Hall, he took her hand and kissed it. "I like you a lot, Cissy Stewart."

Cissy couldn't wait three whole weeks to call Iris. "I think I'm in love," she confided.

"Are you glad?" Iris asked.

"I don't know. Does falling in love feel like you were going a little crazy?"

"I'm afraid so, sweetie. It's a ride on a roller coaster, and sometimes it crashes, leaving you bruised and sore. I hope it works out for you. Remember when I asked you what kind of life you wanted? It's time for you to decide. Are you going to choose for yourself or let marriage choose for you?"

Iris was twenty-three now, in her second year of medical school. She had had lots of boyfriends over the years and even had been engaged once in college and wanted Cissy to be her maid of honor. But the young man had second thoughts about Iris's plans for medical school. Last year, she had gone with a law student at Columbia who planned to enter the diplomatic corps when he graduated. The woman who married him must be willing to spend her life moving from embassy to embassy.

"Where does Randy want to practice?" Iris asked.

"I don't know," Cissy admitted. "But he's considering family medicine. Maybe he could practice in Columbus or someplace close by."

"I thought you didn't want to go back to Columbus."

"I don't know. Part of me feels like I really should. Mama took care of Granny Grace, Grandma Polly, and Grandma Stewart. Who will take care of her?"

"My sweet Cissy, always the good little girl."

twenty-five

It was only three o'clock in the afternoon when Martha Claire returned much earlier than expected from a funeral in Rosenberg for her father's cousin Trudy. Arriving at the store, she found that the lights were off and the door was locked.

With a sigh of disappointment, she fished around for her key and went inside.

She turned on the lights and looked around. The merchandise on the sale table was all in a jumble. She could see by the shoes and shoe boxes scattered about that Buddy had waited on someone in the shoe department.

And the cash register drawer was open.

How much had Buddy taken? Martha Claire wondered. She simply couldn't get it into his head that every dime they took in each day had to be accounted for and deposited in the bank. Records had to be kept. She paid him what she could afford, and he absolutely could not help himself to more money whenever he felt like it. Or to the clothing. He could have clothing at cost, but a sales receipt had to be written and the transaction had to be run through the register. He could not just put something on and wear it out of the store.

He didn't pay rent and ate most of his meals at home, so he should have more than enough money to make payments on his used Ford pickup and to manage his few other expenses. But Martha Claire knew that he was already behind on the truck payments.

Buddy went out with his friends almost every night and didn't come back until all hours. Sometimes he didn't show up at the store until noon or later. He had no interest in inventories and ledger sheets. He was a good salesman, however, when he put his mind to it. Male customers would linger after they had made their purchase—to talk sports, often thinking of something else they needed to buy while they rehashed Dallas's victory over the Dolphins in the Superbowl or Buddy's game-saving tackle in the 1968 Cotton Bowl game. They would critique the high school's first black football coach and speculate about how state players would fare in the NFL draft. They talked about other sports, too, but it always got back to football. Sometimes Buddy even ignored other customers while they talked on and on about football.

It was just going to take time, Martha Claire told herself as she folded the sweaters on the sale table and put the shoes back in their boxes. Buddy still wasn't over the disappointment of being dismissed from A&M. Eventually, he would settle down and assume more responsibility for the store. She certainly wasn't going to give up on him.

Once she had become accustomed to the idea of Buddy's not going back to college, it began to appeal to her. If he had finished school and gone off to play professional football, she would be lucky to see him once or twice a year. But now her son could live here always.

She no longer loved her husband. Iris had run off with Justine. Cissy would probably never come back to Columbus and its tiny hospital—not after living in Dallas for three years and working in a huge, modern hospital with state-of-the-art everything. Besides, Cissy didn't need her the way Buddy did. In fact, when it came right down to it, Buddy was all Martha Claire had left. Without him, whom would she mother? If she had to make excuses for him, so be it. She would look the other way from time to time when he took money he did not earn. He was still just a boy really. He would grow up in due time. He just needed to sow his wild oats and get all that disappointment over A&M and football out of his system.

Grayson didn't agree with her. He kept insisting that Buddy was going to have to leave Columbus. "If he stays, he'll never amount to anything."

Grayson thought Buddy should join the army or learn a trade, like welding or auto mechanics. Only last week he'd told Buddy that he was going to kick him out of the garage apartment if he came home drunk one more time.

"This is my property," Martha Claire reminded her husband.

Buddy had smirked at his father. "Hear that, Dad? Guess we know who wears the pants around here, don't we?"

At five o'clock, Martha Claire decided that it was a good thing she had come home early from the funeral. In spite of a late-afternoon rainstorm, four customers had come in. Jane Myers exchanged a pair of shoes for her son and bought half a dozen pairs of athletic socks and two packages of T-shirts. Millicent Owens put a tweed sports coat on layaway for her husband's birthday. Lanella Willis bought a pair of house slippers for her husband, the sheriff. And Uncle Ezra Washington, with his shiny vintage Cadillac parked out front, purchased fishing line and sinkers. Uncle Ezra had taken care of old Mr. Goodpasture for years, and the old man left his house and the Cadillac to Ezra.

By the time Martha Claire had swept the floor and cleaned the glass showcases, she was tired and ready to go home. It had been a long day, and funerals were such a drain.

Poor Trudy. She hadn't known up from down for decades, but once upon a time she'd been a spirited, handsome woman with fiery red hair and a hearty laugh. When they were growing up, Martha Claire and Justine spent a week with her in the summer, and she would let them play dress-up with her clothes and showed them how to milk a cow and kill a chicken. She had been the youngest of the Mayfield cousins, the last to die. Now Martha Claire was a family elder—she and Justine. Several people asked about Justine today. Martha Claire would say that she was just fine, that she still lived in New York. And Iris, too. Yes, Iris was in medical school. No, neither one of them had been back to Columbus in a good long while.

Buddy probably wouldn't come home for dinner—not if he'd already headed off with his friends. Tonight it would be just her and the television set. Martha Claire wished it were Friday and she knew that Grayson was on his way home. She didn't like going home to an empty house.

This weekend, she didn't want to fight about Buddy. She planned to tell Grayson that. There wasn't anything he could say that would make her send Buddy away, so there was no point in discussing it. Buddy had a good heart. He would come around. Grayson would see. The boy had had a bad time of it. It wasn't his fault that he wasn't bright like his sister.

She would cook a pork roast with stewed apples for Friday night dinner. Grayson often didn't arrive home until eight or later, but always she had a hot meal waiting for him.

He called Friday morning, though, to say he was making a call in nearby Sealy and should be home by six. "Tell Buddy that I expect him to have dinner with us. If you go to the trouble to cook a meal, he should be there to eat it. And I thought we could sit down after dinner and look at some of the brochures I've sent for. There are some excellent vocational programs around the state."

Martha Claire started to snap at him, to say that she had no intention of sending Buddy away, but she held back. She wanted a nice evening. Besides, Buddy wouldn't show up for dinner anyway. He never did when Grayson was home. He didn't want to hear his father's lectures about responsibility and planning for the future.

Sure enough, right before closing time, Buddy left the store—to run an errand, he said. Martha Claire knew she wouldn't see him until he dragged himself out of bed Saturday morning. Sometimes she did half wonder if maybe Grayson was right, and they should use a heavier hand with Buddy. But if they did that, the boy might move away, and Martha Claire could not accept that possibility.

The first thing Grayson said when he walked in the door was "Where's Buddy?"

Martha Claire couldn't help herself. She put her hands on her hips and told her husband that Buddy was having a hard time adjusting. Yes, he drank too much, but he just needed time to get himself straightened out. It just took longer for some young people than others. Buddy needed time. Maybe someday he would learn to drive sixteen-wheelers or become a ferrier or a welder, but it had to be something the boy himself decided and not something his father dictated. And she didn't want to hear another word about sending him away, not for now anyway. Maybe in a year or so, if he still hadn't settled down.

"It probably doesn't matter anyway," Grayson said, tossing a packet of brochures in the trash. "He's probably going to be drafted anyway. He'll end up crawling around a jungle in Southeast Asia."

Cissy was home for spring break when Buddy's draft notice arrived. She felt fearful and relieved at the same time. His presence in Columbus had put a greater strain on their parents' already tenuous relationship. Her father had moved back into Granny Grace's old bedroom, her mother almost never smiled, and Cissy feared that Buddy was on his way to becoming a worthless bum. But young men were coming home from Vietnam in body bags. Already more than a dozen Colorado County boys had been killed. It was such a confusing war—one hardly knew what to believe about it. She certainly didn't believe in it enough to be willing to sacrifice her brother.

That night at dinner everyone tried to put a good face on the situation. Draftees had to serve only eighteen months, and a lot of draftees got stateside assignments. Buddy also had heard that many U.S. Army posts had football teams and that generals really got off on having winning teams. If he could play on a military team, maybe he wouldn't have to go to Vietnam at all. He even knew the name of an NFL player who had once played for some army team.

After dinner, Buddy wanted Cissy to go drinking with him—just for a couple of beers. He and his friends had found a new place to hang out over by Alleytown. However, Cissy insisted they take a walk instead.

It was a beautiful spring night, with seemingly millions of stars overhead and the scents of wisteria and magnolia in the air. They walked downtown for an ice cream cone, then walked over to the Walnut Street bridge. Halfway across, they stopped and leaned on the railing. The moon, full and newly risen, made the river shimmer like liquid gold. The water made a heavy, sluggish sound as it flowed under the bridge. From the banks, a chorus of night birds and insects filled the night. "Remember all those canoe rides and picnics Justine organized?" Buddy said, gazing upriver. "We always had a good time with her."

"Very good times," Cissy agreed.

"It wasn't the same after Iris left."

"No. Iris was our sunshine."

"You still talk to her once a month?"

"Not always. We both have hospital schedules to contend with. But she knows all the important things that happen to us. Next time we talk, I'll tell her about the draft notice."

"Tell her I miss her, will you?"

"Yes, I'll do that."

"I'm a little bit scared," he admitted. "I want to go over there, but at the same time, I don't."

Cissy understood. *Vietnam*. The thought of going to war excited him, but he was afraid. "I think it's always like that, Buddy. Men like the idea of being tested, but they're afraid they won't measure up. And everyone is afraid of dying."

"Yeah. That's about it. Do you pray?"

"Not as much as I should, but I will pray for you every day if you go over there."

"You think it does any good?"

"I don't know. But it can't hurt. It gives a person a way to focus on things."

"Do you hate me for what I said that morning up in Denton?"

"Oh, Buddy, I could never hate you. We've always been close and depended on each other. Like Iris said, it's hard to tell one kind of love from the other."

"You told her what I said? She must think I'm weird."

"No. She thinks you have a lot of love and need to find the right girl to give it to."

"I don't get along with other girls. I'll never love anyone as much as I love you."

"No, you'll never love anyone *the way* that you love me, the way that you love your sister."

They were silent for a time. Cissy took a deep breath, inhaling deeply the clean night air. It was so pretty here, she thought. Her home. Columbus was in her blood, and maybe there was no escaping that. She reached over to take Buddy's hand and realized his shoulders were shaking with silent sobs. She put her arms around him, held him close. He was so big and strong, but a part of him remained a confused little boy still.

She would pray for him with all the strength of her being, even though she didn't believe that God would factor in a sister's prayers when deciding which boys should live and which should die.

When they got back to the house, their parents joined them on the front porch, where they drank lemonade and reminisced. The evening ended with Grayson telling once again the story of how Doc Hadley brought them Cissy and then six months later came back with Buddy. Cissy never tired of hearing it recounted and always got misty when her father said those were two of the three happiest days in his life. Cissy knew without asking that the other happiest day was when he married her mother. But she always asked anyway, marveling that he still felt that way.

Once her parents had loved each other completely. How could a love like that change and die? Cissy wondered. She thought of Randy Calhoune, who now filled her heart and soul. For two years now she had lived for his phone calls, his presence, his touch. True love was supposed to be forever, but the lesson she had learned from her parents told her that was not always so.

Later, lying in bed with her windows open, Cissy heard Buddy's truck back down the driveway, on his way to drink with his ne'er-do-well friends. "The lost boys," her daddy called them.

When Buddy completed his basic training at Fort Hood, he came home for one last weekend before he left for Vietnam. I drove down from Dallas to tell him good-bye.

Mama had cooked enough food for an army, but no one had much appetite. Mama suggested we play cards, but Buddy said he'd promised some of his friends he'd drop by. In the middle of the night, I heard him stumbling up the stairs to the garage apartment. He didn't come down for breakfast or lunch.

I had to get back to Dallas, so after lunch I went up to the apartment and knocked on the door. Buddy looked like death warmed over. We hugged. I cried and told him to take care of himself. All the way back to Dallas I kept wondering if I would ever see him again. I prayed to the god of prayers that I would, and that the army would make a man of him. Something sure needed to. If that war over there didn't destroy him, I feared he would end up doing the job himself.

I tried to call both Iris and Randy before I went on duty that night, but neither one of them was in. Randy was a first-year medical student now and labored long hours in the gross anatomy lab.

He was living at home, in the Highland Park area of Dallas. His parents' house was as big as a small hotel. The Calhounes were lovely people and included me in family gatherings and social events, but I was never quite comfortable in their world. For one thing, I didn't have the wardrobe for it. I never saw Randy's sister or mother wear the same dress twice, and I wore my few good dresses over and over again.

Randy planned for us to get married the week after he graduated from medical school. He had decided to vie for an out-of-state residency when the time came. I asked him to consider a program in New York City, so I would be near my relatives. I hadn't seen Iris and my aunt Justine in all those years—almost ten now. From photographs, I knew that Iris was still slim and fresh-faced. Justine looked older, of course, and more like Katharine Hepburn than ever, with an attractive gauntness and her graying hair never quite tidy. I had sent them pictures of us: big, burly Buddy; my father, who was still a handsome Southern gentleman but without the military bearing of his youth; and my mother, who was still pretty and surprisingly young-looking when she smiled.

I suspected that my father had now taken up permanent residence in the spare room and would never again be welcome in my mother's bed. Their war over Buddy seemed to have eroded whatever goodwill they had reconstructed in the years since Iris left. I often wondered why my father didn't find someone else—a sweet, uncomplicated woman who would not shut him out of her bed, who would hold him in her arms and love him tenderly. Surely women out there in all those little towns he visited noticed him and recognized his kindly soul. I almost wished that one of them would steal him away from Mama, except I suspected that my mother needed him around more than she realized and that her life would be quite empty without him.

After falling head over heels in love with Randy, I found myself pulling back, little by little. I still loved him dearly and hoped to spend the rest of my life with him, but I knew that I wouldn't wither up and die if that did not come to pass.

Randy had given up any thought of a general practice, and he was no longer considering plastic surgery. He was now debating between orthopedic surgery and thoracic surgery, which meant that he would need to be affiliated with a major medical center, probably in Dallas or Houston. He assumed that after we married I would magically turn into a gracious, fashionable woman and take my place in society, as his mother had done. I could not imagine re-creating myself in his mother's image, but maybe it would be absolutely glorious having a closet full of beautiful clothes and a home with a grand entry hall and a curving staircase.

His mother kept asking when she and "the doctor" were going to meet my parents. Soon, I would say.

I finally did take Randy to Columbus to meet my folks. Mama and Daddy had absolutely knocked themselves out to get the house and yard in shape. Randy was actually quite impressed when we pulled up out front. Of course, once he went inside he would surely notice the sagging floors and stained ceilings, but on first impression it was a truly handsome house with its broad porch and gingerbread trim, its round attic window and high pitched roof, surrounded by a stately grove of venerable trees.

No sooner had Randy turned off the motor than the front door opened and Mama and Daddy came out to greet us. I paused there on the sidewalk to take a mental picture of them standing side by side on the front porch, Mama in a new floral silk dress, Daddy in a coat and tie. They looked dignified—patrician even—this son and daughter of old Columbus. My chest swelled with pride, and my eyes filled with tears. God, how I loved them, with all their secrets and complexities. If only I could fix whatever was broken between them and make them happy once again.

My dad had inherited forty acres of bottomland from his mother and sold off most of it to a cotton farmer, saving a river-hugging sliver for himself—for a fishing shack. He used the money from the sale to pay taxes and to buy a newer station wagon, but he saved back enough to bulldoze a narrow lane, buy construction materials, and dig a well and an outdoor toilet.

After my brother left for Vietnam, Daddy built a one-room cabin with a porch that overlooked the river. He slept out there sometimes, but usually not. I think he was looking ahead to retirement and knew that he wanted to have a retreat, someplace to which he could escape from Mama.

My mother was more hurt than angry about the cabin. More and more, my heart went out to her. Her marriage was a shell. Buddy and I were gone. She was still involved at church, but she hadn't had time for any of the ladies' clubs in years. She and Daddy occasionally played bridge on the weekends with old friends, but Daddy was only a part-time resident of Columbus, which limited my mother's opportunities for a life outside the store.

Buddy was assigned to a quartermaster unit in Saigon. He never wrote, but he did call home every couple of weeks. Mama said that he liked it there and actually seemed to be enjoying himself. No one shot at people in the quartermaster corps.

After a year and a half, Buddy returned to Columbus and the rent-free garage apartment seemingly unchanged from his time in a war zone. He still had no ambition and was as irresponsible as ever. Mama claimed he was an immense help at the store, but I knew that wasn't so. I suspected that my brother had become an alcoholic or worse. I knew I should go home and confront him, make him see a doctor or join AA, but I didn't. Sometimes, as I finished up my last year of nurse's training and spent as much time with Randy as our schedules allowed, Columbus and the problems there sometimes seemed very far away.

Randy wanted to give me an engagement ring, but I told him I wasn't ready. I loved him then but thought of my parents and wondered how I might feel about him in fifteen or twenty years—and how he would feel about me.

❧❧

twenty-six

As wakefulness invaded the fog of Buddy's morning hangover, he realized even before he opened his eyes that there was too much light in the room—offending light that energized his headache and made it pulsate with even greater vigor.

Obviously, the window shades were up—not something he had taken note of when he'd arrived home last night, not with his old man sitting on the sofa waiting for him.

His mother must have been up here yesterday. Mom was a great one for sunlight.

Yesterday. That would have been Sunday.

Sunday afternoon, he and some buddies had driven over to Rek Hill—to the cockfights. He'd lost a week's wages, he recalled.

Shit. He'd have to ask his mother for an advance. She'd told him she wasn't going to do that anymore, but he knew he could talk her into it. He'd straighten up the back room before she asked, maybe offer to take her to the movies.

His mom raised the damned shades every time she came up here. When he was a kid, the first thing she'd done in the morning when she came to wake him for school was raise the shades, telling him that God had blessed them with a brand-new day.

He considered it an invasion of his privacy for her to come up here when he was gone. It was nice, though, having the sheets changed once in a while. And she did gather up his dirty clothes and wash them for him. It wasn't right to expect her to do that for him, he supposed. He was twenty-four years old and should be looking after himself.

When he was a kid, he'd had to change his own sheets and gather up his own dirty clothes. He and Cissy and Iris didn't get their allowance on Saturday morning unless they had finished their chores and their rooms had passed inspection. Now, the rules had changed. Mama did everything for him, even put his clean underwear in the bureau drawers. All she expected of him was that he show up down at the store. Five and a half days a week—like a prison sentence.

At least she had given up trying to teach him about stocking and inventory, and about bookkeeping and taxes. Now they had pretty much agreed that she would always take care of the business side of things, but he was to carry his weight by looking after customers. She had to be able to count on his being there, she insisted. She had earned the right to stay home once in a while, to work in her garden and paint stuff. His mother was always painting stuff. She wanted to start playing bridge again and going to guild meetings at the church more regularly.

Since it was Monday, he really should get up and go down to the store, he told himself. And he imagined for a minute the delighted look that would appear on his mother's face if he actually showed up on time.

Sometimes he wondered how long she was going to put up with him. He realized that his parents had hoped the army would transform him, that he would come back a more responsible person who hung up his clothes and showed up at work on time. His father had hoped for more than that—he had wanted Buddy to make the army a career.

But it hadn't worked out. Stuff had been missing from the warehouse where he worked. Tires and car parts mostly—stuff that brought good prices on the black market in Saigon. He hadn't actually taken anything himself, but he had looked the other way a few times and, as a result, almost ended up with a dishonorable discharge. He really lucked out there. The officer who investigated the case had been from LaGrange—a Texas Aggie, even. He remembered the '68 Cotton Bowl game and told Buddy he'd fix things this time. But the officer warned that he would be keeping an eye on him and that Buddy sure as hell better keep his ass clean or he would personally see to it that Buddy did time, Texas boy or not.

His parents didn't know about any of that. They also didn't know about the girl he beat up. He'd really liked her, too. Ha was her name. A pretty little thing. Vietnamese girls weren't stuck up, and they expected a guy to call the shots. He couldn't even remember now why he'd hit her. He'd paid her father five hundred dollars to keep him from going to the military police.

Buddy tried to decide if he should get up and close the shades or just get up.

His dad had been waiting for him last night, sitting there on the sofa when Buddy had come stumbling in the door. Buddy groaned again, remembering. He had promised his dad that he would be home for supper Sunday evening. Afterward they were going to do a little night trolling. And his dad had been hot to talk to him about something. But Buddy had forgotten to show up.

He couldn't believe that his dad had been sitting up here all that time, waiting on him. He'd never done that before. Buddy apologized, of course, and made promises about next weekend.

His dad had not said it was all right, but he hadn't yelled or anything. Dad never raised his voice. Maybe if he did, Mama wouldn't treat him like a hired hand.

His dad told him to sit down. Buddy almost missed the chair, and Grayson grabbed his arm and helped him get situated. Then he sat back down on the little sofa and said his piece. He said he loved Buddy very much and wanted what was best for him. It was time for him to get his act together—past time, in fact. The drinking had to stop, and Buddy was going to need help doing that. There weren't any programs in Columbus to help folks with drinking problems, but Buddy needed to move on anyway.

"Could we talk about this some other time?" Buddy finally asked, trying hard not to slur his speech. His head was spinning. He needed to pee. "I'm really beat," he said, trying to explain.

"And really drunk," Grayson said in a soft voice that Buddy found irritating. "And you need a haircut. You haven't shaved in days. You smell like a locker room. You are pickling your brain, son. I love you too much to let this continue. I mean it, Buddy. You've got to get a real job and get help for your problem."

Buddy hoisted himself out of the chair and staggered into the bathroom to relieve himself. Then, without zipping his pants, he crawled onto the bed. "Mama says I can stay here forever if I want to. And for your information, I am not an alcoholic. I never have a drink until after five o'clock, and all I ever drink is beer. You aren't an alcoholic unless you drink whiskey in the morning."

Grayson stood. "Friday evening, when I get back, I expect you to be here," he said, looking down at his son. "Do you understand me, Buddy? I want you home and sober. We *are* going to talk about this."

"Yeah, yeah, yeah," Buddy said, closing his eyes.

He felt the bed sag as his father sat down beside him and put a hand on Buddy's arm. "We are going to work through this. I have some ideas I want to try out on you, ideas about job training and getting off the booze. I'll help you all I can, but you have got to leave here, Buddy. Nothing is going to change as long as you stay here and let your mother give you money for doing not much of anything. You are wasting yourself here when there are lots of things you could be doing with your life."

"Yeah, maybe I can follow in my old man's footsteps and be a sales rep for Happy Feet Shoes. Talk about a wasted life!"

His father looked away. As soon as he'd said the words, Buddy wanted to take them back, to say he was sorry. His father led a shitty life, but he was doing what he had to do to support his family. That made it different. Not a waste. Buddy wanted to explain why he couldn't leave Columbus, not a third time. He'd flunked out at A&M and almost ended up with a prison sentence when he went to Vietnam. He didn't have the courage for a third time. In Columbus, he was safe. He needed to stay here. He was going to start showing up on time down at the store and put in regular hours, not lock up and leave the minute his mother left him in charge. Really he was. He wasn't going to fuck up a third time. A guy had just so many chances. He wanted to explain that to his father.

But Buddy hadn't said anything. He was starting to feel really bad and needed to sleep. He rolled toward the wall, pulled a pillow over his head, and waited for his father to leave.

Finally, he heard the bed creak as Grayson got up. Buddy held his breath until he heard the door open, then close, and his father's footsteps going down the wooden stairs. As he let out his breath, he whispered, "Go to hell." But he hadn't meant it.

And now, the next morning, he thought about the promises he'd made to himself last night. It was time, he told himself. Starting today, he was going to put in a full day down at the store. When Dad got home Friday evening, Mama would tell him what a good job Buddy was doing. Then they wouldn't have to talk about laying off the booze or career choices or his moving away.

Buddy rolled his feet onto the floor and pushed himself to a sitting position. Then he had to sit still for a while, letting his head adjust to being upright. He considered taking another leak and crawling back into bed. Tonight, he would drink less beer and be ready for tomorrow, when he would turn over the new leaf.

Maybe it was now or never, though, he decided. Even his mom wasn't going to put up with him forever.

He took a long shower, shaved, put on a clean shirt. His head still throbbed, but he felt like he had a purpose.

His mother didn't look so much delighted as relieved when he walked in the back door of the store even before she'd unlocked the front one. It was sidewalk sale day, and he helped her move tables and sale merchandise outside. He spent the day out front, which wasn't so bad so long as he wore sunglasses. People stopped by to talk sports, the only world in which Buddy was comfortable. Some folks assumed since he'd been in Vietnam he kept up with what was going on in the war over there. He'd act like he knew what they were talking about when they mentioned My Lai or Haiphong, and then he'd turn the conversation back to sports at the first opportunity.

Friday night, his dad presented his list of career options for Buddy: welder, ferrier, oil field roustabout, longshoreman, truck driver, bricklayer, bulldozer operator, firefighter, policeman, highway patrolman, barber—the list went on and on. He even had brochures and application forms for training programs.

"And who is going to support him while he learns a new trade?" Martha Claire demanded.

"We will."

"He needs to work at the store. It will be his someday."

"Martha Claire, the store makes less and less money each year. With the new highway, people are driving to Houston or shopping at the discount stores in Yoakum and El Campo. It's only a matter of time until they build a Kmart or the like in Columbus."

Buddy sat watching his parents argue about his future, talking about him as though he weren't there. His dad thought he would turn into the town drunk if he stayed in Columbus. His mother said it was ridiculous for him to move away when he had a rent-free apartment here and a home-cooked meal whenever he wanted it. And she had ideas of her own. The town was starting to get a lot more tourists. They could turn the store into a gift shop that catered to the out-of-towners. And they could take out a mortgage on the house, turn it into a bed-and-breakfast. They would need Buddy more than ever to help manage things.

In the end, nothing was decided. Grayson thrust the brochures and forms into Buddy's hand. Back in his apartment, Buddy tossed them on the table and pulled a six-pack out of the refrigerator.

The last Sunday in May, my parents and Buddy drove up to Denton for the Texas University for Women commencement ceremony. Even though my nursing class had spent the three years in Dallas, we were honored alongside the rest of the class of '72.

During the ceremony, looking out at the sea of faces, I found myself thinking of my birth mother. I never wanted to meet the woman, but I would have liked for her to know that the baby girl she had birthed and given away had grown up to be a nurse. I graduated with highest honors and even won the Florence Nightingale Award for most exemplifying the highest ideals of nursing. I had worked hard to make my parents proud.

Randy Calhoune sat with them. He had given me a birthstone ring as a graduation present. A friendship ring, he called it, which meant we were engaged to be engaged. My mother seemed as happy about that prospect as she was about my diploma.

I had worried that Buddy would feel resentful. After all, I had succeeded at college, and he had not. But he told me how proud he was, and with tears in his eyes.

And back home, after the celebratory dinner my mother prepared, she and Daddy presented me with a hope chest. Inside were my Granny Grace's wedding dress, a tablecloth crocheted by Grandma Polly, and Grandma Stewart's sterling flatware.

I had already opened in private my package from Iris and Justine. Inside was a gold watch from Tiffany's that must have cost enough to buy five or six hope chests. Never in all the years since have I worn that watch in my mother's presence.

Buddy gave me a book on the history of nursing. He had called a bookstore in Houston to order it. It had been his own idea, and he was quite proud of himself. Tucked inside the book was an envelope. "You can read that later," he said.

Later, sitting on the side of my bed, I read Buddy's note, which was carefully printed and without a single misspelled word. He wrote that I was the smartest, sweetest person he had ever known and that no other girl would ever measure up to me, that he would do anything for me, even die for me.

I knew that my brother would always love me. I wasn't so sure about Randy.

The friendship ring on my finger was supposed to have been an engagement ring, but once again I had asked him to wait. He had not protested greatly. There was plenty of time, he supposed. He still had years of training ahead of him.

Eventually, of course, my foot-dragging turned into a decision of sorts, and he found someone else. Even as I suffered the pain of rejection and the genuine sadness that comes at the end of a relationship, I felt as though a burden had been lifted from my shoulders. My future no longer was laid out in front of me like a road map, a situation that was a bit frightening but also exciting.

I was a better nurse after that. I became a professional, not just a girl biding her time until the wedding bells rang. Dedication surged through me. A sense of renewal buoyed me. I felt myself taking crisper steps as I walked down the hospital corridors. My hands became more deft as I ministered to my patients.

I began to think about additional training—to become a nurse-anesthetist maybe. Or I could earn an advanced degree and join a university nursing faculty. With Randy out of my life, whichever option I decided to follow, I could do it in Houston. With the interstate highway, Columbus and Houston were now just an hour apart.

I actually looked forward to being the dutiful daughter once again. My parents needed me, and I needed them. They were a part of me as nothing else in my life.

If Buddy had been a more devoted son, if Iris wasn't lost to them, if Justine still came to visit, if they had a joyous marriage and hordes of close friends and money in the bank, I might have felt less connected to them. As it was, I was needed. One of my favorite hymns had always been "Blest Be the Tie That Binds." I can still remember my daddy and Iris singing it, with Grandma Polly accompanying them on the piano.

twenty-seven

Over the years, uniformed army officers would always garner a second look—just in case. It wasn't that Justine was expecting or even hoping to see Cameron Russell again. A military uniform just made her think of him, and after all, most men in uniform were worth a second look. She admired their bearing, their spit and polish, their leanness.

Dozens of uniformed men were lunching at the Anderson Air Force Base Officers' Club, most in air force blue, but some in army green. Out of habit, she scanned the room.

And there he was.

Justine caught her breath and quickly moved her chair a few inches to remove herself from his line of vision.

Very carefully, she leaned forward for a second look. It was truly him. Truly Cameron Russell.

Justine felt as though she had been jabbed by a cattle prod. *Cameron Russell, after all these years!* She put her hands to her face, rubbed her temples. Beloved Cameron. *Oh, my God.*

Once again, she leaned forward, cautiously peering around the handsome black officer at the next table. Cameron had been a major back then, now he was a major general with two stars on each shoulder. His hair was gray. He was lean, tan, magnificent. And with his family—a handsome wife in an impeccably tailored suit, two teenage daughters who looked like their mother. Had it really been that long?

But then Iris had been almost seven when the Korean War ended and she and Cameron began their affair. Iris was almost thirty now. Almost two dozen years had gone by, and she still thought of him during late, lonely minutes while she was waiting for sleep. Sometimes her thoughts were laced with regret. Sometimes she just wished she could see him again.

And here he was.

A wave of light-headedness washed over her, and she reached for a glass of water.

Her hand was trembling. She put down the glass and clutched her hands together in her lap.

The last time she had seen him was that bittersweet day at West Point, the day she could have said yes—and ruined his life. Or hers. Either there would be no stars on his shoulders, or she would have turned into the perfect lady at his side.

But, oh, how she had loved him! She hadn't realized then just how much she loved him, how painfully she would miss him.

No man since had ever captured her heart like Cameron.

Justine tried to hold back the flood of memories, but they came anyway. The first time they'd made love was in a traditional Japanese inn at the base of Mount Fujiyama. He had a week's R&R. She had followed him there, to that oasis from the war. Surrounded by ageless beauty, they had primed themselves with sake and lolled in the private bathing pool adjoining their room. Their futons had been rolled out and waiting for them. She had imagined lustiness, but that first time had been tender. So tender. Every touch. Every kiss. It had filled them with wonder.

Then there had been all those weekends in New York, dancing, drinking, laughing, loving. And a leisurely week spent exploring the coast of Maine. She had put off visiting him at West Point, not wanting to see him in his element, not wanting him to see what a misfit she was in his world.

"Are you all right?" Maggie Harrison asked. Lovely Maggie, who had opened her heart and home to Justine over the last week. Maggie would be a general's wife someday, now that her POW husband was coming home.

"I'm fine," Justine said.

"But you haven't taken a single picture in the last ten minutes."

Justine laughed. All she'd done for the past week was take pictures of Maggie and her children, and of her father-in-law and parents, as they prepared for this incredible day. She had taken pictures of them cleaning and cooking, going through photograph albums, bathing the elderly Labrador, praying at church, visiting the grave of the mother who had not lived to see her son come home.

A plane carrying air force pilot Colonel Billy Harrison and sixty-four other prisoners of war released from North Vietnamese prisons was scheduled to arrive in little more than an hour. Justine would be there to capture the first hugs and kisses as Colonel Harrison's family welcomed him home. Out of the hundreds of pictures she had taken, the editors of *Life* would select the ones that best captured the excitement and nervousness of the past week and the joy of a hero's homecoming.

And now, Justine's own bit of drama had injected itself into this remarkable day. *Cameron*. A married Cameron. A husband and father. She could have married him and had children with him.

But she had not done that.

Throughout the room, women were starting to gather up purses and children. Men were taking their last sips of coffee, the last bites of pie. It was time to go to the airfield. Justine knew it would take all of her concentration to get herself out of this chair and walk across the room.

"Do you know them?" Maggie asked.

"Who?" Justine asked as she pushed in her chair and hung her camera bag from her shoulder.

"You keep glancing at that family over in the corner."

"I knew the general once upon a time."

"General Cameron's son is coming home today with Billy—without one of his legs, apparently, but alive."

"Oh, God," Justine said. Suddenly, the room was spinning around her, and she grabbed the back of the chair.

Maggie took Justine's arm and helped her stay on her feet. "She ate something that didn't agree with her," she told her family. "There's plenty of time. Meet us in the hall."

Maggie helped Justine to the ladies' room. "Take deep breaths," she told her. "It will pass. I did the same thing when they called to tell me Billy wasn't dead after all."

Maggie put wet paper towels on Justine's forehead and spoke sooth-ing words. It would pass, she said again. Justine was a professional. Her automatic pilot would kick in, and she would take wonderful pic-tures of Billy's homecoming. Maggie didn't ask any questions. She was too much of a lady for that, Justine realized.

The family was waiting. Justine had fallen in love with all of them over the last week. They were a true family, a reminder of what she had missed.

Stephanie, the thirteen-year-old, burst into tears, and Maggie gath-ered the girl in her arms. "What if Daddy's not on the plane?" Stephanie asked. "What if it's all a mistake?"

Maggie soothed the girl and smiled at them all over Stephanie's blond head, Justine included. "It is time, my darlings," she told them.

"Hallejulah," said Maggie's father, a retired army officer, uniformed once again for this most special day, perhaps the most special of his lifetime.

"I want to tell you all thank you and good-bye now," Justine said. "I'll take my pictures at the airfield and disappear. I can't tell you what a privilege . . ." She stopped, her voice breaking. She really couldn't tell them. She was too overwhelmed.

Maggie's mother took Justine's arm, and they all marched out to the waiting cars. On the short drive to the airfield, Justine dug around in her camera bag and pulled out a wadded-up khaki hat and a pair of sunglasses. She didn't want to be recognized. She would not intrude on the homecoming of Cameron's son.

As the ranking POW on the flight, a gaunt Billy Harrison was the first returning hero to appear at the door of the transport, to wave and start down the ramp. Maggie ran like a girl across the tarmac, the oth-ers following. She literally flew into her husband's arms, and Justine was able to capture their first kiss with her zoom. Then the colonel em-braced his children and his widowed father, who was shaking with emotion, then Maggie's parents. Justine took thirty-six exposures with one camera and grabbed another. Whether that damned war was right or wrong had nothing to do with this day. She was photographing joy and dreams that came true for this remarkable family. Never in all her years of taking pictures had she felt more privileged.

The Harrisons were whisked away to privacy, and Justine doubted if she would ever see them again. But she knew she would never forget them, and she knew even before developing the pictures she had taken of them that they would be among her finest.

She stayed on to photograph the rest of the men being greeted by their loved ones. She would have done that even if Cameron's son weren't among them. He was the last POW off the plane, carried down by two medics, placed in a wheelchair at the bottom of the ramp. Cameron kneeled to embrace his son. His wife took her boy's face in her hands and covered it with kisses. His sisters caressed their brother's arms and hair.

Later that evening, Justine was drunk when she called Iris. "I just wanted to tell you that I am so glad I had at least one kid, and I'm glad that kid is you."

"Emotional day, huh?"

"Like no other."

"Come on home. I'll mother you."

"I'm the mother."

"Sometimes you are."

The pictures of the Harrisons occupied a four-page spread in the next issue of *Life*. The picture of Major General Cameron Russell kneeling to hold his son accompanied an editorial about the POWs' return.

The day after the magazine hit the newsstands, Cameron called. "Justine, this is Cameron Russell," he said, as though she would not have recognized his voice. "You're a hard person to track down. No one wanted to give out your phone number."

"I hadn't realized your son was one of the POWs. But then, I guess I hadn't realized you had a son. And two daughters. It must have been rough for you and your family."

"Yes, but we're okay now that Mike is back."

"What will he do now?"

"He's going back to school. He'd like to be an architect. He's a wonderful young man. So strong and brave." His voice broke, and he paused. "We knew that he was alive, but we didn't know that he'd lost a leg until three days before he was evacuated. It was a wonderful picture, Justine. I was stunned when I saw the credit line."

"I kept out of the way. You didn't need an old girlfriend hanging around on that day of all days."

"Yes," he agreed. "Thank you for that. How are you, Justine, besides famous?"

"How am I? Well, my daughter is a physician. I had a falling-out with my family back in Texas, so I'm pretty much a full-time New Yorker now. My friends are crusty old broads who have rallies for the Equal Rights Amendment. And that's pretty much it." She paused, then added, "I was proud to see those two stars on your shoulders. I'm glad everything worked out for you."

"Yes, I've have a good run. You were right; the good wives of West Point found me a wonderful wife. Barbara's father was a general. She knew how it was done. But it wasn't without pain, for her and me, until I learned to love her. We ended up with a good marriage, though, and a beautiful family."

"It was hard for me, too. You and I had a good thing going, but it wasn't meant to be permanent."

"I suppose. I wish I could have at least seen you at a distance the other day. I really don't want to go the rest of my life without ever seeing you again."

"It's better that way."

"Not even a drink for old time's sake?"

"Not even that."

"I can't just say good-bye."

"Yes, you can. Good-bye, Cameron."

"Good-bye, Justine."

Justine considered throwing herself on her bed and weeping. Instead, she walked in Central Park—all afternoon.

Cameron had wanted to see her again. Perhaps they could have begun anew. But she had already destroyed one good woman's happiness, and she didn't plan to ever do that again to another.

But then, when she turned in the picture of Cameron and his family along with the ones of the Harrisons, she had known the magazine would find someplace to use it. She had known Cameron would see it and the credit line, had known he probably would call. Had she wanted him to tempt her just so she could like herself better when she did not succumb? Or had she just wanted to reassure herself that he still cared?

Justine sat on a bench, closed her eyes, lifted her face to the sun, allowed her mind to wander.

Surprisingly, her thoughts did not immediately seek out Cameron Russell. Instead, she imagined her sister coming down the sidewalk and sitting here on the bench beside her. She imagined Martha Claire telling her that she'd come here to tell Justine that she could never forgive her, but she had decided to stop hating her. And Justine could, at last, come home.

Home. That word still evoked images of Columbus. Of Courthouse Square. The house on Milam Street. Huge, spreading live oak trees that made deep, wonderful shade on a sultry summer day.

twenty-eight

Bob Anderson regarded Martha Claire from behind his large, very cluttered desk. "What does Grayson think about this?" he asked.

Martha Claire shifted in her chair. Grayson wanted to sell the house. He called it an albatross. "He's not crazy about the idea," she admitted. "But it is my house."

The portly bank officer picked up Martha Claire's loan application. "This is a lot of money you're asking for."

"That's what it will take to fix up the house," she said, trying to keep the nervousness out of her voice.

When they were growing up, she and Justine used to play kick the can with Bob. He had spent a fortune fixing up his own family home.

"The plumbing has to be replaced and new bathrooms installed," she continued. "The kitchen will have to be modernized. I'll want to finish out the attic and put two bedrooms, a bathroom, and a sitting room up there. The estimates are all attached."

"A lot of money," Bob said again, glancing through the attached paperwork. "And what if this bed-and-breakfast idea starts catching on? Other folks with old houses could decide to fix up their houses and rent rooms. The town could end up with more guestrooms than it can support. I know the local tourist business is making some gains, but we're never going to be in a league with Galveston or New Braunfels."

"Mine would be the best," Martha Claire said with a lift of her chin. "I have the finest yard with all those wonderful old shade trees and my rose garden. Folks are always stopping to take pictures of my roses. I'm going to put an iron fence around the property, like it used to be before the war, and I plan to rebuild the gazebo. I also intend to build a pavilion on the east side of the house for parties and weddings—the estimate for that is attached, too. I'll do the catering myself. I can make the house pay its way, Bob. I know I can."

"Maybe so, maybe not," he said, leaning back in his chair, regarding her over the top of his reading glasses. "Do you really want to be starting something like this, Martha Claire, at your age? A place like that would be a lot of work, and we are getting on, you know. I'm looking forward to less time behind this desk and more time fishing and golfing."

"I don't fish or play golf. My house has always been my hobby, only I've never had enough money to do it right."

Bob nodded, acknowledging her point. "I do like to see Columbus folks hanging on to the old houses. So many of them are being sold to out-of-towners."

"I couldn't bear to sell the house. My people have been living there ever since my great-great-grandfather built it in 1852. But I might have to sell it if I don't get this loan. It's in desperate need of restoration. I can't fix its problems with more paint and wallpaper."

Bob picked up the paperwork again and stared at it. "If the bank does agree to finance this project, I'll have to have a mortgage on the house, Martha Claire. And I will need for Grayson to sign the note."

"But the property belongs to me," she protested.

"Yes, but it's going to take both of you to make this project work, and we've got to have a co-signer. The bank has to protect itself, you know."

Martha Claire narrowed her eyes. "And what if Grayson wanted to borrow money against the store? Would I have to sign that note?"

Bob grinned. "Ah, you modern ladies, always making sure you're being treated fairly. Yes, Martha Claire, indeed you would have to sign a note for any money Grayson borrowed. In most cases, our policy is to have both spouses sign. If you really want to do this thing, you'd better sit down and talk it over with Grayson. It's a big undertaking and a big debt to assume. Unless you both are completely behind it, I think you better forget about this loan."

She felt hot anger rise to her cheeks. As a child, Bob Anderson had been such a sissy, always running home to his mother. Once his mother had come bursting out of the house to call Justine a bully. And now that irritating little ninny suddenly had control over her life, had the right to tell her that no, she could not fulfill her dream. She wanted to swear at him, to tell him never mind, that she would take her business elsewhere. But if her hometown bank wouldn't loan her the money, how could she expect anyone else to?

She stood. Bob followed suit. "I'll talk to Grayson," she said.

"You do that," Bob said, extending his hand. "Then the three of us need to get together and go over these figures."

Martha Claire walked across the square to the store. The Closed sign was still hanging in the window. Buddy had promised he would open for her so she could keep her appointment at the bank.

Martha Claire turned over the sign and turned on the lights before she called Cissy.

Nurse Stewart would have to call her back, a terse female voice informed Martha Claire. It was after two when Cissy returned the call, breathless. Two nurses on her shift had called in sick, she explained.

Buddy finally had come in and was waiting on two men in the sports corner—hunters, from out of town. One of them had just told an off-color joke; she could tell by the way they were laughing and looking sideways in her direction.

When she finished telling about her visit to the bank, Cissy asked, "Are you sure you really want to saddle yourself with that much debt?"

"You know how I've been trying to fix up that house since before you were born, but it's been a losing battle. The only way I can get the money to restore it is to turn it into a business."

"And Daddy doesn't have a clue?"

"I wouldn't say that. I've been talking about it off and on for a couple of years, but he always changes the subject. I don't care if he likes the idea or not, but I do need for him to sign those papers, and I'm so afraid he won't do that."

"Why don't you ask Justine?"

"*Justine!*"

"It was her childhood home, too. She might want to help save it from being sold to strangers."

"It is your father's responsibility to help me. If he doesn't, the house will just have to fall apart around me. I will not move, and I will not go begging to Justine for help."

"I didn't say anything about begging, Mama. Can't you just call her up and ask her what she thinks you should do about the house? Or offer to make her a business partner. It would be an investment."

"I haven't talked to Justine in years—more than twelve years now."

"Why, Mama? I never did understand what happened between you two. Was it because she never helped you with Granny Grace and Grandma Polly, because you had to take care of them on your own? Or was it because she decided to take Iris away? Or was she mad because Grandma Polly left the house and all the furniture to you? Are you still mad because she left her emerald ring and Grandpa Walter's pocket watch to Justine? Whatever it is, don't you think it's time to deal with it?"

"No, I don't. And I'll thank you never to bring it up again."

Without bothering to say good-bye, Martha Claire hung up the telephone and stood there behind the counter, staring at the floors that Buddy had not swept, at merchandise that needed straightening, fingerprints on the showcases, a light fixture with a burned-out bulb. In the back room were boxes of underwear and fishing tackle that needed to be put out. She would like to turn the sign on the door back around and go home to her garden, where she could find comfort in chopping weeds, picking caterpillars off the tomato plants, standing with a hose and watching the graceful arc of water as she sprayed her plants— plants that had begun with seeds she had planted and nurtured. But she would not go home. She closed the store only for illness and bereavement. The only day she had closed the store on a whim was the day Buddy arrived home after being kicked out of Texas A&M.

Martha Claire and Grayson still had their Friday evening dinners—just the two of them. Buddy was seldom around on Friday evenings. And Grayson had given up on ultimatums.

He was going out with his friends, Buddy would say, which meant he was going drinking with whomever he could find. Two of his old high school buddies were divorced and usually available. Otherwise, Martha Claire supposed, anyone sitting alone in a bar became his friend. But as much as she hated Buddy's drinking, she liked Friday night dinners with just her and Grayson.

Strange how she still looked forward to them. She doubted if she and Grayson would ever again sleep in the same bed. They never kissed, never touched. But Friday morning she would wash her hair, and Friday evening she would rush home to prepare something nice for dinner. As she listened for his car in the driveway, she remembered the anticipation of waiting for him to arrive for a date all those years ago. Such memories were bittersweet. Their love had not endured. At least hers had not. She wasn't sure what his feelings were.

Over dinner, they would share any conversations they'd had with Cissy. Martha Claire would give him a report on the store and catch him up on town gossip. He would tell her about his week on the road, relating funny stories about people Martha Claire almost felt like she knew after more than a decade of hearing about them. They would discuss current events: the war in Vietnam was finally winding down, Nixon's presidency was unraveling, and gasoline prices were shooting sky-high in the wake of the OPEC embargo. Buddy would be mentioned only in passing. If they talked about Buddy or spending money on the house, they would argue. And they tried not to argue on Friday evenings.

After dinner, they would take a walk, play a few hands of gin rummy, and have a beer or a high ball while they watched television. Friday nights were an oasis in an otherwise unsatisfactory marriage. Unpleasantness was saved for Saturday or Sunday.

This Friday night, however, Martha Claire couldn't wait. She passed Grayson the bowl of mashed potatoes and told him all in a rush that she needed for him to stop by the bank in the morning and co-sign a mortgage so she could turn the house into a bed-and-breakfast establishment.

"Right now we are without debt, Martha Claire," he said, putting down the bowl, shoving back his chair. "That is one of the few things we have going for us. I know how much you love the house, but we're too old to take on a debt like that. I'd never be able to retire, and I'm tired—tired of life on the road, tired of traveling around year after year to the same little towns. If we sold the house, we could start over. We could buy a smaller place and travel some—maybe go to Europe. Just think of how tied down you would be with a bed-and-breakfast, how hard you would have to work. And don't tell me that Buddy would help you run it. Or that he'll run the store so you can be free to run it. We both know better than that."

"I want it more than anything," she told him. "And you owe me this, Grayson."

He met her gaze. "So, if I sign this note, does that mean an end to my penance?"

Martha Claire regarded her husband of more than thirty years. His hair was thinning, and he was a bit on the thin side, but she could still see in him the fine-looking young man she had set her cap for all those years ago. All she had ever wanted out of this life then was to marry Grayson Stewart and have children with him. Her only stipulation was that they stay in Columbus and someday live in this very house.

They never had been truly happy. At first it was the prospect of war hanging over their heads, then came the years of separation. After the war, he had resigned himself to a life of her choosing, and she had spent year after year dying a little every month when her period came. When she learned that her husband was the father of her sister's child, any chance they'd ever had for coming to terms with their disappointments and finding their way into a contented middle age vanished like a puff of smoke in a hard wind.

If she had never discovered the truth about Iris's birth, she could have lived the rest of her life in blissful ignorance—not gloriously happy but still in love with the man she had married. Her beloved Iris would still be a part of her life. She would still be able to reach for her husband in the night. If her children had grown up in a household with two parents who loved and respected one another, maybe they would be married themselves by now, and she would have grandchildren to love unconditionally. Then maybe this dilapidated old house wouldn't have become so important to her. As it was, however, all her hopes and dreams were invested in it. The house had become her lover, and it was her future. Her only chance for happiness was to turn her family home into a bed-and-breakfast. Mayfield House, she would call it. It would be a dignified establishment with a dignified history.

But Grayson wanted to strike a bargain. He would sign the papers at the bank if she would agree to renew their marriage. He knew she could never forgive him, but she could put his sin in a box and bury it out of sight. How remarkable to think that he still cared about her enough to want that. She should be flattered, she supposed.

She could tell him yes, that she would wipe the slate clean if he would only sign that note. He could return to her bed and her arms. They would forget the past and concentrate on the future.

But he had made love to her sister, and for twelve years she had had to live with that image. The two of them meeting someplace, kissing, undressing one another, exploring each other's bodies. She could see her husband's mouth at her sister's breast. Had he buried his face between her legs? Had Justine teased him with her mouth? When he finally entered her, they would have cried out in ecstasy. Their bodies would have glistened with sweat while they moved closer and closer to a climax. Oh, yes, she could see it all. She could see the act that had given her sister a baby when she herself would never have one.

She had never forgiven him, but for a time she had begrudgingly allowed sex because her body wanted it, and she had no other outlet for those desires except a husband she didn't love. She would close her eyes and turn him into some vague faceless lover, not Grayson, not the man she despised. Sometimes she couldn't help herself, and thoughts of him with her sister would force their way into her mind. Then she would push him aside and promise herself that she would never let him touch her again.

But she was weak. She would relent, telling herself that unsatisfactory, marginally disgusting sex was better than no sex at all. Even that ended when they started fighting about Buddy. Actually, it had been a relief of sorts. She could stop thinking of herself as a sexual being. That part of her life was over.

twenty-nine

Cissy's elderly landlady stood in the middle of the tiny apartment and clasped her hands to her meager bosom. "You have made it very pretty," Mrs. Tran said in her very precise English.

Cissy looked around, seeing it though Mrs. Tran's eyes. In the past week, she had painted the walls and ceiling, installed a ceiling fan, sanded and varnished the floors, hung wallpaper in the miniature bathroom, painted the table and chairs, and refinished the headboard on the bed.

"My goodness, where did you learn to do all this?" Mrs. Tran asked.

Cissy laughed. "I spent my childhood scraping and painting our old house in Columbus. I even know how to fix leaky faucets, lay tile, and install a windowpane."

"Well, I was skeptical when you said you wanted to do all this, but you have done a wonderful job, my dear," Mrs. Tran said, examining freshly painted window frames and the freshly starched curtains.

It did look nice, Cissy decided. A garage apartment, no less, just like back home. It was only a ten-minute drive to Houston's Baylor Medical Center and cheap enough that she didn't have to have a roommate.

She had disappointed her mother terribly when she accepted a position in the intensive care unit at Baylor. It was nursing at its most intense, triumph and loss on a daily basis. Maybe someday she would be satisfied with working in a small-town hospital, but right now she wanted challenges. She yearned to grow in her profession and learn all that she could.

Cissy remembered those wonderful train rides to Houston with Justine, Iris, and Buddy. The city had changed so much from those days as to be unrecognizable. The old buildings were gone, replaced by soaring towers with mirrored facades. Houston had become as cosmopolitan as Dallas, with a plethora of restaurants from international to barbecue, a symphony orchestra, a fine art museum, and people from all over the world. Mrs. Tran was Korean. Cissy's supervisor at the hospital was Filipino. Many of the physicians and residents were from South America.

Cissy had been lucky to find an affordable apartment close in. It was just one big room really, with a kitchen nook and a tiny bathroom, like the apartment Buddy lived in back home. She had considered renting something larger and farther out and inviting Buddy to live with her. She agreed with her father; Buddy needed to move away from Columbus and do something with his life other than being Mama's sometime assistant and errand boy. A big strong man like Buddy would have no trouble finding some sort of work in Houston, and maybe he'd find a wife, too, or at least a steady girlfriend.

Cissy worried, however, that living with Buddy would change the careful relationship they had established since his declaration of love four years ago in the Denton bus station. She felt young and lighthearted. She was excited about living alone for the first time in her life and about making friends. It wouldn't be the same if she assumed responsibility for her brother.

Her mother had insisted that Buddy was doing better, though, that he was drinking less, dating some, running the store on his own two days a week so she could garden and work at the house. There was always so much to do, her mother would explain, and Grayson would rather head out to his shack on the river than help her.

The dynamics of her parents' marriage had shifted once again since her father had refused to mortgage the house and let Mama start a bed-and-breakfast. Her father no longer automatically did everything her mother asked and spent more and more time in his fishing cabin. He had bought an old generator, and now the place had electric lights and even a television. He would work at the store on Saturday, but he refused to spend his weekend replacing rotting boards and patching leaks in the roof of his wife's house. He believed that Martha Claire needed to sell it while it still had value. It a few more years, he would tell her, it was going to be ready for a bulldozer.

Cissy's parents hadn't seen her new apartment yet. Buddy had helped her move up here, his truck full of odds and ends from the attic, much of it stored up there after Grandma Stewart died—dishes, kitchen utensils, a kitchen table, and a bed. Cissy had purchased a secondhand pull-out sofa, thinking her parents might stay over sometimes, but probably if they ever came, it would be one at a time. Buddy could come for overnight stays, however. She could handle one night, Cissy decided, if he didn't drink too much.

In reality, though, she realized that she would be the one to do the visiting, making frequent trips to Columbus to see her family, and maybe that was best. It was only an hour's drive on the new highway. She could keep her life here separate.

In September, her father did drive over for a weekend. Her mother felt they shouldn't both be away at the same time, he explained, in case Buddy had a problem at the store. "Of course, she could have closed the store for a few days, and no one would have known the difference. The truth of the matter is she feels like she's supposed to be at home in the evening in case Buddy decides to show up for dinner."

Cissy took her father through the intensive care unit where she worked, and they toured the Astrodome and Ima Hogg's home on Buffalo Bayou with its vast, beautifully landscaped grounds and wonderful collection of American antiques.

At the Houston Museum of Fine Art, he lingered in front of the paintings by European masters and told her how, after the war, he had spent many afternoons in the Louvre and traveled to Rome to see the Vatican art treasures. In Italy, even small churches in out-of-the-way towns often housed a masterpiece. Of course, when he was last there, much of Europe had been in ruins. But not all. There was still such splendor and history all around. Beautiful cities. Quaint villages. Wonderful farms. Kindly people.

"You always said you were going to go back to Europe someday," Cissy said and immediately wished she hadn't. The look of pain on her father's face made her look away.

"Yes, I always wanted to take your mother there, but I don't think she really wants to go. Once maybe, but not anymore."

"I'll go with you," Cissy said. "We can start saving our money right now. We'll rent a car and visit all the battlefields and all the museums."

Her father looked at her for a long moment. And smiled. "Yes, I believe you would like that."

They had dinner at a Mexican restaurant and drank more margaritas than they should have. She asked him more about Europe and the war and wondered why she never had done so before. He didn't talk about battles and killing, just about places—hill towns in Italy, seacoast towns in France, the whitewashed villages of Luxembourg. "I really meant that about going over there with you," she said.

"I know you did. And maybe we shall someday. But just knowing that you would like to do that is a wonderful gift."

"Maybe Iris could even go with us," she said, getting caught up in the fantasy. "Mama wouldn't need to know."

"Do you still talk to Iris?"

"Yes, but not like before. She's doing her residency, so she's as busy as I am. We're lucky to catch each other every other month."

"Please tell her that I think about her every single day."

Cissy realized her father had tears in his eyes and reached for his hand. "I will," she promised, then she added, "I love you, Daddy. Iris does, too. She says you are the finest man she's ever known."

Cissy didn't arrive home for Thanksgiving until almost eleven o'clock Wednesday evening, but her parents had been watching for her and came out to greet her, like always.

Her father carried her bags up to her room, and her mother insisted on putting out milk and cookies. The Thanksgiving pies were lined up on the counter, the turkey thawing in the refrigerator. Buddy was out, they explained. He had left directions to a roadhouse on the Brenham highway if Cissy wanted to drive over and meet his friends. Saturday night, she would go, Cissy promised herself. Tonight, she was tired. And she wanted to be here with her parents.

They sat with her at the kitchen table, quizzing her about work, the performance of the used Volkswagen bus she had bought, Houston traffic. Her mother promised she would get over for a visit soon. She would like to see where Cissy lived and worked.

As she watched her parents, she thought how handsome and digni-fied they were—aging certainly, but not old. Life had disappointed them, but as they sat here talking to her, their faces were filled with the pleasure of her company. Cissy felt guilty that she didn't come home more often. After all, she had decided on Houston so she would be close to home.

Cissy's bedroom was spotless, with a bouquet of dried roses on the dresser and her favorite picture of Grandma Polly newly framed on the bedside table. Lying in bed, she found herself remembering both good times and bad in this old house. The best had been family dinners when Iris was still with them and Granny Grace and Grandma Polly were still alive. The worst were after Justine took Iris away and her mother didn't come out of her room for three weeks.

Cissy awakened in the night to the sound of the phone ringing. She rolled over and stared at the clock. Three-fifty-seven. Then she looked out the window to see if Buddy's truck was parked by the garage. It was not.

She rushed out into the hall, but her father was already hurrying down the stairs, an anxious expression on his face. Her mother had come out of her room. Cissy stood with her mother at the railing. *Let it be a wrong number,* Cissy prayed, *or a fire at the store.* Or maybe Buddy had been arrested. A barroom brawl, perhaps, or drunk driv-ing. Nothing worse. *Please, nothing worse.*

When he hung up the phone, Grayson looked up at them. "There's been an accident. Buddy was coming back from Brenham. They're tak-ing him to the hospital there."

"Was he badly hurt?" Martha Claire asked, her voice trembling.

Grayson nodded.

Cissy drove, with her mother in the front seat and her dad in back, heading up Highway 109, the same county road she drove to College Station for all those study sessions with Buddy during his freshman year. Near Kearney, they passed a wrecker towing Buddy's hideously twisted pickup. It had been rolled. Martha Claire cried out, "Oh, my God!" and began to sob.

Cissy clutched the steering wheel and prayed with all her might that her brother would survive. Buddy had a good heart. He was just mixed up about things. She should have driven to Brenham tonight to meet him, no matter how late it was. She should have let him move to Denton. Insisted he come live with her in Houston. He had no business coming back to Columbus after A&M didn't want him anymore, after Vietnam. Buddy wasn't strong like she was. He needed her to take care of him. Yes, she would do that, when he was well enough. She would move to a larger place. She would nurse him back to health, help him get himself straightened out.

The nurse looked up as they rushed into the emergency room and paged the doctor. Cissy knew at once that Buddy was dead. It was too quiet. There was no activity, no ER staff racing around, no voices coming from a treatment room.

The slim, young doctor introduced herself and explained that Buddy had been dead on arrival. He had been thrown from the car, his neck broken. He had not suffered.

"Where is he?" Martha Claire demanded.

The doctor walked over to a door and opened it for them. "I'm sorry," she said and stood aside to let Martha Claire and Grayson enter.

Watching from the doorway, Cissy gasped as her mother pulled back the sheet exposing the face of her dead brother.

Martha Claire lovingly caressed Buddy's lifeless features, kissed his brow. Like a mother crooning to her baby, she called him Mama's good little boy, Mama's sweet little boy, the dearest little boy in the whole wide world. Then suddenly, she whirled to face her husband.

"Go ahead," she challenged. "Say it's my fault. I should have sent him away before it came to this."

Tears streaming down his face, Grayson shook his head. "No, it's my fault. I saw this coming and didn't stop it. I should have taken him a thousand miles from here and told him that he could only come home for Christmas."

Then Grayson approached the body of his son with halting steps and leaned forward to kiss his lips. He lifted Buddy's hands and kissed them, too. He stroked his hair. "Oh, God, my poor Buddy," he said.

"My poor little Buddy. We didn't do you any favor when we made you a member of this family. No favor at all."

Cissy realized her mother's knees were giving way and reached for her. The doctor pulled a stool over for her to sit on.

Then with sobs that felt as though they were ripping open her chest, feeling the worst pain she had ever felt in her life, Cissy approached her brother's body and lay her own across it. She was so sorry. So very, very sorry. And there was no way to make amends.

thirty

Their visit to the Brenham hospital lasted only minutes. After they said their farewells to Buddy, Cissy told the nurse the name of the funeral home in Columbus. And then there was nothing else to do but go back home.

A fine drizzle had cooled the air and left a sheen on the surface of the parking lot. *We are changed,* Cissy thought as they walked toward the car. *We are a family of three, when once we were five, with Granny Grace and Grandma Polly rounding out our household and Justine swooping in from time to time.*

Even then, through the intensity of her grief, other thoughts were threading their way into her consciousness. What was going to happen now? How was she going to manage the rest of her life? What was her responsibility to her parents now that Buddy was dead? They would need her more than ever now. Already she could feel that need sucking at her.

She drove away from the hospital, desperately trying to remember the way back to Highway 109. She glanced in the rearview mirror to see if her father might help, but he had retreated inside himself. Her mother was huddled against the door. Cissy was on her own.

Finally she found a road sign pointing the way. As she drove south, the first light of dawn erupted into a startlingly vivid sunrise, aglow with pink and orange and purple. Should she comment on it and try to make something spiritual out of the beauty revealing itself to them on this first morning of Buddy's death? But she didn't feel spiritual, and probably the sunrise had no greater meaning beyond the optic phenomena that had created it.

Cissy found it somewhat amazing that she was able to drive, to avoid potholes and brake at the occasional stop signs, when her entire body felt as though it had been emptied of substance. Everything seemed surreal, like the paintings by Dalí and Miró that she and her father had been drawn to in the Houston art museum. It was the same world out there—but somehow not the same. She was the same person—but not the same. Nothing would ever be the same again. The thought cut off her air and made her choke, made her eyes fill with tears. She needed to pull off the road and weep for Buddy and for herself. All her life there had been Buddy. They were Martha Claire and Grayson Stewart's adopted children. Now her brother was no more. She had lost a part of herself.

She drove on, of course, her weeping saved until later, until she had her parents safely home. They were almost to the Frelsburg turnoff when her father broke the silence and began a rambling monologue. "I never should have let him go to A&M. He should have played football at some small college where he had half a chance of getting through. If he'd gotten some sort of degree, he could have taught driver's ed and coached high school ball. He needed football. It gave him an identity, but I let him set his sights too high when I knew that his chances of succeeding were piss poor. And I knew he was never going to have a life down at that damned store. The store should have been closed years ago. People don't shop at little family-owned stores anymore. Buddy needed to drive trucks or move furniture. He could have found something respectable to do, something that let him like himself again."

He stopped as suddenly as he had started, and the car fell silent again.

Once home, her mother said she wanted to be alone. Cissy helped her up the stairs and onto her bed. While she was covering her with a quilt, Cissy heard her father's heavy footsteps on the stairs. The door to his room closed.

Cissy went downstairs and picked up the phone. It wasn't Sunday. It hadn't been a month since she had last talked to Iris. She didn't hide in the closet. She didn't call collect.

Iris answered at once with a crisp "Dr. Dover."

Cissy began to cry. "It's Buddy, Iris. Oh, dear God, Buddy is dead."

She heard her mother's door open, then her father's. She knew they were standing up there looking down at her as she told Iris, the banished child, what had happened to their Buddy, heard her pour out her heart, how she could have saved him, how she could have taken him in and watched over him. How she could have kept him from drinking and didn't. How Mama and Daddy never should have let him come back to Columbus and turn himself into a worthless freeloader. Now they were all prostrate with guilt and grief and couldn't even hug and cry together.

"Yes, you could have become his little wife," Iris said, "but would that have turned him into a man? In the end, Buddy had to take care of himself."

"No, you're wrong. The strong have to take care of the weak. I didn't do that. I was too selfish to help my own brother."

"Cut out the self-flagellation, Cissy," Iris said, her tone harsh. "Any fault on your part was doing too much for him, and now you're saying you should have just bellied up and been his nursemaid forever. You need to remember all the reasons why you love him and bury the rest. Honor his memory with clean, straightforward grief, without all that other crap messing it up."

When Cissy hung up the phone, she heard first her mother's door close and then her father's. She sat there in the hallway of her childhood home, where three happy children once had lived. She could almost hear their voices, their laughter, their footsteps on the stairs. Why had it all changed? Where had happiness gone?

Later in the day, Cissy called the few out-of-town relatives they had left—cousins and a great-uncle. She wrote out the information for the obituary and made the arrangements at the funeral home. She selected a modest casket for the son of a modest family. She wanted him buried beside his Grandma Polly.

The morning of the funeral arrived bright and fair. Cissy insisted that her parents come downstairs and eat breakfast. She stood over them, making sure they drank coffee and nibbled on some toast. When the funeral home limousine arrived, they were ready.

Cissy wanted her parents to hold hands or walk arm in arm, but there was no touching between them, not as they walked down the front walk, not in the limousine. Not a word passed between them as they rode to their son's funeral. They bore their misery in stoic silence.

The sunlight was white and intense, and once inside the church, it took Cissy's eyes a minute to adjust to the dusky interior, a minute to realize the smart-looking young woman standing in the vestibule was Iris.

Stunned, Cissy's hands flew to her mouth. *Iris!* She took a few halting steps, then suddenly they were embracing. It was really Iris! Her Iris, after all those years.

The tears flowed once again, her profound sadness mingling with such joy. Iris had come to help them bury Buddy.

Cissy kept saying her name over and over. *Iris.* Surely the most beautiful word in the English language. In the entire world.

Then Cissy felt Iris pull away and stood to one side so she could approach Martha Claire and Grayson—the aunt and uncle who had raised her. Martha Claire was standing erect. Grayson looked as though he was about to faint, his face white, his hands shaking.

"I had to come," Iris explained. "Buddy was like my little brother. Mother and I cried together. I am so sorry and know how you both must hurt."

Martha Claire nodded and allowed Iris to hug her, to kiss her cheek. Then Iris turned to Grayson. He stood like a statue while she embraced him, but tears were running down his cheeks.

They sat together in the front row, in front of Buddy's open casket, the five of them united once again. Cissy clung to her cousin's hand on one side, her mother's on the other. Her poor father was left with no hand to hold, no one to cling to.

Behind them, every seat was taken, and men were standing in the back. They had come to bury the boy who helped give them some of the best years of football Columbus High School had ever had. The musical selections included the high school alma mater and the "Spirit of Aggieland"—and, at Martha Claire's request, "Come to the Church in the Wild Wood." Grandma Polly had taught Buddy that song, and he was always wanting her to sing it with him—over and over again. Iris squeezed Cissy's hand to let her know that she remembered.

At the graveside, Martha Claire grew faint and almost fell off her chair. Grayson grabbed her and held her close, but soon she pulled away and sat rigidly in her chair, her gaze fixed on Buddy's casket. Reverend Huxley hurried to the end of his prayer.

The ladies of the church brought lunch to the house, and people came throughout the afternoon to offer their condolences and to see Iris.

"I remembered them all," Iris said later as she sat with Cissy at the kitchen table, drinking first coffee, then bourbon. "Even the people I hadn't thought of in years—I knew them all. God, it was as though I had never left. Some of them asked about Mother, but only when Martha Claire wasn't listening. Mrs. Lawson from the courthouse said how sad it was for family not to get along. They all must wonder what the hell happened."

"Don't we all?" Cissy commented.

They sat there into the night, reminiscing about Buddy, about life as it once had been. "I used to think this was the best house in the whole town," Iris said, looking around the kitchen—at the worn linoleum, the outdated appliances, the cracks in the ceiling. "I felt proud walking up the front walk and climbing the steps. I thought I was so lucky to live in such a wonderful house. It makes me sad to see it like this. What about the bed-and-breakfast project? Do you think she'll still want to do that?"

"I'm not sure if she'll have the heart for it now. They'll probably just keep patching it up."

"Maybe they should sell it and move someplace newer and smaller."

"That's what Daddy says, but I don't think Mama will ever sell it. She was going to leave it to you someday, since you're blood kin, but then you went away."

"And you don't want it?" Iris asked.

"Probably not. I don't really know what I want. Sometimes I think I should move back home. Other times, I would like to live on the other side of the world and come home every other year."

"Are you still carrying the torch for the medical student?"

"Randy's a doctor now. I'm no longer in love with him. I do wonder, though, if I made the wrong decision. What if there is never anyone else? I would like to have children someday."

Iris reached across and stroked Cissy's cheek. "There will be someone else, sweetie, if you allow it. Did Randy marry the other girl?"

"Oh, yes. I read about it in the Dallas paper—a real society wedding. She had a ten-foot train and eight bridesmaids, a reception at the Petroleum Club with music provided by a ten-piece orchestra. I'm sure Randy's parents were relieved when we broke up. We loved each other but not enough to overcome our differences. What about you? Will you ever allow someone else in your life?"

"I'm like you. I want to have children, but what if marriage made me as miserable as it's made Martha Claire and Grayson?"

Cissy nodded. "It's so hard to understand how love can just end. After we got back from the Brenham hospital, they went to their separate rooms to cry. They couldn't even share their grief."

"Don't sacrifice the rest of your life for them, Cissy."

Cissy sighed. She didn't try to explain her need for atonement. Iris would not even try to understand that. She had failed her brother, and now he was dead. She didn't want to fail her parents, too.

They listened while the mantel clock struck twice. Then Iris pushed an envelope across the table.

"What's this?" Cissy asked.

"An open-ended plane ticket to New York. You can use it any time. I'm not leaving here until you promise that you will."

Cissy picket up the envelope. "I always wanted to come visit, but I knew how it would upset Mama."

"I realize that, but I feel I have some claim to you, too. And I'm tired of just talking about someday. I'm tired of only phone calls. Martha Claire's not going to disown you, honey. You're all she has."

"Don't I know it," Cissy said with a sigh. "I *will* come, though. I promise, but I have to get things settled here first."

They both stretched out on Cissy's bed and slept for a while, then took a walk at dawn around the square and down to the river. "It wasn't the same town after you left," Cissy said. "All my good memories have you in them. And Buddy."

Iris linked arms with her. "I want our good memories to start again."

"Do you really have to leave today?"

"Yes. I must go. I need to get my things together and tell them good-bye."

Martha Claire shook Iris's hand and thanked her for coming, but she said nothing about hoping to see her again.

Grayson wished her the best and hugged her. Martha Claire turned away and went back up the stairs.

At the curb, Cissy and Iris embraced. "I still love them," Iris said, "but mostly I love you and my mother."

From her bedroom window, Martha Claire watched the two cousins embrace. How lovely they were. Iris was long-legged and slim, her golden hair pulled back in a tight bun. She was more like her mother than before, less like Grayson. Cissy was smaller, her hair a cap of dark curls shining in the morning sunlight. They were grown-up young women now, when not so long ago they had been skinny little girls jumping rope and climbing trees, with Buddy never far away.

Those years went by too fast. Martha Claire wished she had appreciated them more while she was living them. She should have spent more time with them—wading in creeks, making forts under the porch, having impromptu picnics at the end of some country lane, stretching out on a blanket in the backyard at night to watch for shooting stars. As Justine had done. But someone had to cook the meals and look after things. Someone had to watch over the old folks and keep the house from falling apart. That someone was always her. Justine should have helped her more; then maybe they both could have had more time to enjoy the children. Martha Claire remembered the hurt she had felt at being left behind while Justine drove off with the children for yet another excursion—a small hurt, to be sure, compared to the pain that was yet to come.

The only feeling she now had for her sister was hate—endless, exhausting hate that had not been softened by the passing years. She no longer hated her husband, but she would never stop hating her sister. Justine had ruined her marriage and stolen away Iris. And poor Buddy had never quite come to terms with his reconfigured family, with parents who did not love one another.

Martha Claire sighed. Her sister had ruined her life. Now, all she had left was Cissy.

She saw that Iris had taken a small camera from her purse and was posing Cissy with the house in the background. Before Martha Claire had a chance to step back, Iris looked up at the window and saw her standing there. She waved, then put a hand over her heart and mouthed the words *I love you.*

Martha Claire backed away, then fell across her bed and buried her face in her pillow. But just for a minute. Suddenly she was on her feet, throwing open the door, racing down the stairs and out on the front porch. But Iris's car was already turning the corner. Cissy was coming up the walk. "Are you all right, Mama?" she asked

"Not really. I'll think I'll sit out here for a while. Maybe you could bring me a cup of tea."

"Do you want me to clean Buddy's apartment before I go back to Houston?"

"No, I need to do it myself." She walked over to the porch swing and seated herself, folded her hands in her lap, and looked up at Cissy. "Do you think he's in heaven?"

"I don't think much about heaven, Mama. All I know is that he's dead when he didn't have to be."

"I want to believe that I'll see him again. I need that. More even than my parents, I need to know that I'll be with Buddy again."

My daddy drove off with his sample cases the Monday after Buddy's funeral, and I decided to stay with Mama through the week. Then another week passed. How could I leave my mother alone in that big empty house? Finally, though, my supervisor said that I would lose my job if I didn't report for duty the following evening. My mother accepted my departure stoically. I promised to return in two weeks. And I promised I would be better about coming home than before.

As I drove away, I felt almost euphoric about the prospect of returning to my little apartment, to my regular work schedule and routines. But as the weeks went by, I understood where the expression "heavy heart" came from. That was how I felt—heavy-hearted. If Buddy had been killed in Vietnam, we could have eventually come to terms with our loss. As it was, I doubted if we ever would.

This heavy-heartedness carried over into every facet of my life. My tiny apartment no longer felt quite so homelike. My job was less satisfying than before. I found myself less and less inclined to accept invitations to parties or even to the movies with one of my fellow nurses. How could I enjoy myself when my brother was dead?

I drove home every other weekend, finding solace in being the good daughter once again. My presence comforted my parents. When I was there, my father slept under my mother's roof and not out in his riverside shack. Maybe if I came home often enough he would move back home altogether. Even if they never again shared the same bed, I hated to think of them eating solitary meals and sleeping alone in an empty house.

Out of necessity, Mama gave up the idea of a bed-and-breakfast. No financial institution was going to loan her the money without her husband's signature, and Daddy refused even to discuss it. Buddy would have been proud. It always upset him so the way Mama ruled the roost. Our father was the proverbial henpecked husband, and everyone in town knew it.

I almost wished Daddy had not drawn the line just yet, though. With Buddy gone, Mama needed something. If it wasn't the house, I wasn't sure what it would be.

❧❦

thirty-one

Buddy had been dead more than two years when Iris called to say it was time for me to see if that plane ticket was still good. If it wasn't, she would send another. She was getting married.

I was shocked. In our phone conversations since Buddy's death, she had never said a word about a man in her life. I knew she kept company with an older German physician who had been one of her teachers in medical school, but I had envisioned a kindly old soul who took a fatherly interest in my cousin, an older man who enjoyed her companionship at the symphony and museum exhibitions.

"But isn't he the man who was in a concentration camp?" I asked.

"Yes. Hillel lost his wife and baby. And his parents, his brothers, everyone. He was the only one of his family to survive. He was able to finish his medical education here. He's quite brilliant really—a neurologist."

"So he's Jewish?"

"Yes, but our beliefs are more alike than different."

"Are you in love with him"

"In a romantic way? Not really. I'm not sure I believe in romance anymore. But I do have tender feelings for him. He's a good person, and I respect him terribly."

"Why did you decide to get married?" I asked.

"Because we need each other. We'll make a baby or two. Or maybe adopt a child or two. Or both. He hasn't had a home and family for a long time. You have to come, Cissy. It will be just a small wedding at

Mother's apartment. You will be my only attendant—my maid of honor. I couldn't possibly have anyone else."

"Is Justine okay about this?"

"I think so. She said he wasn't the man she would have chosen for me, but she was beginning to worry that I might never produce a grandchild. Now, tell me that you will come and stay for weeks and weeks and weeks."

"Don't you need to spend time with Hillel?"

"I already do that. We'll both spend some time with him. And Mother. I have some friends I want you to meet. But mostly I want to show you my city and see it anew through your eyes. I need to be with you, Cissy. I want to feast my eyes on you and link arms with you while we stroll down the avenue. I want to watch you talk and smile. I want to take you to the top of the Empire State Building and to see *A Chorus Line*. And I want you to know Hillel and see the kindness in his eyes. I want the two of you to be friends. He already calls you our 'little cousin Cissy.'"

I agreed to go, of course. But it was going to be difficult. It wasn't the trip itself I feared, although I had never flown anyplace, never been outside the state of Texas except for weekend trips to Louisiana and a couple of forays into the Arkansas Ozarks with nursing school friends. It was telling Mama that I dreaded.

We were having a cup of coffee at the kitchen table when I explained that Iris was getting married and I was going to be her only attendant. She looked out the window for a long time. "From the time she was just a little thing, I used to dream about her getting married in the rose garden—as I had done."

I wanted to ask if she had ever thought of me getting married in the rose garden. But I didn't. Instead I asked the larger question even though I knew she would not answer it. "What happened, Mama? Why did it all end?"

She pushed her chair back and took her cup to the sink. "Go to New York, if you must. But don't send me any postcards and don't come back with a bunch of wedding pictures for me to look at. I don't want you to speak of it at all."

Before I left, I tried to give her Justine's phone number, in case there was an emergency, but she said not to bother. She didn't want to know anything of Justine, not even her phone number.

"But what if you need me?" I protested.

"If I need you, you won't be here," she said.

For many years I'd dreamed of my brother's death—a different sort, though, than the one that eventually claimed him. In my dream, in my recurring nightmare, it was far worse than a highway accident.

The dream came infrequently. I believe the first time was shortly after Justine took Iris away, but maybe it was before that. In all, I probably had the dream only six or eight times. Sometimes I could wake myself in time to avoid the final agony. It really didn't matter, though. I knew how it was going to end. Awake in my bed, I could feel and see it being played out. And even if I went a year or two without experiencing the actual dream, it haunted me. A phrase in a book or a word in a conversation would push it to the forefront of my mind, and I would have to force myself to think of other things, to remind myself that it was only a dream.

It always began with me chasing Buddy through the deep shadows of a thick woods, calling his name, begging him to stop and wait for me. He ran on, though, through tangled underbrush that reached out and caught my clothes and scratched my bare legs.

Finally, the trees gave way to a clearing. In the middle of the clearing was a remarkably large building, soaked in sunshine so brilliant the building itself seemed to glow. It must have been ten or twelve stories high—not a building I had seen before, not a building that would even exist in deep woods with no roads or sidewalks, no parking lots, not even any people that I could see. The building was crisscrossed by a white wooden fire escape that climbed from floor to floor, from landing to landing, making it possible to climb all the way to the top floor without going inside.

Buddy ran across the clearing and started up the stairs. Shading my eyes against the sun, I watched him climb higher and higher and yelled his name over and over again.

I could hear the thump of his footsteps on the wooden boards, higher and higher. *Buddy,* I called. *Buddy, Buddy, Buddy.* My throat hurt from yelling at him, but still I kept calling his name. He kept climbing higher and higher, though, until finally he reached the top, where he climbed onto the railing and, without even an instant's pause, launched himself, his arms outspread, like a bird.

I screamed his name one last time, then stepped aside to avoid his falling body. The thud of his body hitting the bare earth would wake me.

It was the thud that stayed with me, keeping me awake for the rest of the night. I would try to go back to sleep, try to find the dream again. Even if I wasn't able to change the final outcome, I wanted to do more than just call out my brother's name. I wanted to race after him, up those many stairs, back and forth across the face of the building. I wanted to feel my heart pounding in my chest, my lungs bursting, as I tried to catch up with him. Even if I reached the top too late to grab him and hold him back, even if I found myself sailing though the air with him, I would at least have tried to save him.

To try to save him, though, meant that I would have had to know the reason why he was climbing those stairs. Did my dream self know that he was heading for self-destruction? Or did I think that he was just being an ornery older brother taking perverse pleasure in aggravating his little sister?

I wanted to think that the "me" of that dream had been concerned but not alarmed by my brother's actions. I had wanted to walk through the woods with him, but he ran ahead. Buddy could always run faster than me. No matter how hard I had run, how ferociously I had attacked all those stairs, I would not have caught up with him. I must have known that. That was the reason I did not try.

As I faced the reality of my brother's death in the Brenham hospital, I understood that even though the sound of Buddy's dying came not from his body hitting the ground but from his head hitting the windshield of his truck, my brother had plunged to his death. The plunge had taken years rather than seconds, but the result had been the same. And in reality as well as in the dream, I had been a bystander.

Buddy and I probably had not been related by blood. Doc Hadley had tossed that piece of fiction into the pot to make sure my mother would take in another foundling. But with Buddy and me, blood did not matter. We were Martha Claire and Grayson Stewart's adopted children. Everyone in town knew the story of how Doc Hadley had brought first me, and then six months later two-year-old Buddy, for the Stewarts to raise. Because of their childlessness, our parents were regarded as tragic figures. Iris was, after all, a borrowed child and not really theirs. Even so, folks considered them either saintly or crazy to take in two children of unknown origins. Our being adopted connected Buddy and me to each other more profoundly than we were to our parents or even to Iris. As much as I loved and needed Iris, it was Buddy who was the other half of myself. And the thud of my nightmares had taken him away.

As much as I wanted to believe that Buddy's death had been preordained by an unfeeling God or that he had been irreversibly locked on a downward course from the moment of his dismissal from A&M, I knew that it was I and no one else who could have saved him. I had always been my brother's keeper. Buddy had begged me to continue in that role on any terms, and I had chosen freedom—freedom from him, from Columbus, from my parents. I had wanted to think of the three of them always in the big old house on Milam Street, frozen in time, and I could swoop in for visits as Justine had once done. The knowledge of them there would allow me to move unhampered into a larger, more exciting world that would fill my intellect in a way that they and the town never could. Now I know that such freedom from one's beginnings is never a possibility. I was rooted in Columbus as firmly as the magnolia tree my great-grandfather had planted in the front yard when my mother and aunt were little girls in pigtails.

If I had chased Buddy up those symbolic wooden stairs, I could have lived the rest of my life with less regret. If I had grabbed his legs and pulled him back from the railing, he would have belonged to me forever. I could have found joy in that. Perhaps as much as Buddy, I, too, had been confused about what we were supposed to mean to each other, but somehow, I could have navigated the maze. I could have found a way to take care of my brother but did not, which was and would always be my burden.

Two weeks before Iris's wedding, Cissy boarded a plane for New York. Justine, Iris, and Hillel were all at the airport to greet her.

Justine was an older version of herself—long, lean, graying hair going every which way, wrinkled white shirt tucked into expensive brown slacks. She engulfed her niece in a huge hug. "You didn't grow much, honey. You're still little Cissy." Then she had to reach into her purse for a handkerchief.

Hillel backed away, leaving the three women to their tears. Cissy felt sad for him. He would never be reunited with his family. All the memories of his childhood came to a dead end.

He looked like her idea of a typical professor, with a tidy beard and a baggy brown suit and tie. His hair and beard were sprinkled with gray.

He kissed Cissy's cheeks, then her hand, and told her was honored to know her.

They had dinner at Justine's vintage apartment. With its high ceilings and wooden floors, the apartment reminded Cissy of her mother's house in Columbus. Justine's photographs covered the walls of the long, well-lit hallway, but the walls of the spacious living room were covered with handsomely framed drawings and watercolors, obviously all by the same person. A friend of Justine's, Iris said. Over the mantel, however, was a large, handsomely framed sepia-toned photograph of the Colorado County Courthouse.

Justine had prepared curry for dinner and wanted to know if it was the first time Cissy had tasted East Indian cuisine. "Actually, one of my favorite neighborhood restaurants in Houston is Indian. It's right next door to a Thai establishment."

"I guess everything in Texas isn't just like I remember it," Justine said sheepishly.

Over coffee, Hillel explained to Cissy the high regard he had for her cousin. "I know you think that such an old man as I should not be marrying a woman as young and beautiful and intelligent as your cousin Iris. I want you to know that I would have been content the rest of my life simply to be her good friend."

"Getting married was my idea," Iris interjected. "I was looking for a nice, safe man to have children with, and one night we were at our favorite little Chinese restaurant down on Bleecker Street. We had just gone to a silly little off-Broadway play about lesbian gladiators from hell that we were still laughing about. And I looked across the table at him and thought, Why not Hillel? He came to America with nothing. He doesn't have a single photograph, a single memento of his childhood. The neighborhoods where he grew up and where he lived with his wife and baby no longer exist. There are no grave markers for his family in any cemetery. He needs a family, too, and his biological clock was also ticking away. Our kids will be smart. I'm going to insist he speak only German to them. And Mother will teach them to take pictures and really to see the world. And when they are old enough to understand, we will tell them what happened to this whole other family in Europe they will never know but must never forget."

"And what about the family in Texas they will never know?" Cissy asked. "What will you tell them about Columbus?"

Iris said nothing for a minute, then looked to her mother.

Justine said, "I will tell my grandchildren about two sisters who didn't get along and spent the rest of their lives being sorry. Or at least one of them was sorry."

Then she opened a bottle of brandy, and they sat out on her little balcony, which overlooked the treetops of Central Park. Cissy closed her eyes and listened to the street sounds. She was actually here, actually in New York. With Justine and Iris. It seemed a miracle.

Iris had already moved to Hillel's apartment on Roosevelt Island, but she and Cissy would share her old bedroom at her mother's until the wedding. It was decorated with more of Justine's photographs, including one of the three cousins sitting on the top step of the front porch of the house on Milam Street. Throughout her visit, Cissy would find herself drawn to the picture, to the three youngsters in dungarees, their feet bare. With Cissy in the middle, they had linked arms for the picture. With his spare hand, Buddy was waving. They were all smiling. Cissy touched Buddy's face with a fingertip. She should have let him stay a boy forever.

For Cissy, the next weeks passed in a blur as Iris showed her the sights. They went to the Metropolitan Museum of Art, Empire State Building, Statue of Liberty, Russian Tea Room. They prowled through

Greenwich Village, Little Italy, Chinatown. They toured the UN and saw the Mets play the Phillies.

Cissy spent the second week of her visit at the women's clinic Iris had helped establish in a poor section of Brooklyn. The clientele was mostly immigrant, some from countries Cissy had never heard of. The clinic was a storefront located in a former grocery, with shelves still on the wall. Curtains had been hung from the ceiling to create examination rooms. The first day, Iris and two other female obstetricians saw more than a hundred pre- and postnatal patients and forty-seven sick children. They desperately needed a pediatrician, Iris said.

"Our major problem is low birth weight," she explained as she examined a Honduran woman. "Women who have had prenatal care and some semblance of adequate nutrition throughout their pregnancies deliver healthy babies more than ninety percent of the time."

The wedding was starkly simple. An elderly judge officiated and made no mention of religion in his legalistic explanation of marriage. Iris and Hillel offered their own simple vows. They would be honest and treat each other with respect. A friend of Justine's played a cello. The woman who had painted the pictures in Justine's living room had made the wedding luncheon. Astrid was her name. She looked like Ingrid Bergman—Scandinavian, large-boned, incredibly beautiful.

The apartment filled as the evening went by—people coming to offer their congratulations and drink the night away. It was the most eclectic group Cissy had ever seen—artists, actors, rabbis, professors, physicians, students, nuns, nurses, restaurateurs, social workers, storekeepers. Cissy watched as Iris and Hillel moved among the well-wishers with complete ease, but as the evening went on, she saw Hillel begin to weary. Iris saw it, too, and began telling people good-night. She and Hillel needed to get some sleep before they left for a brief honeymoon trip to Toronto. And Cissy had an early flight in the morning.

Finally it was time for the two cousins to say good-bye. "I'll pay your way through medical school," Iris whispered as she hugged Cissy.

"Don't be ridiculous," Cissy said, wondering how many years it would be until she saw Iris again. She was going to miss her more than ever now.

thirty-two

"With your grades and experience, any medical school would have to accept you," Iris insisted.

"But what would I tell Mama?" Cissy said. "She would consider it charity—an editorial comment on the fact that she and Daddy could not pay my way. I would, too, I guess."

Cissy stared down at the four-page application form that Iris had had sent to her. It had arrived two days ago, but they hadn't been able to catch up with each other until now. The application form had been like another presence in Cissy's small domicile—a siren promising things that she had never even allowed herself to imagine.

Cissy had come in just as the phone started to ring. Even though it was late evening, Iris was still at the clinic, getting caught up on paper-work.

"Just tell Martha Claire that you won a scholarship," Iris said. "She doesn't have to know I had anything to do with it."

"I never said I wanted to go to medical school," Cissy said, kicking off her shoes. She carried the application form and the phone to her bed and wearily propped herself against the headboard. The flu was going around. She had worked a double shift. She often worked double shifts, though, to keep her weekends free for trips home. Tonight she'd barely had the energy to climb the stairs to her apartment, which was in sad need of cleaning. More than a year ago, she had moved into a larger apartment, one that felt more adult and permanent than a garage apartment and even had a small patio area. But all the fixing-up she had planned to do remained undone. And she couldn't remember the last time she'd dusted. Or changed the sheets. The hamper was overflowing with laundry. She needed to wash her hair and pluck her eyebrows. She really should have her car serviced before she drove another mile. And she had promised her mother she'd be at the church in Columbus by six o'clock for the covered-dish supper honoring Reverend Huxley, who was finally retiring to his books and fishing. He had a standing invitation out at her father's place on the river as long as he didn't preach or bring up the issue of Grayson's immortal soul.

"You always said you were going to be a doctor when you grew up," Iris reminded her. "I remember the very fine doll hospital you established up in the attic. When you were in high school, you told me you'd like to be a pediatrician, but it would cost too much and you'd have to go to school until you were thirty. You settled on nursing because it took less time and you had a scholarship to Denton. Well, here's your chance, with no strings attached. You don't have to move to New York and practice with me, although that invitation will always be there for you. I just want you to have what I have, Cissy. It's really quite selfish of me. I can't enjoy my life until I get yours straightened out."

"I wasn't aware that my life was crooked," Cissy said dryly, and was immediately sorry. Iris only wanted the best for her. "Look, Iris, I truly appreciate your offer. I really can't believe you made it. But I don't have the time or energy for medical school."

"You would if you didn't go home every weekend," Iris pointed out. "Martha Claire and Grayson are never going to be happy, Cissy. You need to look after yourself. That's why I decided on a school in Dallas instead of Houston. I thought about an out-of-state one, but I figured you wouldn't go for that. Dallas is far enough away that Martha Claire and Grayson can't expect you to come running home all the time."

Cissy closed her eyes and stretched out her aching legs. "I don't go home *every* weekend, and they don't expect me to. Going home whenever I can is a burden I've put on myself. At least when I'm at home, Mama and Daddy sleep under the same roof and sit down at the same table. It's really quite selfish of me. I can't enjoy my life until I get theirs straightened out," she said, parroting Iris's words.

"Well, aren't you cute!" Iris said sarcastically. "Martha Claire and Grayson have forgotten how to be anything but miserable. And you're not doing much better. You can't help them come to terms with Buddy's death, and they can't help you. You each have to find your own peace. If it makes you feel better, specialize in psychiatry and dedicate your life to healing alcoholic young men before they kill themselves behind the wheel of a car. You also can make enough money to fix up Martha Claire's house and endow something at A&M in Grayson's name. So many more things are possible, Cissy, if you have an M.D. after your name and some money in the bank."

"You don't make much money."

"I could if I had another sort of practice."

"How can you afford to pay my tuition?"

"I have Hillel now. Mother would help, too, if I asked her. Money isn't the issue."

"Why isn't it good enough that I stay a nurse?" Cissy demanded. After all, most of the time she loved what she did. At times, of course, she would like to know more about the diseases and conditions that affected her patients. And sometimes she got tired of following orders and wondered what it would be like to be the person giving them.

"I've already told you—I want you to have what I have. I feel guilty, too, sweetie. We all are suffocating under piles and piles of guilt. I could have told Mother that I didn't want to leave Columbus. After all, Martha Claire and Grayson raised me and loved me as though I was their own. They were the ones who changed the sheets when I was sick and held me when I had nightmares. Martha Claire taught me about flowers, and Grayson taught me about birds and history. They were the ones who saw to it that I grew up with good manners and respect for my elders. They taught me to be honest and kind and to listen and ask questions. I loved my mother dearly, but Martha Claire and Grayson were the constants in my life—them and you and Buddy. Martha Claire and Grayson made us into a family—a wonderful family. I don't know why our mothers started hating each other, but maybe if I had stayed things would have turned out differently. As it was, I crept away in the night without even saying good-bye. I left you and Buddy there to deal with all that misery by yourselves."

Cissy closed her eyes and rubbed her forehead. "I'm too tired to talk about this now. I'll call you in a few days, okay?"

"It's Friday," Iris said like an accusation. "You're going to Columbus, aren't you? My God, Cissy, you sound exhausted. Can't you just say for once that you need to look after yourself?"

"Reverend Huxley's retirement dinner is tonight."

There was a pause before Iris said she was sorry, that she just worried about Cissy, that of course she had to go to Reverend Huxley's retirement dinner. "He caught me and Jane Whitmore smoking behind the church and didn't tell our parents," Iris recalled. "He didn't even make us promise never to do it again or tell us we were awful girls. He sat on a sawhorse and said if that was the worst rule we ever broke, we'd grow up just fine. Then he told us smoking would make our teeth yellow and give us bad breath. Tell him thank you for me."

"For what?"

"For being wise. For my white teeth. You will go to medical school, won't you?"

"I don't know."

"At least tell the folks that you've been thinking about it, that you've been offered a scholarship. Let them start getting used to the idea, in case you do decide to go."

"It's not a scholarship."

"Yes, it is. I am awarding a one-time-only scholarship to a practicing nurse who graduated from Columbus High School and Texas Women's University."

"I'm a good nurse."

"I know you are, Cissy. I'm sure you are the most competent, compassionate nurse Baylor Medical Center has ever had. But you need something more, and nurses are so underpaid it's criminal. You'll never be able to fix up that old house for Martha Claire on what you make, and don't try to pretend that isn't important to you. You were born to take care of people, Cissy. You will always be Florence Nightingale, but you can be Marcus Welby, too. You'll be a better, wiser physician because of the time you've served in the trenches."

"If I do this, and I'm not saying I will, but if I do, I'll pay you back someday—with interest."

"Fine. Whatever. Fill out the application. I need for you to do this."

Reverend Huxley didn't remember the cigarette incident, but he was touched that Iris thought him wise. "The older I got the more I realized how arrogant I was to parade around as a man of the cloth," he told Cissy. "Maybe it *was* a bit of wisdom that got me through."

Telling herself that it was more to appease her cousin than because of any pressing desire on her part to enroll in medical school, Cissy filled out the application form and tried to write the required one-page essay that explained why she wanted to be a physician. The essay almost made her toss the application in the trash and tell Iris thanks but no thanks.

She spent long evenings at her typewriter, casting about for an approach. First she wrote about her brother's death and needing a new direction. Then she wrote about the inspiring work of her physician cousin among the poor of New York City. Then she tried the inspiration of old Doc Hadley, the consummate family physician.

She wanted to help people, to live a more interesting life, to better herself, to make her parents proud, to be a role model, to give back to society. She wanted to practice on an Indian reservation. In a big city. In her hometown. To take care of migrant farmworkers. The wastebasket was full of wadded-up sheets of paper. If she was having such a difficult time defining herself, then maybe the whole thing was a bad idea.

Then she wrote about her lifelong fascination with the science of medicine and how her study of nursing had only whetted her appetite to learn more.

Was that true?

Partially, she supposed. Each approach she had tried had been partially true.

Finally, she explained that she had always wanted to be a doctor, but she hadn't had the money or the courage to go down that long and difficult road. Now she was older, less fearful, and her physician cousin had offered to pay her tuition. As a nurse, she had the opportunity for meaningful and flexible part-time employment to help meet her living expenses.

The next step was a trip to Dallas for an interview. She still hadn't told her parents. Maybe it wouldn't be necessary. Maybe her application would be denied.

She was interviewed by a panel of five men who had been at their task for hours and were obviously weary with the process. The panel chairman—Dr. Gibbons, a Dallas GP—introduced himself and the other panel members, then explained that they were one of a dozen panels conducting the interviews of the hundreds of applicants. The panels were made up of alumni who volunteered their time as a service to the school.

A portly ophthalmologist from Fort Worth asked the first question. "Don't you like nursing?"

Cissy explained that she loved nursing. Being a nurse had made her want to learn more.

"I suppose you are one of those nurses who think they know more than the doctors," he observed dryly.

"I have the greatest respect for the medical profession," Cissy said.

"Have you ever questioned a physician's judgment?" an Austin pediatrician asked.

"On occasion I have felt the need to supply more information that might help a physician make decisions about a patient's treatment. None of them has ever complained."

Dr. Palmer, a strikingly handsome young surgeon from Abilene, pointed out that, if accepted, Cissy would be taking a place in the class that could be occupied by a man. Since men have the responsibility of supporting their families, she would, in effect, be robbing a family of a physician's income.

So that was how it was going to be, Cissy thought, feeling her spine stiffen along with her resolve. She could accept their denying her admission for writing a dumb essay or having taken only three hours of organic chemistry—but not because she was a woman.

"I suppose that some men might wish to become a physician so that they can support their family with a 'physician's income,'" she said, speaking slowly, composing her words carefully. "But surely others have more altruistic reasons. My cousin, for example, earns only a modest salary practicing in a clinic where poor women come for obstetrical care."

"Is your cousin a woman?" Dr. Palmer wanted to know.

"Yes."

"Is she married?"

"Yes."

"Well, then, she can afford to be 'altruistic' because she has a husband to pay the bills," the surgeon said with a shrug. "She doesn't have to support a family. With the advent of this so-called women's movement, medical schools are being inundated by female applicants. Every woman who is accepted means some man won't be."

Trying to keep her tone calm and reasonable, Cissy asked, "Are you saying that men have a greater right than women to practice medicine?"

"I am discussing an economic reality," the surgeon responded. He seemed less handsome than before. A toad, actually, with beady eyes and sallow skin.

"You are still a young woman, Miss Stewart," he continued, with a glance down at the open folder in front of him. "Only twenty-seven years old and rather attractive. You may yet marry and have children. If you earn a medical degree, then decide to stay home and raise children, your medical education would have been a waste."

"I don't think anyone in their right mind—male or female—would go through four years of medical school plus years of postgraduate training and not bother to practice their profession."

"Most women do want to raise their own children," he countered. The other men had pushed their chairs back and had taken the posture of spectators, obviously willing for their Abilene colleague to handle Cecelia Stewart's interview.

"My mother worked in the family store," Cissy said. "No one ever accused her of not raising her own children."

"Ah, but a storekeeper doesn't have emergency calls in the middle of the night," he insisted.

"When that happens, the children's father would look after them," Cissy countered.

The surgeon leaned across the table. "What if he is a physician, too?" The question was asked with a certain gusto, like a bridge player who takes a trick with an obviously forgotten trump.

Cissy looked toward Dr. Gibbons, but the panel chairman averted his eyes. She was on her own. Probably they were all hoping she would burst into tears and go racing out of the room. She took a breath to calm herself. "If I and this husband 'I may still find' were both physicians, we would determine the best way to provide for the care of our children under such circumstances. My family doctor in Columbus was a widower who raised his three daughters on his own from the time they were quite small. No one thought he was being a bad parent because he had a live-in housekeeper. The Sunday afternoon he set my collarbone, two of his daughters came with him and watched the entire procedure."

"Ah, but that was in a small-town hospital," the Abilene doctor said. "Things would be different in a large city."

"Who's to say I won't practice in a small town? I am curious, gentlemen. Do you ask male applicants how they plan to manage child care if the woman they marry is a physician? If their wife becomes incapacitated or dies?"

The surgeon threw up his hands and pushed his chair back from the table. A white-haired family physician from Burkburnet spoke for the first time, responding to her question. "Your point is well taken, Miss Stewart. I fear that Dr. Palmer has been overly strident," he said with a frown in Dr. Palmer's direction, "but I'm sure he just wants to make sure you are serious in your intent to practice medicine. Sometimes young women apply to medical school with a rather romanticized notion of the profession."

"I'm sure some young men do the same, but including my nurse's training, I have spent the last eight years in hospitals and seen medicine at its best and worst. And I ceased being a romantic at age eleven."

Dr. Gibbons stood and extended his hand. "Thank you, Miss Stewart, and good luck. You should hear from the dean within the month."

Cissy muttered "*Fuck you!*" under her breath as she walked toward the door. "*Male chauvinist pigs!*" She wished she knew where their cars were parked so she could write epithets on the windshields with lipstick. She hoped they triple-bogeyed every golf hole for the rest of their lives. That their children all flunked their college entrance exams.

That their wives all ran off with tennis instructors. That their Mercedeses and Cadillacs were all made on a Monday.

She drove away almost blinded by her anger and ended up hopelessly lost in an unfamiliar part of Dallas. She pulled into a Holiday Inn parking lot and went straight to the bar. After two bourbon and sodas, she called Iris. "I hate men," she said, "especially if they happen to have 'M.D.' after their names."

"It didn't go well, I take it."

"They were all pricks. I wish I had given them the finger. Did you know that for every woman who gets into medical school, some poor male will be denied the God-given right to become a physician and join a country club."

"You know they're not all like that, Cissy. You just drew a bad panel."

"You can say that again. I'm sorry, Iris. Really sorry. The more I thought about it, the more I wanted it."

"Are you sure you won't be accepted?"

Cissy laughed. "I have about as much chance of getting into that medical school as finding the Hope diamond in my next drink."

"There are other medical schools."

"I am not that stubborn."

"You aren't going to drive home tonight, are you?"

"I have the seven A.M. shift."

"Oh, Cissy, you sound like your tongue is two inches thick."

"Part of it is just anger. I've only had two drinks. I promise I'll drink two cups of coffee and a gallon of water before I head out."

The letter from the dean's office arrived exactly four weeks after the interview. Cissy started to toss the unopened envelope into the trash, but paused. The envelope was fat. It took only a one-page letter to turn her down.

She tore it open and read with amazement the dean's letter of congratulations on her acceptance for the fall of 1977. Enclosed was orientation information and her class schedule. Would she please fill out and return the health profile and parking application as soon as possible?

Iris was in delivery when Cissy called. She left a message and called her mother. "I thought I'd drive over for dinner if you're going to be home," she told her mother. "I've got something I want to tell you."

"Are you engaged?" Martha Claire said hopefully.

"No, Mama, nothing like that. Is Daddy there?"

"No, he's out at that place on the river."

"Would you drive out and ask him to come home for dinner?"

"I don't know the way."

Cissy gave her directions. "Please, Mama. I want to talk to both of you together."

"It isn't bad news, is it?"

"No. At least I don't think it is."

"What would you like for dinner?"

"Just go get Daddy. I'll stop on the way into town and pick up a pizza."

They seemed almost relieved when she told them her news, even when they realized she would be moving to Dallas. Apparently her parents had been worried that she had become too dependent on them since Buddy's death. A young woman needed a social life and friends her own age, they said.

"Maybe you'll find a nice young man in medical school," Mama said.

"Our little Cissy is going to be a doctor," her father said with such pride it brought tears to Cissy's eyes. For an instant she thought he was going to reach for Mama's hand. But Martha Claire got very busy closing up the pizza box and stacking the plates.

"How did you find out about this scholarship?" he wanted to know.

"A doctor told me about it. It's for a practicing nurse."

They sat on the porch for a while. Several neighbors called out hellos, and Martha Claire had them come sit for a while and hear their news.

"I probably won't come home for a week or two," Cissy said apologetically as she hugged them good-bye. "I'm going to drive up to Dallas and spend a few days—you know, figure out where I'm going to live and see about getting a part-time job at one of the hospitals—probably at Parkland, where I took my nurse's training."

"Don't worry about us," Grayson said. "You're the best daughter parents could ever hope for. We just want you to be happy, honey. It does my heart good to see a smile on that pretty face."

Before she left town, Cissy drove to the cemetery and walked to her brother's grave. In the moonlight, she knelt on the damp grass and touched his tombstone. If she had taken care of Buddy, she probably wouldn't be going to medical school. Nothing made any sense. Maybe one just had to accept that and move on down the road.

As she drove east on the interstate she allowed the euphoria to rise in her breast. Her parents were pleased! Everything was going to be all right. She was going to be physician. *Cecelia Claire Stewart, M.D.*

thirty-three

"Well, well, well, if it isn't our soon-to-be Dr. Cissy Stewart," Doc Hadley said, holding open the screen door for her.

Cissy was stunned at the sight of him. The man who had looked after the health of their town for half a century was himself wasted and ill. She hadn't seen him in years but had found herself thinking about him more now that medical school and a medical degree were in her future.

He led her past the parlor, where his daughter Trudy's collection of Chinese porcelain was displayed, and down the hall to the kitchen. He now lived with Trudy, the oldest of his three daughters and the only one to make her home in Columbus.

"Trudy said you'd called," he said. "She's off at one of her meetings, but she left lemonade and cookies."

Doc Hadley never had officially retired. After he'd brought another physician to town, he had gradually phased out his own practice. Trudy said some of the old-timers still came by to have him listen to their hearts and poke at their bellies to make sure the "young doc," who had been in practice for more than twenty years, was getting it right.

"Well, well, well," he said again as he poured the lemonade. "Your folks are certainly busting their buttons over you. You know, over the years, lots of youngsters told me they were going to be a doctor when they grew up, but you're the only one to actually do it. 'Course, you were always the most inquisitive. Just listening to your own heart wasn't enough. You wanted to listen to mine and your mama's. You had to look in my eyes and ears and watch when I lanced your brother's boil and cut out his ingrown toenail."

Cissy smiled. "You remember all that?"

He nodded. "You and your brother weren't just any other patients, you know. I had a hand in your family like no other and always felt a special responsibility toward the Stewarts. I was almost glad when you kids got colds and measles so I had a chance to hover. Oh, yes, I remember. I remember charming little Iris and oversized, rambunctious Buddy. I remember how you would sit there with your big serious eyes asking one question after another."

Cissy carried their lemonade out to the backyard, where they settled themselves on two lawn chairs. "Did you always want to be a doctor?" Cissy asked.

"No. I had grown up thinking I would be a vet. Then one summer I worked for one and got kicked in the head by a sick mule. They thought I was going to die for a time. I figured it was a sign of some sort and decided I'd better find something else to do."

"But why medicine?"

"Same reason as you, I suppose. You want to do something more than just make money. If I hadn't been a doctor, I would have been a farmer."

"What about when people died, though?" she asked, remembering him at Granny Grace's and Grandma Polly's deathbeds. "Didn't that bother you?"

"Depends. Sometimes letting people go ahead and die is the only cure you can offer. You welcome death like an old friend and wonder what in the hell took the old buzzard so damned long. Other times, you know you'll wonder for the rest of your life if you couldn't have done something differently that would have saved a patient, 'specially the young ones. That's a real burden. And after I'd have a mama bleed to death during childbirth or a hurt young'un die on the way to a surgeon in Houston, I'd swear I was going to pack up and move to a city where there was a real hospital with fancy machines and specialists and a blood bank, but I never did. People in little towns need someone to look after them and do the best they can with what they've got. Now it's a bit better, with the interstate to Houston and helicopters than can come fetch the severe cases, but in my day I had to manage as best I could."

They talked for a while. She let him ramble on a bit about Buddy and the glory years at Columbus High School. Then she helped him back up the steps to the house and got him settled in front of the television. She shook his hand and thanked him for everything he'd done for her and her family and promised to come back next time she was in town. She walked down the hall toward the front door but paused at the screen door, staring out at the shady street.

Her life had been set when Doc Hadley bundled her up and found her a home. Now he was old and at the end of his life. She might never see him again.

She retraced her steps down the hallway. He had turned off the television and was waiting for her. "If you're going to ask me about your birth parents, don't bother," he said with a dismissive wave of his hand.

"I'm not even sure I want to know," Cissy said from the doorway. "Buddy wondered about them more than I did. I thought it was disloyal to my parents—especially Mama—to think much about them. But sometimes I wonder if my birth mother knows about us or if she even cares."

"And now you're wondering if this is your last chance to find out."

"Something like that," Cissy admitted.

"Buddy got to where he asked me every time he saw me. The last few years, he kept trying to get me to say that you and he had different parents, that you two weren't related by blood. But secrets are the one thing I get to take with me. Physicians usually end up with lots of them, 'specially docs like me with a small-town practice. I've been in most houses in this town and know the good and the bad about most everyone who lives here. Hippocrates even put keeping secrets in his oath for us docs. We all have to promise not to divulge the things we see or hear in the lives of men."

"But have you ever talked to her over the years?" Cissy persisted, realizing that this dying man was her only connection to that empty, faceless specter of motherhood that had hovered about the corners of her life. "Did Buddy and I have the same mother? Does she know that he died? Will you tell her that I'm going to medical school?"

He shook his finger at her. "You go on now, Cissy Stewart, and make the parents who raised you proud. You'll be a fine physician."

Doc Hadley died the following month. The funeral was held in the high school gymnasium, with the bleachers filled to overflowing, whites and blacks keeping with their own.

At Doc Hadley's request, the service was conducted by the pastor of Freedmantown's Redemption Baptist Temple. Pastor Ulysses Bell had been a fishing buddy of the doctor's since childhood, ever since the pastor's mother cleaned house for old Mrs. Hadley. The music was provided by the temple's Redemption Choir and surely uplifted the souls of even the most bigoted among them. The service concluded with a message to the town written by the good doctor himself and read by his daughter Trudy, with her sisters at her side.

"I've been in most of your homes," his letter began, "and put my hands on most of your bodies. I've delivered most of your babies and tended the dying of most of your departed." He went on to describe how he'd been paid in chickens, pies, house and car repairs, and sometimes with prayers and even money. He officially forgave the debts of those who still owed him. He admonished those who needed to mend their ways that no good ever came from drinking and carousing around or from physically hurting another human being, especially wives and children. He apologized to his daughters for never taking them on that trip to the Grand Canyon, and concluded by saying it had been a privilege to serve them all, even the ones who never took his advice. Now it was time for him to join his darling Beatrice in death. "I'm not sure there's a hereafter, but for me it's enough to know that my earthly remains will lie next to hers for eternity."

The service ended with the singing of "Swing Low, Sweet Chariot." Everyone cried, of course. Cissy had come prepared with pockets full of Kleenex. She shared them with her father. Her mother had brought her own.

She cried for the loss of the man himself and for the thread he represented to her beginnings, to her birth mother. That thread was now forever broken.

thiry-four

With her parents' help and a rented truck, Cissy moved her possessions to Dallas, back to the city where she had lived during the three clinical years of her nurse's training. She had rented a three-room duplex in a shabby neighborhood near the medical center campus.

Martha Claire cooked their meals in the tiny kitchen and saw to it that Cissy had a full assortment of spices, condiments, and canned goods. Grayson installed chain locks on the doors. He wanted to plant a tree in her barren little yard, but Cissy insisted that she would forget to water it. She didn't want houseplants, either.

They stayed for three days, with Martha Claire sleeping with Cissy in the bedroom and Grayson on the sofa. When they finished cleaning and painting, the place looked livable in a basic sort of way. Her mother wanted to hang curtains, but Cissy insisted the bare blinds were just fine. She didn't want to spend her time washing and ironing curtains.

The three of them agreed that Cissy would not come home until Thanksgiving. It was a six-hour drive from Dallas to Columbus—too far for a weekend visit, and Cissy would need to use weekends for her studies and nursing. "I wish you didn't have to work," Martha Claire said.

"Mama, lots of medical students have jobs. It's no big deal."

They all blinked back tears when it came time to say good-bye. Grayson insisted on giving her a wad of bills and made her promise that she'd call if she was running short of money. "I don't want you skipping meals," he said.

Cissy stood on the curb and watched her parents drive away. She didn't know if she should feel liberated or miserable. Both, she decided. She would miss them terribly, but she had been cut loose for a time. She wouldn't have to go home on weekends to bear witness to their sadness.

At least her parents hadn't closed the store yet. Even if it didn't turn much of a profit, it offered structure to their lives. Without the store, they wouldn't have to communicate at all. As it was, they had to decide who would work when, what lines of merchandise to carry, when items should go on sale.

For the most part, though, they lived separate lives. Grayson was active in the county historical society and was compiling a history of Columbus's Courthouse Square. He still drove up to College Station for the home games and drove to Houston every couple of months to prowl around the used-book stores and buy a stack of newspapers— *The New York Times, The Washington Post, The Dallas Morning News, The Herald Tribune.* And he fished, of course, which wasn't so much a sport as a way of life for him. Grayson had become a part-time hermit. When he wasn't working in the store, he wore wrinkled old clothes. He went too long between haircuts and carried a book or a newspaper with him everywhere. He would read between customers. Read sitting on a bench in the square. Prop a book up in front of him while he ate his meals. He preferred history and biography, which distanced him from the world in which he actually lived.

Martha Claire had rejoined two bridge clubs and had taken up mahjong, which had become all the rage. After five years, she still didn't like the "new" minister and was thinking about joining the Christian Church after a lifetime of being a Methodist. Her yard was more beautiful than ever. People stopped by on their evening strolls to walk among the flowers and shrubs and marvel. With such a garden, if the house itself were ever to be restored, it would be the jewel of the annual home tour. Cissy wondered how much of her motivation to attend medical school came from her desire to restore her mother's house and have it be included on the Magnolia Homes Tour. She dreamed of seeing her mother proudly showing tourists through the home her great-great-grandfather had built as a wedding present for his daughter.

Her dead brother, though, provided her principal motivation. She would never stop feeling guilty about Buddy, never be able to balance the ledger sheet. But if she did good work in the world, if she became a healer of her fellow human beings, if she became a very competent and compassionate physician, she might come to terms. At least, that was her hope.

Cissy had told Iris that she wanted to have children someday. And at some deep elemental level, she supposed she still did. But that dream was dimming in the face of the task at hand. She would have to see how she felt about marriage and children after she finished medical school and completed her postgraduate training. Would she feel too bound up in her medical career to raise children? Too old to start bearing them?

She did long for a male presence in her life, however. Other than Randy Calhoune, there had never been anyone. In high school, she had been a little sister to all Buddy's friends and certainly had her share of crushes, but whether it was due to Buddy's hovering presence or her own shyness, no boy had ever walked her home from school or called her on the phone. Joey Huffman would sit on the front porch with her sometimes but never got up the courage to ask her to the movies or anyplace else. She read novels about pirates and Indian braves ravishing stolen-but-willing ladies and felt an almost painful and very real longing deep inside of her.

Randy had gone so far as to buy condoms, but they had never used them. They petted for hours but never went all the way. Cissy had thought it was proper at the time; now she was sorry. She still had all that to go through. Because she was still a virgin, she could not slip easily into a casual but fulfilling relationship that would cure her longing.

Or could she?

With her parents gone, the three rooms that were now her home seemed deafeningly quiet. Cissy turned on the radio and stared at the clothes her mother had hung neatly in her closet, pondering what she should wear to tomorrow's orientation. What if she wore a dress and all the other women students showed up in pants? She finally decided on a sleeveless black dress and sandals.

She ate a bowl of tomato soup, washed her hair, shined her shoes, filed her nails. And felt like she had gone backward in time, preparing for the first day of school. The biggest day of the year. New notebooks and books. New teachers. A new beginning. Just like when she was a kid. All that was lacking was a new pair of loafers and a new cigar box for pencils and scissors.

The first-year class was welcomed by the dean, who told them they could expect to work harder over the next four years than they had ever in their lives. Their vocabularies would increase by over ten thousand words. They would acquire more information in just their first year than most people learn in a lifetime. It was their job to turn that information into knowledge.

Then he gave a rundown of the class demographics. Of the one hundred twenty class members, one hundred two were men and one hundred ten were residents of the state of Texas. Ninety-eight had come directly from an undergraduate program. The remainder included six military veterans, two accountants, a commercial pilot, five paramedics, four pharmacists, two schoolteachers, a Presbyterian minister, and one nurse.

The dean concluded his remarks by telling them that medical school wasn't all hard work. They were supposed to have fun and make friends for a lifetime.

"Are you the nurse?" one of Cissy's classmates asked during the break. She had noticed him earlier—the good-looking guy wearing a sport coat, jeans, and well-worn cowboy boots.

"Does it show that much?" she asked, reaching up to pat the top of her head. "I could have sworn I left my white cap at home."

"Just a good guess. The rest of the females look hopelessly young and affluent."

He looked to be about thirty, with white teeth, a square jaw, and close-cropped blond hair. With his lean, tan body and west Texas drawl, she would cast him as a cowboy, but there weren't any cowboys on the dean's list. "Are you a veteran or the pilot?" she asked.

He saluted. "Captain Joe McCormack, at your service."

At lunch, they went through the cafeteria line together and sat at the same table. He had grown up on a cattle ranch outside of Lampasas and gone into the army after college. His undergraduate degree was in biology.

Cissy gave a perfunctory rundown on herself, including the part about her cousin paying her tuition. "I am definitely not one of the affluent," she said. "I put my name on the special-duty roster at every hospital in the metro. I'll be doing most of my studying at the bedside of the comatose and dying."

That afternoon, they were introduced to their cadavers in the gross anatomy lab. Cissy and her three lab partners were assigned the body of an elderly black woman who had died at age eighty-seven. Her lab partners were the pilot and two young men freshly graduated from the University of Texas, one of whom was the only black member of their class. It was disquieting for Cissy to see the cadaver's emaciated, unclothed body exposed for all to see. She was as flat-chested as a boy, and the formaldehyde had turned her skin a leathery gray. Her face was expressionless; her lifeless features seemed more like those of a statue than a human being. The white UT grad laughed nervously. "This old gal looks like she's been rode hard and put up wet."

"Shall we name her?" the pilot asked.

"What's a good name for a teacher?" Cissy asked. "We will need to learn a great deal from her."

"What about 'Grandmother'?" the black student asked.

The others nodded. "Grandmother" it would be.

At the end of the day, Joe McCormack caught up with her in the hall and invited her out for a hamburger. Cissy had planned to get acquainted with her *Gray's Anatomy* but heard herself saying yes. It pleased her to think that she had already made a friend.

They sat on the outdoor deck at a west Dallas restaurant and talked the evening away. His group had named their cadaver Teddy Roosevelt, for obvious reasons. "The old guy must have weighed three hundred pounds," Joe said. "I've heard that adipose tissue is the pits, especially when it comes to dissecting out the nerves."

Cissy told him about Grandmother. "It's all a little emotional," she

admitted. "When I saw that woman's body, I realized what a tremen-
dous responsibility we all have to learn and to use what we learn."

He lifted his glass. "To Grandmother and Teddy," he said solemnly.
"May we do them proud."

Over their second beer, they talked about aspirations. Joe wanted to
be a family doctor back in Lampasas or some other west Texas town.
He would run a few cattle, raise a few horses and kids, have family dinners every night at a big round table in a kitchen with wooden floors.
Cissy told him about Columbus and Iris's clinic in New York. She
wasn't sure which she wanted. Mostly she was concentrating on the
present, on not failing.

Joe laughed when she told him about her admission interview. Cissy
tried to remember if anyone had ever laughed when she told a story before. "I've always been so serious," she confessed.

"I forgot how to laugh for a while," he said.

"Vietnam?"

He nodded and called for the check. Cissy thought about her father,
who would not talk about his war either.

Joe drove her to her car. "You okay about driving home alone at this
hour?"

She nodded. "I enjoyed the evening."

"Me, too. Can we be friends?"

"I hope we already are."

"I'm in the middle of a divorce. She said I changed too much in
'Nam. She didn't care for the nightmares, I guess."

"I'm sorry. That must have been difficult for you."

"Still is. What about you?"

"Almost engaged once—to a medical student. Sometimes I have regrets. I hope I'm more suited to be a doctor than a doctor's wife."

He touched her cheek with a fingertip. "Good night, Cissy Stewart
from Columbus. I hope we're both still around four years from now."

"Me, too."

It had been a good day, Cissy thought as she drove home, in part because of Joe McCormack. But he wasn't someone she would get serious about, not a man who wanted a wife at home to look after the kids

and horses and serve dinner every night on a big round table. Maybe that meant they really would be friends.

Cissy was surprised at the ease with which she made friends with her classmates—especially her three anatomy lab partners. But then, they saw each other several hours a day, often seven days a week, as they slowly dissected Grandmother. Cissy gave up trying to scrub away the smell of formaldehyde, which clung to her hands and the inside of her nostrils. She even gave up washing her lab coat every week and followed her lab partners' lead, wearing it smelly and stained. Their evening sessions in the anatomy lab were often followed by a beer, often with Joe and his roommate, another Vietnam vet. When she lifted the glass to her lips, the aroma of beer mingled with the smell of formaldehyde.

It took her weeks before she told Joe about Buddy. "I don't want to talk about him," she explained. "I just need for you to know."

She often studied with Joe, sometimes just the two of them, sometimes with others. They quizzed each other constantly. *Name the ligaments of the hand. The nerves of the axillary. What is the function of the angular gyrus?*

If her special-duty patient was in a coma or a drug haze, Joe would put on a white jacket and brazen his way into the hospital room for a study session. Cissy hadn't known there was room in her brain for all the things she learned in just that semester. She dreamed in diagrams and charts. She never listened to the radio or watched television, never read a newspaper or a book that wasn't a textbook. She emerged from the world of medicine only long enough to call home every Sunday evening. She didn't watch Carter debate Ford, didn't see *Rocky*. She kept wondering who Laverne and Shirley were. Sports, politics, current events all but ceased to exist for her as she immersed herself in anatomy, physiology, biochemistry, genetics, pharmacology, neurology, embryology. She grew thinner and smarter. She stopped wearing makeup and learned to ignore dirty dishes and bathtub rings. She wore only clothes that didn't have to be ironed and grew a ponytail because she didn't have time for a haircut. She could hardly wait to become a physician but loved being in medical school. It was intense, exciting, wondrous, challenging, frightening. It was everything. She was aware of the existence of other worlds, but they had no relevance to hers. She would go for days without thinking about Buddy, which troubled her immensely, but she didn't have time even for guilt or grief, so she tucked them away for now. She consumed black coffee by the quart, ate junk food, learned to drink shots. She could party into the night and make it to class by eight in the morning.

It wasn't until she was on the highway, driving to Columbus for Thanksgiving, that she came up for air, that she got all emotional thinking about her parents preparing for her visit. Her mother was preparing a traditional Thankgiving feast for the first time since they lost Buddy. Tomorrow was the fifth anniversary of his death.

Her backseat was covered with books and notebooks, but she wouldn't do that to them, she promised herself. For four days, she would belong to just them.

"God, it's good to be home," she said when she arrived just before eleven. In spite of the hour, the three of them lingered at the kitchen table, drinking milk and nibbling on cookies, while they plied her with questions about school, her friends, her life. Cissy enjoyed telling them about Grandmother and Teddy Roosevelt, about her classes and friends. She didn't mention Joe.

The next day, her father carved the turkey like always, but there weren't enough people at the table, not enough words and laughter to fill the room, too much food for three. Cissy knew her parents, too, were remembering other Thanksgivings with family all around—good memories that made the present poignant and sad.

Their past—with its lessons and mysteries—had created their present, and they were sentenced to live always under its spell.

thirty-five

She didn't start sleeping with Joe until after spring break.

They had talked about it off and on all through that first year. They both confessed to being horny. Joe said he had been all but asexual since he and his wife split up. Now, oddly enough, as consumed as he was by school and studying, he was always having sexual thoughts. He said he hadn't masturbated this much since he was fifteen.

Cissy was tired of her virginal state, tired of being the only one who hadn't done it. Initially, she thought she would save herself for marriage, but now she wondered if she would ever be any man's wife, or if she even wanted to. She certainly didn't want to be the sort of wife Joe said he wanted.

Most men didn't think about equality or inequality. They simply accepted that someone had to be the mother of the children and keeper of the home, and that person was not going to be them.

Cissy's cadre of male friends concurred. They wanted what Joe wanted—a chief-cook-and-bottle-washer sort of wife—which was, they agreed, definitely not fair. They didn't know where all this women's lib stuff was going, but they hoped it all got worked out by the time their children grew up.

"So describe the future," Cissy challenged. "How will things be when your children are grown? Describe male-female relations at the beginning of the next century."

It was a Friday night. The second round of beer had been ordered. Timmy Stevenson, a baby-faced genius from Tyler, insisted that women could never be equal to men. For that to transpire, men would have to make less money so women could get more. And men were never going to step aside and let that happen. They were too selfish, too egocentric. Furthermore, he insisted that the survival of the species depended on men being in charge. If they weren't, they would suffer from low self-esteem and become sexually dysfunctional.

Jerry Virtue, a psychiatrist's son from Houston, claimed that there would be more professional couples in the future, and they would manage their lives by hiring nannies and housekeepers.

"*Female* nannies and housekeepers, I assume," Cissy said.

"Well, sure," Jerry said with a teasing grin.

"You tell us, Cissy," Joe said. "Tell us about the perfect marriage."

Cissy couldn't. Maybe there was no such thing. Her parents certainly didn't have one. Her aunt Justine had never married. Iris had bypassed passion and settled for a man who was safe, gentle, and grateful. Iris insisted that soul-searing sex was for the courting young, that the marital bed was for comfort and predictability.

Cissy didn't want courtship, but she was going to have to do something about sex—soul-searing or otherwise. She had had numerous volunteers for the breaking of the hymen but trusted Joe to not make too much of the act. She didn't have time for dating, for "going with" someone. What she wanted was Saturday night sex, which would be the best way to deal with the distracting, turned-on state in which she found herself. She had mentally auditioned every one of the men crowded around the table, including Benjamin Watson, the TU grad who had named Grandmother. Someone she didn't like as much as Joe might be a wiser choice, but she felt herself responding when Joe touched her arm and when their thighs touched under the table. She liked it when he grinned at her and was always pleased when it was his voice on the phone. He was the first guy she had met in medical school, and she had spent more time with him than anyone else. It seemed only right that he do the honors.

She got a prescription for birth control pills, and they tried to decide on a date for her deflowering. She had a busy work schedule. Joe's brother was coming for a visit. There were midterms looming on the horizon. And the gridiron. Joe had a role in their class skit, playing the part of their anatomy professor singing a parody of "You Gotta Have

Heart." Finally they agreed on the following Sunday evening—at her place. There would be no romance, no candlelight or soft music, no pretty words. They would each consume two beers, turn off the lights, feel each other up, get naked, and finish in time to study biostatistics.

When the time came, however, he asked if he could leave a light on. Just the little lamp on the bureau.

"No. That would make it too personal. This is supposed to be generic sex."

"But it's your first time."

"So?"

"Don't you want to see what's going on?"

"Not really."

He shrugged. "Whatever. Are you ready?"

She took the phone off the hook. "As ready as I'll ever be, I guess."

Joe switched off the lights, and they stretched out on the bed.

Cissy got up to close the blind. But the glow from a nearby street-light still seeped through. She covered the window with a blanket and plunged the room into velvety darkness.

"Ouch," Joe yelped when she sat on his leg. Cissy jumped off and fell on the floor.

When she didn't get up, Joe turned on the light and sat on the floor beside her. "Cold feet?"

"Is that what it's called?"

"Let's go in the other room and study," he suggested.

"Then I would just have all this to go through again."

He helped her to her feet, turned off the lamp, and they arranged themselves again. Joe took her in his arms and found her mouth. They kissed for a long time. "Are you feeling it yet?" he asked.

"Definitely," she murmured. "How about you?"

"Oh, yes. When do we get to take off our clothes?"

"Soon. Kiss me some more."

He obliged and began feeling her through her clothes, then putting his hand inside her clothes. She did the same. Still kissing, they began to undress each other, which was a bit like a tug-of-war and was made more difficult in the complete absence of light. Cissy had to unhook her bra for him.

"Oh my!" she said when their nude bodies came into contact.

"Touch me," he said, his voice low and husky as he took her hand and placed it over his engorged penis.

"That is really amazing," she said.

"Thank you."

When he put his mouth on her breasts, she gasped, and found her hips moving up and down of their own accord. "I think I'm ready," she whispered.

They did not study biostatistics until the small hours of the morning, and then not for very long.

Instead of solving their mutual problem, they started having sex at every possible opportunity. They would meet in his van for a quickie between classes. When she drew a night shift, they would make out in the bathroom of her patient's room. Other nights, he spent at her house, going to his own place only to change clothes.

"We have created a monster," Cissy said finally. "I fell asleep in class again today."

They rationed themselves. They'd have sex on Wednesday and Saturday nights only. Cissy missed his presence in her bed but was relieved. She didn't like feeling out of control. She didn't want to think about him and sex all the time. She was here to make a physician of herself.

But when she wasn't with Joe, she still thought about him, and the thoughts began to take a different turning. Forbidden thoughts. She imagined herself in a wedding dress. Every song she hummed was about marriage and forever. And she thought about a baby in her belly, a baby in her arms.

But when Joe asked if she thought they should get married, Cissy didn't know if she should feel hopeful or unbearably sad. They were making an evening visit to the embryology lab, taking one last look at tray after tray of microscopic slides in preparation for their final. The shelves that covered three walls of the room were lined with hundreds of jars of various sizes. In each jar floated a grossly malformed fetus. The monster gallery, it was called, "monster" being the official designation for such specimens. Or simply "product of conception." No one ever called them "babies." Many didn't seem even remotely human.

"Did you select this setting intentionally to have this discussion?" Cissy asked. "Or did the thought just pop into your head?"

Joe glanced around the room and shrugged. "Sorry. I was just thinking about things. I'm distracted. We either need to cool it or get on with it."

Cissy gathered up her things. "Well, you certainly managed to break my concentration," she said and left him there.

It would be funny if it wasn't so awful. Embryology was a microcosm for marriage and life, she decided. Embryonic development usually went according to plan, but screwups could be monumental.

Given her state of mind, she would marry Joe in a flash if she thought it would work, but she feared she was no more the right woman for Joe McCormack than she had been for Randy Calhoune. She liked Joe better, loved him more, resented him just as much— resented the fact that he wanted a traditional wife who would look after him and the kids, keep a clean house, have clean underwear in his dresser drawer and meals on the table. If she were Joe, though, she would have wanted the very same things.

If she did have children, whoever their father was would have to have a different set of expectations than Joe, than the men who had conducted her admissions interview. The truth of the matter was, in spite of Gloria Steinem and Betty Freidan, in spite of the National Organization for Women and women's studies programs on many college campuses, in the waning years of the 1970s men and women still hadn't figured out how to share parenting, how to manage a marriage so that women could have what Betty Freidan had called "a life of the mind."

The irony was that even while she railed against society's expectations, she was just as guilty of pigeonholing women as Joe and the physicians on her interview panel. She couldn't imagine a family without a mother in the kitchen, as her own mother had been. What was a family without a mother to organize everyone and make a house a home and bake birthday cakes? Cissy loved Justine but found it hard to admire her because she was not such a woman.

Her father was the sort of man she needed. He was more nurturing than her mother. Even after he went on the road, he managed to spend significant time with her and Buddy. He hugged and listened. He did dishes and laundry. But Grayson Stewart was not a physician. There was nothing life-and-death about selling shoes. And his son had borne him no respect for being a gentle man, no respect at all.

For Cissy, there was no going back. Unless she didn't make the grade, she was going to become a physician. There would be an M.D. after her name. She hungered for the respect and challenge that would bring. She longed to diagnose and heal. If she had to choose between Joe and becoming a physician, she would choose the latter. What she truly wanted was to practice medicine *and* for Joe to change his expectations for marriage.

The morning of the embryology final, she had parked her car and was crossing the street to the basic sciences building when she saw Joe being dropped off by a young woman driving a new Mercedes. He pretended that he didn't see Cissy as he raced up the steps into the building, but she knew that he had.

She didn't realize she had stopped in the middle of the street until a car honked at her. Very carefully, as though her body were made of glass, she walked to the curb, then to the steps. She lowered herself to the bottom step and put her head between her knees. Her head was spinning, her skin clammy. Her heart had slowed to a weak flutter. Someone—a female—stopped to ask if she was all right, and Cissy waved her away.

She took several deep breaths and convinced herself that she wasn't going to die, that somehow she was going to get herself up the steps and to the nearest ladies' room.

The cold water felt almost erotic on her hot face. Again and again, she splashed her face and patted her wet hands on her bare arms. Then she studied her face in the mirror. Wet hair was plastered to her forehead. Her mascara was running down her colorless cheeks. "Okay, Cissy Stewart, you get your ass down that hall and make a better grade on that test than Joe McCormack."

She was the last one in the room before the proctor closed the door. She slid into a seat and never once scanned the room to see where Joe was sitting.

It was almost midnight when he called. He was speaking so softly that at first she thought it was an obscene phone call. He wasn't alone, she realized. *She* was there with him, asleep or in the bathroom. "Coward," she said. "You could at least come tell me in person."

"My wife wants us to get back together," he whispered. "She's moving up here."

"With some of Daddy's money, I take it. How nice for you—home cooking *and* a Mercedes. You can't beat a deal like that."

"Don't, Cissy. I am really sorry, but I guess I never stopped caring about her. She's a good person. She will devote herself to me and our children. Maybe I'm a selfish son of a bitch to want that, but I do."

Cissy hung up and threw her coffee cup against the wall. And the saucer. She went to the kitchen and broke more dishes. Then she called the pilot. His name was Barry, but everyone called him Bear. "I need a house call," she told him.

Bear accepted her rules. He had to be invited. She would take care of birth control. He was to supply the booze. And the word *marriage* was never to be mentioned, which was fine with him. He planned to find a trophy wife when he became an uptown plastic surgeon with a major bank account and a Porsche. His wife would be tall, redheaded, and have big breasts. He didn't care if she could cook.

Bear was pretty businesslike about sex. You do it and then you sleep. Cissy decided that sex with him was like taking aspirin when what she really needed was codeine. But codeine was addictive, she reminded herself.

Eventually she added another rule. No falling asleep. He had to go home afterward. "No way," he told her.

She stopped inviting him for a while. When she started once again, it was like before. He fell asleep after sex, only now she moved to the sofa.

thirty-six

When the first year of medical school ended, Cissy ranked fourth in her class. By the end of the second year she had slipped a few notches but was still in the top ten. Her classmates and professors all knew who she was—Cecelia Stewart, the nurse from Columbus who had made top ten two years running. Her biochemistry professor invited her to work with his research group, which was investigating the chemical changes that led to diabetic retinopathy. She showed real promise, he told her. There weren't enough women in biomedical research. Maybe she should change to a Ph.D. program. She could write her own ticket.

As intrigued as Cissy was by the prospect of medical research, her dream was to help one person at a time. She wanted to *practice* medicine, as Doc Hadley had done.

Iris insisted that the days of horse-and-buggy medicine were over, that modern-day physicians practiced near major medical centers, with the newest technology and practitioners of every specialty and subspecialty close at hand. "Houston's a lot closer than it used to be," Cissy insisted, quoting Doc Hadley's own words about how people in little towns needed someone to look after them, too.

"You just can't cut yourself loose, can you?" Iris's voice challenged. "You're going to spend your life looking after your dysfunctional parents and treating sore throats to pay penance because you weren't your brother's keeper."

"Oh, come on, Iris. I want to practice in a small town instead of a big one. Don't make it into something more."

"You're delusional, Cissy. It *is* something more."

"Are you sorry you talked me into this?" Cissy asked.

There was a pause before Iris said, "Of course not. I suppose I knew all along how it would turn out. I just had this dream of you and me working together. I need you more than you need me, it seems. And I'm one to talk. I'm paying your way because I ran off and left you and Buddy to fend for yourselves."

With the two years of basic sciences out of the way, Cissy and her classmates knew about the structure of the human body and the cells that composed it. They knew about the chemistry of living organisms and the germs that infect the body. Now the time had come to leave the classroom and the academic faculty behind and enter their clinical years. For the next two years, they would follow attending physicians around, learning from them at the bedsides of actual patients.

Cissy's first clinical rotation was surgery. The first day, she and another third-year student scrubbed in on the amputation of a fifty-five-year-old diabetic male's left leg—just above the knee. She had scrubbed in on numerous surgeries during her nurse's training but nothing so brutal as an amputation. The sound of the saw and the putrid smell that rose from the gangrenous limb were too much for the other medical student. Jared Franklin, the son of an Austin urologist, started weaving back and forth, then grabbed hold of a nurse's arm for support. The assisting surgeon yelled at him to get the hell out of there.

The operation lasted more than two hours. Cissy concentrated on the hot shower she would take as soon as she got home—a very long shower that would wash away the smell of rotting tissue and the tension that pressed like a vise across her shoulders and neck.

But she also felt satisfaction. Because of her nurse's training, she was better prepared than her classmates for the experiences that awaited her over the next two years. She had thought this would be the case, and now she knew it.

For most of Cissy's classmates, this was their first foray into the front lines of medicine. The time had come to see if they could relate all that knowledge they had crammed inside their heads for the last two years to the actuality of disease and trauma and begin to discern where it was on medicine's diverse landscape that they themselves would eventually land.

The day after the amputation, Cissy stopped by to see the patient. He was groggy with painkillers. And weepy. Why had this happened to him? His wife reminded him that he was lucky to be alive. The doctors had been telling him for years it was going to come to this if he didn't stop smoking and get his diabetes under control. "I'll bet this young lady doesn't smoke," the woman said, nodding toward Cissy. "Nurses know better."

Third-year students were allowed to introduce themselves to patients and their families as "doctor." Even so, no matter how emphatically Cissy said the word, patients continued to mistake her for a nurse, which she still was when she worked at her paying job and would always be in some basic way. But when she wore her white jacket with a stethoscope in the pocket, her hair pulled into a severe bun, she wanted the respect of her new station in life. She was a physician-in-the-making, but patients still would ask her to get a bedpan or to fill their water jug.

Her second rotation was internal medicine, which was run by the first and only female department chair in the history of the medical school. Daisy Cunningham was barely five feet tall, pushing sixty, and formidable. Students, residents, clinical faculty, and even the dean himself snapped to when Dr. Cunningham addressed them.

The first day of the rotation, Dr. Cunningham marched her new crop of students from bedside to bedside as she examined patients and questioned them about their symptoms in a kindly voice.

At the conclusion of rounds, she encouraged the students to speculate about the patients and describe any significant symptoms they had noticed. When one hapless young man referred to a patient as the fat lady at the end of the hall, she told him in a frosty voice that the woman had a name. "On my service, *all* patients have names. They are not room numbers or diseases or body types. They are human beings and will be treated and spoken of with dignity. Now, does anyone remember this patient's name?" Dr. Cunningham asked.

When no one answered, Dr. Cunningham looked in Cissy's direction. "Dr. Stewart?"

"Mary Sinclair," Cissy answered.

"What else can you tell me about Mrs. Sinclair?"

"Her diagnosis is acute pulmonary edema brought on by congestive heart failure."

"No, no, no," Dr. Cunningham said impatiently. "I mean, what else can you tell me about her as a person?"

Cissy shrugged. "She is a retired church secretary, married, and has three living children."

Dr. Cunningham nodded. "And how do you know these things?"

"They were on her chart."

"Did you learn anything else about this patient at her bedside?"

"She has the beginning of a bed sore on her right elbow, and I suspect that she is lonely," Cissy said.

"What makes you think that?" Dr. Cunningham asked.

"She was admitted last Monday, and there are no get-well cards on her dresser, no flowers, no magazines that people have brought by."

"Now, you may tell me what therapy you suggest for this patient and speculate about her prognosis."

Cissy recited what she had read the night before and added some of her own observations gleaned from patients she had taken care of as a nurse. When she finished, Dr. Cunningham said, "Thank you, Dr. Stewart. Would you please come see me this afternoon?"

It was after three when Cissy arrived at the administrative offices of the internal medicine section and was escorted into Dr. Cunningham's cluttered office. The first thing Cissy noticed was the quilt that hung on the wall behind a worn leather sofa. Another was draped over the sofa's back.

"The wedding ring pattern," Cissy said, indicating the quilt on the wall. "It's beautiful. My mother has one. My great-grandmother made it for her as a wedding present. She still keeps it folded at the foot of her bed. Who made this one?" she asked, examining the fine stitches.

"I bought it at an estate sale. The one on the sofa was made by my quilting circle—a group effort. I have more at home. I change the ones here in my office every month or so. They comfort me, especially the old ones made from feed sacks and old clothes. When I think of the women who made them to warm their children and beautify their homes even if the home had a dirt floor and sod roof, I am reminded that people are more than systems and symptoms."

"I keep the one my grandmother made for me folded on the foot of my bed—on the days I get around to making my bed. The pattern is kaleidoscope."

Daisy Cunningham nodded. She knew the pattern. "My grandmother used to say a woman had to quilt or crochet in order to leave something of herself, that all the other things a woman did—cleaning and cooking and laundry—never stayed done. Well-placed stitches, on the other hand, stay put for generations."

"I've always thought more women should be surgeons," Cissy said. "They've got smaller hands and are accustomed to precision."

Dr. Cunningham offered a small smile and waved Cissy to the sofa. She poured water from an electric kettle into two waiting china cups and bobbed tea bags up and down. Dr. Cunningham placed the cups on a wicker tray next to a plate of sugar cookies. She set the tray on a small, gate-legged table, pulled her chair from behind her desk, and sat across from Cissy. "I've been waiting for you, Cecelia Claire Stewart," she said.

"I'm sorry," Cissy said. "I didn't think you had specified a time for me to come."

Dr. Cunningham shook her head. "I wasn't talking about today. I've been waiting for you for two years."

"I don't understand."

"I was a nurse, too. I don't have a nursing degree like you do. I'd never even heard of a college degree in nursing back then. I went through a three-year hospital program when I got out of high school. I put myself through college nursing. And through medical school, like you're doing."

Cissy nodded. "I earn most of my living expenses. My physician cousin paid for my tuition and books the first two years. Now I've got a scholarship."

"How many hours a week do you nurse?"

"It varies. Usually about twenty, mostly night shifts, obviously."

"Is that why you never joined the Women's Student Medical Association?"

Cissy knew that Daisy Cunningham was the founder and sponsor of the organization's local chapter. Still, she answered honestly, "Not really. I prefer to think of myself simply as a medical student, not a *woman* medical student. And I've never been much of a joiner."

"There are too few women in medicine," Dr. Cunningham pointed out. "We have to band together. If we don't, we're overlooked. Women aren't elected president of their medical school class. They don't serve as medical school deans. The best residencies go to men. Chief residents are seldom women. That has to change."

"How can a club do that?"

"We can do that by supporting each other, by meeting successful women physicians and learning from them. The next meeting is at my house. Thursday evening at seven. Here is my address," she said, writing on a memo pad. "Our speaker will be a family physician from Oklahoma—a classmate of mine. Agnes and I graduated from a women's medical college. That was easier. No one compared us to men. But it was hell getting a decent residency. If you don't learn anything else from me, I want to teach you to look after other women and not be one of those nasty creatures who claws her way across the drawbridge, then pulls it up behind her."

Dr. Cunningham lived in a vintage house in a lovely old neighborhood near Southern Methodist University. Her home was indeed full of quilts. The walls of the hall and stairwell were lined with them, and they were folded on benches and draped over the arms of chairs. A large second-floor loft area held a quilting frame circled by an assortment of ladder-back chairs.

The rooms of the spacious house were filled with American antiques—from early colonial to art nouveau. The backyard was shared in equal parts by a swimming pool and a vegetable garden. The guest speaker, Dr. Agnes Hanover, poured tea from a silver tea service. In appearance at least, the gathering wasn't greatly different from a ladies' club meeting in Columbus. Rather than conversation about recipes and children, however, these women discussed coursework, hospital rounds, residency prospects. And there were lively discussions about how difficult it was to find time for boyfriends and the despair of unkempt apartments and never-ending piles of laundry.

After dessert and coffee, Agnes Hanover told them about her life. Her husband had been on the faculty at the University of Oklahoma. She had raised two children with the help of a string of housekeepers. Her husband was a fine vertebrate paleontologist but totally incompetent—perhaps by choice—in most other endeavors, including the balancing of checkbooks, washing of clothes, hammering of nails, care of children and pets, opening of cans of soup. She practiced in her home so she could kiss ouchies and feel like a better mother. She had been there when her son fell out of a tree and broke his arm. Her neighbors often fed her children when she was tied up at the hospital and her husband forgot to come home from his lab. Life was better now that the children were grown. Her husband was retired now, but he still went to the vertebrate paleontology lab every day, including Sundays.

"Not being able to keep a definite schedule is the worst part for a physician who is also a mom," she admitted. "I often wished I'd specialized in dermatology and had primarily an office practice—or become a radiologist and read X-rays until five o'clock, then gone home to my children. But when it comes right down to it, I can't imagine being contented with any life other than the one I have led. What I would do differently, however, is demand more of my husband. If he had covered the home front for me instead of leaving it to hired help and the neighbors, he would have gotten to know his children better. When Daisy and I started out, though, the only women who worked were old maids or widows—and occasionally a woman whose husband was an invalid or a drunken bum. We had no role models. I always worried that I was shortchanging my children and raised them apologetically. My husband could spend ten or twelve hours a day fondling old bones in the lab or off hunting them for weeks on end with his students and colleagues and never suffer a pang of guilt. That wasn't fair. I know that now, but I wish I had come to that conclusion sooner. Ironically, my daughter is married to a cardiologist and is the perfect doctor's wife. And my son went out of his way *not* to marry a girl just like the girl who married dear old Dad. His wife is an avid golfer and organizes benefit galas, but she's there when her children come home from school and has never missed one important moment in their lives. For what it's worth, however, my seven-year-old granddaughter says she's going to have six kids and be a brain surgeon. And through it all, I still love the old fossil I married. He didn't help me, but he didn't hinder me, either."

After the talk, Dr. Cunningham served sherry. At the end of the evening, she put her arm around Cissy's shoulders.

"I hope you'll come back."

"Yes, I will," Cissy promised. "It was a wonderful evening."

Cissy now spent most of her waking hours in hospitals, either rotating through her current clinical service or working a shift as a special-duty nurse, usually at huge, sprawling Parkland. Sometimes she and Joe would pass each other in a hospital corridor, not even hesitating as they asked "How's it going?" and rushing on by.

In various configurations, the Friday night crowd still gathered, but Joe had dropped out when his wife moved to Dallas. Cissy tried to go every second or third week, just so she wouldn't lose touch. More and more, though, she welcomed the solitude of her messy little duplex. She wanted to eat her bowl of soup or whatever, spend three or four hours going over charts and checking textbooks in preparation for the next day's rounds, then take a hot bath and crawl into bed alone. She was too tired for sex. Bear complained about that. And he complained that she never had any food in the house, never wanted to share a six-pack. If they went to a movie, she fell asleep. If they watched television, she fell asleep. When they did have sex, she longed for it to be over so she could fall sleep. "You could at least do me the courtesy of faking an orgasm," Bear told her. "Is that what your other girlfriends have done?" Cissy asked.

Even so, they saw each other once or twice a week, fearful that something was better than nothing, Cissy supposed.

Finally, one morning she stopped by his apartment on her way to the hospital. He came to the door in his underwear, made coffee in his underwear, but he put on a pair of jeans before sitting with her at the kitchen table with its clutter of books and papers.

"So, you've come to tell me in person," he said.

"How did you know?"

"You have never just dropped by. The very few times you've come up here, you've been either on your way to or returning from a hospital and desirous of a quickie. And it's been obvious for some time that you are no longer interested in quick sex with me or slow sex or any sex at all."

"It was great while it lasted, Bear, but we've run our course." Cissy took a deep breath, followed by a sip of coffee. Telling him hadn't been as bad as she thought it would be.

"Is Joe coming back?" Bear asked, stirring a second teaspoon of sugar into his mug.

"To me?" Cissy shook her head, puzzled. "Joe has a wife."

"Yeah, but I hear that she moved back home to Lampasas."

"I didn't know that," Cissy admitted.

"So, there's no one else? I'd almost rather there was. I'd rather come in second than simply be rejected whole cloth."

"You're a great guy. The problem is with me. I never should have started up with you in the first place."

"You were just using me, huh? Bear, the sex object?"

"Oh, come on," Cissy said with a glance at her watch. "We were using each other."

"Well, it could have been more than that for me, but you never changed your damned sheets."

"You could have changed them yourself."

He pondered this for a minute. "I never thought of that."

At the door, they hugged. Cissy clung for a bit. They had indeed run their course, but it had been a comfort knowing that there was someone out there for a kind word or a "quickie."

She sat in her car for a time before starting the engine, feeling sad about Bear and digesting the news that Joe's wife had left. She would have preferred not to know that particular piece of information—not that she wanted to take up with him again. She had known it was going to end between her and Joe sooner or later, she supposed, but she hadn't been ready, hadn't seen it coming. Just thinking about him brought a dull ache to her chest. *Heartache.* No matter what medical science said, the heart was more than a pump. And she'd thought she was over him. That's what Bear had been about. In truth, she *had* used him—to get over Joe.

When her shift at Parkland ended, she decided she would go for a swim in Daisy Cunningham's pool. Daisy was out of town, but Cissy had a standing invitation to swim anytime she wanted and to help herself to vegetables from the garden.

Since that first WSMA meeting, Cissy had dined in her mentor's lovely home many times, sometimes with club members, sometimes just her and Daisy. "Are you happy living alone?" Cissy had asked her one evening over sherry.

"No, but I wasn't happy living with a man, either. A man wants a woman to fuss over him. I never fussed."

"My mother liked doing that for Daddy and us kids," Cissy said. "I always thought I would grow up and be just like her."

"Why didn't you?"

"The fussing over all came to an end. My parents fell out of love and have spent the last sixteen or so years making each other miserable. Now I wonder if it wouldn't be better to be like you and go it alone. Maybe I'd never be gloriously happy, but I'd be spared all that hurt. I guess I'm using medicine as a substitute for marriage."

"Some women do both."

"Yes, but they need to have husbands who want them to do both. I suspect such men are hard to find."

Daisy nodded. "That certainly was true for my generation. Probably still is. And how can you blame men? I'd like a lovely, competent person to look after me and have a wonderful meal on the table every night at six. And there's still a part of me that would like to be that person for some man and a couple of kids. It's better now that I'm past childbearing age, but the feeling hasn't gone away."

"I came very close to marrying a medical student back in my nursing school days," Cissy said. "I would have put my nursing degree in a drawer and devoted myself to being a good doctor's wife and a good mother to his children. It might have been okay. It might even have been wonderful."

"Do you still think about him?" Daisy asked.

"No, I think about the man who came after him," Cissy had answered. Randy Calhoune was history. She would go for days, even weeks, without thinking about him. But she did still think about Joe McCormack.

After her swim, she took a short detour on the way home, driving by Joe's house, then circling the block and parking across the street. His van was in the driveway, an even older van than her own. Maybe his wife hadn't left at all. Her Mercedes was probably in the garage.

Light came from a side window and pooled itself on the lawn. A dining room window, perhaps. They could be having dinner right now. A lovely home-cooked meal for the harried medical-student husband.

She wondered what service Joe was on now. And at which hospital.

Such a pretty little house with a steeply pitched roof and diamond-paned windows. Joe and his wife were probably deliriously happy. She probably baked bread and changed the sheets twice a week.

Cissy put her head against the steering wheel. What if there was never another Joe in her life? What if she never felt like that again?

thirty-seven

I once asked Daisy Cunningham why she had never married. She had come very close, she explained.

We were sitting by her pool, as I recall. We often did that on a summer's eve, drinking iced tea garnished with fresh mint from her garden, discussing the patients we had seen that day and sometimes other things, like why we had turned out the way we had. Her home had become my retreat. And her mind. She patiently answered my questions, even enjoyed doing so, I suspect, using our friendship as a means to reflect and put her own experience and knowledge in perspective.

Daisy had fallen in love with a widowed pathologist with two grown daughters who were dead set against their father's getting involved with anyone, especially a woman close to their own age. Their mother had been a saintly woman who had founded a shelter for the homeless and done all manner of other good works in the community. Their father was supposed to live out his years as a grieving widower.

The pathologist kept telling Daisy that his daughters just needed time to become accustomed to the idea of his remarrying. They would learn to love her. They would want him to be happy.

Daisy saw the professor in secret, always at her house. She parked her car on the street, so his Lincoln would be discreetly out of sight in her garage. They would spend the evening and night together, but he would get up before dawn so he could drive home in the dark. He didn't want his neighbors to know he'd been out all night and possibly mention the fact to his daughters.

"I kept giving myself ultimatums," Daisy recalled. "After my next birthday, I would tell him that we were finished and then get on with my life. After his next birthday. After Christmas. After the tenth anniversary of his wife's death. After he recuperated from back surgery, then from a heart attack. Then one morning I saw his obituary in the newspaper. By then, I was forty years old.

"As awful as it sounds, his death came as a relief—not at first, of course. I cried a lot and allowed myself to be bitter over not being able to attend his funeral. I didn't keep any of his stuff, though. I threw out his bathrobe and toothbrush, his razor and pill bottles. Not long after, I bought this house. I don't even think about him much anymore, just when I see one of his daughters' pictures on the society page. Last year, they endowed a chair in pathology in honor of their parents."

There had been other men in Daisy's life after that, some quite wonderful, others less so. But after the professor died, she was shocked how much she enjoyed not having to factor him into her busy schedule—not that they had spent every night together, but she always tried to keep her evenings open, just in case. With him gone, her life became more spacious. She had time for a garden, for cultivating women friends, for taking up quilting. She bought season tickets to the symphony and SMU basketball games. She didn't have to agonize about whether or not she really needed to go back to the hospital at midnight or could handle a crisis over the phone and stay with her professor.

The men who came after him were allowed only a well-defined corner of her life. If they did not agree to her terms, they were dismissed. They were seldom allowed to stay the night; mostly she went on trips with them. Trips were nice—honeymoonlike. Even now, she traveled some with a history professor on the Rice faculty. They had toured Europe, ridden the train across Canada, skied in Colorado. Lovely trips, but she was always glad to get back to her house and routines. And the poor old darling was getting a bit dysfunctional. More than a bit, actually. If he got it up, it seldom stayed. She had to decide if his company alone would be enough.

Her reminiscing completed, Daisy had reached over and patted my hand. "I've often wondered if some of us women seek out medicine because it distances us from the more traditional relationships that our parents and everyone else expect of women and gives us an almost no-ble reason to avoid them—almost like joining a religious order. We are healers and therefore too busy to look after a husband. Kids, too. If I had it all to do over, however, I would have adopted a couple of kids from Mexico or wherever. And hired a nanny. If you're saving kids from starving to death or a life on the streets, you don't have to feel so guilty about not being the perfect All-American mom."

Daisy's words made me think of my cousin Iris, who had chosen a dear but damaged man who felt privileged every time she touched his hand or kissed his cheek. He expected nothing of her, therefore every minute he had with her was a gift. By her own admission, Iris had mar-ried because she wanted a baby.

And I thought of my relationship with Joe McCormack. In the be-ginning, I hadn't wanted a love affair, just an affair. But I wasn't as modern a young woman as I had wanted to believe. In my heart of hearts, I believed then, and maybe I still do, that sex is supposed to mean something, that sex should be about love.

When Joe went back to his wife, I used anger to salve my wounds. *He was a son of a bitch. Men were no damned good.* After a time, I considered myself healed, sadder but wiser, a veteran in the relation-ship wars. I would be more careful next time. I would hold back and not get hurt.

With Bear, I succeeded for a time. We would engage in sex and friendship, when actually—except perhaps in a few rare marriages—the two don't mix. Bear and I might have been friends for life if we had avoided sex.

The fortress I had erected around myself began crumbling the minute Bear told me that Joe's wife had gone back to Lampasas. As soon as the words were said, as I sat there in Bear's cluttered kitchen taking that last sip of coffee, the walls were already beginning to crack.

☙❧

Sitting in front of the house that Joe shared with his wife, Cissy felt as though she was incapable of turning the key in the ignition and moving on. For an indeterminable time she sat there, with no plan in mind, no hope of anything. Finally, the pressure from a full bladder forced her to head home.

The next day she began dialing Joe's phone number. Every time Cissy had a chance, she dialed—to see if *she* answered. Cissy didn't even know the woman's name. She was simply Joe's wife.

Did this nameless wife know that Joe had been with someone during their separation?

With her finger hovering above the disconnect button, Cissy would listen as the ringing went on and on. She imagined the ringing penetrating every corner of the house. Given its vintage, its rooms probably had high ceilings and wooden floors. Were they tidy or cluttered? Had Joe's wife decorated with moiré or chintz?

What sort of person was this wife? Was she sexy or the girl next door? Spoiled, certainly, with her Mercedes and upscale home, when other medical students and their spouses lived with cockroaches in crummy little apartments.

Even if Joe's wife truly had gone back to Lampasas, that didn't mean she had left for good. She could have gone home for a long visit. A parent might be ill or a sister getting married.

Monday night, Cissy once again drove by Joe's house. The driveway was empty, the house dark but for one dim light on the side of the house. Once again, she parked across the street and studied it, trying to discern the interior floor plan. Was their bedroom in the front or the back?

Suddenly she was startled by the flashing light of a patrol car. She waited while it parked across the street and a uniformed policeman approached her car, shining a flashlight in her face, demanding to see her driver's license, wanting to know why a young woman in a van was parked along a tree-lined street in this affluent neighborhood.

Cissy stammered that she had felt dizzy and had pulled over for a few minutes. No, she had not been drinking. Maybe she was coming down with something.

The policeman studied her driver's license for the longest time, then returned the beam of light to her face.

"You know someone in this neighborhood?"

"One of my professors lives two streets over," Cissy said. "I was on my way home from visiting her."

Finally, the policeman sent her on her way with a warning. Folks get spooked when someone sits in front of their house in a van. Don't do it again.

Cissy's hand trembled as she turned the ignition. In bed, she wept. She was out of control. She had to get a grip on herself.

All day Tuesday, even though she had promised herself that she wouldn't, Cissy once again repeatedly dialed Joe's house. His phone number became a litany, replaying itself endlessly in her brain.

What if she became this distracted a couple of years from now when she was a physician with patients under her care? She wouldn't be capable of making good decisions for them. She might cause them grave harm or even kill someone.

Why hadn't medical science come up with a medication for whatever it was she had? An obsession—that's what it was. Levelheaded, sensible Cissy Stewart was obsessed with a married man who had dumped her.

She had to work her way through it.

Should she talk to someone?

But who would understand? She had always told Iris everything, but this was so embarrassing, so unlike her. She tried to imagine what Iris would say. What Daisy Cunningham would say. Her parents. Joe himself. They would be so shocked. Not Cissy. Sane, sensible Cissy would never act this way.

She was alone on the entire planet, in the middle of a vast, empty desert, dialing the same phone number over and over, driving by a forbidden house, sobbing into her pillow.

After the fourth day of such insanity, she bought a bottle of cheap wine on her way home. Sitting on the back step, she drank from the bottle and watched thunderheads form overhead.

When the rain began, she carried the bottle inside and watched from the kitchen window as torrential rain and then hail the size of Ping-Pong balls beat down on her tiny, treeless backyard. The claps of thunder were so loud and startling, she jumped each time. The lightning seemed close enough to strike the roof. Maybe that was how this all would end—a small story on page 2 of the Dallas newspaper: MEDICAL STUDENT DIES IN HOUSE FIRE.

Was there a heaven? Would she really see Buddy again? And the others? Grandma Polly. Granny Grace. Even relatives she'd never known.

Her birth parents even.

But how would she know these other parents? And they her? She imagined passing them on the golden streets of heaven and not even knowing who they were. Would they be the age they were when she was born? Or the age they were when they died?

Maybe Buddy would be a little boy again, and she could look after him. She hoped Granny Grace and Grandma Polly would be young again, not old and sick.

It all seemed so fanciful, though. Not even in her drunken state could she convince herself that she would have a second chance with Buddy. She wouldn't even have a second chance at Joe McCormack, and he was still alive.

With her wandering mind and the noise of the storm, it took her a minute to realize the phone was ringing.

It was Joe. He was just around the corner. Could he drop by?

Cissy didn't know what to do first. Comb her hair? Pick up the clutter? She just stood there clutching an empty wine bottle until he came to the door.

The door wasn't even locked. The safety chain her father had installed was not engaged.

Joe was drenched, his hair plastered to his head, a puddle forming around him on the floor.

"Did she leave you?" Cissy asked.

"No. She's pregnant and throwing up every fifteen minutes. She went home so her mother could look after her."

"Then what the hell are you doing here?" she screamed at him over the sound of the pelting rain.

"I can't stop thinking about you."

"Just leave, will you, before I throw this bottle at you?"

"Are you sure that's what you really want? I saw you sitting out in front of the house Monday night, saw that policeman shine his flashlight on your face. I haven't been able to think about anything else since."

Of course, she didn't really want him to leave. What she wanted was for him to stay forever, but she couldn't have that, so maybe she should just take what she could have. Probably that was one more night, one more time with his body in hers. "I hate you," she said as he grabbed her and wrapped his wet arms around her.

It felt so good to say those words that she said them again and again. She did hate him. More than anything, she hated him. But her body didn't know that. Her body felt as though she had just come home after a long and perilous journey.

Afterward, he told her that she was beautiful.

"No, I'm not. I'm ordinary."

He propped himself up on one elbow and looked down at her. "No, you are not ordinary. You are the most extraordinary woman I have ever known. You are lovely and so brilliant. God, so brilliant. You learn things at a glance that I have to read five times. You master one piece of information and are able to deduce the next one, and the next. Do you have any idea how in awe of you the rest of us are?"

"So, why did you leave me if I am so extraordinary? Is *she* extraordinary?"

"No, she's not. But I knew if I survived that fucking war, all I wanted was an ordinary life. I wanted a sweet wife who would look after me and our kids. A pretty house. Financial security. The whole package. That's not the way it would be with you and me. Lynette needs me, Cissy. You don't need anyone."

Lynette. She had not wanted to know that name, she realized, had not wanted to hear it spoken in her bed. "So you get what you want, and I don't? Do you love her that much?"

"I love her," he said, "but not like I love you."

"I hate you," she said again, trying to push him out of the bed, but he began touching her again, pushing his face against her belly.

Finally, they both lay paralyzed, a sheet pulled over their damp bodies. Two thoughts flitted about her mind as she fell into a drunken, bottomless slumber. She wondered if she had done this to herself. Because of some deep, self-destructive flaw, had she deliberately fallen in love with a man who would abandon her, who would break her heart and, therefore, leave her less likely to trust and believe?

She knew he wouldn't be there when she woke up. "Don't come back," she told him. "Not ever."

In the night, she heard him leave and knew she was supposed to feel sad. But the pain of too much wine throbbing behind her eyeballs precluded other feelings. She needed to sleep some more, then she would feel sad or angry or whatever. She went to the bathroom first, locked the front door, set the alarm clock. Put her poor head carefully back on its pillow. Life went on.

Toward morning, she awoke again, and it occurred to her to wonder when her last period had been. After she broke up with Bear, she stopped taking birth control pills. But she wasn't mid-cycle. She was sure of it. Close, maybe, but days off. Surely she was in the clear.

Surely.

But a shiver of fear shot through her body.

She looked at the clock. It was still early. She would go back to sleep until the alarm sounded. Then she would look at a calendar and convince herself everything was okay.

Her body was finished with sleeping, however. With a groan, she lifted her head and planted her feet on the floor.

The calendar was in the kitchen, hung over the phone. She stared at it, trying to remember. She had had her period when she scrubbed in on that appendectomy. She remembered wearing double pads to see her through the procedure. That had been on the first of the month. It was now three days short of two weeks. Which should be all right, shouldn't it?

Maybe she should pray.

Praying wouldn't do any good if fertilization had taken place, though, unless she prayed that the conceptus would fail to implant.

Was it wrong to do that? Did God even care? After all, it wasn't God's fault. She was a third-year medical student and certainly knew where babies came from.

She was sure that Joe knew she'd been sleeping with Bear. He'd probably assumed she was still on the pill.

She should have at least insisted on a condom.

She tried to replay the evening, making Joe go to an all-night drugstore and buy a package of condoms, which would have destroyed the mood, ended the madness. They would have calmed down, come to their senses. He would have realized he didn't want to be unfaithful to his pregnant, ordinary wife and her rich daddy. Cissy would have realized how destructive it was to have a one-night stand with an ex-lover with whom she was still in love. Joe would have left. She would have locked the door, turned out the lights, gone to bed alone, as all third-year, female medical students who are not on the pill should do.

She stood under the shower for a long time, symbolically and literally washing away Joe. "No baby, please," she whispered out loud in the shower stall, offering up a prayer after all.

thirty-eight

Had she really been in love?

Love? She remembered how she had behaved that fateful night, remembered thinking that she was in love with Joe, but she could not conjure up the feeling itself. All she felt now was stupid.

In the name of love she had had unprotected sex with a man whom she knew—regardless of all the emotion leading up to that night—was just passing through her life.

She had risked her future, or certainly risked greatly altering that future, for a couple of orgasms with a married man who planned to stay married.

The prospect of a pregnancy was grim beyond measure. She was years away from completing a residency program and entering practice.

And she was tired.

Any time she had left over in her daily life, after fulfilling her school and job responsibilities, she needed for sleep.

Cissy had nothing left over for a baby—not time or money or energy. And she wasn't tough enough to deal with the censure a pregnancy would bring, with people wondering how a smart woman like Cissy Stewart could have been so stupid, so completely irresponsible.

But all this panic was premature, she kept telling herself as days turned into weeks. One night of unprotected sex did not necessarily a baby make. She had not been mid-cycle. Not quite. Probably nothing was going on.

Odds were, she would be just fine, with no microscopic blastula lurking down there to complicate her life beyond measure.

What she needed to do was to calm down, to stop thinking about it. Which she did for long stretches of time. Then a wave of disquiet would ripple through her body, and she would find herself praying again, not so much to God as to her own body. *Don't do this thing to me. Please.*

Each day that passed was ominous, pushing her closer and closer to the brink.

She simply could not have a baby. Not for years and years. Maybe never. A person missed a lot by not having kids, both pain and pleasure. Christmas would be a downer, but you didn't have to worry about phone calls in the night.

She thought of her own mother's constant hovering presence in her childhood. And even now, their weekly phone calls were a reaffirmation of abiding love. Someone on this planet cared whether she was eating vegetables and taking a multivitamin every morning. Her mother had spent a week here last summer—to "deep-clean" the duplex, mend Cissy's clothing, prepare wonderful summertime meals with fresh cantaloupe and vegetables picked fresh and brought from Columbus.

Even as a woman almost thirty, Cissy missed her mother's presence in her life, missed the mothering things, missed having someone care whether she was getting enough sleep or not, whether her head ached or her stomach hurt.

Cissy knew that any baby of hers would not have a mother like Martha Claire Stewart. Or a father like Grayson Stewart.

Every child needed a father who would take him or her fishing and discuss all manner of things, from the habits of owls to the Norman Conquest. So often when some obscure piece of information would pop into Cissy's head and she would ponder how she happened to know that female hawks are larger than the males, that President William Henry Harrison died thirty days after his inauguration, that Eskimos had no system of government, she would trace the fact back to a discussion she had had with her father while they were fishing on the river, weeding the garden, walking home from the store.

Cissy waited three weeks before giving up hope. And then, in spite of morning nausea, tacked on another week just in case.

Then it became impossible to put it out of her mind. A feeling of panic was her constant companion as she performed her various shifts—Dr. Stewart and Nurse Stewart, going from ward to ward, hospital to hospital, switching roles like other people changed clothes. But she was distracted. She lost her place in conversations and forgot why she had walked into a room. People kept asking her if she felt all right. When she crawled into bed exhausted, needing sleep more than anything, sleep eluded her. She would stare into the darkness, agonizing over her fate.

She wanted to hate Joe, to blame him for all this suffering. But when he called that fateful night, she had allowed him to come over. She hadn't told him to stay away. She hadn't even locked the door.

An early abortion was the only way out of this mess. It was legal now, in the wake of *Roe v. Wade*. None of the hospitals allowed the procedure, but there were clinics. She would find the money someplace. Not ask Joe. Or Iris. She would borrow it from Daisy Cunningham. Dr. Cunningham wouldn't ask questions. She would simply get out her checkbook and ask how much Cissy needed.

But what if she never married? What if this was the only time her body would ever be pregnant?

And Cissy thought about her own origins. She wondered if her birth mother had found herself with an unwanted pregnancy and considered abortion. Every woman in those circumstances must consider it, even those who had professed moral revulsion to the procedure. At the least, every woman with an unwanted pregnancy prayed for a spontaneous abortion—a freebie, with no lifelong burden of wondering if it had been the right thing.

Maybe this pregnancy was an opportunity for Cissy to come full circle with her own life—a paying back of sorts for her mother's not ending the pregnancy that resulted in her own birth. Cissy could carry the child and give it up for adoption as her birth mother had done before her.

Cissy also thought about Justine and Iris. If Justine had given Iris away, how different her own life would have been. Iris had been the most joyous part of her childhood. Iris was the reason she was in medical school. Iris believed in her. If Cissy screwed up medical school because she had gotten herself pregnant, she would be letting Iris down.

Iris was pregnant now—and deliriously happy, as pregnant women should be.

Cissy's thoughts led her around and around in an endless, confusing circle. There was no easy answer. No answer to be found by reexamining the past. The past was a maze of secrets and unhappiness. So much unhappiness, and she didn't even know why. It had killed Buddy. It had made Justine take Iris away. It made her too afraid to make this all-important decision about her own life.

Her mother would never explain the past. Martha Claire would insist that nothing had happened, that marriages wear out just like cars, that hers and Grayson's was simply an old, tired marriage.

Finally, sick with indecision, Cissy made the six-hour drive home to Columbus—not to the house on Milam Street, but to her father's cabin by the river.

When Grayson heard the crunching of car tires on gravel, he thought that Paul Huxley had been able to get away after all.

The retired minister came most Sunday afternoons. To fish. And to sip a bit of Jack Daniel's—their little secret. After all, where in the Bible did it say not to drink whiskey? Paul always brought a lemon to suck on while he drove home. Even though he was retired now and liberated somewhat from the watchful eyes of parishioners and deacons, his wife, Amanda, was a lifetime member and past state president of the Women's Christian Temperance Union. If Amanda thought he'd had so much as a sip of demon whiskey, she would probably kick him out of the house or at least make him sleep in the attic, all of which made those clandestine sips by the river, often with a fishing pole in hand, all the more pleasurable for the aging clergyman.

Amanda had fallen last week, however, and broken her hip. She was hospitalized in Houston. Martha Claire had talked about driving over with Paul to visit her this afternoon. Grayson hadn't been expecting him, hadn't decided on a topic for today's discussion. Last Sunday they had argued about the Virgin Birth. It had been delightful.

Grayson was sitting on his covered porch. A stereo just inside the open window serenaded him with baroque melodies by Bach. The porch offered a fine view of the river, and the ceiling fan he'd installed overhead helped stir the air and discourage mosquitoes.

He put down his book and walked through the cabin to greet his visitor. The cabin was less primitive now, with interior walls, shelving for canned goods and clutter, a secondhand refrigerator, a pump mounted over a metal sink.

Monday, Wednesday, and Friday were now his days to tend the store. He always had dinner with Martha Claire on Friday evening and stayed over, and sometimes other nights, especially if the weather was bad. The narrow track to his cabin was often impassable after a big rain.

They now kept the store open more because it imposed a needed structure on their days and weeks than for the modest income it produced. Grayson was surprised that they had any customers at all. The store wasn't outdated enough to be quaint. Martha Claire insisted on keeping clothing on the racks long after it should have been sold at the sidewalk sale at fifty percent off the last marked-down price. Not even the sports corner attracted much business. Fishing lures and shotgun shells were cheaper at Wal-Mart.

Grayson was surprised to see Cissy's battered Volkswagen bus—and not the reverend's vintage Buick—rolling to a stop behind his own elderly pickup.

He smiled and waved, but apprehension prickled its way across his forehead. He hadn't seen his daughter since her visit this summer and hadn't expected to see her again until Thanksgiving.

Had she come to tell him that something had happened to Martha Claire? To Iris? That she was having problems in school?

"This is an unexpected surprise," he told her, wrapping her slight body in his arms, laying his cheek against her soft hair. How he loved this darling girl—the only child he had left to love.

She touched his hair. "A few more gray ones, I see," she said, teasing. "You look very distinguished."

He looked down at his ragged T-shirt and cutoffs and laughed. "Yes, Grayson Francis Stewart, Esquire, at home on his country estate."

Cissy looked toward the cabin. "You painted the door."

"Yes, and there have been a few other improvements since the last time you were here," he said, linking arms with her, walking up the gravel path. "Busy hands are happy hands, your great-grandmother Grace used to say."

Cissy smiled. "I remember."

"I wish I had known you were coming," he said as he opened two cans of beer to take out on the porch. "I would have squeezed some lemons for lemonade and had fish ready to fry."

"I can't stay long. I just drove down for a few hours."

"You didn't spend the night with your mother?" he asked, surprised.

She shook her head. "No, I came to see you."

Grayson felt a heaviness settle in his chest. *Something was wrong. Just let it be something they could handle. Nothing serious, please.*

"It really is pretty here," Cissy said, staring out at the river. "And still so warm. We've already had our first frost in Dallas."

"Sit down and tell me what's on your mind," he said.

Cissy leaned back in the dilapidated wicker rocker and closed her eyes for a long minute. The air from the fan played with a wisp of hair on her forehead. When she opened her eyes, she said, "I came to ask what happened to our family."

Grayson opened his mouth to speak, then closed it for lack of words. He tried to clear his throat but could not. His hand would not relinquish the can of beer to the table beside his chair. He just sat there, motionless and mute, feeling like an old fool.

Had he actually thought he might live out his life without his daughter's asking that particular question of him?

Maybe he should have left years ago to prevent just such a moment as this. Or died. Death almost seemed preferable. To have been spared this. And Buddy's death. What a blessing that would have been.

"Have you talked to your mother about this?" he managed to ask, his voice coming out in a croak.

"No, but she wouldn't tell me if I did."

"No, I suppose not."

"I've reached an impasse, Daddy. I need to know what happened before I can get on with things. I know that Justine was banished because she took sides with you against Mama. But what was it that Justine forgave and Mother could not. God, how I've wondered. Are you my birth father? Or Buddy's? Was that what Mama found out?"

Grayson sucked in his breath and then let it out slowly. A heron rose gracefully from a stand of cattails with a silvery fish in his mouth. From across the river, a crow cawed noisily from a grove of buck-thorns. A perfect day. A peaceful place. In the summer, it was too hot for comfort and the mosquitoes were ferocious, but even then he stayed out here to avoid the pain and censure that still resided in his wife's eyes. Even now, after all these years. For so long he had hoped that he would be able to work his way back into Martha Claire's heart, but he had hurt her too deeply for any hope of redemption. Maybe if he'd known that forgiveness would never be forthcoming he would have driven away and never come back. He would have taken up with Loretta in Tucker or Clara in New Braunfels, finding what comfort there was in another woman's arms. But he never could bring himself to abandon Cissy and Buddy to a mother whose spirit he had shattered.

He hadn't thought much about leaving since carving out this little place of his own. And the truth of the matter was, he still held on to hope, still loved Martha Claire, or at least the memory of that other Martha Claire—the girl he had fallen in love with, the girl he had married, the girl whose image he had kept next to his heart throughout the war.

He stayed out here more nights than not, however. When he did stay at his wife's barny, old house, he slept alone. For years, he hadn't set foot in the room he had once shared with his wife.

Slowly, like the old man he was becoming, he rose from his chair and went inside.

Such a cliché, to keep money in a coffee can hidden under a floor-board. His secret cache. He tucked away bills now and then, telling himself he was going to take that trip to Europe someday, with Martha Claire or not, a pilgrimage to the battlefields and cemeteries of his war.

But there would be no trip to Europe, no trip to anyplace. His only traveling would be up and down State Highway 109 to the football games in College Station. As a student there, he had made fun of the tottering old geezers who came back, year after year, decked out in their A&M regalia for as long as they were able. Now he was one of them.

He didn't know what had happened in Cissy's life to precipitate her question, but the need in her eyes was real. He only hoped that when she had her answer she could forgive him, if not completely, then a lit-tle. He had lost Iris and Buddy. The prospect of living the rest of his years cut off from Cissy was too sad to contemplate.

He handed her a wad of bills. "Go see Justine," he said. "I'll let her know that you're coming."

"Is it that difficult for you?" Cissy asked.

He nodded. He had gotten medals for bravery, but he didn't have the courage for this.

He couldn't just let her come and stay ten minutes, so they went out on the river, drifting down to the highway bridge, then rowing back, talking about not much of anything.

"Will you stop by your mother's house?" he asked as he walked her to the Volkswagen.

"No. She would ask too many questions."

With her hand on the door handle, she paused. "Iris is pregnant," she said. "I know she would want for you to know."

"She'll be a wonderful mother," Grayson said.

"Yes, she will, won't she?" She hugged him. "I'll forgive you, no matter what, even if you were a Nazi spy."

He tried to smile. "I hope so, honey."

"We didn't talk about Buddy at all," Cissy said.

"I think about him all the time."

"Me, too. I love you, Daddy."

Grayson wondered if it would be the last time he would ever hear her say those words.

Back inside his cabin, he stretched out on the bed. Suddenly, he felt lonely. Very, very lonely.

He wondered if he would ever see Iris's child. His grandchild. Perhaps the only one he would ever have.

thirty-nine

At the airport, Justine almost didn't recognize Cissy coming down the ramp. She seemed deflated, older, less the lovely young woman who had come to Iris's wedding. And so thin.

Justine opened her arms and felt awash with memories of the precious little girl who had followed Iris around all those years. And she wondered if this would be the last time she would be allowed to embrace her niece. How would Cissy feel about her when she knew the truth about her family?

"Are you all right, honey?" Justine asked, reaching for Cissy's carry-on.

Cissy smiled. "Sure. Just tired. I've started my OB/GYN rotation. I don't understand why babies insist on being born in the middle of the night. And they come in clusters. The head nurse swears it has something to do with the phases of the moon."

"That's what Iris says, too. Can you believe that after years delivering other women's babies she's finally going to have one of her own?"

As they headed for the car, Justine explained that they were going to spend the weekend at her friend Astrid's beach house—out on Shelter Island.

"It's not a long drive," she promised, glancing over at her niece.

"I'm fine. Really," Cissy insisted.

Justine found herself talking about Iris, of course. She was so thrilled about the baby and worried about Iris—four months pregnant and taking a trip to Europe.

Hillel had sworn he would never return to Germany, but last year he had located an elderly male cousin who had survived the Holocaust—the last living person on this earth who had known his parents and sisters, his wife and son. The man was in failing health; if Hillel was ever going see a member of his family again, he would have to journey back to the place where they all had died. Iris wasn't about to let him face that emotional journey alone.

"You know how pragmatic she is," Justine said. "She insisted that pregnant women travel all the time, that it was no big deal. And she's right, I suppose. But I'd given up hope of being a grandmother. I don't want her to go up and down stairs, much less fly off to Germany. When she didn't get pregnant, they tried to adopt, but Hillel was too old. I tried to tell myself that it didn't matter, that I'm close to Astrid's grandchildren, but when Iris told me she was pregnant, I cried like a baby."

"Me, too," Cissy said. "I'm so happy for them. She told me how Hillel found out he was going to be a father and that a member of his family was still alive all in the same week."

"Yes, it was overwhelming for him," Justine said. "He was filled with joy and the horror of remembering all at the same time. I'm sure you realize that I was never in favor of Iris's marrying Hillel. I don't care a squat about the Jewish part, but he was too damned old and had been through too much. He suffers from bouts of terrible depression. Iris says he's never gotten over the guilt of being spared when all the people he loved were not. But Iris wanted a baby, and he wanted a safe harbor, I suppose."

It began to rain, and Justine became preoccupied with traffic and wet highways, then on finding the right turnoff. Usually, Astrid drove, she explained. They had been together for twenty years now. The beach house had belonged to her parents.

"Sometimes I wish I could just be a lesbian and be done with men altogether," Justine said, peering through the drizzle. "I love Astrid a lot, and she loves me, but not in that way. We tried it for a while, convincing ourselves it merely took getting used to. Then we just decided to be friends for life. No sex, or whatever it was we were trying to do. It was such a relief. Now I can hug her all I want and have it just be a hug. It was like having a sister again. I had missed having a sister more than I realized."

"Iris was a sister to me," Cissy said. "I missed her so much after you took her away, but at least I had all those phone calls. I cycled my life around those once-a-month calls in the back of the closet. Events and feelings became relevant only when I ran them by Iris."

Justine glanced over at Cissy. She sat with her hands in her lap, her face blanched an unnatural white in the light from oncoming traffic. "You two don't talk as much as you used to, do you?"

"No, not like before. She has a husband. Our lives are different now. Most of the time when I call, I get her answering service. And I'm never at home myself. I never have any time to just sit, any time to spend with my parents. Sometimes I'm not so sure I want to be another Doc Hadley after all. Dermatology is starting to sound pretty damned attractive. Dermatologists don't have emergencies in the middle of the night. No one is going to die because you didn't make the right split-second decision when you are so damned tired you can't see straight, much less think straight. But Mama and Daddy are living for the day I hang up a shingle in Columbus. I'm not sure I really want that, but I do want to make them happy. Every time I go home, I find myself wishing that they'd head for the same bedroom at night. They both seem so alone."

Justine could hear the weariness in Cissy's voice, and more. She was disheartened. Little Cissy, with her big heart, who had always tried so hard to make everything all right for everyone, had finally realized she couldn't do that and wanted, at least, to know the reason why.

Justine had begged Grayson not to send Cissy up here. Cissy was *his* child. *He* could explain their sordid history himself. Or lie to her. Whatever. The truth did not set you free, she pointed out. They had taken a vow with Martha Claire that their children were never to know the secret that had destroyed their family.

"I know," Grayson said. "But Buddy is dead, and Iris escaped. Cissy is bearing the burden of the past on her own, and it's gotten to be too much for her."

"What if she never speaks to you again?" Justine was in her darkroom, bathed in the red glow of the safelight. She almost hadn't picked up the phone, but it might have been Iris calling from Europe. Grayson's was the last voice she expected to hear, but she had recognized it almost at once.

"I can live with that if it helps Cissy get on with her life. Please, Justine, talk to her. I don't have the courage."

"Then let Martha Claire do it."

"Martha Claire's version would be vindictive."

"And my version?" Justine demanded. "How will it be?"

"Kinder, I hope, than Martha Claire's."

Justine sank onto a high stool and stared down at an enlargement of one of her wartime London photographs as it slowly materialized in the developing tray—a man carrying the limp body of a child in his arms, the rubble of a bombed building behind him. It was painful to look at it even after all these years. The child was certainly dead. The man might be, too, after all this time. And if he was alive, his memory of that horrible day would have lost focus with each passing year, the pain softening into something endurable. Yet, in the photograph, the image of that day was just as sharp as it had been when it was being lived.

A Manhattan gallery had scheduled a retrospective exhibition of her work: "Justine Mayfield-Dover—Thirty-Five Years of Photojournalism." For months now she had been spending hours every day in her darkroom making enlargements and reliving three wars, along with the Texas City disaster, floods, fires, hurricanes, political campaigns, presidential funerals, and just plain people going about the business of everyday life—including the everyday life of Columbus, Texas. And she would include a few of her more recent photographs in the show. She had wearied with traveling, with chasing the story. She now photographed celebrities to pay the bills and nature to fill her soul. Soon she would have a grandbaby to fill her lens.

She didn't want to do this thing that Grayson was asking of her, didn't want to relive those confusing two days when she had tarnished her soul and created the daughter who had given her life meaning.

"This is the first time we've had an actual conversation since Dover," she told Grayson.

"Yes, we carefully avoided words—and eye contact, being in the same room alone."

Remembering, Justine closed her eyes and leaned against the wall. They had talked for two days in Dover, baring their souls; that was what Dover had been about. Not sex. The sex just sneaked its way in, so to speak. Not even great sex. It was the words that had been profound as they tried to draw maps for the rest of their respective lives, maps that didn't take them back to Columbus. Then for the rest of their lives, because they had drunkenly stumbled over that line into forbidden territory, they were sentenced to silence. Silence was how they tried to keep the secret and avoid the shame. If it hadn't been for an unwanted pregnancy, the secret would have been buried so deeply they might have escaped from it. They *would* have escaped from it. It would have shrunk in dimension over the years to something no worse than a misdemeanor—shameful but not life-altering.

But then there would have been no Iris.

"I avoided thinking about that time," Justine told Grayson. "I trained myself not to. Sometimes suddenly, out of the blue, I'll remember that you were Iris's father and feel such shock and loathing—not for you, but for myself. I've told the story about the British soldier who was supposed to be her father so many times that I almost believe it. I feel as though I should go find his grave and put flowers on it. I even thought about putting one up for him in some cemetery over there so I could take Iris to it. She used to talk about going over there to search for relatives. I finally told her that I had to get married, and it never would have lasted. I was prepared to tell her that I made up the whole thing and didn't know who her father was, but it never came to that. She sensed it was a sore subject and let it drop. Iris has always been so sensible. Such an incredible person. A wonderful daughter. The greatest blessing of my life. I can't wish that Dover had never happened because of her. It's too confusing to think about, so I don't. *I just don't.* And now, here you are calling me up, breaking the silence. Damn you, Grayson Stewart! Damn, damn, damn."

"Will you talk to Cissy if I send her to you?"

Justine sighed deeply. "No promises," she said. "I don't know that I have the courage, either."

The next phone call had been from Cissy herself. Had her father called yet? She had already booked a flight and would arrive the following Sunday.

To keep from weeping, Justine had put on her walking shoes and gone down to the park. She could call Cissy back and tell her that she had to work, she had decided as she walked. After all, she had a major exhibition coming up. She could tell her that the past was none of her damned business. Tell her to talk to her mother if her father didn't have the guts.

Maybe, though, this was a part of her penance, Justine thought. Maybe by telling Cissy the story she could absorb most of the blame and leave Cissy's feelings for her father intact. It didn't matter so much if Cissy hated her aunt, but she needed to love her father.

On the ferry, Justine babbled on a bit about the island. How property values had soared. How it made her think of Galveston. Astrid had spent summers out here when she was growing up. The house had once been a farmhouse. "We were so busy being busy that we hardly used it for years. Now we come out here a lot. I take pictures and she paints."

After they had carried in the suitcases and groceries, Cissy said the house reminded her of her father's place on the river. "Of course, it's much larger and has indoor plumbing, and the porch overlooks the sound instead of a sluggish Southern river, but it's a retreat and not meant to impress anyone," she said, taking in the cast-off furniture, rough wooden floors, open shelves stacked with books, magazines, and dishes.

Justine showed her Astrid's studio, in a second-floor garret with windows all around. "We open up the windows and sleep up here when it's hot," Justine said, pointing to a pair of cots. "The breeze from the ocean is like a blessing."

Cissy admired Astrid's work in progress, of two children hunkered down on the beach watching a hermit crab, their mother in the distance, sitting on a blanket with her nose in a book. "It reminds me of William Chase's work," Cissy said.

Justine nodded. "Yes, it does a bit, but Astrid's picture glows more.

You almost expect an angel to burst through those clouds. She's too traditional to be trendy, but she's finally getting some recognition."

They put away groceries and prepared a simple meal. Justine lit candles and poured wine. "We'll eat first and save the serious stuff for later," she said. After she had several glasses of wine, Justine thought, wine to calm her nerves and take the edge off her sorrow.

Cissy only took tiny sips of the wine but ate a bowl of pasta and two slices of the chewy French bread. She looked fragile, Justine decided, with weariness in her eyes and purple smudges under them. She wondered where her niece found the stamina in that small body to face the rigors of medical school and long hours of special-duty nursing.

"Tell me about my sister," Justine said. "I have a hard time imagining her as a woman of sixty. Of course, I'm not far behind, but she was always such a pretty little thing."

"She's more handsome now than pretty," Cissy said, "a little thick around the middle, but not much. Her hair is mostly gray, and she wears it short and brushed back from her face."

"Everyone always seemed to think that I should be jealous of her, but I never was," Justine recalled. "I loved watching her lovely, lively face as much as everyone else. I was certain that she would be a famous actress someday. I loved it when she acted in plays or did dramatic readings. It absolutely broke my heart when she decided she was going to marry Grayson and live in Columbus for the rest of her life. We were going to experience the world together, to become the rich and famous Mayfield sisters. She settled for kitchen duty instead. What are her days like now? What gives her joy?"

"Well, she has the church, of course," Cissy began, "but it's less important to her now that Reverend Huxley has retired. She doesn't have much use for the new pastor—he won't let her run things like Reverend Huxley did. He told her it was time for the younger women to have a chance. She claims the man has no soul—she actually said that! She tried the Christian church for a while and then drove over to the Methodist church in Schulenberg for a couple of months, but she missed the familiar trappings and came on back. And she still loves to garden. She was never able to turn the house into a showplace, but the yard is on the annual Garden Club tour."

"Iris tells me that your father spends most of his time out by the river."

Cissy nodded. "Yes, he and Mama see each other, though. They trade off days at the store, but sometimes they are there together. And he has dinner at home on Friday nights and stays over—in his own room."

"Does she ever go out there—to the river?"

"Not that I know of."

"They got married out by the rose garden," Justine recalled. "I kept wishing for rain, for them to call it off. I didn't even bring my camera downstairs. Then when I saw them together, Martha Claire in Grandma Polly's wedding dress, Grayson in his uniform, with such hope in their eyes, I thought my heart was going to burst inside my chest. I still hated Grayson for stealing my sister, but they were so beautiful and so much in love. I knew that no one was ever going to love me the way they loved each other. I wish they could rekindle some of what they were feeling that day."

"Me, too," Cissy said, "but I don't think they ever will. Mama is not one to forgive."

Justine nodded, with a heavy heart. Yes, her sister was not the forgiving sort. But then, Justine wasn't so sure if she herself would have been able to forgive such a crime if their positions were reversed. And now the time had come for her to confess that crime to her sister's child.

forty

The rain had put a chill in the air, so after they tidied up the kitchen, Justine built a small fire in the stone fireplace. She brought a cup of tea for Cissy, more wine for herself, and a plate of *biscotti* from her favorite Italian grocery.

They pulled their chairs close and stared at the flames for a time. If she were a praying woman, Justine would ask that Cissy change her mind and let sleeping dogs lie, that they would just nod off in their chairs, lulled to sleep by sounds of the waves, the crackling of the fire, the creaking of the old house as it settled in for the night, then rouse themselves to shuffle off to bed. Tomorrow they could walk by the water, and she'd show her around the island—just a nice visit between an aunt and her beloved niece. But Cissy was gathering herself to speak, and Justine waited with a heavy heart. Then she offered up a prayer of sorts: *Help me get through this.*

"Since I was twelve years old," Cissy began, still staring at the fire, "I've been navigating a maze without knowing how I got there. I have tried to heal my parents without knowing why they're the way they are. I have tried to make up for not being Iris and tried to help us all come to terms with Buddy's death, all the while wondering if I had been a real daughter and not an adopted one if things would be better. And wondering if I am going to end up old and lonely and scared just like my mother and father. What happened to us, Justine? I need to know. I'm pregnant, and I have to decide what to do about it."

Then she burst into tears. Justine knelt beside her and held her, smoothed her hair. "Precious little Cissy," she said, her voice soothing.

"You were always trying to be the best little girl in the world so we would notice you and maybe love you as much as we loved Iris."

Justine handed Cissy a napkin and watched while she wiped her eyes. "No, I never expected to be loved like Iris," Cissy said. "Buddy and I always accepted that she was the adored one. We adored her, too. I just wanted to feel that Buddy and I were significant and not just add-ons—like two stray dogs who were allowed to live alongside the beloved family pet."

"What about the man who got you this way?" Justine asked, her knees creaking as she rose and returned to her chair.

"I got myself this way," Cissy said wearily. "It was so dumb. But to answer your question, he's married. He doesn't have a clue about what's going on, and I intend to keep it that way."

Justine put a hand to her chest, feeling herself sigh. "Dear Lord, I had this very same conversation with my mother when I came back from the war. Does Martha Claire know?"

"You're the first person I've told," Cissy said. "Before I decide what to do, I want to know what happened to our family. Why has Mama never been able to forgive Daddy for whatever it was that he did? I spent my whole life trying to make my mother love me, but she was more dedicated to *not* loving Daddy and you and Iris than she was to loving Buddy and me. She needed Buddy and me because she didn't have Iris anymore. Iris had been a substitute for the babies she could never have. We were all substitutes for something else. Now, I wonder, if I have this baby, would Mama think that it is yet another way that one of us had failed her, that I was a misbegotten child bringing another misbegotten child into the world for her to deal with?"

Cissy stopped talking and, with her hands folded in her lap, waited for Justine's response.

Justine took the last sip of wine from her glass and filled it again—to the brim. "I don't know where to begin," she admitted.

Cissy began for her. "I grew up believing that you were a widow, that a British soldier named Philip Benston Dover was Iris's father. But since there was never one shred of information about this man, not one photograph, not one letter from him, not one memento, I decided that you had to get married and didn't really love him. I thought that was why you never talked about him. Now I wonder if he ever existed at all."

"He didn't," Justine said softly. "Your grandma Polly made him up out of whole cloth, and Martha Claire put his obituary in the newspaper. That's all Philip Dover ever was—an obituary in the *Citizen*."

"Does Iris know?"

Justine shook her head. "No. I let her believe that the marriage never would have lasted if he had lived, that he was a nice man doing the honorable thing, but we never planned to make a life together. One day, she just stopped asking. If she had wanted to visit his grave, I would have provided one."

"I also thought for many years now that Daddy was my birth father," Cissy continued.

Justine held up a hand, calling for a pause, and replayed Cissy's words in her mind. *Cissy thought that Grayson was* her *father*. "What made you think that?" she asked.

Cissy shrugged. "I was casting about for a damning secret. That one seemed to fit the bill. I decided that Doc Hadley knew all about it. Maybe Daddy even asked him to give me to them so he could raise me. Probably it was Doc Hadley's idea to tack Buddy onto the deal—I could see him pulling something like that. Then in those last weeks of Grandma Polly's life, Mama somehow found out. When you came home for the funeral, you stuck up for Daddy and told Mama she should forgive him. The older I got, however, the more difficult it became to believe that story, too. I couldn't imagine Daddy sneaking off behind Mama's back. Still, I thought of every lady in town who might possibly have stepped out with my father and given me birth. Eventually, I gave up. No one could hide a pregnancy all the way to term in Columbus."

Cissy paused, took a breath, then continued. "Or maybe he hadn't fathered a bastard child. Maybe Mama found out that he had been unfaithful without that added complication. But with whom? I couldn't imagine him sneaking over to the whorehouse at La Grange or taking old Miss Woodson back to the storeroom for a quickie before they opened in the morning. I think I considered every white woman in town—and some black ones, too. But we always knew where Daddy was. If Mama sent me to look for him, I could always find him. He was either at the store, at Grandma Stewart's, the library, fishing, or talking football with other businessmen at the Sandwich Shop."

"So now what do you think?" Justine asked, her fingers curling around the arm of the chair, waiting for the ax to fall.

Cissy hesitated, as though unwilling to say the damning words out loud. "It wasn't until Daddy told me I had to come see you that the pieces began to fall into place. Now, I think my daddy fathered a child, but it wasn't me. I think he is Iris's father."

"Why do you think that?" Justine asked, not yet able to acknowledge the truth of her niece's words.

"Mama has never forgiven him," Cissy explained. "If he'd had an affair with anyone else, she would have given him a hard time but eventually gotten over it, even if he'd had a baby with another woman and convinced Doc Hadley to pass it off as a foundling."

There were other things, too, Cissy went on, carefully explaining why she now thought that her cousin was also her sister. "Iris and Daddy both got hiccups when they laughed too hard, both chewed on their thumbnails when they were puzzled about something." She paused, then asked, "Did you ever hear them sing 'La Vie en Rose?' And 'Don't Let the Stars Get in Your Eyes'? Their voices blended so perfectly, like syrup and melted butter."

Cissy paused, waiting for Justine to confirm or deny. Justine sat motionless, saying nothing. She felt as though she were turning to stone. Like Lot's wife. No, Lot's wife turned into salt. A pillar of salt. That's what happened when one looked back.

Finally Cissy broke the silence. "How did Mama find out?" Cissy asked softly.

Justine took a deep breath. "I think the same way you did. She realized how alike they were. Then she started looking for proof until she found it."

Cissy lifted her chin. "Were you in love with my father?"

Justine wondered, if she had been in love with Grayson, would that mitigate her sin or worsen it?

The night they sought shelter from the bombs in the cellar under her favorite pub, as she clung to him for what she thought was the last bit of human comfort she would ever feel, maybe then she understood that Grayson Stewart was a man she could have loved if he weren't married to her sister. But did such feelings have any relevance now?

Then Justine began to speak in a great outpouring of words, trying to explain how it was during the war, how she had reveled in the intensity of that other time and place, how euphoric she had felt coming up out of the shelters after a night of bombing, alive for another day. But when the young Aussie airman she had fallen in love with was killed, everything changed for her. She told Cissy about that awful night, waiting in the pub for Billy to come through the door like he always did, with his hat at a jaunty angle and a grin on his darling face, with each tick of the clock making it less likely that she would ever see him again. Finally, two mates from his wing came to give her the news. Her Billy Boy was dead.

"I never made love with him," Justine said. "In the middle of a world war, with planes being shot out of the sky on a daily basis, I had clung to my virtue like it was the most important thing in the world. My sister had been a virgin on her wedding night, and I would be, too, by golly. I would hold myself to a higher standard than all those other girls. I had played hooky from church more Sundays than not, but I knew what God and my parents and sister expected of me."

Justine took another sip of wine, then put down the glass. No amount of wine was going to ease her way through this. "When Billy died," she went on, "I slept with every man who came along. For months and months I did that. Then I picked up my camera and took pictures instead."

She had her camera with her the evening she saw Grayson in London, she explained. He was in England for medical treatment. He had a bandaged eye when they met for a drink. Then the bombs started falling and they were trapped for hours, clinging to one another as the rubble shifted above them and the fire from burning buildings crept closer. She told Grayson about the boy she had loved and the men she had slept with since his death. He told her that he didn't want to go back to Columbus, that he wanted a different sort of life but knew that Martha Claire would never agree to it. He dreaded going back to Columbus, more than he'd ever dreaded marching off to war.

When they finally were rescued, they dusted themselves off and spent the rest of the night and the next day walking through the ruins. She took pictures until she ran out of film. Then they found an open pub where they could drink and talk until it was time for him to leave. The next day he was heading back to the front to rejoin his unit.

"It was an extraordinary twenty-four hours," Justine said. "We had faced death together and shared our innermost secrets. After the armistice, Grayson came back. I took a train to Dover and met him there. The war in Europe was over, but we were still scared. I was scared that, after all my bravado about wanting to live a different kind of life, about striking out on my own and making a name for myself, maybe I didn't have the guts, that it had been only a foolish daydream. And Grayson was afraid of going home, afraid of spending the rest of his life tending the family store. He wanted to stay in the army, and he wanted me to tell him that he had a right to start anew now that he had fought a war and was a different man, that he had the right to do that even if it meant not going home to his wife."

Justine turned her face toward the fireplace, feeling the heat tighten her skin. "I told Grayson that he didn't have to live in Columbus, but whatever he did, it had to be with Martha Claire at his side. I told him he would never find anyone who loved him as much as my sister, but he had to make her understand how he felt. He should tell her they were going to give military life a try—for three years or five years or whatever. At the end of that time, if she wasn't happy, they could renegotiate. Then I went home and realized how determined Martha Claire was to put Grayson behind a counter and stay in Columbus."

"Did you go to Dover knowing that you would make love with him?" Cissy asked.

"I don't think so," Justine said, rubbing her forehead. "No, I'm sure I didn't. We planned to go just for the day, but we missed the last train back. The lady at the inn assumed we were married. We had downed one too many pints. Columbus seemed so far away, like another world, another lifetime. We weren't the same people we had been back then. But excuses don't count. It was the worst thing I could have done—my own sister's husband. The fact that Martha Claire adored Iris from the moment she was born just made it worse. It took me seven weeks to fall in love with Iris, but Martha Claire loved her from the minute she was born."

"When you discovered you were pregnant, did you think about not having the baby?"

Ah, so now they had arrived at the heart of things, Justine thought. She would have to go carefully into those deep waters.

"Of course, I thought about it," Justine said. "That was my plan. I wasn't about to have my brother-in-law's child. As soon as I got home, I would go over to Freedmantown for a kitchen table abortion, but my mother decided otherwise. And I must admit it was a great relief to have her take charge. When Martha Claire and I were in high school, a neighbor girl had died after having an abortion. The principal said it was appendicitis, but her father dragged a blood-soaked mattress out back and burned it. I didn't want a baby, but I didn't want to die, either. Eventually, I resigned myself to having it, but I never intended to love it. Strange how things turn out. Being Iris's mother has been the best part of my life."

Justine leaned forward. She wanted to take Cissy's hand but didn't dare. "Before you decide on an abortion, you need to ask yourself why. Would you be doing it because it's what you really want or because you are afraid to tell your mother?"

"Both, I guess. I don't want a baby unless I have a husband and my mother can hold her head up. I'm all that Mama and Daddy have left. How can I disappoint them like that?"

Cissy stood abruptly, putting an end to the discussion. Justine rose to her feet, and the two women stood facing each other, the room barely lit by the last glow of the embers. "Thank you for talking to me," Cissy said, her tone formal. "I know this has not been easy for you."

"Your parents and I swore to each other that you children would never know who Iris's father was," Justine said. "I still don't want Iris to know. And please, don't tell your mother that you know. She hates me enough the way it is." She paused. "Do you hate me, too?"

"A little," Cissy admitted. "Just like I hate myself. But I have loved you for my entire life. And Daddy. I can't go back and change that. My mother did that, and look what happened to her."

At the door to the guest room, Justine wasn't sure if a hug was in order, so she kept her distance. "Let me know what you decide. Either way, I'll pay your expenses."

Cissy started to protest, but Justine wouldn't let her. Whether she had the baby or not, she would need money.

"Should I tell Iris?" Justine asked.

"No. She would want to have a say. I need to decide this on my own."

"I love you, Cissy," Justine said. "I haven't told you that in years, but I do, and I've always felt guilty about taking Iris away from you. I know how difficult life was for you in the aftermath of all that. I know how you suffered for what your father and I did."

"Yes, but what you and Daddy did gave me Iris in the first place. I don't so much forgive you as accept that it happened. Okay?"

"May I hug you?"

Cissy slid into Justine's arms. God, such a little slip of a girl, Justine thought once again. An image of Cissy as a child flashed into Justine's mind. A skinny little girl in pigtails, holding her aunt's hand as they walked downtown for ice cream cones. Justine had always loved her niece but probably never more than she did at that moment.

I suppose I had gone to New York thinking I was somehow entitled to have the sins of the past revealed to me so that I could find some justification for the mess I had made of my own life.

I learned that my father and my aunt made love while my mother was anxiously waiting for their return. I ached for my poor mother but wished she had been valiant enough to rise above what had been done to her, to either send my father packing or help him earn her forgiveness. My father had stayed on in their loveless marriage out of remorse, and because of his love for me and my brother. Together, our parents condemned us to bear silent witness to their rotting marriage. All Buddy wanted out of life was to play football and not be like his father. Maybe all I wanted out of life was not to be like my unhappy mother.

I tried to imagine how it might have been for Justine and my father in Dover. Had they simply allowed liquor to push guilty thoughts of Martha Claire right out of their minds? Or had they acted out of anger at my mother's unwillingness to go forth with them into the larger world?

I had not asked those questions of Justine. But then, I'm sure she could not have answered them. One doesn't keep the memory of such deeds fresh in one's mind. She would not have been able to recall her exact feelings, her exact motivations. Just as I had no earthly notion of why I had thought I would die if I did not have sex with a man whom I knew loved and admired his wife and was committed to living the rest of his life with her.

But at some level, though, my father and aunt had knowingly committed a vengeful act against my mother, just as Joe and I had figuratively screwed his wife. We had been raging against the person who represented limits for what had been seemingly limitless lives.

forty-one

Cissy took the middle road. She would have the baby and give it up for adoption. Her parents must never know. Nor should Joe. Or Iris. Anyone who might try to change her mind.

She did, however, long for a miscarriage, which in medical terms was a *spontaneous* abortion. Except she tried to help it along. She would climb up on her kitchen table and jump off. Over and over again, she made the jump, trying to disrupt the pregnancy and create a less-than-spontaneous end to her problem. She didn't have the courage to tumble down a flight of stairs.

The thought that Joe would find out about her pregnancy filled her with heavy, heart-pounding dread. Different nightmarish scenarios pushed their way into her mind. What if he saw her pregnant and realized how she had gotten that way? What if he thought the pregnancy was intentional on her part, that she was trying to tie herself to him, trying to make him leave his wife?

She imagined him demanding that she have an abortion and thrusting money into her hands.

She also imagined him offering to perform the procedure himself. He would come to her duplex apartment, lead her meekly to the kitchen table. Their shared secret. A secret that would bind them for life.

One evening, she heard two residents talking about the baby of a third-year medical student one of them had just delivered and realized they were talking about Joe's baby. A case of *placenta previa*. A live birth, but at only twenty-three weeks. The infant wasn't expected to live.

Cissy waited several hours, until the wards had battened down for the night, before making her way to the neonatal intensive care unit. She glanced around furtively, fearful that Joe would find her there. Or his wife. But only a portly nurse was in attendance, keeping watch over her Lilliputian charges. She glanced in Cissy's direction, nodded, then went back to her charts.

Cissy stared at the tiny little thing in its incubator. Baby Boy McCormack was no bigger than her hand. He was the smallest one they'd had in a long time, the nurse told Cissy. Most his size, if they lived at all, would take a few gasps or two and expire in the delivery room.

It was painful to watch the baby's fragile chest move up and down. He was already blue, already in the final hours of his minuscule life span. Cissy felt genuine sorrow. This baby had been wanted. His parents would have been preparing a nursery for him, buying a crib, making plans.

Then suddenly in the middle of her sorrow, a new fear struck arrowlike through Cissy's heart, a new reason why Joe must never know she was pregnant with his child. With the death of this infant, Joe might hire a lawyer and lay claim to the one she carried. If Cissy wasn't going to raise it, he and his saintly wife would.

With her hands on her abdomen, Cissy backed away from the dying preemie. No, they could not have her child. She did not want this baby raised by a mother who would always have a reason not to love it. This baby's history would be erased. It would go untainted to strangers who wanted it more than anything, to a mother who could not use it as a weapon against a husband who had betrayed her.

Suddenly panic rose up in Cissy and began to choke her. She could almost feel Joe's wife rising from her bed, demanding to be taken to her baby. She should already be here, spending what time there was with her dying child. Cissy backed away and, remembering to nod at the nurse, hurried out the door and down the hall. Like a thief, she took the stairs and crept out into the night.

· · ·

Daily, Cissy inspected her body from all angles, trying to decide if anyone might guess. Naked, she could see her waist losing definition. Dressed, she looked normal. She could make it to the end of the semester, she decided, then go someplace else before she began to show.

Other than Justine, the only other person she would tell was Daisy Cunningham, and that was only because Cissy needed her help in salvaging the second half of the academic year.

Cissy often had dinner with Daisy on Tuesday evening, sometimes just the two of them, other times with other medical students or faculty members, usually women but not always.

It was a kitchen meal for just the two of them the evening Cissy chose for confessing.

"I wondered when you were going to tell me," Daisy said.

"How did you know?" Cissy sat up straighter and sucked in her middle.

"All of a sudden, you stopped wanting a glass of wine with dinner or a cup of coffee afterward."

"Yeah, my stomach doesn't like alcohol and caffeine anymore."

"So, what happens now?" Daisy asked, breaking eggs into a bowl for omelets.

"I don't want anyone to know, including my parents. Is there any way I can transfer to an out-of-state medical school for just one semester?"

"It would be unusual, but I'll see what I can work out."

"You must be terribly disappointed in me," Cissy said.

"Not so disappointed as shocked," Daisy said. "You're not some dumb little high school girl, Cissy. You know better than to have unprotected sex. What in the hell were you thinking?"

"I wasn't," Cissy said.

"Next time, take a pill or give him a condom."

"There won't be a next time, at least not with this particular man."

"And the baby?" Daisy asked.

"I'll give it up for adoption."

"You're sure?"

"Yes, quite sure."

Daisy nodded her agreement. "You won't have time for motherhood—not for years," she said as she fished around in a drawer for an eggbeater.

"No time or money," Cissy added. "I have to work at a paying job to pay my rent and eat. And there will be more and more night shifts in my life. Already there are twenty-four-hour stretches when the only time I'm at home is to shower and change clothes. I've gone too far to just give up on medical school."

"I would think that went without saying," Daisy said.

"I know I've been stupid and irresponsible, but I will have this baby—not because I think it's the moral thing to do but because, for me personally, it just feels like the correct thing to do. Maybe I'd feel differently if I weren't adopted myself. Maybe it's payback time. My birth mother didn't have an abortion. I have a life. This baby will, too, but I don't want to raise it. I don't want to be reminded of its father every time I look at it. When I'm in practice, I may or may not have children, but right now my first priority is finishing my medical training."

Daisy held up a hand to call a halt to the outpouring. "Hey, you don't have to do all this justifying for my benefit. I agree with you."

Cissy shrugged and offered a small smile. "It helps to say out loud all the words that have been bouncing around in my head."

Daisy poured herself a glass of wine and Cissy a glass of iced tea. Cissy dutifully asked if Daisy needed any help but didn't protest when told to relax. From her perch on a bar stool, she sipped the tea and watched Daisy bustle around her wonderful kitchen. Cissy loved the room—and the rest of the house, with its curving staircase and spacious, antiques-filled rooms. Maybe someday she would have a lovely home herself. And perhaps, like Daisy, she would live in that someday house alone. Hopefully, she would be able to fill it on occasion with people, as Daisy did. Daisy collected people as lovingly as she collected antiques and quilts. Not a bad life, Cissy decided. A worthy profession. A lovely home. A safe existence. No great joy, but no agonizing pain, either. And maybe, Cissy thought wistfully, she would enjoy this good, safe life more knowing that out there someplace there was an anonymous child to whom she had given life.

. . .

The following Thursday afternoon, Cissy received a summons from Daisy. When she arrived at her office, Daisy closed the door. "You will spend a semester of clinical training in Tulsa. The University of Oklahoma medical school has opened a branch campus there for third- and fourth-year students. One of my former students is an assistant dean. You're being offered a special one-semester student fellowship in family medicine. I'll see to it that credit for the semester transfers back here. You will have to pay out-of-state tuition, though."

"My aunt has offered to help me financially."

"Well, let me know if you need any additional help," Daisy said.

"I hope I can do something wonderful for you someday," Cissy said.

Daisy waved her away. "Go finish up your shift over in the baby factory, then go home and get some sleep. You look like a scarecrow with two black eyes."

Cissy had worried needlessly about what she would wear when she went home for Christmas. Other than snug waistbands, her clothes still fit just fine. If anything, they were a little loose.

She bought some concealer for the circles under her eyes and warned her mother that she'd had a bout with an intestinal virus and didn't have much of an appetite. Actually, though, with the arrangements for second semester made and the nausea of early pregnancy fading, Cissy arrived home feeling reasonably well. Her mother's pork roast and mashed potatoes had never tasted better. And the apple pie would have won first place at the Colorado County Fair.

Christmas Eve was one of those balmy evenings that frequently present themselves during south Texas winters. After dinner, the three of them walked down to the square to admire the town Christmas tree, then over to the Catholic church to view the living Nativity scene.

Christmas morning, her parents emerged from their separate rooms. Grayson fixed waffles and sausage, which they ate in the dining room so they could see the lighted tree in the parlor. Cissy wished she had brought home her stereo. Christmas carols would have softened the quiet.

After breakfast, they gathered around the tree. Just the three of them. Cissy remembered when their family had filled the room. Her mother sighed and said, "What this house needs is children."

Cissy felt infinitely sad and vowed she would always come home for Christmas. If she didn't, she doubted if her parents would even put up a tree and go through the motions. Rituals tinged with sadness were better than no rituals at all.

The next morning, before she started back to Dallas, she explained about next semester, about Tulsa. It was a wonderful opportunity—a fellowship program. Her expenses would be paid. She planned to sublet her duplex. Of course, she would be incredibly busy, with no time off to come home.

"Tulsa is so far away," Martha Claire protested. "We'll never get to see you."

"It's just for a few months," Cissy told them. "I'll still call home every Sunday. This summer, I'll only have a couple weeks off before I start my fourth year, but I'll spend every minute of them with you. I want us to go someplace together. The Grand Canyon maybe. Or New Orleans."

Cissy enjoyed her solitary journey to Tulsa. With each mile that rolled by, she felt calmer. Tulsa was six hours from Dallas and twelve hours from Columbus. Her secret would be safe there.

The backseat was piled high with clothes. Her stereo and television were wedged in the back of the van with towels and blankets.

She stopped just across the state line for lunch in the pretty little town of Durant. It reminded her of Columbus, with lots of trees and a courthouse square.

She arrived in Tulsa before dark and had no trouble finding the rooming house where Daisy had arranged for her to live. Her room was Spartan, with a tiny bathroom and a window that overlooked a church parking lot. She spent the evening putting away her things and mentally declaring herself at home. Pictures of her parents and Buddy occupied the top of the bureau. Her quilt was spread on the bed. She put a Carly Simon tape on the stereo.

She had allowed herself a day to settle in and learn her way around before beginning the semester. She located the campus and the clinic where she would begin her family medicine rotation. Then she drove around a bit, exploring the downtown and an area with stately old mansions that reminded her of the Highland Park area in Dallas. Both areas had been created by families who had made their wealth during the oil boom of the early 1900s.

By the end of the first week she had settled into a routine, spending her days at a freestanding family medicine clinic on Utica Avenue and at sprawling St. Francis Hospital, where she usually ate lunch. At night, she would have a peanut butter sandwich. She still didn't have much appetite. She bought fruit that went bad sitting on her dresser waiting for her to eat it.

She was able to conceal her pregnancy much longer than she would have thought possible. The mandatory white jackets that all medical students wore helped. And she never wore makeup or jewelry, never called attention to herself.

The attending faculty and her fellow students assumed she had transferred to Tulsa for the remainder of her medical training. She did not correct them. In fact, she volunteered no information about herself at all, other than that she had transferred from Texas, not even saying which medical college she had attended unless asked.

It wasn't until her seventh month that women started asking when the baby was due, whether she wanted a boy or a girl, if she had selected names. Men seldom commented.

Justine had insisted that Cissy not do any special-duty nursing in Tulsa, and sent more money than Cissy really needed. Cissy was grateful. She felt well enough but was always tired, so very tired. She wondered if it was caused by pregnancy or by the state of limbo in which she found herself. She hadn't watched a television program without dozing off since arriving in Tulsa. Sometimes when she had a break from her clinic or hospital duties, she took catnaps in her car.

At the women's clinic where she went for prenatal care, the word *confidential* was written in red across the front of the folder holding her medical records. The nurses were brusque with her—no smiles and chitchat, no "How are we doing today?" Such pleasantries apparently were saved for women who weren't giving away their babies.

When she felt the baby move, Cissy did not allow herself to feel wonder. She did not study pictures in her embryology textbook to determine what the fetus looked like at each stage of development. She did not talk to her belly or caress it. She wanted no bonding at all. This was not her baby to keep. She was carrying it for someone else. She did not want to see it or touch it when it was born.

Justine called often. *Was she all right? Did she like her doctor? Had she talked to Martha Claire this week? Did she need more money?*

"You don't have to feel responsible for me," Cissy told her.

"Yes, I do. I abandoned you once before. I'm not going to do it again. Are you still going to put the baby up for adoption?"

"Yes. The arrangements have all been made. They will whisk it away the minute it is born."

"Are you truly all right about this?"

"I'm fine, Justine. You don't need to worry about me. I got myself into this mess. With your help, I'm getting myself out."

Justine called from the hospital after Iris had her baby—a beautiful little girl with big eyes and long fingers, a future surgeon, maybe, or a pianist. Cissy talked to Iris, who sounded exhausted but happy. "You'll have a baby one of these days," she told Cissy. "Our children will grow up together. If you have a little girl, they will be like sisters."

For the first time, Cissy felt the sting of regret. But she dismissed it. Any children she might have would see their cousins once a year, if that. The infant she was carrying would have another family. She wondered if some worthy husband and wife had already been told their baby was on the way.

Now that she was in her last trimester, she went to the women's clinic every two weeks. At seven and a half months, during her regular checkup, the physician who examined her also delivered a lecture. Hadn't she learned anything during her OB/GYN rotation? She needed to take better care of herself. She was anemic. Her blood pressure was elevated. She hadn't gained enough weight. Getting enough rest? Drinking a quart of milk every day and eating plenty of fruit and vegetables? Just popping a prenatal vitamin every day was not enough.

Cissy used the leftover money from Justine's checks to buy a tiny refrigerator and stopped by the grocery for juice, oranges, milk, carrots, apples. The landlady wasn't happy about the refrigerator and said that Cissy would have to pay five extra dollars a month for the additional electricity. But she and the retired gentleman who lived across the hall from Cissy carried it upstairs. Cissy put away her groceries, poured a glass of milk and downed part of it, then fell across her bed, exhausted. She'd eat an apple later. Did all pregnant women feel so lethargic? she wondered.

The doctor had said the fetus was in a transverse lie. Yes, she could tell, as she probed with her fingertips, visualizing the position of the baby in her uterus. It would weigh about two and a half pounds. Just a tiny little thing.

She reached over to where she'd tossed her white doctor's jacket on a chair and pulled her stethoscope from the pocket. For the first time, she listened to the baby's beating heart.

Having an abortion was one thing, but since she had signed on for the duration, she had a responsibility to the life she carried. She had failed to keep her brother alive. She would not fail this child, too. She roused herself long enough to finish the glass of milk and brush her teeth.

Under the covers, she closed her eyes and carefully choreographed her presleep musings, pushing aside thoughts of a baby in a transverse lie. And no thoughts of a man, not even an imaginary one. She put herself on her bicycle, riding alongside Iris and Buddy down the tree-lined streets of Columbus.

forty-two

The following Friday afternoon, Cissy began experiencing intermittent Braxton Hicks contractions. The OB/GYN resident who examined her said she was threatening to go into premature labor and prescribed a few days of bed rest.

Cissy went back to the rooming house, put on her robe, and prepared to sleep away the weekend. She lay across the bed with her hands on her belly. No contractions now. Later she would read about their implication in her OB textbook.

She reached over to where her white jacket hung on the back of the desk chair and pulled the stethoscope from the pocket. The baby's heartbeat was fine. One hundred forty beats a minute. Nice and strong.

She put the stethoscope on the bedside table and eyed the blood pressure cuff on the bureau. She'd check that later, she decided, and rolled onto her side, curling her body around her belly and feeling sleep already beginning to fall.

Monday, the doctor said she could resume her duties but to take it easy. No lifting. Avoid stairs. Lots of rest. Lots of fluids. Her feet and ankles were swollen, her blood pressure still elevated, so she should stay off her feet as much as possible.

Trouble was, when she sat down she dozed off. Sometimes she even wondered if she had narcolepsy and kept meaning to read up on the disease. She felt as though she could sleep around the clock. Sleep was beautiful. She lived to sleep, loved falling asleep. Maybe it wasn't narcolepsy at all. Maybe she was running away. But she was too sleepy to analyze her condition.

The following Monday, the contractions were back. A different resident gave her a shot of terbutaline and prescribed bed rest with bathroom privileges for the rest of the pregnancy.

Cissy protested. She couldn't just go to bed, she told the attending physician—this time a middle-aged female faculty member who wore her glasses parked on the end of her nose. Cissy explained that she needed to finish the semester. And she didn't have anyone to look after her while she lolled around in bed.

The woman stared at the incriminating red word on Cissy's folder. "No one at all?"

Cissy nodded. "I came to Tulsa to have this baby. I live in a rooming house."

"Try bed rest for a week, and we'll see how you're doing," the physician said, compromising.

How much time could she miss without losing credit for the semester? Cissy wondered as she headed for her car. Maybe she would just go ahead and deliver. At this stage, the baby was viable. It was almost six weeks further along than Joe's baby had been.

The thought cheered her a bit. Maybe all this would be over with sooner than she had expected. Usually infants born at thirty-one weeks did just fine, she told herself.

Not always, though. She knew that every week a baby spent in utero enhanced its chances of being healthy and normal. Abortion was one thing, but once she had opted to carry the baby to term, she knew she had a responsibility to see it through. And she had not done a very good job of taking care of herself.

She wondered if a mother's not wanting a baby could affect its development. Did happy mothers have better babies?

Images of the embryology lab's grotesque, floating forms flashed across Cissy's mind, forcing her to stop mid-stride.

Suddenly the world was spinning around her. She put a hand on a dusty pickup for support. Then she gave herself a mental slap on the wrist. *Stop being melodramatic. Get on with things.*

On the way home, she stopped at the convenience store for a quart of milk and a ham sandwich. Later she would make a grocery list. Tomorrow morning, she would make a quick trip just to the grocery. The rest of the weekend would be spent in bed.

She dozed through the evening news, then ate part of the sandwich with a glass of milk. She thought about taking a shower but felt herself drifting back to sleep. Maybe it wouldn't be so bad, spending an entire week in bed. All this bed rest gave her a backache, but when she was asleep she didn't feel it.

She woke a couple of hours later and watched a *Lucy* rerun while she nibbled on the rest of the sandwich. Then she took a shower and tried to study a bit.

The next time she woke, she felt a bit queasy and chewed on a couple of antacid tablets. She tried to go back to sleep but lay there feeling her stomach grow progressively more rebellious. She was relieved when she finally threw up.

When next she woke, she hurried to the bathroom to deal with a bout of diarrhea.

Then she threw up again.

It was the sandwich, she realized—either the mayonnaise or the ham had gone bad. Maybe both. It hadn't been out of the refrigerator that long—only a few hours. Maybe it had been old, though. Had there been a date on the wrapper? It had tasted okay, she supposed. Just a sandwich. Just something to eat. The doctor said she didn't eat enough.

By tomorrow she would be fine, as soon as she passed the microorganism that had taken up temporary residence in her digestive tract. Salmonella, probably. It shouldn't hurt the baby at all. She just needed to stay hydrated.

She drank half a glass of water and went back to bed.

The water stayed down less than five minutes.

She rinsed out her mouth and took just a few more sips, then carried the glass to her bedside table.

She awoke the next morning to her neighbor tapping on her door. She had a phone call.

Her mother, Cissy thought. And prepared to sound chipper.

"What took you so long?" Justine's voice asked.

"I was in bed," Cissy said.

"Why? Are you sick? You don't sound like yourself. Are you okay?"

"I ate a sandwich that made me sick. The worst is over. I'll be fine."

"You sure?"

"Yeah. I just need to drink water and sleep."

Cissy listened for a minute while Justine raptured a bit about Iris's baby. She had mailed Cissy the latest pictures. Then she stopped midsentence. "Would you rather I didn't talk about the baby?"

"Of course not, but right now I need to get back to the bathroom," Cissy said.

"Call me tomorrow," Justine demanded.

Cissy barely made it to the toilet.

Before she went back to bed, she dutifully took several tiny sips of water, waiting several seconds in between each one to give her stomach time to accommodate. Hopefully, some of it would stay down. If it didn't, she would have to go to the emergency room for IV fluids.

She woke several times during the day, going to the bathroom, sipping water, throwing it up in the metal wastebasket she had parked beside her bed, but not all of it. She was sure of that. She wasn't dizzy and was still putting out urine.

When she woke to darkness, she turned on the lamp and looked over at the alarm clock. But she couldn't seem to focus her eyes. Reaching for the glass of water, she knocked it over.

She needed to eat something, she decided, and managed to stumble across the room to her refrigerator, which contained milk, stale bread, apples, carrots, and tomato juice. She closed the door and found a couple of packages of restaurant crackers in her purse. Perfect, she thought. A pregnant woman's mainstay. She ate one and drank more water.

She crawled back into bed. It felt so good. She loved her bed. Loved her pillow. Everything was fine.

She tried to remember if she had called the family medicine clinic to tell them she wasn't coming in all week. She remembered thinking about it. But couldn't remember if she had. She'd better call and make sure. Was this Monday or Tuesday morning?

At first light, she looked in her purse for change for the pay phone and found only pennies. It was too early to be knocking on her neighbors' doors, asking for change.

She ate another cracker and crawled back into bed. The crackers had been a godsend. Next time she woke up, she would get dressed and go across the street for a whole box. And get some change for the phone. And ice. She'd give anything for a piece of ice to suck on.

The next time she struggled to wakefulness, the sips of water came back up the minute they hit her stomach. She was dizzy. Her head throbbed. She had spots in front of her eyes.

She crawled from her bed and managed to put on her robe. She pulled some bills from her purse. She would ask the lady across the hall to go buy her some crackers, ice, and Seven-Up. And get her some change. With money in hand, she stumbled across the hall. The woman did not answer her knock. Or the man across the hall.

The landlady. She would ask the landlady. But that meant getting down the stairs. She could do that, she told herself. But she needed to rest a minute first.

She was quite proud of how well she got back to her room. She took just a sip of water and crawled back into her bed. She was even able to focus on the clock. It was four-thirty. The landlady wouldn't have been home if she had gone downstairs. She didn't get home until after five. Mrs. Hamburger. Such a funny name. But no, Hamburger was the name of the woman who owned the duplex in Dallas. The landlady here was Mrs. Wilson, which wasn't a funny name at all. Cissy patted her belly. "Wilson is a very serious name, don't you think? Like Woodrow Wilson or the observatory out in California."

Next time she woke, she was retching, and her head hurt like hell. Her stomach, too—high on the right, under her ribs. Really bad pain.

She half crawled to the desk chair and used it to pull herself to her feet. She took three shaky steps to the door but collapsed against it. She knew exactly what the trouble was. After all, she was a third-year medical student. She was suffering from serious dehydration. Food poisoning. And she supposed she would have to add malnutrition to the diagnosis. But her main problem was the toxemia of pregnancy. She had all the symptoms. Lights were even flashing in front of her eyes, and her legs were beginning to twitch—just like the textbook said.

She put her hands on her belly. "I think we're in trouble," she said.

She raised up one elbow and called out, "Help! Will someone please help me?" She could barely hear her own voice, though. How was anyone else supposed to hear her?

There was something hurting her left arm. Cissy reached down and tried to pull it out. But whatever it was, it was covered by a piece of tape.

She opened her eyes and stared up at a bag of IV fluids. She was in a hospital. A patient. She'd never been a patient in a hospital before. It was good that she was here, she thought as she allowed her eyes to close again. She remembered how sick she had been.

But what about the baby? She reached down and touched her stomach. It was soft. Very soft. Like a pillow without its stuffing.

"It's a boy," a voice said. Her father's voice.

Cissy opened her eyes. "Daddy?"

"I'm here, sweetheart. You gave us quite a scare."

"How long have you been here?"

"Since yesterday."

"How did you know? What happened? When . . ." Her voice trailed off. It was too confusing. Her father was here.

"Justine tried to call you. She made the landlady unlock your door and check on you."

Cissy touched her stomach again.

"Yes, you had the baby. He's a tiny little thing but moving about. They have him in an incubator, but he's breathing on his own."

"Does Mama know?"

"Yes, Cissy, your mother knows."

forty-three

The ring of the phone in the middle of the night had cut through Martha Claire's chest like a dagger. With heart pounding, she rushed down the stairs, thinking of the last time the phone had rung in the night—of the night that Buddy died.

Her hello was breathless. Then she listened while a woman explained that she was Cissy's landlady up in Tulsa and Cissy had been taken to the hospital in an ambulance.

"Why?" Martha Claire demanded. "What happened to her?"

"I'm not sure," the woman said. "She was unconscious. Her aunt insisted that I look in on her when she didn't answer my knock."

"Her *aunt?*"

"Yes. She had called several times, but Miss Stewart never seemed to be in her room. Finally the aunt asked to speak to me and said she was worried about her niece and asked me to check on her. Miss Stewart was unconscious, lying on the floor right next to the door. I thought she was dead. Scared me half to death. We called the police, and they took the door off the hinges. When I called the aunt back, she asked me to call you and gave me your phone number. They took your daughter to St. Francis Hospital. I do hope she's all right." The woman paused. "And the baby, too."

"The *baby?*"

"Yes. Her aunt said you didn't know. Your daughter was pregnant, Mrs. Stewart. She came to Tulsa to have the baby and was planning to put it up for adoption. Maybe I shouldn't be telling you, but you'd find out anyway when you got up here. She's a lovely young woman, your daughter. So polite. Never plays her television too loud. And a medical student. Not the type at all you'd think would get herself in a situation like that."

Martha Claire hung up and immediately called New York information for the number of Justine Mayfield-Dover. It was listed under Justine Dover.

With a trembling hand, Martha Claire punched in the numbers. Justine answered immediately.

"What is going on with my daughter?" Martha Claire demanded without identifying herself.

For two heartbeats, there was no sound. Then Justine began to speak slowly, cautiously. "I talked to her the day before yesterday and thought she sounded shaky. Then I kept calling back to check on her. Finally I convinced the landlady to unlock her door and see if she was in there."

"And just why is it that you know about my daughter's situation and I don't?"

Martha Claire listened while her sister sighed. "She came up here last November, wanting to know the family secrets. She told me then that she was pregnant."

"The family secrets?" Martha Claire's throat was dry. It was suddenly hard to speak. "What did you tell her?"

"She had pretty much figured out things on her own. All I did was confirm them. She seemed to think that understanding what had happened between you and Grayson would help her make decisions about her own life. She was trying to decide if she wanted an abortion or not. The only thing she knew for sure was that she didn't want you to know. Oh, Martha Claire, your little Cissy spent her whole life trying to please you, trying to make you love her half as much as you loved Iris, then trying to take Iris's place. She couldn't bear the thought of disappointing you."

"You had no right to tell her," Martha Claire said, clutching the receiver so tightly that a painful cramp took over her hand. She stared at the picture of a young Buddy and Cissy that hung on the stairwell wall, in the space where the picture of the Mayfield sisters once had been. "We swore on the memory of our mother that those children would never know."

"Cissy asked me. I wish I had told her years ago. She has suffered because of what happened. She has a right to know why her mother hates her father, why her brother turned into a drunken bum who ultimately managed to kill himself, why I ripped Iris out of her life. She has a right to know why her mother's love is conditional, why no matter how hard she tries she will never be able to make you happy. Good Lord, Martha Claire, how could I not tell her?"

"If the past was so damned important to her, she should have asked me."

"She knew you wouldn't tell her. She went to her father, but poor Grayson didn't have the nerve. He won medals for facing the Nazi war machine, but you have managed to suck all the courage out of the poor man, and now he's empty inside. He didn't have the guts to go against you and tell Cissy what she wanted to know, so he asked me to do it. You should have divorced him back then, Martha Claire, but I guess that would have been too kind."

"You have talked to Grayson?"

Once again, Justine sighed. "Yes, I talked to him. It was the first real conversation I'd had with him since England. He was all torn apart inside back then, and he still is. You've really done a number on that man. I'd think you'd be tired of it after all this time."

"Don't you go heaping blame at my doorstep. You committed adultery with your own sister's husband. You took Iris away from the only home she'd ever had. You were the one who took the ax and chopped this family in half."

Martha Claire could hear Justine draw in her breath. "Yes, I did those things. You have every right to hate me. But you should have forgiven Grayson."

"Why?" Martha Claire demanded, spitting out the word.

"Because, God help him, the man still loves you, or at least the memory of you, the memory of the way you used to be. He still hopes that someday you'll let him come home."

"He can come home anytime he wants."

"But only as a visitor. Are you going to Tulsa and see about Cissy? Because if you're not, I will."

"You leave my family alone!" Martha Claire said, spitting out the words. "I will look after my daughter."

"Good-bye, Martha Claire," Justine said, and the phone went dead.

Martha Claire slammed down the receiver. "I hate you!" she screamed, her voice echoing in her big, empty house. "I hate you! I hate you! I hate you!"

Grayson awoke to the beam of headlights shining through his curtainless window. He pulled on his pants and grabbed his shotgun. A couple of weeks ago he'd had to scare off some teenage boys intent on pushing over his outhouse.

Martha Claire was standing in the beam of her headlights. "Cissy's in the hospital," she called across the yard. "We have to go to Tulsa. I have your brown suit and dress shoes."

"What happened?" he asked, stepping down from the porch.

"I'll explain on the way. Pack some things and let's go."

Grayson hesitated. "Would you like to come in?"

"No, I'll wait in the car."

"She's not going to die, is she?"

"I don't know. Please hurry."

Grayson stumbled up the steps, then stood in the middle of the room trying to think of what he should do first. But his only thoughts were of Cissy. She was in the hospital. In danger. *Please don't let anything happen to her,* he silently implored to a god he had not addressed in years.

Then he spoke out loud. "Don't you dare! Not Cissy, too."

He didn't have a suitcase out here, so he emptied a box of magazines and threw in some underwear, a few shirts, a pair of khaki pants. He packed a shoe box with his shaving things and toothbrush. Then he put on shoes and a shirt, picked up the two boxes, and looked around his humble dwelling, making sure the windows were closed, the door to the back deck padlocked. He was glad Martha Claire hadn't come inside. She would have found fault.

She had only been out here once before, at Cissy's request. Cissy had wanted them both to be at home when she drove over to tell them that she had been accepted to medical school. Martha Claire hadn't come inside that time, either. She'd delivered her message and left. Not that she wouldn't have been welcome. In fact, sometimes he imagined her sitting out back with him, watching the river go by.

Martha Claire had moved to the car's passenger side. Grayson put his boxes in the trunk and got in. "Tell me," he said as he backed down the rutted lane.

"Did you know she was pregnant?"

Grayson shook his head. "No, I didn't."

"She went to Tulsa to have the baby and put it up for adoption. I called the hospital. She was unconscious and convulsing when they brought her in. She had an emergency C-section and is in intensive care. The doctor I talked to said her kidneys had shut down."

"Will she be all right?"

"He wouldn't say."

"And the baby?"

"Alive."

"A boy or girl?"

"I didn't ask."

He heard the rest of the story in bits and pieces. About Justine getting worried. The landlady checking Cissy's room. Martha Claire had called Justine—not a good conversation, apparently. His wife was angry at him for sending Cissy to Justine, angry at Cissy, angry at Justine. But her anger was tinged with weariness. And fear.

They did not speak of their fear, but it filled the car. Their entire life had been about loss. Now there was only Cissy. Without her, they would be two aging, lonely people filled with their regrets.

Whenever they stopped, Martha Claire would call the hospital. "No change," she would tell him.

Grayson wanted desperately to talk about the baby, but he didn't dare. As he drove, his thoughts twisted back and forth between his daughter and her baby. Such a long drive it was. Endless. His body ached from sitting. Whenever he got out of the car, it took several steps for his legs to loosen up. He was getting old. Martha Claire was more agile than he was, her body still strong and youthful—from all that gardening, he supposed. When he wasn't tending the store, all he did was fish, tinker, listen to music, read. He'd become an old man. But what did it matter?

Unless there was a child.

He must not even think about that, though. He had to concentrate on Cissy. He would gladly die himself if it meant Cissy could live. She could have his kidneys, his heart. Anything.

Cissy. The dearest person in his life. He wouldn't want to live in a world without her.

Should he have known she was pregnant? She had been despondent last fall, but at Christmas she had seemed fine. She was such a lovely young woman, the center of their lives. He and Martha Claire had talked about that after she drove away, before he went back out to his cabin. They talked about how proud they were going to be when she graduated from medical school, how much Martha Claire wanted her to practice in Columbus. He wanted that, too, but he would never say so. Cissy had to decide on her own. She must not move to Columbus to please them.

A baby. Cissy had a baby. His thoughts kept coming back to that. Why had she kept it a secret? Had some boy hurt her? Was that why she wanted to give it away? Grayson's hands tightened on the steering wheel at the thought. He would want to kill anyone who hurt Cissy. He probably wouldn't actually do it, but he would want to.

Finally, he had to ask. "How do you feel about the baby?"

"Angry that she got herself that way. Angry that she didn't tell me. Angry that she told Justine instead."

"But the baby itself. How do you feel about it?"

"I don't know."

Mostly they drove in silence, with only the radio softly playing on whatever station they could find to help him stay awake, with country and western singers lamenting the trials and tribulations of love and life. Mile after endless mile. Hour after hour.

They had breakfast in Huntsville, lunch along the Dallas loop, dinner in the Oklahoma town of MacAlester. It was late afternoon when they reached the hospital in Tulsa. Grayson was so stiff he wasn't sure he could walk across the parking lot.

Cissy was still unconscious, but alive. They stood by her bedside, weeping, caressing her sweet face, begging her to live on. "We need you so," Martha Claire said, clinging to her daughter's limp hand.

Then they went to the nursery. Martha Claire tapped on the door next to the viewing window. Five bassinets were lined up in front of the window. Two pink name tags. Three blue. Grayson stared at a baby in an isolette that was pushed into a corner, separated from the other babies. The word *confidential* was written across the name card in thick black letters.

When the nurse opened the door, Martha Claire explained that they were Cissy Stewart's parents, that they had been driving most of the night and all day from south Texas to get here, that they wanted to see their daughter's baby.

"It was a confidential delivery," the nurse said, glancing over her shoulder at the lone infant in the corner. "I can't let you see the baby."

"Our daughter is in a coma. We need to see this baby," Martha Claire said, then she added a soft, imploring "Please."

"Go stand in front of the window," the nurse said. "I may need to move the babies around. His isolette might happen to pass by the window."

"Then it's a boy?" Grayson asked.

"Yes. A boy. A scrawny little thing, but holding his own."

She firmly closed the door, and they watched while she bustled about, rearranging her charges. Then she looked around furtively and pushed the isolette to center stage.

Grayson watched his wife. Not that he wasn't interested in the baby, but he knew that any future he might have with this infant depended on what happened in the next few seconds. He watched his wife standing as still as a statue in front of the window, watched as tears began streaming down her cheeks, as her face took on a look of such rapture he had to look away. Only then did he focus his attention on his grandson, who was stretching, thrusting tiny legs with tiny feet and toes, clutching tiny little fists over his head. Then the baby yawned, opened his eyes, looked around with seeming wonder at this place where he found himself. Martha Claire was weeping now, holding on to Grayson's arm for support.

. . .

They waited through the evening. About ten o'clock, Martha Claire went downstairs to find them some coffee and sandwiches. When she got back, Grayson was standing by the bed. Cissy's eyes were open.

Martha Claire took a deep breath and offered a silent prayer before joining her husband at their daughter's bedside.

"Oh, Mama," Cissy said. "I'm so sorry. I didn't want you to know."

"Shhhh," Martha Claire said. "We went to see him. He's a beautiful baby."

"Oh, God," Cissy whispered.

"You go back to sleep, honey," Martha Claire said. "We'll talk about it in the morning."

They waited until after the nurse had checked her vital signs, assuring them that she was "out of the woods" and even putting out a few drops of urine. The nurse urged them to get some sleep and come back in the morning. She directed them to a nearby motel. One of the nurses would call if they were needed.

"Do you want me to get two rooms?" Grayson asked as he pulled up in front of the motel office.

"Two beds will be fine," she said.

Martha Claire waited until she was sure Grayson was asleep, then put on her robe and went to sit by the window. She parted the drapes and stared across the highway at the massive shape of the hospital, where Cissy was. And the baby.

Martha Claire hadn't wanted to leave her daughter's side, but Grayson looked as though he could sleep standing up. She needed to get some sleep, too. She had to be clearheaded when they talked to Cissy in the morning. And Grayson—she would need to talk to him first. He had to be a part of this. Yes, she had to decide exactly how she would present her plan to both of them.

She realized her hands were resting on her belly, over her useless old uterus that was surely dried up like a prune by now. Even now, after all this time, she could feel her barrenness as surely as she felt hunger or thirst.

If God would let them have Cissy's baby, though, she would never think about her uterus again. She made that solemn promise to herself and to God.

A baby could heal them. A baby could make them happy again.

She thought of the tiny little boy in the hospital nursery and felt such a longing to touch him and hold him in her arms, to kiss each of his fingers and toes. She loved him already.

"Please," she whispered into the dank darkness of the cheap motel room. "I'll forgive Grayson if you'll let us have that baby."

forty-four

Grayson watched from the corner of the hospital room while Martha Claire explained. She was standing at Cissy's bedside, holding her hand. "Your father and I have it all worked out," she said, leaning forward to smooth Cissy's hair. "We will take care of the baby while you finish school and serve your residency."

Cissy was so pale and thin, her wonderful dark hair lacking its usual luster. Of course, she looked considerably better than she had when they arrived, when she had been comatose, with tubes and monitors. When they first saw her, Grayson had been certain she was going to die, that the doctor had waited for them to arrive so they could give permission to pull the plug.

Cissy was frowning now, trying to work through this new option in her life. "But what would you tell people?" she asked her mother.

"That you had a baby," Martha Claire said with a shrug.

"When Justine had Iris, you made up a story," Cissy challenged. "You told people that she'd been married and her husband died."

"Times were different then," Martha Claire said. "If a girl had a baby out of wedlock, her life was ruined and her family could never hold their heads up again. Bea and Jim Hawkins's daughter isn't married, and they're all there at church on Sunday morning, proud as peacocks, with their granddaughter all dressed in ruffles and bows. But we can make up a story if you like."

Cissy's forehead creased in a puzzled frown. "You've always been so concerned with what people think."

"Yes, I have been, haven't I? I admit that I was appalled the first time Bea and Jim brought that child to church. But what were they supposed to do? Hide that pretty little thing in a closet? I'm sure folks do gossip about them, just like they gossip about your father and me, with Buddy dying like he did and Grayson living out by the river in a shack and me living all alone in a big old house with a sagging front porch and a broken garage door. But the gossip just doesn't matter as much as it used to. Every family has complications to be worked through."

Cissy sighed. "I don't know, Mama. I don't want to be a single mother, and marrying the baby's father is out of the question."

"It's not like you'll be raising the child alone, honey. Your father and I will be there till the day we die."

Cissy had to reach for a Kleenex and blow her nose. "I thought you'd be so mad."

Martha Claire reached for a Kleenex herself. "I was at first. But it's hard to be mad at a baby."

"That baby would connect me to a man I'd just as soon forget. I'd always worry that he would find out and that someday the baby would demand to know who his father was."

"Neither the child nor the man will find out unless you tell them," Martha Claire said. "Don't anticipate trouble. Just deal with it when the time comes, and don't forget, the baby would be living in Columbus, at least until you've finished your medical training. It's not like you'll be wearing him around Dallas in one of those baby slings."

Cissy grabbed another tissue. "I feel so stupid about getting pregnant in the first place. I'm not sure that I want a constant reminder of my own stupidity hanging around for the rest of my life."

"You can't hold an innocent child responsible for what you did."

Cissy stared out the window. "Do I have to decide right now?"

Grayson watched while his wife sagged a bit, worry creeping into her expression. "No, of course, not," Martha Claire said too brightly. "You take your time, honey. This is a very important decision."

Grayson thought of the trip to Target this morning. Martha Claire said she needed stockings and shampoo, but what she really wanted to buy was baby clothes, diapers, baby bottles, and yarn so she could crochet a baby blanket. She was presuming too much, he told her, and amazingly, she agreed with him. But she bought yarn and a crochet hook. She was always needing a baby gift, she had told him.

Grayson stood. "It's time that we leave, Martha Claire. Cissy needs her rest."

A peeved look descended onto Martha Claire's face. She glanced toward her husband and back at Cissy. She didn't want to leave. She wanted to wait until Cissy promised she would not give away that baby.

The room was silent. From outside came the sound of distant thunder, an ambulance siren. Across the hall, a phone rang. Martha Claire sighed and picked up her purse.

Cissy seemed not to notice their motions to leave. "Are you sure you and Daddy want to take on a baby?" she asked. "You're not as young as you used to be. What about night feedings and all that?"

"We have had a great deal of experience," Martha Claire said softly, hopefully.

"And the expense. We're poor as church mice."

"I'll sell the house if I need to," Martha Claire announced.

Cissy let out a little gasp. "You'd do that?"

Martha Claire pulled back her shoulders. "In a flash."

Again the silence settled over the room while Cissy digested that piece of information. Then she looked at her father. "What about you, Daddy? You haven't said a word."

Grayson stepped to his daughter's bedside, took her hand, cleared his throat. "I think you should listen to your heart. It might help for you to see the baby, but that's up to you." Then he half pulled Martha Claire from the room.

"We can't just leave her there," Martha Claire sputtered as he guided her toward the elevator. "What if someone from the adoption agency comes with forms and a fountain pen? If Cissy gives that baby away, I'll hire a lawyer, Grayson. I'll sell the house and fight her with every breath in my body."

"I know you will, Martha Claire. And that might even be the right thing to do. But let's wait and see how things play themselves out first."

From Cissy's room, they went to the nursery. The isolette with

Cissy's baby had been returned to the far corner. This time Martha Claire couldn't talk the nurse on duty into giving them "just a peek."

From the hospital, they went to Cissy's rooming house. Martha Claire had called the landlady this morning and arranged for them to stay there while Cissy was in the hospital. A fold-up cot was already waiting in the corner.

Martha Claire was a caged lion for the rest of the afternoon. Keeping the door ajar so she could hear the phone, she paced about the small room, stopping periodically to crochet a row or two on the baby blanket she had started, change the television channel, rant at her husband for making her leave her daughter alone at the hospital to make this monumental decision alone. When she didn't eat the peanut butter sandwich he made for her, Grayson realized her gesture was intended as a punishment. She glared at him when he ate it himself. The drying sandwich was supposed to sit there on the desk, a symbol of his incompetence or insensitivity or whatever.

Whenever the phone rang, she raced down the hall, then would dutifully knock on the appropriate door, slip a note under it if the person wasn't home. He had made a deal with her that they could return to the hospital after dinner if they hadn't heard from Cissy. She waited until five-thirty and prepared the next set of peanut butter sandwiches herself. Silently she ate hers and pretended to watch a few minutes of the evening news, then went into the bathroom to groom herself for what lay ahead.

Cissy was out of bed, sitting in a chair, the IV still in her arm. "Is it all right for you to be out of bed?" Martha Claire asked.

Cissy smiled. "I'm fine, Mama. Did you have a nice afternoon?"

Martha Claire glanced at Grayson. "We rested."

"Good," Cissy said. "Me, too. And I saw the baby."

Grayson held his breath. Martha Claire's hand flew to her breast.

"He's a skinny little thing, isn't he? I hope he doesn't stay that way. I've always hated being skinny." She paused, as though she expected them to say something.

Grayson was afraid to speak. Martha Claire, too, apparently.

Cissy laughed. "You both look like you're waiting for a judge to tell you if it's life or death."

When neither of them said a word, her expression softened. "You poor darlings. You really want this baby, don't you?"

Like two puppets, they both nodded.

"I guess it will be okay then."

"Thank God," Martha Claire said softly, sinking onto the side of the bed.

Grayson knelt in front of his daughter and put his hands on her shoulders. "I hope you're not doing this just for us."

"I'm not, Daddy. I promise that I'm not."

"Well," Martha Claire said, "we need to think of a name."

Cissy actually laughed. "Mama, something tells me you have a name already picked out."

"He's such a little angel," Martha Claire said, clutching her folded hands in her lap. "I was thinking about Gabriel. We could call him Gabe."

Grayson drove back to Columbus to tend the store and prepare for the arrival of his grandson, with Martha Claire staying behind to look after Cissy and the baby. It was with much pleasure that he refinished the crib, Polly's rocking chair, and a chest of drawers.

He chose Buddy's room for a nursery, rather than Iris's old room with its pink-and-white wallpaper or Polly's room at the back of the house. Buddy's room was across the hall from Martha Claire's, and it was time to close down the shrine.

Clearing out the room had been heart wrenching. Even though Buddy had lived out in the garage apartment the last years of his life, this had been his room throughout his childhood, and the possessions of his childhood remained pretty much as he had left them. Grayson felt as though he was somehow erasing his son's life by taking down all the posters and boxing up trophies, athletic paraphernalia, yearbooks, photographs, model planes, baseball hats. Boxes of memories. As he cleared out the room, Grayson would cry and talk out loud to his dead son, telling him how well he remembered this or that day or game, telling him how much he had loved him, apologizing for not being a stronger father, for not keeping him alive.

Once he had everything out of the room, he varnished the floors and painted the walls and ceiling a soft white. He put the crib by the window so Gabe could see the trees and the sky. He found a braided rug in the attic. And in the back room down at the store, he found the picture of Buddy in his Texas A&M uniform that Martha Claire once had displayed in the store window. Grayson carried it home and hung it over the chest of drawers. He didn't think Martha Claire would mind.

He told everyone who came into the store that Cissy had had a baby. *No, she wasn't married. He and Martha Claire were going to take care of the baby while Cissy finished her medical training. The baby's name was Gabriel, but they were going to call him Gabe.*

He found himself singing to himself when no one was in the store. Songs he hadn't sung for years. "Mockingbird Hill," "If I Knew You Were Coming I'd-a Baked a Cake," "Dear Hearts and Gentle People." Sometimes he laughed out loud just for the sheer pleasure of it.

Grayson called Martha Claire and Cissy every night, first at the hospital, then at the rooming house after Cissy and the baby were discharged. Gabe was doing just fine, sleeping in a dresser drawer. The phone calls were a foolish luxury, Grayson supposed, but after spending most of his evenings alone for the past fifteen years, he found he needed a daily connection with his wife and daughter and through them the baby. Martha Claire did not chastise him.

He drove back to Tulsa when Gabe was four weeks old, to bring him and Martha Claire home. Cissy had already returned to her duties. She was worried about getting credit for the semester but promised she would not overdo.

On the drive back, they had just crossed the Red River when Martha Claire asked him to move back into the house. "The boy will be needing his grandfather," she pointed out.

"Yes, I'd like that," he said.

They drove straight through, pulling into the driveway in the middle of the night. "I hope that's the last time I have to make that drive," he said, but actually he would love to go back someday—a leisurely drive with Gabe, to show him where he was born, to poke around the Oklahoma countryside and visit local museums and historical sites. He was ready for new vistas after years of knowing what lay over the crest of each hill, around each curve in the road.

He heated water for tea while Martha Claire fed and fussed with the baby. Gabe was all eyes, looking around. Such an alert little guy. When he was fed and changed, Grayson carried him upstairs and rocked him to sleep in his great-grandmother Polly's rocking chair

Martha Claire seemed pleased with the baby's room. She watched while Grayson carefully lowered Gabe into the crib and covered him with the baby blanket she had crocheted in Tulsa. "It was hard going through all of Buddy's things," he admitted. "Is the picture all right?"

"It's perfect."

They stayed there for a time, side by side, staring worshipfully down at the tiny boy who already filled their hearts.

Later Grayson stood under the shower for a long time, trying to bring some ease to his aching muscles. In his room, he gingerly stretched out on the bed. *Home,* he thought. He was home to stay. Maybe he'd buy a new mattress. He closed his eyes, wondering how long the baby would sleep, and felt his own body ease into slumber. He was surprised when the bedroom door opened. Martha Claire stood in the doorway, the light from the hall backlighting her body in her nightgown. "You don't need to sleep in here," she said.

Would I really have given away my son? That's a question I often ponder. If I hadn't almost died there at the end, if Justine hadn't set my rescue into motion, if my parents hadn't come to Tulsa, as hard as it is to fathom now, I probably would have dutifully signed the adoption forms and sent him off to another life.

According to the woman from the adoption agency, my son's adoptive parents had already been selected—a physician and his wife who'd been married for eleven childless years, who had a fine home in a mid-sized Oklahoma community, who were well respected in that community, in good health, and devout church members. This fine couple had already been called, already been told the baby they were to adopt was a boy, born more than a month early, but healthy. The doctor and his wife already had a crib and diapers and had selected a name. The birth announcements were written and ready to send. I thought of those two people as I wrestled with my decision, thought how brokenhearted they would be—not, however, as brokenhearted as my parents, for whom the baby represented the final chance for a lifeline. The physician and his wife would have other opportunities, I told myself. Still, I grieved for them and felt as though I had done them a genuine disservice, getting their hopes up like that.

Part of me wants to think that, if I had given birth secretly as I had planned and the woman from the agency had come with her forms, I would have had second thoughts and been unable to sign them. Maybe, even without my father's urging, I would have asked to see the baby first, and after touching his sweet face I would have felt such a well of maternal love rising inside of me that I would have sooner cut off my arm as given away my child. But probably, even if I had seen him, I would have signed him away. My plan for the rest of my life did not include that particular child—some other child, perhaps, but not that one. And life would have gone on. He would have been lovingly raised. I might have thought about him with regret, but I would have gotten on with my life. I might even have entered a longer residency program, become a pediatric urologist or a neonatologist instead of a primary care pediatrician.

But that's not how it happened. I almost died. My aunt Justine saved me with her phone call. My parents rushed to my side and saw the baby they were never supposed to know about. When it comes right down to it, I kept the baby because I could not bear to deprive them of something they wanted and needed so desperately. And, of course, I came to love that baby more than life itself. That's a given, I suppose.

I loved to hear Daddy tell about the first time Mama saw Gabe. He had several different versions of that day. Sometimes he claimed that the instant Mama saw Gabe in the hospital nursery, the heavens opened and the light from on high illuminated the nursery and Mama's face, which at that particular moment had never been more beautiful, the face of a grandmother angel. Other times Daddy told the story with the Mormon Tabernacle Choir marching down the hospital corridor singing the Hallelujah Chorus to accompany Mama's rapture. Other versions had her tears of joy flooding the hallway and the fire department having to come to rescue all the babies and nurses from drowning. Or Mama growing ten feet tall, sporting horns, and telling the nurse if she let that adoption lady anyplace near that baby all hell was going to break loose. Gabe would laugh, of course. His grandpa had a near-perfect record at getting a laugh out of him. Gabe's laughter was a cherished blessing in a house that had known no such sound for so many wasted years.

Not that we were completely healed. Any mention of Justine and Iris was still not allowed. My mother and I were alienated for months after I took Gabe to New York to show him off to them, to meet my niece Tovah for the first time. Mama told me that if I took Gabe to New York, I shouldn't bother coming home. Daddy moved back out to the river. I had to put Gabe in a day-care center in Houston, where I was serving the first year of my residency. Mama still hated her sister that much, even though it was Justine who had set the wheels in motion that brought a grandchild to her lap and life.

But finally my daddy got sick of it all and came for Gabe. He took him home to Columbus and dared my mother to turn him and the boy away. She couldn't, of course. She was probably mad that Daddy hadn't taken the bull by the horns sooner. My mother loved Gabe completely, as completely as she once loved Iris.

forty-five

Martha Claire's decision to invite Grayson back home had been carefully thought out and carried out with full intent. She needed his help and support to care for Cissy's baby, and a fatherless boy needed a close relationship with his grandfather.

She had not planned, however, to invite Grayson back into her bed.

The sweet moments they had shared putting the baby to bed had softened her, she supposed. Shoulder to shoulder they stood by the crib Martha Claire had bought secondhand after Iris was born. Grayson had brought the crib down from the attic after Doc Hadley brought them Cissy. When Buddy joined them, they had bought him a low cot, but for the longest time he carried his pillow and blanket to the floor beside Iris's bed. Often as not, she would pull him up into bed with her and sleep with her arms around him. When Cissy was old enough for a regular bed, he would crawl into bed with her.

Those had been good days, Martha Claire thought, with three children and a husband to look after. She hadn't realized how good until they ended. She could have been an easier mother, though, less preoccupied with cleanliness and on-time meals. She could never have been as silly and carefree as Justine, but she could have laughed and smiled more.

With Gabe, she would do better. She wanted to enjoy this baby more. She imagined herself leaving the kitchen untidy to take a walk with him or read him a story. She wouldn't have so many rules this time around. She would let Gabe play in the dirt and maybe even have a pet.

She watched while Grayson stroked Gabe's tiny back until he fell asleep. Grayson had always had all the patience in the world with children.

She leaned down to kiss the baby's downy head, to touch his soft cheek, to marvel that he was theirs to love and help raise. How could a mother be glad that her daughter had disgraced herself? But she was. God help her, she was.

She wanted to touch Grayson's arm and tell him she was remembering their first night with Cissy. She didn't, though. She had stopped touching her husband during the years they warred over Buddy's future, had not reminisced with him since they lost Iris.

From her room, she heard Grayson come out of the bathroom, heard the squeak of the floorboards as he walked down the hall, the sound of the door to his room closing behind him. Her husband had been a once-a-week visitor in her home for so long now. Occasionally he would stay over after a late night of taking inventory at the store or if there was a heavy enough rain to flood the dirt lane that led to his shack. Usually, though, he used the room only on Friday night, and he always closed the door, as a guest would do.

Martha Claire had left her own door ajar, to hear the baby. Maybe Grayson should have set the crib up in here until the baby was older, she thought.

She had bragged to Cissy about their experience tending babies, but she was out of practice. When her children were small, she heard every whimper in the night. She had known when they were sick before they knew it themselves. She had known if their fussing was due to discomfort, hunger, sleepiness, or just wanting to be picked up. But that was a long time ago. Iris was almost thirty-five. Cissy would soon be thirty. Buddy would have turned thirty-one last May. What if she had lost her knack? What if she didn't wake up when Gabe cried? The poor little thing might cry on and on before she heard him. She couldn't bear the thought of him crying with no one rushing in to offer comfort.

If both she and Grayson left their doors open, one of them would surely hear the baby when he woke for his feeding.

She got out of bed, padded across the hall, tapped on the door. "Grayson," she said, turning the knob.

The light from the hall fell across his bed. He had propped himself up on an elbow and was waiting to see what she wanted. She meant to tell him to leave his door open, but those other words had come out of her mouth. *You don't need to sleep in here.* Words that indicated she wanted him to sleep in her bed.

She went back to her bed with her heart pounding. *What had she done?*

Maybe he would not come, she thought, pulling the blanket up to her chin.

She lay with her back toward the open door, heard him coming across the hall, felt his weight on the side of the bed, waited while he settled in—on the wrong side of the bed, she realized. In the past, when they shared this bed, their positions had been reversed.

"Good night," she said.

"Good night," he responded.

She wished she had her robe on. She was naked under the thin fabric of her nightgown.

She lay motionless, not daring to move, hardly daring to breathe, even when the muscles in her legs and shoulders began to cramp. Any movement on her part might seem an invitation.

She would not be able to sleep with him there. It had been too long. She would have to tell him to leave.

But she said nothing, maybe even dozed a little.

Then she heard an odd sound coming from his side of the bed, the sound of muffled sobs. Grayson was crying into his pillow.

She sat up and touched his arm.

"I'm sorry," he said into the pillow. "Oh, God, Martha Claire, I've missed you so. God, how I've missed you."

She rubbed his arm, trying to comfort him. It had been an emotional three weeks, she said in a soothing voice. Things were different now, with the baby. Their lives would be better.

He grabbed her hand and kissed her palm. "I wish I had died in the war," he whispered. "Then I wouldn't have hurt you like that."

Martha Claire drew in her breath and pulled her hand away. They did not talk of such things. It was not allowed.

"I love you, Martha Claire," he said. "I've never stopped loving you and hoping that someday I could make things right with you."

"Don't say any more," she told him, lying down again, positioning herself on the very edge of the mattress, on the wrong side of the bed. Tomorrow night, she wondered, would they sleep like this or return to the old way?

Tomorrow night?

Did she really want him here tomorrow night? And all the nights hereafter?

She did not love him, but he was her husband still. For years she would have liked to see him bloodied and dead at her feet. She had gotten over that, but she continued to jab at him, to let him know in small ways that she had not forgiven him, did not expect ever to forgive him. He had been unfaithful to her. With her own sister, he had betrayed her and allowed her to love the child begotten by that betrayal. That knowledge still brought such pain, still made her heart feel as cold and hard as a stone.

She needed him now, though, not just for the store and to saw dead limbs off the trees, but to help with their grandson, with little Gabe. She didn't have as much energy as before. She could not do it all alone.

She did *not,* however, need him to sleep in her bed. Maybe she would tell him tomorrow she hadn't slept well with him there. He should return to his own bed but leave the door ajar in case she needed him in the night.

With that option formulating itself in her mind, she felt herself relaxing, drifting, felt sleep overtaking her. "Good night," she said once again.

Grayson did not respond.

Later, she struggled back to wakefulness when Grayson touched her shoulder. The baby was awake. He would see to him.

Martha Claire could remember him doing that the first night with Cissy, telling her he would take the first feeding. When he came back to the bed, they had made love. Tender, beautiful love filled with such promise.

She had loved him that night, but that was because she didn't know what he had done. She had still loved Justine then, too, and loved her sister's child who was also Grayson's child.

If she had known the truth about her sister's child back then, she never would have allowed herself to love Iris. It was all too confusing to think about. She'd never stopped loving Iris, but she had learned to stop thinking about her.

The next morning, they bathed the baby in the kitchen sink, dressed him in a blue sailor suit that was sized for a newborn but was still miles too big, and took him to church. Martha Claire insisted that she had to get it over with, that if she waited, people would think she was ashamed.

She had not expected Grayson to go with her, which seemed a miracle of sorts. She realized it probably was just this once, that he broke his moratorium as a special favor to her because this was a special day and he didn't want her to face all those people alone. But still, in spite of the glances and whispers, it was nice to be at church with a husband at her side and a grandbaby in her arms. Grayson even sang the hymns —"Nearer, My God, to Thee," "What a Friend We Have in Jesus," "O God, Our Help in Ages Past." She had forgotten what a wonderful voice he had. He and Iris would harmonize while Polly played the piano. So many memories had come floating back in the past few days. She felt as though she were standing on the crest of a hill, able to see both where she had been and where she was going.

After the service, Grayson followed her to the fellowship hall, where she reintroduced him to the minister, who said he was glad to see his most elusive parishioner.

Grayson stood beside Martha Claire as she showed off the baby and explained that Cissy still had years to go on her medical training, that she had planned to give the baby up for adoption. "Of course, Grayson and I would have none of that," she told people, adding that they would raise the baby until Cissy was in a position to care for him. Bea and Jim Hawkins, with their little granddaughter, came to stand with them.

"You were magnificent back there," Grayson told his wife as they walked to the car.

Martha Claire felt herself blush. "What were you and Reverend Miller talking about over in the corner?" she said.

"Fishing. Apparently Paul Huxley has been telling him about the great fishing out on my bend in the river. I told him the big ones only bite on Sunday morning."

"You didn't!"

"Yes, ma'am, I did."

At Grayson's suggestion, they had dinner at Schobel's, along with all the other churchgoers, with Gabe displayed in an infant carrier. People stopped by to admire him, to satisfy their curiosity. Martha Claire knew the whole town would be talking about them. Well, maybe not the whole town, but all of old Columbus would talk.

Of course, she and Grayson already were a common source of gossip, with him living out by the river like some latter-day Thoreau. Cissy's out-of-wedlock baby would top that, of course. The looks on people's faces said they wouldn't have thought such a thing of Cissy, of that quiet little girl who had never caused anyone a moment's trouble in her entire life.

Martha Claire wouldn't have thought it of Cissy, either. Not that it hadn't occurred to her that, as a young woman on her own in this day and age, Cissy probably had gone to bed with a man. What bothered Martha Claire more than the pregnancy itself was that Cissy had been afraid to tell her about it. Martha Claire had no illusions. She fully realized that Cissy had been prepared to give away her baby primarily because she didn't want her mother to know.

It made shivers run up and down Martha Claire's spine, made her blood run cold in her veins, to think how close she had come to being denied her grandson. Like her mother before her, Martha Claire wanted her fatherless grandchild. She wanted Gabe no matter what people thought or said, no matter that Cissy wasn't married, that the baby would not have a father's name. But how could Cissy have known that her mother was going to feel that way? Martha Claire herself could not have anticipated such feelings.

Back home, she and Grayson both admitted to exhaustion. Neither one had slept very well last night, she supposed, and each of them had gotten up for a feeding. They and the baby slept away the afternoon, with Grayson on the sofa, the baby in its crib, and Martha Claire on her bed, with her grandmother's quilt across her legs.

That evening, Gabe ruled over the dining room table from his infant carrier. He was such a beautiful baby; Martha Claire delighted in watching him. She and Grayson marveled at how alert he was, how he responded to their voices, how wonderful it was to have a baby in the house again. They laughed together at his silly sounds and expressions.

Laughter. God, how long had it been since she had laughed, really laughed? She liked the feel of it in her mouth and belly.

Her hand and Grayson's touched as they handed the bowls of food back and forth, as they cleared the table and tended to their grandchild. And again when Grayson handed her a glass of wine.

Martha Claire felt girlish. Giddy. Feverish, even. She couldn't quite allow herself to consider the reason why. Grayson kept looking at her as though she were rosy and young. She caught a glimpse of herself in the hall mirror and was transfixed. She *did* look rosy and young.

She ran her hands over her waist and thighs, enjoying the feel of her own touch. And there was Grayson handing her another glass of wine. She took the glass but told him no more. They had a baby to look after.

It wasn't like those years when she begrudgingly allowed sex because her body wanted it. She no longer thought about sex, no longer needed or wanted it. That part of her life had ended long ago.

How could a *grandchild* change that?

It was crazy. Ludicrous. Grayson was still Iris's father. That would never change.

Grayson said he would rock the baby to sleep while she took a bath.

She rummaged around in the linen closet and found a bottle of bath oil that probably had been there for years. She felt so strange, so alive, as she took off her robe and settled into the water. She thought of that sweet child in her husband's arms, of Grayson once again coming to her bed. She lingered for a long time in the bathtub, shaving her legs, soaking in the sweet-smelling water, touching her breasts. After she dried herself, she examined herself in the mirror.

She wasn't fat, but her skin no longer fit her body as it once had. Her body was old, her face was old—but she wanted to feel young again.

Once again, she stood beside Grayson in the baby's room while they worshipfully stared down at their grandson.

In bed, she lay on her back. Grayson, too. Side by side, their shoulders almost touching, staring up at the dark ceiling.

She was almost relieved when Gabe began to fuss. Maybe she wouldn't have to betray the long-held animosity she felt for her husband, a feeling that had become such an important part of who she was. She wouldn't be able to recognize herself without it. But Gabe's fussing was the sleepy sort and grew softer until it stopped altogether. Martha Claire realized she had been holding her breath.

Grayson wasn't going to do anything unless she gave him a sign. Her heart felt like a teeter-totter thumping up and down in her chest. Maybe all this excitement wasn't good for her. Maybe she was too old for lust. She had a baby to raise and needed to look after herself. Carefully, so Grayson wouldn't notice, she took a deep breath, then another, and willed her heart to calm itself.

As it turned out, she didn't need to give him a sign. He said her name. Softly. As though it were the most beautiful two words in the world. Then he asked if he could hold her in his arms.

She said yes. There were no more words after that. He sensed that she did not have any for him and did not want to hear his. They kissed for an incredibly long time, as they had back in their courting days, kisses that went on endlessly and would leave her lips swollen and bruised the next day. Then she could reach up and touch them with her fingertips and remember.

She felt beautiful, like that girl back then, like she had been on their honeymoon before her husband went to war, before he went to England to be with Justine.

Their honeymoon on Galveston Island—that's where she would take herself. Not to the motel in Sugar Land. That first night had been passionate and special—but not like the second night, when they crawled inside of one another and became a new being. Yes, she was on Galveston Island, with the sound of the waves, the smell of the sea, the night breeze coming through the open window and cooling her warm young flesh as she made love with the man she had loved since he was a boy, the only man she had ever loved.

forty-six

Martha Claire bent over to pull an offending shoot of nut grass from the lawn, then climbed the front steps, put her pruning shears and straw hat on the table, and seated herself in her favorite wicker rocker. She picked up her hat and began to fan herself, trying to decide if she should go inside and start breakfast or just wait out here for Gabe and Grayson.

The scent of brewing coffee reached her nostrils—from the Williams house across the street, she decided. Every window in the house was open. Ethyl never used the air conditioner her daughters had installed. She lived alone now, with Clark in the nursing home and the children scattered.

Martha Claire rocked back and forth, surveying her domain, enjoying the busyness of a pair of black-headed sparrows who were building a nest in the magnolia tree and the merry splashing of her resident male robin in the birdbath.

The robin finished his splashing and perched on the porch railing momentarily, peering at her with his beady eyes before flying back to his family duties.

The chair made a rhythmic squeaking sound as she rocked. She remembered the same monotonous sound when her father had sat there. This had been his chair, where he read his newspaper and dozed. Her mother and grandmother preferred to sit in straight-backed chairs while they snapped green beans or black-eyed peas, peeled potatoes, shucked corn, crocheted, embroidered as they watched the occasional car go by and called greetings to the neighbors. As long as there was daylight, neither one of them would just sit idly. She herself had been like that, and still was, she supposed. But not like before, though, not since Gabe had come to them.

The broad front porch was what Martha Claire loved most about her house. No one built houses with porches like this anymore. Porch-sitting had passed from the culture. Folks nowadays preferred to stay inside with their air conditioners and televisions, as she did herself midsummer, except in the mornings and evenings. Every day, no matter how hot and muggy, she needed to be outside, to hear the rustling of the leaves, watch the birds, inhale the scents of her little corner of the world. Spring was best, with the heady fragrances of wisteria and magnolia. Later came the aroma of roses and freshly mowed grass. Autumn smelled of burning leaves. And the cooler air of what passed for winter in south Texas smelled brisk and clean.

When Gabe was a baby, Grayson would sit out here rocking him. Even that first winter, he would bundle the baby up and bring him to the porch for his daily dose of fresh air.

Surely no baby had ever been rocked more than Gabe. Whether on the porch or inside, Grayson rocked him by the hour, often singing the old songs that they once had sung around the piano: "Jacob's Ladder," "On Top of Old Smoky," "She'll Be Coming 'Round the Mountain." It was only in the past year that the boy had finally learned to fall asleep on his own, without his grandfather rocking and singing or stretched out with him on his bed, and then only because Martha Claire reneged on a previous ruling and let Puppy Dog sleep with him.

Puppy Dog had been a tiny little thing when they found him along the road out near Grayson's shack. The poor animal had been half dead, with every rib showing and one of his paws badly cut, but he made a beeline for Gabe and started licking his face. Probably they should have thought of another name for him, but it was too late for that. Puppy Dog was now a big, ungainly creature who left a trail of slobber and fine yellow hair everywhere he went, but Martha Claire often found herself wishing she'd let Buddy have a dog.

She paused a minute in her rocking, studying an overgrown branch on a holly bush. But she resisted the urge to take up her shears and snip it off. The offending branch would still be there tomorrow. Cissy liked to say that she and mother both made rounds in the morning. Cissy marched up and down hospital halls with a stethoscope in one pocket of her white coat and an ophthalmoscope in the other, and her mother marched around the yard with her pruning shears and basket. It was true, Martha Claire thought. That was how she started every day, grooming her yard, harvesting her crops.

And such a wonderful yard it was. The crepe myrtle were in full bloom now, and the rose of Sharon. The beds of coleus, caladium, and impatiens were in full foliage under the trees. And the fence shown whitely with a fresh coat of paint. Cissy and Grayson had painted it last month, with lots of eager assistance from Gabe. It took days for the paint to come out of his hair. Cissy said that one of these days, when she had finished her residency and was finally in practice and making all that money that everyone said she was going to make, the first thing she was going to do was replace the handsome iron fence that had marched its way around the yard in all those old photographs. Cissy wanted to do all the things to the house that they never had been able to afford, and sometimes Martha Claire let herself revive the old dream of restoring the house to its former glory, but mostly she lived from day to day, enjoying what blessings came her way. When the time came, she probably would tell Cissy to put on a new roof and forget about the fence.

Martha Claire lifted her apron and wiped the sweat from her brow. Already, at eight o'clock in the morning, it was muggy and still. But then, what else could one expect in south Texas in the middle of July? In July, she could almost understand why folks packed up and headed for the mountains in Colorado or New Mexico.

Grayson said they were going someplace cool next summer, if only for a week. Last summer, they'd taken Gabe on several little trips—to Six Flags in Arlington, an Indian powwow in Oklahoma, a rodeo at Bandera—none of which were cool. Martha Claire didn't like to leave her yard for more than a day or two in the summer, but she supposed she could find someone to water and look after things. Wherever they went, Puppy Dog would have to go along. She didn't want the dog thinking he'd been abandoned again.

She put down her hat and picked up the newspaper that Grayson had left out here last night, using it to fan herself while she waited. Cissy planned to put a ceiling fan out here. That would be nice, Martha Claire thought, imagining the lazy turning of wooden blades slicing through the still air.

Soon, she saw them coming up the street—grandfather and grandson, with Puppy Dog loping along behind. Grayson was carrying the tackle box and had their fishing poles over his shoulder. Gabe saw her sitting there and began to run, holding up the morning catch. "I caught two, Grandma! I caught two!"

At four, Gabe was an undersized little boy. He had started life small and would always be small, like his mother. Small but mighty, his grandfather liked to say. Mighty curious, for one thing. Gabe was a boy with a million questions about everything under the sun. He kept his grandfather constantly going to the encyclopedias to find out what was the largest bug in the world, how many kinds of birds there were, why Texas was named Texas. Gabe wanted to know if fish kissed, why worms didn't have legs, why someone didn't feed the starving children in Africa, why there wasn't a bridge over the ocean, why people got sick, what held up the moon and sun. On and on, his mind formulating the next question as the previous one was being answered. Gabe was the exact opposite of Buddy, who had been a big, athletic boy with few questions.

Gabe came running up the steps holding his catch in the air. "Can we take the fishes to Houston and show them to Mommy?"

"They would smell up the car, honey, but we'll sure tell her about them. We could take her some vegetables, though. Why don't you and I go around back and pick some things for her. I bet she'd like some tomatoes and corn and okra."

"My mommy likes okra a lot," he said.

Martha Claire had to take his dirty, sweaty little face between her hands and kiss it. Such a dear face, a dear boy. She loved him without reservation. Her love for this child filled her up and made her a calmer, better person. If only she could have allowed herself to love her children this way. "Yes, your mommy really likes okra," she agreed. "But do you know what she likes even better than okra?"

His face broke into a big silly grin. "She likes me better than anything," he said proudly.

"Oh, indeed she does. That mommy of yours is looking at the clock right this very minute and thinking that in only three more hours her Gabe will be there to spend two days with her. She's thinking how she'll take you to visit the children in the hospital and down to the shipping channel to see the big ships."

"And after two days, she's going to put me in the car and drive us both back to Columbus, and she will stay here for five whole days. And we'll pick blackberries and go to the beach in Galveston and visit Reverend Huxley at the nursing home and practice writing numbers and put on a show for you and Granddaddy in the attic and drive out in the country to see chickens and buy fresh eggs and put a penny on the railroad track and watch the train come along and smash it flat so that it's bigger around than a quarter."

"You got it!" Martha Claire said. "Now, give those fish to Granddaddy, and let's go pick those vegetables."

"And some strawberries, too. Strawberries aren't vegetables. They're a fruit."

"My, what a smart boy you are!" Martha Claire said, taking his hand and remembering another summer day when she had waited on the porch for Grayson and Iris to return from an early-morning fishing excursion. She and Iris had gone around back to pick vegetables to take to her mother, back in the days when Justine was working for the newspaper in Houston.

It couldn't have been too long after that when Doc Hadley brought them Cissy, a day that Martha Claire had come to realize was the most important in her life. What would she and Grayson be now if it weren't for Cissy and her precious child? Martha Claire looked at her husband, thinking to share her memories with him, but he was still standing there, staring down at the fish, the poles still over his shoulder, a puzzled look on his face.

"Grayson, are you all right?"

He shook his head, as though to clear it, and looked at her with questioning eyes.

"Are you going to clean the fish?" she asked.

"The fish? Yes, I'll clean the fish," he said gratefully and followed her and Gabe around back.

The party was Cissy's idea. She insisted that Stewart's Dry Goods could not close its doors after more than eighty years without a bit of fanfare.

After the last bit of merchandise had been sold off or given away, they cleaned the old store for the last time. Cissy decorated the walls and shelves with old snapshots she'd had blown up to poster size—of Grayson's grandparents standing behind their cash register, of his parents behind the same cash register, of the salesladies who had worked there over the years, of Martha Claire and Grayson in his army uniform standing in front of the store. She'd also had posters made from some of the old newspaper ads—shoes for two dollars and fifty cents a pair, thread for a nickel, men's socks for a quarter. And she'd borrowed the picture of Buddy in his A&M football uniform from Gabe's bedroom.

They'd run out of punch and cookies the first hour. Cissy rushed off to get more. Then she went to the nursing home to fetch Reverend Huxley—and ended up making several trips back and forth to the nursing home when other residents wanted to come. The store was a part of their memories. A steady stream of people came all day. Some even brought things they'd bought at the store over the years. Others had old sales receipts and sale circulars.

The photographer came from the newspaper to take Grayson's and Martha Claire's picture beside the punch bowl. And a young reporter skillfully interviewed them, probing for poignant memories. Grayson recalled washing the storefront windows every Saturday morning until he went off to college, and he told how people would just drop by the store for a visit, whether they planned to buy anything or not. Martha Claire recalled the war years, when she worked at the store after her father-in-law's heart attack. Back then, they would sell more fabric than ready-to-wear. Ladies would spend hours looking at pattern books, calling her over to ask her to help them decide between a Butterick and a Simplicity pattern. And Martha Claire found herself rambling on about Buddy, how her dream had been that he would take the store into a fourth generation. The reporter promised that the picture and story would be page 1, even if there was a hurricane or war was declared. He had his memories, too, of coming here with his mother to buy a new shirt and jeans to wear the first day of school—and with his father to buy shotgun shells and gun grease.

When the last of their guests had finally taken their leave, they took down the posters and folded the tablecloth. Grayson took the trash out back one last time. "I feel like we should say a prayer or something over the old place," Martha Claire said.

"I always felt close to my father here," Grayson said. "I'll miss that."

Cissy and Gabe left first, to return the punch bowl to the church and pick up some Kentucky Fried Chicken for dinner. Martha Claire cried as she locked the door. Wal-Mart finally had put them out of business. She hated Wal-Mart and had vowed she would never set foot in the ugly, sprawling store that was ruining downtowns all over America. However, in spite of the sadness and hating Wal-Mart and their like, she felt a sense of relief. She didn't want to spend her days down here anymore, and Grayson no longer could manage the store on his own. He would forget how to make change and sometimes got lost on the way home. She needed to look after him and Gabe now, and her garden.

The store had represented such a major part of her life. It became who she was—Martha Claire Stewart from the dry goods store. Even so, they probably should have closed the store when Grayson's father died. She should have let Grayson have a go at another sort of life. She told him that as they walked home.

Grayson didn't answer for the longest time. Martha Claire wondered if he'd even heard her. He wasn't hard of hearing, but these days he didn't always listen. They walked half a block before he said, "I never was a good storekeeper, but maybe I wouldn't have been a good army officer, either. What I should have been was a teacher."

"You could have had a fine military career," Martha Claire said, taking his arm, "but you would have been a good teacher, too. You could have taken students on school trips to all those places you never got to go."

"Cissy wants to take me to Europe," he said.

"She what?" Martha Claire said, slowing her stride, not sure she had understood correctly.

"She told me just a little while ago. She found a tour just for veterans and their families. I always dreamed of going there with you someday, until . . ." His voice trailed off, leaving words unsaid. Martha Claire wondered what they would have been. *Until she found out about him and Justine? Until she discovered that he was Iris's father?*

They walked along in silence for a while, past the house where he had grown up, past the little house where they had lived as newlyweds. So, here they were, she thought, two old people walking down the street toward what was left of their lives. So much time wasted, so many regrets. And such a sense of missing. She missed her parents and Granny Grace, but time would have taken them from her no matter what. Most of her missing was for Buddy and Iris, who both should still be a part of her life, along with Iris's daughter and any children Buddy might have had. And she missed having a sister in her life.

"You should go," she told him as they turned into the white gate of their own home.

"To Europe?"

"Yes, you should go. You tell Cissy all about the war. Tell her all the things you felt and thought and learned, and someday she will tell her son."

"I love Gabe," he said.

"I know you do," she said, linking arms with him as they climbed the steps.

For years, I had thought of taking my father to Europe, since before I went to medical school. Then, when Gabe came along, I thought maybe I'd wait until he was old enough to go with us. I began to realize, however, that Daddy couldn't wait that long. He often forgot what he was about to do, stopping in his steps, a puzzled frown creasing his forehead. He forgot where the silverware was kept and what year it was.

So we made the trip, joining our fellow travelers in Rome—old men, some with old wives, others with sons and daughters. There was a pair of aging brothers who had traveled together from Wisconsin. A middle-aged woman from Oklahoma had come alone, fulfilling a life-long promise to herself that she visit the place where her father had died. She had been studying French for years, knowing that someday she would make this pilgrimage. In all, there were forty-five veterans, two dozen wives, twenty-one children, and two grandchildren. The men moved with shuffling steps and apprehension in their eyes. After years of thinking about this journey, they were finally there. And maybe it was going to hurt more than it helped to put their memories of that monstrous and occasionally glorious time in perspective. They had come seeking to ease the grief they had carried all these years for fallen comrades and the guilt of having lived into old age when others had died so young.

A sometimes suffocating blanket of poignancy hung over our bus journey through Italy, Germany, Luxembourg, and France.

The buses were decorated with division insignias, and farmers stopped in the fields, pedestrians on sidewalks, to wave at the busloads of aging American veterans. I had not anticipated the welcome we re-ceived along the way, with *vins d'honneur*—receptions with wine and speeches and gifts in towns we visited.

Strange how Daddy couldn't remember yesterday's news, yet he re-called quite vividly his war years and recognized many of the places he had been: *That little stream was red with blood when we waded across. We slept over there in that stone barn. Over the crest of the next hill is the town where my sergeant got hit. I prayed in that church.*

It was the cemeteries, of course, that tore us all apart. These were surely the saddest places on the planet. Cemetery after cemetery. Seas of white markers, each one representing a young man who didn't get to go home to the rest of his life, most of them very young men, some not even twenty.

When we were planning the trip, I had asked Daddy if there was anyone buried over there whose grave he wanted to visit, and he told me about Fenton Crutchfield, the young driver who had died in his arms. It was the first time I'd ever heard him speak the name of any of the men he had known and fought with over there. Fenton had grown up in an orphanage in Iowa and planned to marry a girl named Sally when he got back home. He was an artist who drew sketches of the places they visited but never of the war itself. "I don't know what happened to those sketches," Daddy had said. "I would have liked to have one of them."

I had done my homework and knew that Fenton Crutchfield was among the ten thousand servicemen buried in the American cemetery outside of Lorraine. You can't imagine what it was like climbing down from that bus and looking out over ten thousand markers. Even after four decades, sadness seemed to radiate from the green grass, the white headstones, the stately chapel. The fact that the men buried there were so far from home somehow made the place even sadder. I thought of Buddy, of how I felt the day he died, and multiplied that sadness by ten thousand. All those sisters and parents and wives and children who had never seen these men again, never even had a funeral for them.

My poor father was overwhelmed to the point of speechlessness. With a map sent to me by the American Battle Monuments Commission, I led him up and down the rows until we found Fenton's grave, where he would pay homage to the driver who had died in his arms and to all the men he had known who died. For all those years, he had carried that unbearable burden, of living while most of the men in his command had died. I knew my father well enough to know that he had cared for them, loved them, even the ones who were with him for only a few days before the shell or grenade exploded, before the bullet came. Some died quickly and cleanly. Others died of hideous wounds. "I would have died to save any one of them," he told me. "And always I wondered, if I had made better decisions would fewer of them have had to die?"

He knelt in the grass and embraced the cross that marked young Fenton's grave and wept. I wept, too, of course. How could one not? I wept as I backed away, leaving my father to his grief and remembering. I wept for the burden my father and all these men had carried with them into old age. I wept for Fenton and for all of these young heroes buried so far from home.

I watched from a distance as Daddy spent almost an hour at Fenton's grave. He sat with his back against the stone, his hands between his knees.

Finally, it was growing dark and the buses were loading. I went to him, to pull him to his feet and hold him in my arms. I felt privileged to share my father's sorrow, but my mother should have been the one to make this journey with him. Maybe then she might understand how otherworldly, how hideously difficult the war years had been for him, how he might have sought refuge in a woman's soft arms, even if that woman was his wife's own sister. Or maybe it was because she was Mama's sister that he sought her out, because being with her was the next best thing to hearing Mama's voice, to being in her arms. I myself fully forgave him; I would have forgiven any of the men on our bus just about anything. They had suffered for me and my son.

Daddy told me that he had seen hundreds, maybe thousands of dead—Americans and Germans, soldiers and civilians. Toward the end of the war, he refused to even learn the first names and hometowns of the replacements, of raw recruits who didn't even know to keep their heads down. Daddy's company had turned over the equivalent of three times through death, wounds, and frostbite.

If my mother had made this journey, maybe she could have finally understood the incomprehensible burden that he bore and would have finally been able to forgive him for Dover.

In Paris, with hugs and tears, we bid our traveling companions farewell and stayed on for four more days of sightseeing.

Our last night, we went to the top of the Eiffel Tower and looked down on what must be the most beautiful city in the world. It was a magic moment that Daddy had dreamed of sharing with my mother.

While I had forgiven my father, the sinner, I found it difficult to forgive my mother. I blamed her more for what had happened to our family than I blamed him—or Justine. Which wasn't fair. Technically, Mama had done nothing wrong.

I remembered asking Mama about inviting Iris to my graduation from medical school. Mama wouldn't hear of it. She said she wouldn't come if Iris did. And there would have been no point in participating in the ceremony if my mother wasn't there.

"What did Iris ever do to you?" I had demanded.

"She left."

"But Justine was her mother. When Justine said she couldn't stay with us anymore, what did you expect Iris to do?"

"She should have told Justine that she belonged here in Columbus with you and me and Buddy," Mama had replied, real anger in her voice. "I was the one who raised her while her so-called mother went trekking all over the world. Whatever time Justine had left over from her career was what she gave to Iris and me. Family was an aside with her. Iris was sixteen years old. She could have told Justine that she wouldn't leave us."

I never told Mama that my medical education had been Iris's idea and that she had helped me financially. And I never told her that Justine had provided the money for me to live in Tulsa until Gabe was born. I suppose I was afraid that she might withdraw her love from me the way it had been withdrawn from them. Maybe being adopted had altered me more than I realized, but I needed for Mama to love me, no matter how conditionally. I had lived my entire life seeking her approval.

When it came time to decide if I would continue my postgraduate training or enter private practice, I decided to go home to Columbus. It had been foolish for me to ever think I might do otherwise. I wanted to be with my son and didn't have the heart to take him away from my parents. I would make them happy and tuck my son into bed at night in the room that had been his since birth, the room that had once been my brother's.

Martha Claire Stewart might not have given me birth, but as surely as if she had, perhaps even more so, I was and always would be my mother's daughter.

forty-seven

In those earlier years, through monthly phone calls, I had shared every facet of my life with my cousin. Iris knew about Buddy's drinking problem, Daddy's comings and goings as a traveling sales-man, any changes that Mama made down at the store. Iris knew about my unrequited crush on one of the Simpson boys who had lived up the street and how I had lots of sort-of friends but longed terribly for a best friend. She would tell me about her classes, dates, plays, concerts, celebrity sightings. Her life seemed so much fuller and richer than mine, but she insisted that she missed so many things about her old life. She missed dinnertime with all of us around the table and the times we gathered around the piano. She missed frog choruses, the smell of the magnolia blossoms, digging in the garden, fishing from the bridge, vis-iting with folks on the street corners and in the square.

"And I miss the cemeteries," she said. "Maybe that's weird, but I loved the hours you and Buddy and I spent roaming through them, speculating about the lives of the folks who were buried there, pulling weeds away from untended graves. Remember the time when you and Buddy and I spent the whole day in that little Jewish cemetery, pulling weeds, trimming the bushes, hauling off dead branches? We took Grayson down there to show him what we'd done, and he explained about the Star of David and told us that people are more alike than they are different."

The first two years of medical school, I called at the beginning of each semester to thank her for the tuition money. The third and fourth year, I received scholarships from the local doctors' wives organization and the state organization for women physicians and no longer needed Iris's help. But every day, I still reminded myself that I owed my medical education to my cousin. Without her pushing and shoving in the beginning, I never would have had the courage to start down that long and difficult road.

I hadn't told her about my pregnancy or that I was spending a semester in Tulsa. We didn't talk at all during those months. I didn't see the point in telling her about a child that I was going to give away. Or maybe I was afraid she would try to talk me out of it. Worse yet, maybe she would offer to take the child herself, when all I wanted was to banish the baby from my life forever, along with any reminder of it and the insanity that had created it. Only Daisy Cunningham and Justine knew my secret. I wanted to keep it that way.

Finally, though, I called Iris when I realized that Gabe was going to be part of the family. She did not admonish me for my silence but lamented that we had drifted that far apart. We decided we had to do a better job in the future and reinstated the once-a-month phone call tradition. We talked for almost an hour that night. I told her how I had obsessed over a married classmate and how Mama wanted the baby more than anything when I thought she would want to disown me. I did not tell Iris about my visit with her mother at the beach house. I did not tell her that I knew what had destroyed our family. I had promised Justine that the family secret would be forever safe with me.

They were awkward at first—those phone calls for no purpose except that a month had gone by. I now knew things that Iris did not know. I knew that Philip Benston Dover had never existed, that my adopted father was her birth father. I had to be guarded, when before I could say whatever came into my head. Still, the calls connected us once again and made us feel sisterly. And they gave us a new dream— of our babies growing up knowing each other and being part of each other's life.

I did a general internship at Texas Medical Center in Houston, then a three-year pediatric residency, also in Houston. My salary was pitifully small. I still had to work on the side—in the city's various emergency rooms—sending my parents whatever I could. I had become my aunt Justine, sending checks every month and sweeping in and out of my child's life. I missed Gabe terribly and called him several times a week, but I had made my choices. Someday, I would make it up to him.

I did not feel guilty, though. How could I when I saw what my child had done for my parents? He was the greatest gift I ever could have given them. It was as though Gabe had been put on this earth to heal them.

What my parents felt for my son went beyond love. They lived for him, through him. The glorious thing about a child is that you find yourself looking at the world through his or her eyes. Gabe had no knowledge of what had gone before, of family secrets and all that pain and sorrow. He saw only a wondrous world and people who loved him.

My son was already five years old when I bought the building where Doc Hadley had practiced for almost fifty years and hung out my shingle—CECELIA C. STEWART, M.D., FAMILY MEDICINE AND PEDIATRICS. I hoped eventually to limit my practice to pediatrics, but I needed all the patients I could get. At that point, I probably would have treated puppies and kittens.

My parents had sold the building where the store had been and the land by the river that had been my father's retreat. He had a small pension from the shoe company and another from the National Guard. They got by. "Getting by" had become a way of life for us.

But that would change. I already could see that. I would never be rich, but I would earn a good living, even in a small town like Columbus. The bank didn't hesitate to loan the money to buy a clinic to someone with an M.D. after her name. I also borrowed enough money to start the restoration on my mother's house. I considered buying a house for Gabe and me, but the house on Milam Street was the only home he'd ever known. And he was needed there.

The decision to practice in Columbus had not been an easy one. I was offered a fellowship in pediatric urology, which probably would have led to a faculty appointment and the opportunity to practice and teach at a university medical center. For months, every time I drove home, I practiced explaining this to my parents—and that I wanted to buy a house in Houston for Gabe and me, that I wanted to raise him away from the stigma of being a fatherless child, that I loved the challenge of the medical center, loved saving the lives of children who would have died if they hadn't received the level of medical care provided there. In Columbus, I would be the front line of medical defense, not the last resort; I would be the generalist, not the superspecialist with residents following me from bedside to bedside, hanging on my every word. Maybe when it came right down to it, it had been my ambition that kept me from wanting a child. A child changed everything.

In the five years following Gabe's birth, I had only one relationship—with a cardiology resident from Argentina. It was a safe relationship, since he was going back home and I was absolutely certain that my son and I weren't going to move to Buenos Aires. I hoped I also had the resolve not to move to Columbus. But I didn't. My mother had assumed from the very first that I would practice in Columbus, which would make her proud once again. And I was as hopelessly in love with Gabe as my parents were. Without my parents I wouldn't have him at all. How could I turn my back on them and their dream of having me practice in Columbus, of having me and Gabe with them for the rest of their lives?

Iris said I was a fool. After I told her I'd bought Doc Hadley's clinic, we didn't talk for several months. Then finally, she called to apologize. "But it is such a waste," she amended.

It was and wasn't.

Duplicating Doc Hadley's life would not be a waste, and being a good daughter was its own reward. Being a good daughter had been my destiny all along. I would live a full, rich life in the town where I had been raised, in the town where I would practice medicine and raise my child.

❧❧

"Are you asleep?" Cissy asked, sitting on the side of Gabe's bed.

"Not yet," he said, putting his arms around her neck while she nuzzled his.

His flesh was moist and clean. He smelled of youth and health and soap. "I'm sorry I missed your game, honey. Really sorry. I'd so looked forward to the big game."

"We didn't win."

"I know, but I still wish I'd been there." There was enough light from the hall for her to make out the freckles on his nose, the disappointment written on his face. She pushed back his dark hair and kissed his smooth forehead.

"We've got to win our next two games to make the playoffs," he told her.

"I know you guys will do your best."

"I hope you can come to them."

"You know I'll be there unless there's an emergency."

"Yeah. I know. Did the baby die?"

"I don't know. We sent her by ambulance to Houston. I tried to get a medevac helicopter, but there wasn't one available."

"What was the matter with her?"

"She drank some bug killer."

"I hope she'll be okay."

"Me, too," she said, kissing his hand, remembering the fear in the parents' faces as they handed her their lifeless child. She did what she could and sent the child on. That was her role.

"I wouldn't let Granddaddy and Grandma tell me about the game," she said. "I want to hear it from you."

"Granddaddy kept calling me 'Buddy.' He'd yell, 'Nice goin', Buddy,' and 'Keep your eye on the ball, Buddy.' It was embarrassing, Mom. People kept turning around and looking at him."

"Oh, honey, I'm so sorry. He just gets mixed up sometimes. He loved Buddy a lot, and he loves you a lot, and Buddy used to play baseball."

"I know. Buddy hit all those home runs. My coach knew him. He said no one ever hit more homers in a Columbus Little League season than Buddy Stewart. I've never hit a home run."

"Buddy was big and strong, but he couldn't recite baseball stats like you do. Did you catch any pop flies?"

"Yeah, one," he said with a small smile. "And I made a throw to second that put a guy out."

"Cool."

"But I only got on base once, on an error."

"Yeah, but last week you had two singles."

"I wish Granddaddy wouldn't call me 'Buddy,'" Gabe said with a frown. "Can't you tell him to stop?"

"He doesn't know that he's doing it, Gabe. We've talked about this before. Some people get mixed up when they get older. He gets mixed up about the two boys in his life."

"Then I wish he wouldn't come to my games."

"Oh, honey, we all love your games. How could Grandma and I go and not take Granddaddy? Think how it would hurt his feelings. I tell you what, though, next time I'll sit next to him and keep reminding him that the boy out there is named 'Gabe.' And I'll yell, 'Go, Gabe!' I'll try to help him not get mixed up."

"Grandma already does that. She's old, too, and she knows the name and batting average of every boy on the team. How come she can remember my name and Granddaddy can't?"

"He's just unlucky. We have to help him all we can."

Gabe was quiet for a minute, the frown softening. "I wish I could have known Buddy."

"Me, too," Cissy said, feeling her eyes grow moist at the thought. "You two guys would have liked each other a lot."

Buddy's picture no longer hung on the wall of Gabe's room. Cissy had moved it to her parents' room and allowed Gabe to decorate the walls of his room with living heroes—with Cal Ripken, Joe Montana, Carl Lewis.

"Do you still miss Buddy?" Gabe asked.

"Oh, yes, honey, I miss him every day. And having an eight-year-old son makes me remember when he was a little boy. Don't be mad at Granddaddy. That's what he's doing, too, remembering. It's just that he gets the past and present all mixed up."

Cissy nuzzled Gabe's neck again and whispered, "You want to know a secret?"

"Yeah," he whispered back.

"Someone I know is having a birthday next month, and do you know what? I've got tickets to an Astros game for your whole team."

forty-eight

Martha Claire pulled an afghan over her legs and studied the progress she had made on her needlepoint—a wall hanging of Texas bluebonnets—then glanced over at Grayson, who was dozing on the sofa, Puppy Dog curled at his feet. The two of them spent a lot of time on the sofa these days, an old man and an old dog dozing away what was left of their lives.

Martha Claire picked up the remote control and changed the channel from the football game Grayson had been watching to an old black-and-white movie—a mystery with Victor Mature and Richard Widmark. Movies had changed so, she thought, as she returned her attention to her stitches. The old ones like this seemed overly melodramatic, like a high school play, but the stars had such style that she put up with them.

For a time, years ago, she had thought about being an actress herself and setting her sights on a career in films. That notion had ended, though, the day Grayson marched up on a stage and sang "When the Moon Comes Over the Mountain." She had known him all her life, but it wasn't until that moment that she realized she loved him.

Martha Claire felt a smile tugging at her lips. Talk about a life-changing moment! Afterward, she had invited him to a sock hop. Back then, girls weren't supposed to do that, but he didn't seem to mind. From then on, they were together almost all of the time.

The memory made Martha Claire think of Gabe. She wasn't sure she approved of all the time he was spending with the Caldwell girl, whose family lived on Washington Street, across from the elementary school.

But she and Grayson hadn't been much older than Gabe when they had pledged undying love to one another.

Martha Claire glanced at the clock, then put down her needlework. Puppy Dog wearily got down from the sofa and followed her to the kitchen, where she gave him a dog biscuit and put some apple cider in the teakettle to warm. Cissy and Gabe would be home soon from the high school band concert. Gabe had given up football in favor of the band, which was probably a wise move. He played the clarinet much better than he could catch a football.

Martha Claire had decided to stay home with Grayson, who was recovering from a chest cold. She didn't like to leave him alone anymore. He sometimes got panicky when she wasn't around.

She brought a blanket to put around Grayson's legs, then returned to her chair and tucked the afghan around her own legs. Puppy Dog returned to the sofa. A freeze was expected tonight, the first of the winter. She had picked the last of her roses this afternoon and taken them to the nursing home. Last winter, the temperature had dropped below freezing only once, but this winter was predicted to be the coldest in years.

On nights like this, Martha Claire wished for a fireplace so that she could pull her chair close and toast her toes and watch the flickering shadows on the wall.

If she had allowed Grayson his military career, probably some of the houses they lived in would have had a fireplace. She thought of the stately officers' quarters at Fort Sam Houston, each with a chimney, even though it got no colder in San Antonio than it did in Columbus.

No telling how many places they would have lived, moving from army post to army post. As life turned out, though, except for the few years she and Grayson lived in the rented house next door to his parents, Martha Claire had spent her entire life in the house her mother had inherited from her own parents. There was a handsome bronze plaque out front now, mounted next to the front door, stating that the house was a historic landmark in the state of Texas. By next year, Cissy planned to have the house completely restored and listed on the city's annual Magnolia Homes Tour. Martha Claire would get to greet visitors in a dress that Cissy was having copied from the one Martha Claire's grandmother was wearing in the oval photograph that hung in the stairwell. Martha Claire would conduct tours of the house, relating its history—or at least the history that was fit to tell. Mostly her little speech would be about how her great-great-grandfather built the house for his daughter, Mildred Hess, how Mildred had the china cabinet and upright piano shipped to Columbus from New Orleans, how the original iron fence had been donated to the war effort in 1943 and been replaced as part of the restoration. Martha Claire looked forward finally to having her house as handsome as it had been during her childhood and once again recognized as one of the town's finest.

If Grayson had stayed in the army, she wondered if she would have kept the house for them to return to when he retired. That was hard to say. But one thing she did know—if they had not been living in Columbus, she never would have had the opportunity to raise three children. She wouldn't have had those years with Iris and wouldn't have been here for Doc Hadley to drop off two little waifs in need of a family. If she and Grayson had come back to this house to live out their years after retiring from a military career, they would be living here alone, without Gabe and Cissy to warm their hearts. So it didn't do one bit of good to wonder how things might have been. This had been her life, and there was no going back.

Only last week, she and Grayson had been watching a documentary about England on the PBS channel, when suddenly there was a magnificent shot of the white cliffs of Dover. Martha Claire studied Grayson's face, but he showed no reaction at all. "That was where you went with Justine after the war," she told him.

"With Justine?" he asked with genuine puzzlement.

"You don't remember going there with her?" Martha Claire asked.

He shook his head back and forth. "I remember France," he said. "I remember the war. I remember coming home and my father being so sick."

Martha Claire didn't know if she should laugh or weep, if she should be angry or joyous. *He didn't remember Dover.* Did that mean she could no longer blame him for what he had done there?

"Where are Justine and Iris?" Grayson had asked. "Why don't we see them anymore?"

Martha Claire looked over at the man she had loved—and hated— all these years. He was old and frail, and she wouldn't have him much longer. "Justine and Iris live in New York," she said. "Cissy and Gabe go to see them sometimes."

"I miss Iris," he said.

When Martha Claire didn't say anything, he asked, "Don't you miss her?"

Martha Claire had started to say no but changed her mind. "Sometimes," she admitted.

She picked up her needlepoint and glanced over at her dozing husband. *He didn't remember Dover.* She wondered if he had also forgotten the aftermath. Should she ask him?

Before she could decide, the front door burst open and Cissy and Gabe came rushing in, along with a blast of cold air. Grayson blinked himself awake. With tail wagging, Puppy Dog carefully got himself down from the sofa to greet his boy. Life had returned to the old house.

"I've got some apple cider warming on the stove and some freshly baked oatmeal cookies," Martha Claire said, ready to herd them toward the kitchen. "I want to hear all about the evening. How did the presentation for the band director go? I bet he was surprised."

Gabe put his arms around his grandmother and rubbed her cheek with his cold nose. He was taller now than she was, but a slender boy still. He was not handsome, but pleasant-looking, the sort of person you knew by the look of him was kind and good. Not that he was perfect, of course. Gabe had a real lazy streak. He didn't hang up his clothes no matter how much she carped at him. He put off mowing the grass until Martha Claire shamed him by getting out the mower and threatening to do it herself. And he was always running late, always keeping someone waiting. But he was silly and happy and made her heart swell so that at times she thought it would pop right out of her chest. If only she could have loved Buddy the way she loved Gabe, maybe things could have turned out differently for him.

. . .

It got even colder in the night, but Grayson kept kicking off the covers. He wasn't feverish, though, just restless. Martha Claire would pull the covers back up and rub his arms and shoulders to soothe him. "Where am I?" he asked at one point.

"Here with me," she told him.

"With you?"

"Yes, with me."

"Will you stay with me?"

"Always," she promised.

"Thank you," he said, before drifting back into a fitful sleep.

Finally, he stopped thrashing about, and Martha Claire felt herself settling into a few hours of real sleep.

Toward morning, when she woke and reached for her husband's warmth, she knew the instant she touched his flesh that he was dead. In the same instant, the smell of his bowels filled her nostrils.

Quietly, so as not to wake Cissy and Gabe, she went downstairs for rags, a basin, and garbage bags. Then she cleaned her husband's body and changed the bedding, dressed him in clean nightclothes, bundled up the soiled linens, and carried them out to the garbage cans.

Then she washed herself and got back into bed with him, to hold him in her arms and weep and say all those words she never told him in life. She was so sorry for all those wasted years, so sorry for the years she had banished him from his family, so sorry she hadn't let him manage Buddy.

She stroked his hair and kissed his face. She unbuttoned his pajama top and kissed his chest. Kissed his hands and feet. Then she caressed his penis and kissed it, remembering all those times along the river when she had made love to his penis because it wasn't allowed to make love to her, not yet, not until they were married.

"You were the handsomest boy in all of Texas," she told him, remembering how he looked on their wedding day in his uniform. "And you were the best father those children ever could have had. I never told you that, and I should have. Through it all, I always thought you were a fine father."

And he had been so good to her grandmother and mother, who both had loved Grayson like a son. And he had been a good son to his own parents, even though his mother was a silly, difficult woman who didn't deserve a son like him.

Martha Claire remembered how he would sit by her dying mother's bed in the evening and encourage her to reminisce, to remember when she and Walter were young and courting. And she would tell him about dancing at roadhouses and drinking bootlegged liquor from fruit jars. One night, Grayson brought her a few teaspoons of bourbon in a pint jar and held her in a sitting position while she inhaled the aroma of that other time and took a tiny sacramental sip.

Finally, with pale watery light coming through the lace curtains, Martha Claire heard Cissy stirring, heard the toilet flush, and knew it was time for her to relinquish her husband's body and tell Cissy that her father was dead.

Carefully, as though she might wake him, she slid her arm from under his neck, kissed his lips once again, told him she loved him, and went to Cissy's room.

The door was open, Cissy was sitting on the side of the bed, dialing the phone—the hospital, probably, to check on a patient. She looked at her mother's face and returned the receiver to its cradle. "Your father is dead," Martha Claire said, her voice catching.

Cissy looked at her with disbelief, then went rushing out of the room, down the hall.

Martha Claire followed and watched from the bedroom door while Cissy knelt beside the bed, buried her face against her father's chest, and cried out loud. Her cries brought Gabe, who knelt with his mother and tried to comfort her, but he was crying too hard himself.

Grayson had been loved, Martha Claire thought proudly. Her husband had been a good man and he had been loved.

forty-nine

A person's punishment for living so damned long was all these funerals, Martha Claire thought as they walked toward the church. So many funerals. Grandparents, parents, in-laws, other relatives, friends. And Buddy. Buddy's funeral had been the saddest of all. Grayson wouldn't mind her thinking that. Grayson was seventy-four years old, and his time had come.

But, oh, how she would miss him. Never again would she be able to reach for his hand or kiss his lips. Every day, she would think of something she wanted or needed to tell him, and all she would have was a gravestone in the cemetery. And memories. She had lots of those. Trouble was, so many of them were upsetting. It was impossible to filter out the bad and remember only the good. Remembering brought regret along with satisfaction.

It was a cool crisp day. She had insisted on walking the three blocks to church, as she always did.

She was arm in arm with Cissy and Gabe and counted herself fortunate indeed to have them with her. Someday they would be doing this sad task for her. But not for a long time yet, she hoped. She was as strong as a horse and wanted to live on, to see how Gabe turned out and know her great-grandchildren. And she still hoped that someday Cissy would fall in love, and they could have a lovely wedding in the rose garden. She would even invite Iris if Cissy wanted her to.

It was hard to believe that her Cissy was a woman of forty-four. She still looked like a girl.

Of course, who was Cissy going to marry in Columbus? Other than youngsters, the only single men were elderly widowers. Maybe, now that Grayson was gone, it was time to sell the old house—before Cissy sank any more money into it. They could move to Houston and let Cissy get on with her life, if it wasn't too late.

Lots of folks were walking toward the church. The sanctuary would be full, she thought with satisfaction. Some of the men Grayson had served with in the National Guard would be in uniform.

Cissy insisted that Grayson be buried in his dress uniform with medals on his chest. Martha Claire had considered reminding her that her father might have been a good soldier and served his country well, but during his time in uniform he had been an unfaithful husband and brought ruin to their marriage that took years to heal, that took the miracle of Gabe to heal.

But she said nothing when Cissy and Gabe went up to the attic and brought the uniform down, when they arranged for an honor guard to come from Fort Sam. They had the uniform cleaned and pressed and asked the sergeant from the National Guard Armory to go to the funeral home and see that the medals got pinned on correctly.

Grayson's death had been front-page news in the *Citizen*. They had included a fifty-year-old picture of the store and a picture of Grayson that was taken when he won an award from the state historical society a few years back for an article he'd written about the county's last lynching, back in the 1930s. There was even an editorial that called Grayson a "true Texas gentleman," whatever that was. But she knew what the writer was trying to convey—Grayson had a dignity about him that people responded to and trusted. He should have been a leader of men and not a shopkeeper, not a shoe salesman.

Martha Claire paused for a minute in front of the little house where she and Grayson had lived after the war, remembering the time they lived there, remembering how hard she had searched for the young boy she had fallen in love with until finally she realized she had lost him on the battlefields of Europe. Even though she had learned to love the older, sadder Grayson, she never stopped longing for the time when their love had been young and limitless.

She thought of all the people who might be at the funeral—his colleagues from the historical society and the library board, his friends from the Lions Club and the Chamber of Commerce, fishing and hunting buddies, maybe some of the people he knew from the Texas A&M alumni organization. She was sure that Cissy had seen to it that everyone was notified. Martha Claire doubted if his two surviving cousins from Tyler would come. They were teetotaling Bible thumpers, and Grayson had never had much to do with them.

And she wondered if Iris would come. Almost from the beginning she had wondered. She was sure Cissy had called her, probably the first person she had called. Martha Claire wanted Iris to be there—and she didn't. It had been such a shock when she appeared at Buddy's funeral. When Martha Claire had seen her waiting in the vestibule, she had had a hard time breathing, a hard time deciding how she should react. She had been distant, then regretted it afterward. If Iris came today, Martha Claire promised herself that she would not be distant. She would take her arm and march up the aisle with her.

Martha Claire's heart began to beat faster as they turned up the front walk to the church. Was Iris waiting inside?

She paused for a minute to take a deep breath.

"Are you all right, Mama?" Cissy asked.

Martha Claire grabbed Cissy's arm. "I have to know. Did Iris come?"

"I don't know," Cissy said. "She didn't say one way or the other, but her husband isn't well."

Cissy's dark hair shone in the sunshine. There were a few gray hairs, but not many, and a few lines around her eyes, but not many of those, either. It was a dear face, always so full of concern for others. Martha Claire took it between her hands and said, "Do you know what your father's last words were? He said, 'Thank you.' And I want to pass that thank-you on to you—to you and your son. Because of you and Gabe, the last part of your father's life was peaceful and good and full of love. I thank you for that. For the rest of my life I will thank you for that."

Then, with her Cissy on one arm and her Gabe on the other, Martha Claire marched up the steps to her husband's funeral, with a hope, or perhaps a prayer, going forth with each step. *Please, let Iris be there.*

She was.

Just as she had been when Buddy died, Iris was waiting in the vestibule. It took Martha Claire a couple of heartbeats more to realize that the older woman with her was Justine.

At first, before she could absorb this stunning event, she had to digest the fact that Justine was old, almost as old as she was herself. She knew that, of course, but seeing it was different from knowing it. Her younger sister was an old woman—although a handsome old woman, to be sure—and the years were etched on her face as surely as they were on the trunks of the ancient live oak trees in whose branches they used to play.

Iris stepped forward, and Martha Claire opened her arms. The gesture came quite naturally. She wanted to feel Iris in her arms, wanted to touch her face and hair, wanted to kiss her cheeks and lips, wanted to hear her words of condolence and see her tears.

"I loved him so," Iris was saying. "He was like a father to me. I wish I could have seen him one last time."

But because he *was* her father, Iris had not been allowed to see him one last time, Martha Claire thought.

"Oh, Martha Claire, I've missed you so," Iris was saying through her tears, relief on her lovely face that she was being welcomed and not rebuffed by the woman who had raised her and then never forgiven her for sins she did not understand.

"And I have missed you," Martha Claire managed to say, even though she was only a few feet away from her sister, Justine, whom she had not seen for more than thirty years. Justine, who had betrayed her as no sister ever should.

How dare she come here for Grayson's funeral! The bile rose in Martha Claire's throat. The old hate. The old images. *Grayson and Justine.* How dare she come, when all Martha Claire wanted this day was peacefully to put her husband into the ground? Now she had to think about all that other, to be reminded of all that pain.

She felt the air being sucked out of the small space, felt Cissy tense beside her. And Iris.

Justine stepped forward. "I had to come," she explained. "I needed to come back. Not because of Grayson, but because of you."

Martha Claire had to be civilized, of course. She could not make a scene at her husband's funeral. She managed to nod in Justine's direction, to say her name, then to walk by her. Alone, she walked up the aisle to the front row, reserved for Grayson's family. His casket was there. His body. She'd seen him last night at the funeral home, like himself but not. She had kissed his lips and stayed with him throughout the evening.

She had debated about whether to have the casket open at the service. She was glad now that she had said no. Justine would not be able to look on his face and remember the time when they had made love, when they had made Iris.

Martha Claire had thought that she would have the casket open one last time, after everyone had left the sanctuary, just for her and Cissy and Gabe. She wouldn't do that now. She was mad at Grayson. He had made love to her sister. She would punish him by never kissing his lips again, not for all eternity. *Damn him.* And Justine. Most of all Justine.

Old Paul Huxley, leaning on his son's arm, came to offer a eulogy for his old fishing buddy. "Grayson Stewart was not a religious man, but he was a spiritual one," the old minister said. "He knew the name of every bird, knew the habits of God's small creatures. He had such respect for nature and for life in all its forms. He told me once with great certainty that he had no expectation for a hereafter. He had killed men in the war and didn't feel like he had sent them on their way to some great reward. 'They were pretty damned dead,' he said. He liked the idea of his body simply rotting away and becoming a part of the Texas sod that had sprung him, becoming a part of the great cycle of life and death. But those of us who do believe in a hereafter would like to see Grayson there. I myself can't imagine a paradise that didn't have a fishing hole and two spare fishing poles for me and my dear, dear friend Grayson Stewart, who was, in spite of himself, a godly man."

That was nice, Martha Claire thought when he had finished. Such an unlikely friendship: a minister and an agnostic. But it had been a good one.

The rest of the service was meaningless for Martha Claire—just a generic funeral service. The music was nice, though. She had selected music she thought Grayson would have liked. "The Spirit of Aggieland." "Texas, Our Texas." "Stardust." And as a concession to the minister, who insisted that at least one hymn be included, "The Battle Hymn of the Republic."

At the cemetery, as she watched Grayson's casket being lowered into the ground, she was sorry she had not had that one last moment with his body as she had planned. She wanted to cry out, to tell them to stop, that she had to touch him one more time and tell him that she did love him, that she forgave him completely. But it was too late.

The afternoon passed in a blur, with Justine and Iris the center of attention. The kitchen and dining room were full of food, as they should be. Martha Claire had dutifully taken a casserole or a pie to the homes of Columbus's deceased for all of her adult life. Hundreds of times she had taped her name on the bottom of a dish and marched it up to the front door, sometimes even before the funeral wreath had been hung. Often she was one of the women in the kitchen after the funeral, keeping the table replenished, cleaning up afterward.

Finally, when the afternoon had passed and the last of the mourners had told Martha Claire one final time how sorry they were and what a good man Grayson had been, they were alone. Just the five of them. Two old sisters and two younger women who had been raised as sisters. And young Gabe, for whom his grandfather's funeral had been his first.

"Go," she told her grandson. "Go find your friends. Go see your girlfriend. Celebrate life."

He had looked to his mother, who nodded and smiled, and he rushed up the stairs to change his clothes.

Martha Claire had meant to go back to the cemetery alone, but at dusk all four women were in the car, with Cissy driving and Martha Claire beside her in the front seat.

The evening was crisp and still. The four women lined up in front of the fresh gravesite. Martha Claire began to sob first.

Suddenly, with a feeling of panic, she realized that Iris and Cissy were walking away, arm in arm, leaving their mothers alone.

"I don't want to be here with you," Martha Claire told Justine, the first words she had spoken to her.

"I know. I'm sorry I came, sorry I have upset you so. I just thought it had been so many years. When Iris told me about Grayson, all I could think of was coming back here to you. I'd like to start over, Martha Claire, if you will let me."

Shivering a bit, Martha Claire began walking, and Justine followed her. They walked among the tombstones that presided over the graves of their parents and grandparents, of friends and acquaintances. And Buddy.

"Grayson used to come here almost daily when he was still driving," Martha Claire said, with a gloved hand on Buddy's tombstone. "Then I'd bring him whenever he thought to ask, but he started thinking that Gabe was Buddy. Gabe got so he'd answer to the name. It confused Grayson to come here, so I stopped bringing him. It still hurts so much. Grayson wanted to make Buddy leave, to make him grow up, and I wanted him to stay. Grayson blamed himself because he didn't stand up to me. I blamed myself because I didn't have the courage to do what was best for my son. And Cissy seemed to think if she had done a better job of looking after her brother he wouldn't have been driving drunk along that country road. I've never driven down that road since. Or Grayson. When he'd drive up to College Station for the games, he would go the long way around. Until Buddy died, I thought that finding out about you and Grayson was the low point in my life, the worst thing that could possibly ever happen to me. It wasn't. I even wanted to blame Buddy's death on you. After our family got torn apart, things were never the same for any of us. I sent Grayson away, and Cissy had to mother Buddy. I stewed in my own juices for so many years."

"Can you ever forgive me?" Justine asked.

"Not forgive so much as give up," Martha Claire said. "I am weary with hating you."

"I'm not well," Justine said. "When the time comes, I'd like to come back here to die—and be buried here with Mama and Papa. And darling Buddy."

"And Grayson," Martha Claire reminded her.

"Yes, and Grayson. What we did was very wrong. We knew at the time but thought that the war had given us some sort of special dispensation. It ruined our family, though."

Martha Claire led the way back to Grayson's grave. Where did she go from here?

Justine's and Grayson's betrayal had given her Iris. That fact had haunted her all these years. Because of Iris, she and Grayson had the need and the courage to adopt Cissy and Buddy. And in spite of the heartache that children bring, they had defined her life. How does one unravel it all and come to terms? In all these years, she still had not done that.

"I could have forgiven Grayson and saved my family, but it became who I was—a woman betrayed. I became a very ugly person." She paused, then asked abruptly, "Are you really dying?"

"Yes, so it seems."

"Does Iris know?"

"Not yet."

Martha Claire sighed. "Seems like all I do is bury people."

"Then it's all right for me to come home?"

"You couldn't wait to leave Columbus. And now you want to come back. It doesn't make sense."

"A part of me never really left. I thought of you always, Martha Claire. You are my roots. My sister. If there was only some way—"

"Hush up, will you," Martha Claire barked. "I have my sins, too. Every time you went off to some war or faraway place, I thought how nice it would be if you got shot or the plane went down. Then I could have Iris all to myself. I could adopt her like Cissy and Buddy. I couldn't stand it when you took her away. I prayed that you would die so that she would come back to us."

As it turned out, my aunt Justine lived on for almost two years. Iris insisted it was because Mama refused to let her die.

She had come home to Columbus at Christmastime, the month after Daddy died, and she never left. Iris and her daughter came to stay with us the last month or so. Strange how life can be, with sadness and happiness drawn in with the same breath.

My mama's house is still there. My son and his family live in it. I returned to Houston—not to a brilliant career as a university-based specialist, but I am with a medical group that looks after very sick kids. I fight for life when it's possible and welcome death when it's inevitable.

Mama lives with me. I have a beautiful garden because of her. She has all but adopted a young Mexican boy who does the actual labor.

We drive over to Columbus almost every Sunday afternoon, and she inspects the garden there. Gabe earned a degree in landscape architecture at Texas A&M and designs gardens all over the state. But the one in Columbus he keeps just as it was. He wouldn't dare change it while his grandmother is alive.

I ran into Joe McCormack a few years ago at a medical conference. He still practices in Lampasas, a widower now. We see each other once or twice a month and go on trips together. He puts up beautifully with Mama. We never once mentioned that crazy night when I lured him into betraying his wife, not a night I want to be reminded of, except that out of my insanity and my mother's strength I ended up with a son.

Life becomes such a circle. Currents swirling around, coming back upon themselves. Joe doesn't know that Gabe is his son, and I don't plan to tell him.

To this day, Iris doesn't know who her father is, and I will honor the promise I made to her mother. As Justine once pointed out, the truth doesn't always set one free.

With the advent of the Internet and all the possibility for tracking down birth mothers, Gabe wanted to launch a search for mine. I told him no, he absolutely wasn't to do that.

Martha Claire Mayfield Stewart raised me, and I am her dutiful daughter. Every year on my birthday, she still tells me that the woman who gave me birth is thinking of me that day, and I know that if that woman is still alive, those words are probably true. And on that day, I allow myself to think of her and thank her for giving me life.

But the other three hundred and sixty-four days of the year, my allegiance is to the woman who had the courage to take me from the arms of a wise old country doctor who wasn't afraid to play God.